# BREACHER

## JACK LIVELY

*To the Boy and the Wolf*

## CHAPTER ONE

I WAS CROSSING THE STREET, noticing the cross-walk lines on the road, freshly painted, and the foot gear choices of the cruise ship tourists. It looked as if trail walking was high up on the list. New and newish hiking boots, adventure sandals, low-top trail shoes. Then I raised my eyes and caught the guy's reflection in the window of a drug store.

He was walking behind me. Not too close, but close enough. It was a guy I'd seen before.

Specifically, I had seen him during the third bite of my burger, which was about twenty minutes earlier and memorable. I had looked up and there he was at a deuce by the window, looking right at me. Eye contact. An athletic blond man in his late twenties with a trimmed beard. He was drinking from a mug with a string coming out of it. It took me a moment to realize it was a hot beverage called tea. By that point he had looked away. Besides the tea, the other thing was the beard.

In Port Morris, Alaska, beards are not memorable. They are commonplace, but a well-trimmed beard less so. Most beards I'd seen in the last four months working on a fishing boat had been either untrimmed or badly trimmed, but this guy's beard was well-trimmed. Like he had access to a good mirror and good light. Maybe a mirror with lights on it, like in a hotel with a star rating. Good mirror and good light, two things definitely missing in the sleeping quarters of a fishing boat, which tend to be dimly lit mirrorless cavities behind the engine room.

I stopped and pretended to look at something in the window display. The guy swerved, slowed up, and started thumbing through a postcard rack outside of the tourist gift store. His left hand was bandaged, so he was thumbing through the cards with his right hand. I scanned in the reflection for other watchers. Another man was posted by the door to the diner. I hadn't seen him before. He was leaning against the wall, below the stairs. Baseball hat and light blue button-down Oxford. I started walking again, nice and slow this time.

The next intersection was catty corner to a bank with an angled window. I glanced at the reflection before crossing the street. The guy with the well-trimmed beard was moving, now around forty feet behind me. I upped the pace from casual to brisk. Walked a couple of minutes without looking behind me. If there was a team tailing me, that might string them out and break their formation.

I cut left over a footbridge, crossing the creek to go up Lake Road. There was overflow from a bar. Fishermen taking a smoke break from drinking their salmon money. All beards were either badly trimmed, or untrimmed. I asked one for a cigarette, using the interaction to turn and glance down the road. The well-trimmed beard guy was on the bridge, both hands on the worn railing, looking down at the fish running up the creek from the Pacific toward the sweet water spawning grounds.

At the intersection, I saw a crowd of tourists from the cruise ship. Around forty of them packed together like fish in a net, spanning the street and sidewalk. They were coming down Bryant Street, headed back to the boat after a tour of the salmon creeks. I let myself be absorbed by the crowd. Threaded my way in and amongst them, keeping my head low. I dropped down as if to tie my shoe, screened by geriatric vacationers. It only took a couple of gestures and a shrug to pull off my backpack and jacket. I had a ball cap in the bag. I turned the jacket inside out and wrapped it around the backpack. When I stood up again, I wasn't a bareheaded guy wearing a forest green Gore-Tex jacket and a backpack, I was a guy wearing a t-shirt and a black cap and holding a tan package under my arm.

I reversed direction to join the flow of tourists as the group shuffled downhill toward the dock. I smiled at an older lady pulling on the arm of her partner. I said, "Are you with the boat?" She nodded and I turned away. From the hill I could see the cruise ship below. In fact, it was visible from almost anywhere in town. I moved down the street, going with the flow. Like a paper boat in a rain-swollen gutter. I didn't see the first guy from the diner. He was probably still searching for me further up the hill.

A minute later we passed the guy with the Oxford shirt. He was walking uphill, looking like a kid who had lost his teddy bear. I broke out of the crowd below him and stepped into the shadow of a chartered trips office.

I was now a few buildings up from the diner where I'd had that burger, like a full circle. I stayed there for a minute, observing. My baseball cap was pulled low and I figured with the beard I looked just like any other fisherman in Port Morris. Mid-thirties, tall, and jacked from pulling on ropes all season. I hadn't been in shape like that since pararescue indoctrination.

I recognized the girl standing on the other side of the road. She hadn't made me. She was blonde, wearing a tourist bucket hat with a Port Morris logo, and carrying a bag from the souvenir store. Like she was just another tourist. But I was pretty sure that she wasn't just a tourist.

I had met her the night before.

## CHAPTER TWO

The night before I was in the Porterhouse Bar playing pool with Joe Guilfoyle. The Porterhouse is old-school Alaska. Burnished wood fixings. Everything robust and built to survive the harsh elements. Which is to say, the weather and the people, and not necessarily in that order. The music was playing from a jukebox.

The door opened, and the blonde girl came in. Everyone turned to look at her. That was normal behavior, checking out the newcomer. But when the heads swiveled back on necks, they did so slower than they normally would. There were a couple of reasons for that. The most obvious one being the location and corresponding demographics.

Port Morris, Alaska, has a year-round population of five thousand and change. A big town in the southeastern corner of the state. On a very cold and slushy day in February there might be a seven to one ratio of men to women. In late summer during salmon season the population swells by a couple of thousand, and the gender imbalance is more like two hundred to one. So that was one reason why everyone turned to stare at her.

The other reason was that she was good-looking.

Not good-looking like a cute neighbor, more like special-looking, like a model from the city. The kind of face and figure that people get lost in. Mysterious looks that attract fashion magazines, and guys with haircuts and skinny jeans. Photogenic looks that translate weirdly when experienced in three dimensions. Which made the fact of her very existence in Port Morris something along the lines of a big surprise, or an extreme event, like what they call a black swan.

The third reason why everyone was looking at her was because she was anxious, and in a hurry.

By default, most creatures pay attention to rapid movement. And the blonde girl was moving at speed. She came in quietly through the front. Kind of hunched over and nervous. By the time she rounded the other side of the bar she was moving faster. She skirted the outside of the room and hurried into the women's bathroom. The door swung shut behind her.

A minute after that everyone went back to what they were doing, which was playing pool, mouthing off, and drinking beer. In my case I was drinking a chocolate milk shake. Not because I don't drink beer, only because I hadn't yet finished the chocolate shake I'd ordered with my pot roast at the diner.

It was Guilfoyle's shot and he was a slow shooter. I watched him measure up the geometry and the physics. He had an annoyingly painstaking technique of checking the angles, crouching and peering down the pool stick at the ball. Lining it up. Squinting and then calculating the white ball's line to the pocket, and then checking if it was going to hit at an angle likely to scratch, given the inertia and the spin. Besides being the captain of a salmon boat in the summer, Guilfoyle was a physics teacher at a community college back in Seattle.

He was still lining up his shot when the giant came in.

There are some big people in Port Morris, massive guys who do nothing all year but pull on ropes. Sometimes it's salmon, sometimes it's king crab, other times it's herring. But this guy was something else. He was maybe six foot seven and about the same at the shoulders. He had a big beard and long hair pulled back in a pony tail. He wore a black leather jacket and had a spiked wristband around his massive left wrist. He was the kind of guy you'd expect to have a spider web tattoo up his neck, maybe with a couple of tear drops out of his eye, announcing how dangerous he was.

But he had no tattoos, just pure natural menace. When he came into the Porterhouse, everyone's neck did another swivel to the door. But the giant wasn't looking at everyone, he was looking right at me. Staring straight into my eyes. Then he started coming at me fast. Not running but taking very big strides.

For a couple of seconds I stood there holding the pool cue and wondering what was going to happen. I'd never seen the guy before, but that didn't change the fact that he was coming at me with intent. Like every other guy in the room, I had a beard. When I came on board the *Sea Foam* with Guilfoyle I had been clean-shaven. Four months later I had a beard.

So there I was, standing and looking at the incoming giant staring straight at me, about to arrive with speed and force. And it occurred to me that he wasn't really coming at me, wasn't even looking at me. He was looking through me to his real objective. I was just a guy with a beard to him, and he was looking for something else, which was past me at the bathroom. So, I stood aside and let him brush past, which in hindsight was an error. It just prolonged the inevitable. The giant went straight to the women's bathroom and pulled the door open.

Then we all heard the blonde girl scream.

Everyone in the place stopped what they were doing and stared at the bathroom door, vibrating on its hinges. Everyone except for me. I wasn't staring, I was moving. Guilfoyle said something, like a warning. But I was already pulling the door open. Inside there was only the giant's back. Like a wall of black leather. He was reaching into one of the toilet booths. It looked like he had the girl by her hair and her throat, which meant his hands were occupied. She was gasping, trying to scream. The giant was silent. I hammered him in the right kidney. Once, twice, very fast and hard. Then again and another time. That's usually enough, but not in this case.

The guy kind of leaned against the side of the booth, which shook the whole structure. Then he tried to turn. No doubt he was planning to swat me away, like a minor annoyance. But he didn't have the chance. For one thing, he was stuck in the toilet booth entrance. For another, I gave him a vicious swiping kick into the back of the knees and he went down on them. The girl had climbed on top of the toilet, jammed to the back of the booth. I looped my right forearm under the giant's chin. My left forearm went against the back of his neck.

That was it, he was under control.

The guy froze up like a single muscle. Like Coho salmon when they're out of the water and you have them by the mouth. They twitch hard until they die. I didn't kill the giant, but I did choke him out. When he was limp I lowered his head into the toilet.

Lucky for him the toilet was clean. In fact it sparkled with sanitation and cleanliness, presumably because the women's bathroom was so seldom used.

I looked up at the girl. She was looking at me. Her pupils were dilated. But she was not too shocked to have her phone up in front of her, the tiny round camera pointed at me. The flash fired. I stepped back, my vision temporarily ruined. All I could see was her perfectly symmetrical face printed on the back of my eyeballs and the white flash bouncing around in my brain. I got my sight back eventually, but by then the blonde was gone.

And now, there she was again in a bucket hat, part of a little team of people on my tail. Maybe they wanted to give me a medal.

## CHAPTER THREE

Now I was curious.

The blonde didn't see me and wasn't even checking. She was waiting for the others, letting them do the work. Since the guy with the Oxford shirt was now cut out from the group, I decided to stalk him.

I started back up the hill, coming up on his six. None of his buddies were watching or covering. This was not a professionally trained team. So, I asked myself, what were they?

The Oxford shirt guy was walking slowly, looking left, then right, then back up the hill. I noticed the well-trimmed beard guy coming down the hill, on the other side of the street. The two of them made eye contact and I saw the well-trimmed beard moving his lips as he spoke into an ear-piece, which meant they were communicating. Not so dumb maybe. Oxford shirt guy started to walk faster up the hill. Probably following orders from the beard. Which suited me, because I wanted to catch him when he got behind the big tree, right past the dumpster in the alley next to the Porterhouse Bar.

I timed my movements. He was a big guy with a neck like a bull seal, but legs like toothpicks. Classic gym bunny. A guy who trained with weights and rubber bands and mirrors, which meant plenty of muscle up top. Good target. I could hit him there without killing him. All that muscle would protect his spinal cord.

As he stepped into the sweet spot, I swung a hard right hook into that thick neck. It landed well, just above the collar. The punch launched him into the alley, tumbling over thin legs. The guy stumbled a couple of steps and turned to look at me in fear and anger. His hat had fallen off. He started to say something, but by then I had grabbed him by the hair and had the point of my folding knife in his right nostril. I pushed until it drew blood and he winced but didn't make a sound. I kicked his legs out from under him and knelt down without releasing my grip.

"What do you want?"

The guy looked at me and stammered, "We just want to talk to you."

I said, "What happened, did I win the lottery, or inherit a million dollars?"

"No. Just want to talk."

The punch had knocked the ear-piece out of his head. It wasn't fancy, just a regular ear bud from his phone. But I figured they had an open phone line and that others were listening in on the conversation. Which added uncertainty into the equation. Time to move.

I said, "Best to just leave me alone." And nicked his nose with the blade. A minor, controlled slice up the inside of his nostril. Blood ran into the guy's mouth. He licked his lips involuntarily and sputtered. I disappeared, joining the steady stream of tourists down the hill.

But I wasn't done with them. Not yet. I was still curious.

About a minute and a half later I slipped into an ice cream place. It had a nice big window out to the main street, plus I could stand out of sight in the back. I figured the Oxford shirt guy would be returning down the hill. He would meet back up with the well-trimmed beard guy and I wanted to see what happened then.

I ordered a sugar cone with one scoop of chocolate and one scoop vanilla. Chocolate on top, vanilla on the bottom. The guy behind the counter wore a pink uniform with a pink visor. I moved into the shadow at the back of the store while he bent into the freezer to prepare my ice cream.

The front window was like a movie screen. The well-trimmed beard guy entered the frame from the left, moving uphill. He crossed through it, climbing up the grade and then went out on the right side. It was at least the second time he'd climbed the hill. The ice cream was three dollars. I licked the bottom scoop first. Vanilla.

There was one other customer, sitting at a little round table in the window. He was a clean-shaven man with a mustache, wearing a fleece vest over a button-down shirt. He had side-parted hair, which looked like it required regular maintenance and just the right amount of product. The guy was quietly spooning ice cream into his mouth and gazing out the same window.

The ice cream server asked me if it was good. I said it was. He asked me why I'd chosen chocolate on top and vanilla on the bottom. I told him it was the correct order of things, to my mind at least. When the server said that he approved of the chocolate on top and vanilla on the bottom decision, the guy in the window grunted in disagreement. He said, "Two scoops of the same flavor. Avoids all problems."

Looking through the window over his head, I saw the trimmed-beard guy again. He came from the right side, going downhill. But now he was with the Oxford shirt guy, who was holding a balled-up tissue to his nose.

The other customer in the ice cream place was scraping the inside of his cardboard cup with a stubby plastic scoop; he hadn't opted for a cone. I looked over his shoulder through the large window. The two conspirators across the street had stopped on the sidewalk, huddled together, speaking on the phone with someone else, maybe the blonde girl.

The two guys stopped talking and started walking. From right to left, down the hill. The guy in the window stood up slow, and at the same time crumpled the cardboard cup in his fist. He was tracking the two across the street. He didn't bother to look around when he called out, "Thanks for the ice cream."

The guy dropped his garbage in the trash can and walked out the door. I gave him a thirty second head start before following.

It didn't take a genius to see that the mustachioed ice cream eater was following the two guys, and that he didn't know me from Adam. So now I was following him, watching him follow *them*. Like a math equation. Them following me, following him, following them.

I stayed back as far as I thought prudent, while still keeping him in sight. The two across the street were oblivious. They weren't even looking out for a tail. The mustachioed guy slowed down and pretended to look into the window of an outdoor sports store. The two across the street were coming to the bottom of the hill. I walked by the mustachioed guy from the ice cream store. There was a small square of grass to my left. On the other side of it was another foot bridge over another salmon creek. I found a bench facing down to the intersection and sat on it.

The blonde girl was waiting for the two guys at the bottom of the hill, a little above where Bryant crosses Water Street. I put the ice cream cone in front of my face and licked at it slowly. Just a guy with a beard, licking ice cream. The mustachioed man was still at the outdoor goods store, flicking through a rack of sunglasses. He was using the little mirror there to keep an eye on the group.

They had come together now. Looked like the girl was in charge. She was talking, the others listening. She examined the big guy's nose. He was tall, but so was she. Tall enough not to have to reach up to examine the cut. The blood had dripped onto the guy's shirt.

After a minute or two, the three of them turned and walked the short way down to Water Street. The cruise ship loomed at the dock across the road, like a floating city with gangways. One to the right, maybe a hundred yards away. Another to the left, maybe two hundred yards away.

A shiny black Chevy Suburban pulled to the curb. The girl opened the passenger door, revealing a cream leather interior, like the inside of a snake's mouth. The two guys piled in the back and the girl got in the front. I couldn't see the driver. Thirty seconds later the Suburban was gone.

I watched the mustachioed guy walk after them. When he reached Water Street, a Subaru 4x4 pulled up, painted a fancy dark blue green. The word 'teal' crawled up out of some dark recess of my brain, like an unwanted guest. Another guy came out of the Subaru. He had a light-colored beard and long hair tucked behind his ears and wore a John Deere hat. I watched the two of them converse for maybe thirty seconds. The new guy got back into the car. The mustachioed guy stayed. The Subaru took off in the same direction as the big Chevy.

I watched the guy with the mustache. He was looking up at the cruise ship. It was blocking the sunlight. I counted the floors. The ship had eight levels, like an extra wide tower block apartment building. The ship had a name, *The Emerald Allure*. I wondered why anyone would voluntarily walk up that gangway. Looked like the perfect place to catch a virus, like a floating experiment in epidemiology. The guy started walking along the dock.

I concentrated on finishing the ice cream. When I had finished, I turned my jacket back around and put it on. I got up, slung on my backpack, and walked after him.

## CHAPTER FOUR

Them following me, following him, following them. The equation had changed. Now it was just me following him.

The guy represented a group, evidenced by the other guy in the teal Subaru. Therefore, two groups in some kind of conflict. Or maybe not yet in conflict. There was the question of why the first bunch was after me specifically.

Half of me wanted to know more, and the other half didn't. The other half was pretty happy to get the hell out of Port Morris and down to Seattle. The salmon season was over, and I was done with Alaska. It had been a fine experience, but I had already mentally placed Alaska in the past tense.

It had started in Seattle, at Ivar's Fish Bar. Halibut fish and chips had been excellent. I was eating alone, standing on the deck at a high round outside table. Looking out to the ocean. Seattle had been fun. There was a girl. She liked me, and I liked her. She was traveling through the continental United States from east to west. Couldn't go much further west, so next up was Asia. An even bigger continent. From Seattle you strike land on the islands of Japan and you're there, Asia. You can keep going, five or six thousand miles later, you're in

Istanbul, Turkey, standing on the east bank of the Bosphorus, still in Asia, looking across the water at Europe.

I had spent years on the west side of the world's largest continent. Mostly Syria, Iraq, and Afghanistan, with assorted side trips elsewhere. Now I was in Seattle, looking toward the other side, eastern Asia. The girl wanted me to go with her on that trip, which I thought was a fine idea. Island-hopping Japan and then hit the mainland. Maybe an epic trip from Japan into North China. Then over through Mongolia and into Kazakhstan.

The problem was money, more specifically the fact that I didn't have much of it. Certainly, I didn't have enough to go traveling through Asia for a year. So, she was going to leave, and I was going to stay.

Then Joe Guilfoyle stepped in front of me. Guilfoyle was not a big man. Medium size, bearded and red-faced. He had been polite. Asked me how I liked the fish and chips. We started to talk. Turned out Joe had been in the military, 1st Marine Division out of Camp Pendleton. Guilfoyle had participated in Task Force Ripper, the assault into Kuwait City. Before my time. Now Guilfoyle was the captain of a fishing boat. He worked the salmon season in southeast Alaska. He had offered me a job. Said he had four guys for a five man crew, was looking for a fifth. I said, "Why me?"

He said, "Why not? You're staring at the ocean. I can arrange a whole lot of ocean if you're interested."

The truth is, I had already pictured what it might be like working on a fishing boat in Alaska. The picture had been a romantic one. The ocean. The bow of a wooden boat. Spray coming up off it into my face. The mountains, channels, rainforests of Alaska. Whales jumping and turning in the mist. All of that stuff was passing through my mind, and Guilfoyle knew it. He was looking at me with a little smile on his face, like a cherub.

I said, "What will I do on the boat?"

He said, "Web man."

"What's a web man?"

"Three guys on the back. Guy on the left is the weight man. He handles the sinkers that pull the net down. Guy on the right is the floater guy. Handles the floaters to keep the other side of the net up. Guy in the middle is the web man. Handles the net. That's you."

I said, "Thought there were five guys on the boat."

Guilfoyle said, "Me, skiff driver, and three guys on the back."

So I had agreed.

There had been two weeks in Seattle getting the boat ready. Painting and repairs, plus supplies. The crew had gathered. Then we drove the boat up to Alaska. Seventy-two hours, four-hour shifts. That had been in June. There had been no night. Only a twilight at the end of the day, followed by another day. Going up through the inside passage, the water had been calm. We saw porpoises and bald eagles, whales, and orcas. The picture in my head that day at Ivar's Fish Bar had been correct. That is exactly what I got.

Good times, hard work.

Four months pulling salmon out of the ocean with a five-man crew on a fifty-eight-foot purse seiner. Now I was done with that. It was time to leave. I had a plane ticket back to Seattle in my pocket. Departure was scheduled for that afternoon. I also had money in the bank. The season had been a good one, so they said. I had more than enough to get going on that epic trip through Asia. Only question was how to get to Japan. There was air travel, and there was boat travel.

But that was not up to me. The girl was still down there in Seattle. Not exactly waiting, she had used the time to take a couple of college summer classes. She had planned the Asia trip. On top of all that, she was meeting me at the airport in Seattle that evening.

Now this.

THE MAN WAS WALKING out of town, opposite direction from the airport. I thought about turning around. But I didn't.

Why not? I wasn't sure. I was thinking about that while I

followed him. Fact was, I felt like a hound on the scent. Maybe I'm a natural hunter. In the military it had been simple. I was the guy who went in and did the damage. A combat medic in a special tactics unit of the United States Air Force. Medic, but not the kind of guy that cleans up the mess, more like the guy who makes it. *That Others May Live* is the motto. But sometimes you need to clear a path to get to them.

I'd been out of the military a couple years by then. Just bumming around, pretty much. In the beginning I had wanted to feel like a free man. So I started traveling. Eventually most guys will settle down and get their feet stuck into some version of a pair of cement shoes. All the stuff that keeps a person in one place, like planting grain and watching it grow all year, versus hunting and foraging.

I guess I'm not a farmer type. No problem with farmers, I'm just not made for it.

Port Morris wasn't a large town, the curving streets ending halfway up the hill. And when the roads ended, the woods began. Not regular woods, North Pacific rainforest. There was nothing on the other side of the rainforest except channels and islands, filled with more rainforest and then mountains, then glaciers, and after that, more mountains and more glaciers. Eventually, after walking and swimming for months, you might arrive at the boundary of some remote settlement. You might be in Canada. You might be in tribal territory. That is if you hadn't already frozen to death or been eaten by a bear.

After fifteen or twenty minutes, the streets became more sparsely settled and I had to hang back pretty far just so the guy wouldn't notice me following. He was trudging along, moving steadily. Lateral to the south and uphill slightly to the east. The guy turned around a bend and I lost him. I kept on going for a while, but he wasn't there anymore.

It was a neighborhood on the outskirts of town. Maybe three houses deep from the woods. Two-story family dwellings with aluminum siding. Looked like they'd been built in the 1970s or 80s.

Cars out front were the rustic kind. Four-wheel-drives or small and reliable runners that could survive the brutal winter. The asphalt turned to gravel and the road ran sharply uphill. I saw the guy up at the end of it. He turned left and disappeared into evergreen growth.

I went indirect. A bushwhack through the woods. Easier said than done. The rainforest is thick with ferns and mossy roots. A couple of minutes later I was on the edge of a backyard looking at a smokehouse, which resembled an outdoor toilet. Fumes coming out of the chimney smelled like sockeye salmon curing. Smelled good. I shifted position around a big tree and was able to see into the large back window of the house. Looked like a living room on the left through the big window, then a kitchen on the right, giving out to an elevated deck.

I could see the man from the ice cream store. He walked from left to right through the living room and disappeared into the kitchen. Then he reappeared in the window of the kitchen door above the elevated deck. I stepped behind the tree.

Then I heard the kitchen door open and close. I peered around. A different man came down the stairs, and then across the yard. It was the bearded giant from the night before in the Porterhouse Bar. The giant lowered his head and entered the smokehouse. He was armed. A paddle frame holster behind his right hip held a small revolver of some kind.

No big deal. Alaska is pretty much the last place on earth where you'd need to worry about carrying a gun. You don't even need to register your gun. No permit required. I had to admit to myself that it was all kind of mysterious and intriguing. The bearded giant from the night before, the blonde girl, and the mustachioed guy from the ice cream store. Whatever, I was out of there.

I turned around the tree to back out of the woods and came face to face with the barrel of another gun.

Specifically, it was the short and fat barrel of an AR-15 style rifle. My eyes lingered for a moment at the black hole looking right at me, then my gaze moved forward along the fancy ribbed rail in three dimensional space to the rifle stock pushed against a shoulder, which was some kind of tactical military-grade minimalist option from a catalogue. Then I looked up at the face, it was the guy in the Subaru with the John Deere hat. He was looking back at me.

"Hands out and open, buddy."

I opened my hands and put some air in my armpits.

The guy said, "Walk to the house."

I took half a second to scold myself for not being tactically alert. But that was all.

I turned around and stepped onto the back yard grass. Then I started walking over it. The bearded giant was standing by the smokehouse holding a side of salmon. His fist was closed around the hanging wire. He stared at me, but that was it. I was expecting more. But then I figured that the giant hadn't even seen me the night before. He had looked right through me.

The smoked sockeye salmon was a strong and contrasting red against the green grass and the green woods. The bearded guy growled at me, then plucked a bit of flesh off the fish and popped it between his lips and started to chew. I looked away from him to the house. The mustachioed guy was standing in the picture window looking down. He wasn't smiling.

The barrel poked me in the spine, below my backpack and the guy said, "Move."

I considered pushing back at him. What was the guy going to do, shoot me? But I figured it was better to just go with the flow. Maybe I'd learn something.

## CHAPTER FIVE

The mustachioed guy watched me as I came in from the kitchen door on the deck. He was standing in the living room with a smirk on his face.

He said, "So this is the guy who came from town." He looked proud of himself for having said it.

I walked through and said nothing. The deck gave on to the kitchen. To my left was a living room featuring the big window, floor to ceiling. Straight ahead was a hallway and then the front door of the house. It looked as if the house was being used as some kind of dormitory for overgrown children. There were beer bottle empties on the coffee table and a stack of pizza boxes.

The guy with the AR-15 kept the gun on me. The guy with the side-parted hair and the mustache said, "Who the hell are you?"

I pushed the rifle away from me. "Someone who doesn't like guns pointed at him."

The guy in the John Deere hat put the gun back on me and took a step away. "We are still in the gun-pointing-at-you part of the relationship."

I looked at the guy with the mustache. "People follow me, then you're following them. Then I follow you, and then your guy is following me. It's like a snake eating its own tail."

The mustache smiled. It was not a pretty smile. He was all groomed with hair product and clean clothes, but it was exactly like lipstick on a pig. "I like that. Isn't it the symbol of something?"

I said, "Rebirth. Renewal. The cycle of life."

Mustache said, "Well I don't know about that." He pulled a straight-backed wood chair from a desk in the corner and placed it in the center of the room. "You're invited to sit. And let's see some ID."

I said, "It isn't going to go down like that."

The guy with the gun sniggered. "Oh yeah? How's it going down?"

I spread my hands open and spoke in a quiet and reasonable tone. I had in mind something like the emotional tone of a statement of terms and conditions. I said, "We are at a juncture right here. A key moment in the cycle of your lives. Right now, I'm more curious than interested. Curiosity is temporary, it speaks of a fleeting attention that isn't yet in the realm of interest. Broadly speaking, it can still go two ways. Either I'm interested in you, or I'm not. If I am, very bad for you. If I'm not, much better for you. That's my intuition at the moment, not knowing much about you. I have to tell you that I'm leaning on being interested. But you tell me. Should I be?"

The guy with the AR-15 was confused. "Should you be what?"

I said nothing.

Mustache looked at me seriously for a moment. Then his concentration lapsed and he said, "What're you, like a poet or something?"

The barrel poked me again. The guy with the AR-15 said, "Sit."

I don't like being poked with anything, but being poked with a gun barrel is up there on my list of the worst things to be poked with. The man with the mustache picked up a roll of duct tape. He started to unravel a length. I like duct tape. It is an important thing in the world. I've had a lot of uses for it, and plan on using it in the future. But I don't ever plan on having it used on me.

I said, "I'm not going to sit down, and if your friend doesn't stop pointing that thing at me, I'm going to wrap it around his head and then feed it to you."

He laughed. "I'd like to see that."

I turned and looked at the AR-15 guy. He wasn't smiling. I looked at the weapon, it was still pointed at me. I looked back at him. He said, "What?"

I said nothing.

Mustache was watching. He said, "My ice cream-eating friend, let me give you another piece of advice. Willets here is an actual real-life government-trained killer. So, if I were you, I'd just sit the fuck down. But it's a free country."

I looked at the man named Willets, who was looking pleased at the description. I shrugged. "Well, you could have said so from the beginning, would have saved all of us this brief moment of tension."

He allowed a thin smile. "Good man. Now sit your ass down."

I moved toward the chair and noticed that the barrel of Willets' rifle had lowered a pinch. Which was what I was waiting for. Flattery never fails. I took another small step and put a hand on the chair back, like I was going to sit down on it. But instead of sitting on it, I whipped the chair around and hurled it at Willets. He used the rifle to block the chair, which had the effect of radically adjusting his line of potential fire. From me, to the ceiling. That was the whole point, because then I could follow up on the distraction with something more kinetic. In this case, a knife edge strike into Willets' windpipe.

The edge of my hand went into his throat. Hard, fast, like a snake bite. I stood back and watched him. I also looked at Mustache, who didn't react. Willets was silent for a half second, kind of standing there looking lost, then he wasn't silent anymore. When you feel like you might suffocate, nothing else really matters. So, Willets stumbled around for a while coughing and sputtering, turning red and paying no attention at all to the gun.

I stepped over to him, took the weapon in one hand, and kicked him into the sofa with my foot. I was closer to the big window now. Down below, the bearded giant was repairing the smokehouse door.

He looked up at me through the window and we made eye contact. Then he looked away. By then, Mustache had a pistol up. He said, "Who the hell are you?"

I inspected the AR-15 copy. One in the chamber. I ejected the round onto the carpet. Then I thumbed the magazine release and tossed it into the kitchen, heavy with ammunition. I was aiming for the sink, but a couple of beer bottles got in the way and there was a clatter. I dropped the gun onto the sofa next to Willets.

I said, "As I have already said, you should think of me as someone who doesn't like guns pointed at them."

Mustache said, "I asked you who you are."

"None of your damned business."

"I like to be the one who decides on my business."

I said, "I bet you do." I turned back to the window. Willets was getting to his feet. I said, "I think your friend will live. I can't guarantee how long."

Willets coughed. He said, "That was a sucker punch. I'd like to see you in a fair fight."

Just then, a dark-haired thin guy walked into the room from further back. He seemed startled, like he had just woken up. "What's going on?"

The mustache man put up his hand like a stop signal. Didn't even look at the guy. "Get back to your room, Jerry."

Jerry backed off. I heard a door close down the hall. Mustache didn't say anything for a moment, and I could almost smell him thinking hard, like he was burning out the clutch. He looked at Willets. Willets looked at him. He shook his head, as if he were sad. Willets said, "What?"

Mustache lowered the pistol. He said, "No, this isn't happening."

Willets said, "What isn't?"

Mustache said, "This is one of Mister Lawrence's crazy soldiers." He looked at me. "You look like a dumb fisherman, but you're not just a dumb fisherman. Why didn't you just say you work for Mister Lawrence?"

I said nothing. I had no idea who Mister Lawrence was. But it looked like a light bulb had gone off in the guy's head. He'd decided on something and had convinced himself that it was true. I took a stab in the dark.

I said, "Did you expect that we would just let an asshole like you get on with it by yourself?"

He was scratching his head. Like something was really puzzling. "Why the scuffle with the East Coast guy just now? Mister Lawrence said to keep them in check. How does you messing with them help anything?"

I said nothing.

Mustache shook his head ruefully. "You can go back and tell Mister Lawrence that everything's cool and under control. We've got that under wraps."

I figured I could play along. I said, "Doesn't look that way to me. That's not what I'm going to be telling Mister Lawrence."

He was confused. He said, "Look, you could've said something. Mister Lawrence is a good client and I'm fulfilling the task as requested. Okay?" He looked at Willets. Mustache said, "And no hard feelings huh? We're just doing our job here. What would you do if some special operations-looking guy was creeping up on you?"

I turned and walked to the front of the house. A stack of unopened mail was piled up on a floating shelf near the door. I picked up a couple of envelopes. They were addressed to a Mister Deckart. I looked back at the mustache guy.

"Deckart."

He didn't say anything, but it was his name. The other guy was standing now, forlorn next to his superior.

I said their names slowly. "Deckart and Willets." As I spoke, I gave each of them a good look, like a facial recognition machine scanning and memorizing. I went out the door without bothering to shut it. Then I walked down the steps and into the front yard. The gravel driveway tilted to the asphalt road twenty yards away.

I walked down the road, thinking. Mister Lawrence. A bunch of hard guys in a house in Port Morris, Alaska. Another bunch from the East Coast, according to the hard guys. Now was the right time to get out of town before things actually got interesting. It was time to walk away.

Which I did. Down to Water Street, and then hooked a left.

This was Port Morris, Alaska, not New York City. The taxi office was a ramshackle building that looked like it had only barely survived the winter, and the next one was going to be a close call. The office was up a rickety scaffold of worn exterior wooden stairs. The dispatcher was a big guy in a chair eating boiled crabs. He asked me where I was going. I said, the airport. He nodded and pointed outside. Said the car would be along in a minute.

A minute and a half later I was in the backseat of a yellow cab on the way up to the airport. The driver had thoughtfully placed a box of tissues in the elastic net behind his seat. I took one and carefully cleaned the nose blood from my knife blade. The flight down to Seattle wasn't for another couple of hours, but I figured I'd pass the time at the cafe. I yawned and pictured myself asleep in a chair.

## CHAPTER SIX

THE AIRPORT CAFE WAS WARM. Two picture windows faced west toward the sun, hanging halfway up in the late afternoon. Between the horizon and the windows was a single strip runway, empty for now. The cafe was a glorified waiting room. Next door was the only other enclosure on the site, a desk staffed by a man with a walrus mustache. He was wrapped in a flannel shirt. It was a small airport. The guy said the flight was fully booked.

The plane had not come in yet but was expected. The small airplane would land soon and disgorge its nineteen passengers from Seattle. Once they were clear, my backpack would go in the hold. I would go in a seat, along with eighteen others. An hour and fifty minutes later we would hit the tarmac, back in Seattle-Tacoma International Airport, and the girl would be waiting.

I expected that we would head back to wherever she was staying. Maybe we would have some recreational activities right there and then. Afterwards, we might go out and find some place with live music, beer, and barbecue. Preferably a place with gender diversity and a good mix of beard to no beard. The following day I was planning to visit a barber shop and get a hot towel shave.

End of one era, beginning of the next.

But for the time being I was at a cafe counter in the Port Morris airport, one hand resting on the chipped formica, fingers curled through the handle of a coffee cup, fingertips resting lightly against the hot cylinder. The other hand was resting comfortably on my knee. The airport cafe had two big windows, one straight ahead to the runway, another downhill to the approach road from town.

I was looking right out at the runway. A fancy private Lear Jet had just finished unloading its human cargo. A small group of middle-aged men and women. They were dressed in designer outdoor wear, pulling expensive hand luggage. Moving between the luxurious interior of the silver aircraft, and a waiting luxury mini-bus. It was a German twenty-seater, painted a glossy dark green with a white logo that read 'Green Gremlin Tours'. A smiling Gremlin sat on the word 'Green'.

I watched as the bus loaded up and took off, tracked it carving downhill to the south, where it passed another fancy vehicle making the opposite journey.

It was the black Chevy Suburban from earlier, making its way up the hill to the airport. The Suburban was big, shiny, and new, gleaming in the evening light. Like a secret service vehicle, or the personal car of an FBI official. The Chevy eased to a halt right in front of the cafe. The rear door opened and a tall woman came down off the cream leather seat. She was wearing dark aviator sunglasses and I had never seen her before.

This woman was in her fifties and looked rich. The Chevy's windows were tinted so it was impossible to see the driver. The Suburban rolled slowly away, and the woman disappeared from view as she entered next door. She came into the cafe about twenty seconds after that.

The woman stood briefly in the doorway and took in the situation. Me at the counter looking back at her. Nobody else. Behind me, a coffee pot steamed. She was dressed like an important person on a

Sunday. Jogging tights, fleece jersey, jogging shoes. But with the earrings and the hair management of a corporate executive.

She strode toward me. "Where is everyone? I need some of that coffee. Now."

I said, "Everyone is using the ladies room."

She said, "There isn't a ladies room. There's only one toilet, so that makes it an everyone's room."

"Gender neutral. They should paint a fancy sign."

"Could bring the tourists up from California."

"And then where would we go for coffee?"

She said, "Good point. Did she go to the ladies room a long time ago?"

"About three and a half minutes."

"So she'll be out soon, unless there are issues, in which case she might not be out soon. I think I'll pour myself a cup."

The woman walked around the counter. She found a cup and poured coffee into it. She set it on the counter and came back around. She straddled a stool next to mine and extended her hand. "Jane Abrams." Her hand was cool and the fingers were long and well cared-for. I liked her.

I said, "Tom Keeler. But you already knew that."

Jane Abrams ignored that. She examined me. I knew what she was seeing. Worn Carhartt work pants, folding knife clipped to a side pocket, black ball cap with a Purse Seiner Association logo, the beard.

She said, "Yes, but I haven't seen you for myself yet. In person, I mean. Just the photograph of you looking surprised and heroic."

I said, "I saw your vehicle earlier. Who was the blonde girl last night in the bar?"

She said, "What you did last night took courage."

I said, "Not really. You see a smaller person attacked by a much larger person, you do something about it."

"From what I heard it was you who did something, and not anybody else."

"And then what? On that basis you decided I could be useful?"

"Yes. On that basis I asked my team to find you so that I could have a conversation with you. It looks like they found you, but you didn't enjoy being found."

I said nothing.

She moved her eyes lazily to look at me again. "Listen, Mister Keeler. You're here, right now. Right place, right time. Let me pay you three hundred dollars for a private conversation. I'll explain what I want, and you get paid regardless of the outcome. Then you take the plane and go on down to Seattle if you like."

I said, "Not interested in money."

She said, "Money is the only universal truth."

I shook my head. "Doesn't mean I want yours."

She said, "What do you want then?"

"Nothing." I looked at her and drained the coffee cup.

Abrams shook her head. She was beginning to get pissed off, which was a tell right there. A woman who was used to getting her way. But then I saw her relax and control herself. It was like watching the conflict of one personality over another, with the most sensible winning out. I liked that. A couple of early passengers came into the cafe. Abrams looked out the window. The fancy private jet had taken off. The runway was lonely.

For a while we looked at the view. Abrams started to speak, but her voice was drowned out by an approaching aircraft. The sound hit us suddenly and we turned around to watch. The new plane was a small commuter, a Cessna or a Bombardier. The engine roar washed through the window glass, and speaking was impossible until the pilot shut the engine down fifty yards from the terminal. A minute later a guy from the airport walked over and pulled down the stairs. The paint was chipped on the door. The aircraft looked like it had been working hard these last couple of decades. Passengers started to come down off the plane.

Abrams said, "My son is missing and I'm here to find him and bring him back." Abrams pulled a photograph from a zip pocket. It was a picture of a guy in his twenties. Smiling, blond, with a Harvard sweatshirt.

I thought, Harvard, East Coast.

Abrams said, "My son's name is George. Will you help me find him?"

"You already have quite a team. Did you hire some kind of private detective agency?"

She said, "No of course not. These are friends who have known George and who care about him. I asked them to help me." Abrams looked at the glare coming through the window, like she was struggling to contain tears. "And now you saw, we're being intimidated. If I can't find anyone to help us protect ourselves I think we'll have to leave. I'm afraid of what might happen. But it's my son, Keeler. It's George. I can't just walk away."

I looked at Jane Abrams. She was not even aware that her team had been followed by Deckart and Willets. There had been other intimidations. She was completely clueless, in way over her head. Her eyes were wet. Good acting, or real. No way of knowing.

She summoned her courage. "Please, Mister Keeler, let me tell you about George. He is a scientist. He came here on a research project, part of his doctorate. But it's been a month since I heard from him. We're close, it isn't normal that he breaks contact for a month. I became concerned. So, I tried the police, the university, everybody I could think of, but nobody's interested, nobody knows anything."

"What do you expect me to do about that?"

"We need protection while we figure out what's happened."

I said, "You need to go to the police."

She said, "I've already done that. I've gone through the hoops. I have filed a missing persons report but they won't act on it. They said that George is an adult and has every right to go missing."

I said, "And you think there's something else going on."

"I do." She was nodding vigorously. "I came up here, and from day one we are being bullied. So yes. Now I most definitely think that something else is going on."

"Why would your son be in trouble? What was he researching?"

She shook her head. "The only thing I get from George is 'Mom, you would never understand.'"

I said, "Not even a ballpark guess."

"From what I gather, physics isn't a ballpark game. There is no wide general research, it's all extremely specialized. Last I heard from George he was working on acoustic modeling of seismic fissures, whatever that means. But that was when he was doing his masters, and the research was in Kazakhstan."

I said nothing.

Abrams placed her palm on the countertop. She said, "It was a stroke of luck that Amber ran into you last night."

I said, "Last night. The girl took my picture. You ran some kind of search on it?"

Abrams said, "Put a picture into the right computer, with a guy like Jason tapping the keyboard, out comes all kinds of interesting stuff."

She looked up at me, "Jason is the one whose nose you violated, by the way."

"He should have stayed away from me."

She shrugged. "Character building. Jason is a computer genius. He likes to go to the gym, so he looks the part, but he is not an experienced man. Not like you. We are desperate for someone like you."

I said, "Someone like me."

"Yes, Mister Keeler, someone exactly like you."

"And what am I like?"

Abrams examined me critically. "You seem to be someone who doesn't walk away."

I said, "If I were you, I'd go back to the police. Tell them about the intimidation, be insistent. Don't take no for an answer. If you don't want to go to the cops again, you should hire some real help. If you've got the money, they will come. Your computer genius can use his computer."

She looked out at the view. The cruise ship and the great ocean behind it. She said, "I don't have time for that, Keeler. And I can't quit. If you change your mind I'm at the Beaver Falls Lodge. I have the whole place."

I said nothing.

She said, "Do you know it?"

"Heard of it."

Abrams got up to go. "I appreciate that you are reticent to sell your services for money. It is even noble, or something. Unfortunately that does not help my son. If you insist, you can help us for free. And if you do decide to stay, I'll refund the ticket and pay your expenses, of course."

The black Suburban was idling on the other side of the airport building. Jane Abrams walked over to it, climbed into the back and looked at me. She had the aviator sunglasses on again. The driver was the blond bearded guy I'd seen following me from the diner. His bandaged hand was resting on the steering wheel. I pictured the giant giving that hand a twist, maybe breaking a finger or two, Deckart laughing in the background.

## CHAPTER SEVEN

I watched the shiny black Suburban wind its way down the hill. I counted five minutes. New passengers had been collecting at the airport, not quite eighteen of them just yet. It was almost time to get on the plane. But there was an issue with that.

I was interested.

I needed to make a phone call, and I happen to be the last guy on the planet who refuses to carry a phone. A phone in your pocket is like a nagging parent. I loved my mother, but she's dead and I'm not looking for a replacement. So, I dropped a couple of quarters into a phone in the airport building. Pay phones are hard to find and getting harder. Like animals facing extinction. But you can usually find one around travel hubs. Like airports and bus terminals. If that doesn't work, phones can be borrowed from strangers. After all, everyone's got one.

The girl in Seattle answered after three rings. I told her I was going to miss the plane. She said, "Did you meet another girl?"

I said, "Something like that, but not what you're thinking."

She laughed. "You want me to wait or you want me to go?" Her voice sounded good down the line. Happy, unburdened by regret.

"I guess you should go. I don't know how long I'll be, or what's going to happen exactly."

She said, "Alright. You take care of yourself, Keeler."

I hung up the phone. A taxi pulled in and two guys climbed out. They had backpacks in the trunk. When they'd hauled their gear out, I stabbed a chin at the driver. He nodded and I got in. I paid him off ten minutes later, down at the Eagle Cove cannery. The boats were tied up on the other side of the factory. On my way to the waterside I had to dodge a forklift moving hot cans of pink salmon. Which brought me right up against a cluster of Japanese inspectors leaning over a cooler. I figured that was the last batch of sea urchins, or some other delicacy.

There were two kinds of purse seiners in the fleet, the new kind and the old kind. The new ones were million-dollar fibreglass and steel jobs that looked like they'd been designed on a computer, which they had. The old ones were wood and paint and looked like they were held together by glue and screw, which they were.

The *Sea Foam* was one of the old ones. Fifty-eight feet long and painted in blue and white. I found Captain Joe Guilfoyle in the galley, drinking a Seven-Up through the hole in his beard. He was reading a book and looked up when I came in.

Guilfoyle said, "I thought I'd never see you again."

I said, "I was hoping for the same. But here we are."

"Yes, here you are standing in front of me. You must have missed the cooking."

"Don't remember you cooking."

"Well that's true enough. Didn't say *my* cooking, just said the cooking."

I said, "People cook all over. It's a common occurrence. I had a burger for lunch, someone cooked it."

"Fair enough. The salient fact is that it wasn't me."

I sat down across from Guilfoyle and leaned back. "Does the name Lawrence mean anything to you?"

He said, "The long version of the diminutive Larry. Usually Lawrence comes first, and then someone whittles it down to Larry."

I said, "Lawrence as a last name, as in *Mister* Lawrence."

"Means nothing to me." He put the paperback face-down on the galley table. I could see a man on a horse with a gun, upside down. "Thought you'd lost interest in Alaska. Thought there was a girl in Seattle with a plan."

I said, "Yeah, there was and there is. But something came up."

"Mister Lawrence."

I nodded. "That's right."

Guilfoyle shook his head. "Haven't heard of a Mister Lawrence. There's a guy called Larry works at the fuel dock. Not sure anyone ever called him mister—or Lawrence, for that matter."

I knew Larry. He was the guy who pumped diesel into the boats. I said, "Not Larry from the fuel dock."

Guilfoyle said. "Didn't think it was. Is this Mister Lawrence supposed to be from Port Morris?"

"I don't know. Maybe."

"Why don't you ask June? If anyone knows, it's June."

I said, "You planning on using the bike?"

"I'm not. Help yourself."

"Appreciate it."

Guilfoyle said, "You're welcome to stay aboard as long as the boat's here, but I'm thinking of taking her down to Seattle day after tomorrow. If you're done with Mister Lawrence by then, you can drive her down with me."

Guilfoyle went back to his paperback and soda. I went down the ladder and stashed my backpack on the bunk I'd vacated only a few hours earlier. The berth was just rear of the engine room and had the oily smell of diesel. I came up on deck and removed the mountain bike tied down with bungee cords behind the smokestack.

By the time the rubber hit the road it was late afternoon. The bike's fat tires hummed against the blacktop. There were no other vehicles in sight so I had it all to myself. To my left, the rainforest. To my right, the Pacific Ocean. Eagle Cove down to Port Morris is a twenty-minute ride if you're going easy. During the season, the boats docked up at the cannery every couple of days. I would take the bike into town and get dinner. Guilfoyle hadn't worked the galley, that had been another guy, and that guy hadn't been a cook either.

When I got into town I biked along the port to the SEAS office, Southeast Alaska Seiners Association. The building was an unglamorous two-story walk-up on the edge of the long dock in front of town. It was part of a messy cluster serving administrative functions to the maritime activity that made the existence of Port Morris possible. That included the cruise ship and charter offices. The big boat loomed on the other side of the buildings, omnipresent for the past few days.

June was at her desk, as usual. But she wasn't alone when I looked in. There was a man leaned against the filing cabinet holding a wrapped gift. They both looked at me when I put my head around the door.

I said, "Cappuccino from the New York Cafe?"

She said, "I ever say no?"

"No."

"Never going to change, Keeler. Even when you're done and gone, which I thought was yesterday."

I said nothing and let the door swing shut.

Twenty minutes later I was sitting across from June and the guy was gone. His gift was in front of June, unopened. June poured sugar from two paper packets into her coffee cup. I watched her stirring the beige liquid with two nub-nosed plastic sticks. I sipped my coffee, black no sugar.

I said, "What is it, your birthday?"

She looked up from the coffee business and made a face. "Freaking Steve. He forgot my birthday is tomorrow, not today." She touched the gift. "I don't mind, it's the thought that counts."

June was planted in her chair. Part of my job on the boat had been to bring the catch reports to June each week for the past four months. I'd never seen her out of that chair. I asked her about Mister Lawrence.

She said, "Mister Lawrence. Sure. Everyone knows who he is."

"Everyone except me."

"I meant everyone who actually lives here. No offense, but you guys from outside don't count. What do you need to know about Mister Lawrence?"

"Start at the beginning."

June's fleshy arms were laid out on either side of her keyboard. She was looking at me through thick glasses. On the other side of them were watery blue eyes, magnified in the frames. Her hair was lank and brown. Strands of it were stuck to her forehead. She said, "Mister Lawrence owns the property up past the old fire tower. Some kind of business person, I guess. Other than that, he's a big contributor to the town. Paid for the library refurb', plus the new police car upgrades. Donates to us at SEAS."

"The town rich guy."

She nodded. "There are a couple, but yup."

I said, "Made his money in fish or something?"

June said, "No idea. He might be First Nations. Maybe he was here back when the tribes incorporated. So, it might be something like that, but you wouldn't know it to look at him."

"What does he look like?"

She stared up at the ceiling for a moment. "I'd say, he looks like a frog."

"A frog."

"Yup. First off, he's small and doesn't have a beard. In fact, he doesn't have hair at all. I heard he was born with zero hair, like not even eye lashes. Nothing." June was staring at me, and I knew that I was now swimming in the muddy waters of a small town rumor mill. She said, "And no pubes either, according to Randy Pearson."

"How would Randy know?"

"He married a hooker. She heard it from another hooker. Mister Lawrence goes for hookers."

I said, "Past the old fire tower huh?"

June nodded. "Yup." She sipped at her drink. "But you won't even get close. He's got dogs and fences and all kinds of security stuff like that. Mister Lawrence is a very private individual. He moves by helicopter, Hummer, and yacht."

"You ever actually see him?"

"You mean in person?"

I nodded.

She said, "Saw him once at bingo. He wasn't playing, but his wife was doing a charity draw."

"He's got a wife."

"That was a while ago. Maybe he's still got a wife. Maybe it wasn't a wife. Maybe a girlfriend. Put it this way, it was a female woman type of person with tits and long hair and earrings and a necklace in a dress. She was picking out the ping-pong balls from the hopper for about ten minutes. Then he picked her up and put her in the Hummer."

"He's got a Hummer."

June nodded. "Yup. Drives a big gold Hummer."

I said, "You saw him in the Hummer, not necessarily up close and personal."

"You want to get picky about it, I saw him through the window of the bingo hall, which is actually the high school gym, and then through the window of his vehicle. That's as close as I ever got to Mister Lawrence. Me. Air. Window. Air. More window. Mister Lawrence."

"Okay."

"Steve says his boat is filling up."

I said, "Who's Steve?"

"Guy who was just here talking to me. Manages the booking office next door."

"His boat is filling up. What does that mean?"

June said, "Filling up with passengers I guess, which is a good thing for Mister Lawrence, since he owns it, in case you think that's relevant. That's all I meant."

That was interesting. I said, "So, all those tourists walking around. They're coming off a boat owned by Mister Lawrence?"

"Boat hasn't left yet. Those tourists are getting a load of Port Morris while the boat gets ready and fills up. I guess they'll be leaving in a day or two. Not much more than that." June thought of something else. "You can see the place from the top of the fire tower. Save you getting bit by the dogs or electrocuted by the fence."

I raised my eyebrows. "Can you now?"

## CHAPTER EIGHT

The old fire tower was a five-mile bike ride through the woods, the last two of them uphill. Good exercise. By the time I got up there it was as late in the afternoon as you can get without being technically evening.

The tower had nine flights of stairs, framed in a rudimentary steel cage. The bottom started off wide and thick, and by the time I made it to the top, the cage was tight enough to touch on all sides. Up top was a cabin built from split spruce. The stairs came out the floor facing north and west. The sides were open to the air. If you wanted, you could jump out. Nothing to stop a person from falling all nine flights to smash themselves on the bald hilltop below.

The setting sun was bathing the treetops in gold. It was a great view. About a half mile away I could see some kind of a structure poking up out of the woods. A large modern house, with wood and glass glinting in the light. A couple of hundred yards west of that I could glimpse a piece of a lower structure, like an industrial building.

Then the wind died down, and everything got still and quiet, which is how I heard the breathing.

It was coming from the other side of the cabin, the side facing south. I stepped around the stair cage. The cabin was built square, around five paces across any way you chose. Stepping around the stair cage ate up two of those paces. Then I stopped. I was facing out the south side.

If the view north had been interesting with the sunset and architecture, the view to the south was stunning. The edge of the South East Alaskan archipelago faded off into the Pacific Ocean, hit by the late sun. But that was outside. Inside the cabin was a woman. She was cross-legged on the floor, facing me, with her eyes closed. She looked harmonious.

The woman was in her forties with long gray-streaked hair roped in a braid down her back, dressed pragmatically in a wool shirt, jeans, and hiking boots. I figured she was doing something spiritual, like deep meditation, or a special form of yoga. She opened her eyes and looked at me, but said nothing.

I said nothing in return.

Then she spoke. "Nice view, huh?"

I said, "I'm sorry to disturb you, ma'am, I'm leaving."

She said, "You just got here."

Which was the truth. I said nothing again. Walked back around to the other side and looked out at the other view. The house wasn't far from the water, maybe another quarter mile to the west. Because the fire tower was so high, a rocky cove was exposed to view.

The woman stepped next to me. She said, "So you've come to look at that?"

We were side by side looking out over the trees, arms rested on the thick spruce railing.

I said, "House looks new."

"Maybe seven years. Brought in their own people. Outside labor, outside architects, rammed it through the planning commission."

I said, "Sounds like you're an expert?"

She shook her head. "An interested neighbor."

I said, "What else about it is interesting?"

"Well now." She turned to face me. "Built on disputed land, which is always interesting."

"Disputed how?"

The woman pointed. "You see the cove?"

"Yes."

"Just to the south of the cove is a small island that you can't see because the trees are in the way. It's called Bell Island. They built a Navy installation there in the sixties, but it only really got going in the seventies. Became some kind of research installation by the end of the eighties. By the mid-nineties it was hell bent for leather, all kinds of thinking and calculating and measuring going on in there, not that we know what about exactly. Scientists and experts coming in from the lower forty-eight. Hotels were filled up, restaurants had to up their game for more sophisticated customers. Then by the end of the nineties they didn't need it anymore and the Navy quit the island."

I said, "And how does that relate to a dispute about the house?"

She said, "It relates because the property is connected. The Navy requisitioned the island and all the land in proximity. When the property was sold to the present owner, the island came with it. The tribal authorities disputed the sale because it was originally tribal land. It should have reverted to the tribe instead of to a rich guy."

"The rich guy isn't First Nations."

"No, he isn't."

I said, "Where's he from then?"

The woman's eyes were the color of the sea. She was smiling, which made a few lines crinkle around them. It was attractive. She said, "What do I look like, the town ordinance clerk?"

I thought about June in her chair. I said, "No."

"Right." She leaned her hip against the timber cabin framing. "I don't know where the guy's from."

We both looked at the view some more, for maybe two minutes. I looked sideways at her. I already liked the fact that this woman was capable of being in silence. I said, "Sorry to disturb your meditation."

She smiled. "I wasn't meditating. I was sitting down and I had my eyes closed."

"I'm Tom Keeler."

"Lavinia Stone Chandler."

"I don't know if I can say all that."

"Debatable whether it's seven or eight syllables. In any case, people here call me Ellie." I got a chance to sneak a look at her in profile. The light was flattering. She turned to face me again. "Why are you interested in Mister Lawrence?"

I said, "Somebody asked me if I worked for him today."

"Asked in what context?"

"The context was unpleasant, partially physical. Emotionally violent."

The skin around Ellie's eyes went taut, and I had the feeling that she'd shifted in her character. Pragmatic and watchful. She said, "I see."

"There was something else. When they came to the conclusion that I did work for Mister Lawrence, they were satisfied. The issue being, these weren't the kind of guys whose satisfaction is valued, broadly speaking. In terms of civics. So, it left me wondering. What kind of work would a person be doing if he worked for Mister Lawrence?"

She looked alerted to the subject. "Yes, that would be the right question to ask. I guess you concluded that it would not be pleasant work."

I nodded. "Most likely not."

She examined me in the same way as Jane Abrams had, up and down, and then up again. "Fisherman. But not a fisherman."

"Was a fisherman for a minute. Now I'm just a guy."

Ellie shook her head. "Not just a guy."

"And you?"

She hooked a finger in the hem of her wool shirt and lifted it a couple inches. Under the wool, an olive green undergarment was tucked into jeans. The badge clipped to her belt glinted in the light.

Ellie said, "Chief of Police, Chilkat Tribal Authority."

# CHAPTER NINE

Ellie saw something down below and waved. I looked over the railing. A man and a woman had walked into the clearing from a forest trail.

She said, "My friends. I have to go."

We came down from the fire tower stairs together, taking our time. Ellie said, "You know the difference between a puzzle and a mystery?"

"I have the feeling you're going to tell me regardless."

She said, "That's what my son always says. With a puzzle, you know there's something to solve. You just need to find that one piece to complete the picture. With a mystery you don't know what the final picture is going to be. You don't even know if there is one. Solving the mystery means finding the puzzle."

I said, "I was thinking more like I got my foot into someone else's dog shit."

Ellie said, "Another way of putting it."

We came to a platform three or four flights from the ground. I could see her friends now, an older woman and a teenage boy. Ellie turned to me with her hands in her back pockets. "If you've still got your boot heel stuck in dog shit, come see me. Might find something lying around that can help you scrape it off."

I said, "Might come see you anyway."

She smiled. "You do that."

Then we walked down the remainder of the stairs. At the bottom, Ellie made a brief introduction. The woman was Helen, and the boy was Hank. Mother and son. Helen was a distracted, academic type. Tall and thin with her hair wound up around a pencil. Hank looked about fifteen or sixteen, weedy, with yellowish skin and black hair hanging below the ears.

Hank looked at me with a famished gaze. I wondered where the father was in this story. The boy wore a leather jacket over a quilted plaid hunting shirt. I figured it might be tough being a teenager in Alaska. Not much to do except hiking and hunting.

The three of them were going for a sunset walk. The fire tower had been the meeting point. I watched Ellie walk away. Striding downhill. She had long legs and the boots made them even longer. Older than me by a decade maybe, but looking good. The sunlight kicked off against her plaited hair, bobbing as she went.

I was going the other way, to Beaver Falls. I figured I would check in on Jane Abrams and see what that was all about. It would be good to surprise her. Maybe I would learn something.

Now that I was interested.

When I reached the road, I swung the bike onto the asphalt and let it roll downhill, coasting around the ridges until I got to the edge of town. There, the last buildings faded out behind me and the road was a gray line in the growing darkness. It was all Pacific rainforest. I got into a rhythm with the pedalling and breathing. Just me and the bike in the middle of nothing. Maybe a couple of bears were watching. The chain and wheel bearings made only the slightest purring sound. Joe Guilfoyle was a meticulous man.

A mile down the road, I turned up a logging path. The trail cut north across the island, above Port Morris and over to Beaver Falls. My plan was to get there the back way, through the woods. I wanted to take a good look before committing. The logging trail veered off in the wrong direction, so I stashed the bike and walked through the rainforest. An hour later night had fallen. I was up on one knee looking over the Beaver Falls Lodge.

The lodge was an isolated resort in the southeast Alaskan style. All rustic wood with First Nation stylings. The place was a set of connected wood structures looking across the water to Gem Cove on the other side of the channel. The main building had an elevated deck with huge picture windows. The lights were on. Clean smoke came out of the chimney. I could see down to the parking lot. The Chevy Suburban was parked in the guest spot.

I walked down and got under the deck. No lights on downstairs, just upstairs. I went around the corner and down toward the water. The lodge had a dock that pushed out into the channel. A weathered zodiac boat was tied up and waiting. I came around the other side. Still no lights on downstairs. The walkway to the entrance was lit and lined with thick rope connected to wood posts every five yards or so. I walked in the ferns below it and looked up at the deck. Lights on, jazz music playing.

I looked up at the walkway. I was not interested in making an appearance on a security camera video. So, I came around again to the side where I had started and shimmied up the thick deck support until I was able to fold myself over the balcony. I crouched in the dark corner, listening. A few yards away was the picture window and a set of wide sliding doors.

Didn't hear anything besides the music coming from inside, so I moved over and looked in the window. Nothing to see, just embers in the fireplace and an empty room. Nothing moving except the smoke from the hot coals going up the chimney. The sliding door was not locked. I pushed the left side open and stepped in. The volume went up on Nat King Cole singing "Autumn Leaves". To my nine o'clock, polished wood countertops formed a horseshoe-shaped wet bar.

I stepped around the counter. Jane Abrams lay on the terracotta tile floor. Blood had pooled beneath her head. She looked very dead;

her right eye was open. Her left eye had been punctured by a bullet, so was neither open or closed really. There were two more entry wounds at her chest. A whiskey glass had shattered where it impacted in the corner. The place smelled of bourbon. The ice had melted and the water was running up against the blood and starting to swirl in with it.

## CHAPTER TEN

I HELD a palm a half-inch above Jane Abrams' mouth. The lips were slightly parted, showing the tops of even white teeth. There was no breath, but there was warmth. Her internals were cooling down, but that would take time. Eventually the body would be room temperature. Then the decomposition would begin and she'd heat up again. Except by then she wouldn't be a she, she'd be an it. The sound system was controlled from a little box on the counter. I used my knuckle to press the stop button.

Abrams stared up at the ceiling with her one good eye. Good in terms of it being in one piece, but not good in terms of seeing. The unseeing eye stared sightlessly into the burning core of a recessed halogen. I was crouched over the body. The rest of the lodge house made only small and subtle sounds, like the embers in the fireplace, like the sound of the wind outside and the creaking of wood joists.

I stayed still and silent. Counted off two minutes. Which is a long time when you're counting. I eased up out of the crouch and stepped carefully back from the blood. Jane Abrams had been wearing white leather ballet flats. The one on the right foot had come off, revealing painted toenails. The chosen color was black.

I made my way across the open space of the lounge area. By then I had my knife open and held loosely in my hand. Knife against gun does not make a good equation for the guy with the knife. But then it's better than nothing. The fireplace was modern. A big circular pan in the center of the room, with the flue pipe traveling up to the vaulted ceiling and punching through it. The seating was arranged around the hearth, a couple of different areas with appropriate furniture choices for the place and the context. Beyond that was another open space and further on I could see a pool table. I figured that was a games room.

As I crept silently forward I noticed a hand on the floor beneath the pool table. The hand was attached to an arm in a sleeve, and none of it was moving. That was for damn sure. More than that, I couldn't see. There was a doorway off the corridor. It had a sign on it that read 'Sauna'. The door had a little window made of tinted toughened glass. I pushed the door open with my boot. The hinges creaked. It opened into a vestibule containing a simple wooden bench, hanging hooks for clothes, a neat pile of white towels, and a neat pile of white robes. It all looked clean and fresh and smelled like laundry detergent and heated wood.

From the vestibule, there were two ways to go. The sauna, and the bathroom. I toed the bathroom open. Empty and humid. The shower curtain was wet. I pushed the sauna door in. Empty and hot. There was a towel on the bench. I picked it up. Moist. The coals were being cooked by the electric coil below. A pail of water was beside it, the surface flat and unmoving. A wooden ladle lay over the top. The ladle was dry, which didn't mean anything. It was a sauna. Everything was dry. Except the towel, which meant that it had recently contained something wet, like a person who had just showered.

But there was no longer a wet person wrapped in the towel.

I backed out of there and continued down the corridor. At the threshold of the games room I could see bodies, plural, two of them. One was the blonde bearded guy with the bandaged hand. The other was the guy whose nostril I had sliced with my fishing knife.

The sliced nostril guy was sprawled upright into a liquor cabinet. His head rested on a shelf where it shared space with Jack Daniels and Jim Beam. There was also Makers Mark and Wild Turkey. The shelf above had even more exalted characters, like Laphroaig, Yamazaki, and Lagavulin, among others. Beside the nostril cut, the guy had suffered a gunshot wound to his neck that was visible from the doorway. I moved closer and saw another one at the temple, in front of his left ear. That had been the shot which pushed him into the liquor cabinet. The neck shot had been the follow-up, pinning him there. It occurred to me that the neck shot had been a kind of joke. Like the nostril slice guy had been about to fall over and the neck shot had redressed the balance. A third bullet had gone in at the heart. There was not much blood from that one. The blood from the head shot was pooling on the glass shelf, running in and around the bottles, but not spilling over the slightly raised shelf lip.

The blond bearded guy had been playing pool. The shooter had got him first in the back of the head. That shot had killed him. But he had been standing upright and the head is a heavy thing. When the brain ceased to function, it had stopped firing out messages to the guy's muscles. The head was no longer able to defy gravity and had tumbled forward and down. The rest of his body had followed. The head had smashed into the top of the side rail, leaving a nice mark in the polished wood. The body had then crumpled to the floor facedown, where it had stayed. The guy's arm had unfolded beneath the table.

Beside the head wound I couldn't see another entry wound. But given that the others had been shot three times, it was likely that this guy had been as well. Which is why I figured the entry wound was facing the floor, chest most likely. But there was no exit wound at the back. So I guesstimated right then and there that the gun had been a .22 caliber.

There were three drinks in the games room. Two beer bottles on a small table between comfortable lounge chairs. A whiskey glass on a counter near the liquor cabinet. Two dead guys, one dead woman. Four drinks in total if you included Abrams' smashed whiskey glass.

I was thinking about the blonde girl and the wet towel in the sauna. I dipped a finger into the whiskey glass and tasted it. Diluted bourbon. The ice had melted.

But then I was thinking about myself, because I could hear police sirens in the distance. I was thinking that being in the house when the police arrived would be somewhere between bad and catastrophic. Not that I was guilty of anything, but good luck explaining that to a judge.

## CHAPTER ELEVEN

BUT FIRST THERE were things to do, things to know about. There were the bodies and the blood and the smashed glass. There were casings to check for, but no casings to be found. Which didn't surprise me, as the killings had all the features of a professional hit. I figured I had five minutes, tops. Time enough for a rapid tour. The Beaver Falls Lodge had five bedrooms. Four of which had been occupied. One minute per room, one minute for miscellaneous movement and to get out of the house.

I didn't see surveillance cameras. Part of what you get when you can afford luxury is privacy. There would be a camera at the gate, to scan and record vehicles.

I looked out the large picture windows. There were many of them, on all sides. All dark, throwing back reflections from inside the house. I wondered who would have been around to call the police. One answer was the shooter on a burner phone. A corollary to that was the idea that the shooter was watching me now, from the woods. I used up four minutes searching the house.

One minute to go. Sirens approaching fast.

I went out past Jane Abrams, still sightless, still dead. I slid the glass door closed. The wind had picked up and with it came fine droplets of rain moving through the air. I looked out at the woods. Dark and indifferent. Maybe there was someone out there, maybe not. On the other side, water glinted in the channel.

I let myself tumble over the banister. Grabbed hold of the post and shimmied down. At the bottom I crouched under the deck, up against the inside of the post. I saw the flashlights before I heard the people holding them. Two lights moving up in the woods where I'd come from. West to east. Police foot patrol. Problem was, other than the driveway, that was the best way out. They must have parked a quad bike up on the trails and moved in on foot. Vehicles were coming from the south, and the only other land route out was north, along the coast.

No more time.

Two Ford Explorers with flashing lights pulled into the drive. The sirens stopped. The cops inside the vehicles scanned the woods on either side with spotlights. I heard a car door slam, and the crackle of a radio. I slipped between the bushes and the house and started to slowly creep north. I figured I could get away, then double back to the west and get the bike from where I had left it on the logging trail.

But north was not going to happen. Two more handheld lights were coming through the brush. A second foot team. Another radio squawking cop code. Two foot teams plus the approaching cars. Which meant that I was cornered against the house. I crouched at the building foundation, keeping my head down, relying on my hearing and peripheral vision. The police were moving along the ridge, so I moved in the other direction, laterally below the ridge.

When I got clear I saw the opportunity to move behind their position and make it north into the woods. But I stopped. The two foot teams were coming together in a huddle about fifty feet away. I couldn't hear them speaking, but I wanted to hear them. So, I moved back in.

I shimmied into a bush around the foundation corner. Dangerous, but maybe useful. Another cop was coming from the west. Then

I heard the cops from the vehicles. They had found Abrams' body. Footsteps up on the deck. Then a male voice, gruff.

"Shit." A guy came out and leaned over the railing coughing and cursing. The cops below looked up at him. He got his breath and said, "Dead. One dead woman."

A female officer called up to him from the huddle. "Want me to call it in, detective?"

"I'll call it in." When he spoke into his radio there was the weird double sound of a real live voice and its remote twin coming from the two-way radios clipped to the patrol belts. "Dispatch, this is thirteen, I have a one eight seven at the Beaver Falls Lodge. Repeat, one eight seven. Need an ambulance and a supervisor."

The radio squawked twice. The dispatcher's voice came back. "Copy that, thirteen."

The cop upstairs went back inside. I figured thirteen was a badge number. His voice returned in the ghostly form of a radio squawk only. No live sound this time. "Base, this is thirteen again. Let me know as soon as state comes through."

Base squawked back. "Roger that."

One of the cops below the deck said, "Jesus Christ."

I figured they were going to find the games room soon. I started slipping around the other side of the house. I got to the west side of the building and one of the police teams had started to circle round to the north, so that was blocked off again.

I remembered the zodiac.

I moved down to the outbuilding through a gulley below the driveway. The door was open and it was pitch dark inside. I moved slowly and felt around. The police radios were squawking up at the house. It was a matter of minutes before the detective in charge thought to send officers down to the shed.

My plan was to get the boat out quietly. Then, start it up once I was out far enough. But I needed something to get the boat's motor started, since I didn't have a key.

I moved methodically in the dark, feeling my way along a work bench. A cop light beam swung across the shed and shone through the small window on the side. For a brief flash I saw the tool peg board before it went pitch dark again. I started feeling my way along the workbench and running a hand across the tools.

People who are without sight can use touch to see, or echolocation, like bats. I visualized as I passed my fingers along the peg board. First up was a section of pliers. Different types, different sizes. Next were hammers. Then there were rubber mallets in a couple different sizes. After that were the wrenches. Looked like they had a full set of combination wrenches, all the way from eighth-inch to three inches. Finally the screwdriver section. What I needed was a long screwdriver. That way I could bypass the starter and spark the engine up.

I was running my fingers down from the top of the board to the bottom. The top were shorter screwdrivers. The head didn't matter. I needed a long one. When I got to the place where I expected to find one, it was missing. I checked again. Then checked on the work table below the peg board, in case someone had left it there. Nothing.

I stepped carefully around the workbench, feeling with my hands. There was a doorway to a second room. Outside, I could see the beam of a powerful light cutting through the foliage. It was the spot from one of the police vehicles. I waited until it came across again, into the window, and focused my gaze into that room. When the light slashed across the inside of the shed I was able to make out the shape of someone crouched into a corner. There was blonde hair involved.

I spoke into the dark. "You alright?" There was no response. But I heard her breathing. Shallow and hurried. I scuttled over in the dark. I said, "You can hear me. Just say it."

The blonde girl said, "Keeler?"

I said, "Yes."

She said, "You didn't get on the plane."

"No."

The blonde girl said, "I didn't do it."

"I know you didn't."

"Okay."

I said, "I need to get out of here, for a couple of reasons."

She said, "Take me with you." I didn't speak for a while. She said, "For a couple of reasons."

I said, "We need a long screwdriver, or something like that."

She said, "I've got one."

The light slashed again through the shed. I caught a glimpse of her. She was holding the screwdriver. It was precisely what I had been looking for. Maybe she had planned to stab me with it. Her hair was wet, but she had clothes on, which was plus for her because it wasn't a warm night. On the other hand, the clothes were not very substantial. She was going to be cold.

The light came again from outside. This time it was closer, more focused. The police were nearby. I crouched next to her and we shuffled together, back against the wall. She was shivering.

I took the screwdriver from her hands. "What were you planning on doing, stabbing someone with this?"

She said, "Yes. I was frightened."

The police radio squawked again. The light swerved once more and the radio sound dropped off. I felt her moving next to me. I said, "We need to go. Ready?"

"Yes."

We scuttled to the shed door on the other side. The door let out to the dock.

I said, "Wait here until I whistle. Then you go, and you lay down in the boat." I didn't wait for a response.

I slipped into the cold dark water between the boat and the dock. Ten seconds later I had the rope cut. I gave a low whistle. I couldn't see the blonde girl from where I was in the water. But I heard bare feet padding to the dock, then I felt the vibrations in the rigid hull when she climbed in. Then it was still again and I started to inch the zodiac out into the channel. I swam the boat away from the dock, hugging the darkness of the coast and the overhanging trees and rocks. My boots were heavy in the water. The lodge was long out of sight before I climbed onboard.

The blonde girl was there, lying down against the side of the boat, like I had told her to. The zodiac had two seats in the back and the pilot cabin right in the middle. I said, "You can get up now. Sit in one of those seats if you like."

She came up, gripping onto the side of the zodiac, and made her way to the seat. It began to rain a little. Nothing heavy, just an unpleasant drizzle. The motor was behind the seat, so I was squeezed between the girl's back and the stern. The outboard was a very clean-looking Yamaha 250. I got the housing off and found the starter. Crossed the long screwdriver shaft against both contacts and the engine started right up.

It was time to get out of there. I went back to the pilot podium and hit the throttle. The boat surged into the darkness. The light drizzle was suddenly transformed into a painful storm of needles against skin. I took a look at the girl. She was rigid and squinting, her mouth and eyes tightly closed against the wind. We hugged the coast until Mountain Point. Then I brought the boat out mid-channel and idled.

I turned around and examined her. She was shivering and hugging herself.

I leaned my back against the podium.

She said, "How do you know I didn't do it?"

"You were in the sauna when it happened." She nodded. I said, "Are you alright? We need to keep going awhile. Then we can talk."

She said, "I'm okay."

I said, "You look cold."

She smiled weakly. "I'm cold. But I'm okay." She was hugging herself tightly, and released her arms. Maybe to show me that she wasn't that cold. She was wearing an oversized Harvard sweatshirt, like the one that Jane Abram's son, George, had been wearing in the photograph she had flashed me. I went back and checked the fuel. Full, with a couple of spare cans locked down against the hull.

Good to go.

I didn't want to pass through the channel by town. The other option was around Carolina Island, which was not a short trip, but worthwhile, if I didn't want anyone to see us.

I hit the throttle and motored the zodiac southwest out of the channel in the direction of the Three Bears Entrance. Twenty minutes later I turned the boat north around the island. I gunned the engine and the 250 roared. It was impossible to speak. The wind was cruel, whipping around us, but the rain had ceased. The girl was hunched over, clutching herself. I couldn't help the fact that she was cold.

It took another hour to get up around Clover pass, about a quarter mile from the coast on the other side. One of the good things about Alaska is that it is very easy to get secluded, quick.

I gunned it to Carolina island and found a cove that could protect us from both the wind and line of sight from the mainland. I brought the boat around and cut the motor. Then I threw down the anchor. We would be good there for a while. The blonde girl looked at me with wide eyes.

I said, "Let's start with who the hell are you?"

# CHAPTER TWELVE

The blonde girl said, "I'm Amber Chapman, and you're Tom Keeler. The high plains drifter."

I came around and leaned against the pilot cabin. "Okay, Amber Chapman, what did you see, back at the house?"

Chapman said, "I was in the sauna. I didn't see anything. I heard Jane shout."

I said, "Through the door from the sauna to the vestibule, and then the other door to the hall. She must have shouted loudly."

She nodded. "Maybe to warn us."

I said, "And then?"

"Then I stayed in the sauna. I didn't know what else to do." Chapman said, "Her shout was bad, like there was real trouble. You know what I mean? I was scared. She shouted once. Then I heard other stuff but it was unclear, coming from the house while I was in that sauna room, I couldn't hear much. It was like being underwater."

I said, "What kind of other stuff?"

"Maybe something falling. You know. A low bang."

"And then?"

"I waited. I got my clothes on, and I came out. I saw the guys first, dead, in the games room. Then I found Jane."

"And then what did you do?"

Chapman looked at me uncomprehending. "Do? I got out of there. I didn't even think. I came down to the boat house and then you found me."

"How long were you down there in the boat house?"

"I don't know. Less than an hour, I guess. I had nowhere else to go and I was flipping out, Keeler. To be honest, I'm still flipping out."

Not really, I thought. But I said, "So you didn't see whoever killed them."

"No."

"What were you drinking, before you went into the sauna?"

She said, "Huh?"

"In the games room. You were there and you were drinking with the others."

Chapman nodded. "Yes. Jack on the rocks. That's what I drink. Why?"

I said, "No reason." She looked at me weirdly. I pointed to the sweatshirt. "Harvard. That where you went to school?"

"No. I went to MIT." Then she understood. She said, "Yes. This is George's sweatshirt. He's still at MIT. It's close to Harvard, you know." Chapman pulled her knees into her chest. "Jane told you about George. This is all about George, Jane's son. He's missing."

I said, "She told me. Who are you to George?"

"He's my boyfriend. Or at least he was, before he just disappeared."

I looked at Chapman. She was wearing just the sweatshirt and nothing much else. I said, "You're uncomfortable and cold. It isn't going to get better."

She said, "I know that."

I stepped over to the free seat and sat myself down, right next to Amber Chapman. I turned to her. "Alright, take it from the top and go slow. Tell me the story so far. Beginning with your arrival in Alaska."

She took a deep breath, then looked me straight in the eyes. "Keeler, I know what Jane told you. She discussed it with me before going out to the airport to try and get you on board. But I don't mind telling it again."

"Thank you."

She nodded. "We flew out here from Boston. Me, Jane, and the guys. Jane is a money person, affluent. She took care of the car and the house from back east."

I said, "Take it slow. You arrive on an airplane. They don't do direct flights from either Boston or New York, so you transferred through another city. Portland or Seattle, or maybe Chicago."

Chapman bit her lip. She said, "Seattle-Tacoma. Then up here to Port Morris."

"And what did you do first? You went out to eat, you started asking questions?"

She said, "No. First thing we did was go to his apartment building. He wasn't there, and we couldn't get in touch with the super or the landlord. Still can't."

I said, "Alright. What then?"

"We were hungry. Jane refused to eat on the plane because she said the food sucked, so we were all starving when we got here. First thing we did was go eat at the New York café, because Jane liked the name. She's a snob, okay?"

"No doubt. And in the New York café, did you start asking around? Showing photos of your boyfriend to the locals?"

Chapman looked at me for a moment, like a deer caught in the headlights. "Yes. Shit. Jane had a bunch of pictures printed out. We showed them to the people in the restaurant. Then we went straight to the police station, me and Jane. The guys went down to the waterfront. Same thing, they had copies of the pictures."

I said, "What time was this?"

Chapman said, "Late afternoon. I think we landed at 4:00 p.m.

The flight was really long." She looked down at the zodiac deck. "That's it, right? We started poking around too obviously, so the bad guys got wind of us right away. So stupid."

I said, "Only problem was you weren't prepared for them. It wasn't stupid. In some ways it was smart, because now you know. You brought them out of the woodwork."

"Know what?"

"That something happened to George. He didn't have any kind of an accident. Didn't get eaten by a grizzly bear in the woods, or fall into the water while pissing from a boat."

"Right. But Jane and the guys are dead."

I said, "Yes, and now you move on. What happened next?"

Chapman spoke slowly and carefully, as if recounting what had happened was important. She said, "The morning after we arrived, we went to the New York café for breakfast. When we came back to the car, the front left tire had a flat. While we were changing the tire, two men came. I think they punctured the tire in order to delay us."

"A reasonable assumption. Describe the men."

"One guy had a mustache, the other guy didn't. The mustache guy did the talking. He assumed that Jason and Adam were in charge, not me or Jane. Typical macho asshole. He straight up ordered us to get back on a plane and get the hell out of town. Said that if we didn't, then things would go badly for us. Then our men sort of reacted, you know, aggressively. But the two guys knew more about fighting than Jason and Adam. So, the guy with the mustache got Adam's arm behind his back and broke the finger." She snapped her fingers. "Just like that, like dry wood. And after that we got back in the car, but they were laughing at us because the tire was still flat."

"Nice guys. You and your crew were like fish out of water. That's for sure."

"Yeah, I guess so."

The night had cleared up. The light rain had blown out to sea and now the water was still. The cover on Carolina Island was rocky, with big trees swarmed in thick greenery. Giant trunks leaned over the waterline. Over on the other side of a spit of land was Port Morris, a haze of electric light above the trees.

I said, "So what do you want to do now?"

Chapman looked down and examined her bare feet. She said, "It isn't right that they just kill three people and win like that."

"No. But the police will investigate."

She looked up at me. "I don't think so, Keeler."

"What makes you say that?"

"Only that we were already in touch with the police. They were not interested. I believe that whoever killed Jane and the guys is a professional killer, and that the police will find nothing useful to investigate. Except ..." She paused.

I said, "Except what?"

Chapman said, "Except maybe you and me."

Which was pretty much what I had been thinking. Smart girl.

I said, "What was the plan, before this. What were you going to do next?"

She said, "Seeing as you were supposed to be on the plane. We knew how vulnerable we were to the men harassing us. The plan was to fly under the radar if possible. George has an apartment in town. We haven't been able to get in because we don't have the key and it's owned by an absentee landlord. So, the plan was to try and break in, see if there's anything there that can help, like his phone or his computer or something."

"The police haven't looked there yet?"

She shook her head. "Like I said, they weren't interested in our problem. Maybe now that Jane's dead they will be."

I said, "So maybe we want to get there first."

"Now?"

I nodded. "Now. But first we need to do something about this boat."

Chapman said, "What do you mean?"

"Best case scenario, we simply have nothing to do with what

happened at Beaver Falls. No connection at all. You weren't there. I wasn't there. Which means that this boat needs to be gone."

"Which means what, exactly?"

I said, "Couple of things, first of which is a question: can you swim?"

"Sure. I was on the swim team in high school."

Sometimes you get lucky.

I had Chapman pull the anchor. We cruised away from the island and swung south and east. I cut the engine when we were a quarter mile from town, across the channel and above Carolina Island. I stripped two wires from the outboard battery and cleaned up the exposed parts. Then I detached a spare gas can and poured a little pool of it into the engine well.

Chapman was watching me. She was concerned, but she hadn't asked any questions. I turned to her.

I said, "We're going to get wet. That includes our clothes, but since you're a swimmer you can appreciate that it's best if we aren't wearing them and swimming at the same time."

She looked at me for a few moments then she nodded. I showed her the way. I got my boots off first and then the socks. Then the pants and the underwear and the t-shirt. Socks, underwear and valuables like my wallet and my knife went into zipped jacket pockets. So did my t-shirt. The jacket got rolled into a fat tube, tied around my waist by the arms. I tied the boots onto the jacket tube with the laces. I got it pretty secure. Chapman followed my lead and pulled the sweatshirt over her head. She was only wearing the sweatshirt, over panties and a t-shirt. No pants, no shoes, no socks. The t-shirt went into a sweatshirt sleeve and that went around her waist. Made her look like one of those Japanese pearl divers, except blonde.

I said, "Good to go?"

She said, "Yup."

The girl was a trooper.

One of the stripped wires got tucked around each terminal, then I crossed them above a little pool of fuel. The spark set the gas on fire.

By the time the boat exploded in full force and fury, we were a hundred yards away, treading water. Hadn't done much of that since pararescue induction. I figured Amber Chapman never had. I looked at her. In the hot light of the burning boat, Chapman was grinning broadly. She glanced at me and I caught sight of a kind of crazed pleasure at being in harsh circumstances that only people like me are supposed to feel. So, maybe she was someone like me.

Closer to shore we lay on our backs in the water. The swim had been tough. I wanted to clear my head. Up in the sky there were stars. Bright and sharp, with no moon yet.

Time to take it to the next level.

## CHAPTER THIRTEEN

We came out of the water on the far side of Lake Road. Where the creek begins, but away from the footbridges and tourist spots. The place was rocky and the waves were pretty strong, which made it hard to get a foothold. I had to help Chapman out of the water. She was having trouble with her balance initially. I told her to sit down and get her equilibrium back. Look at the horizon. Her skin was pale against the dark water. Small breasts, and a long, spare body. But this was no waif, she was athletic and strong and had the figure of a high jumper.

At first we both lay there against the rocks, spent. But it was cold, and we had things to do, places to be. There was not much to say just then. We unwound the clothes from around our waists and did the best we could to squeeze the sea water out of them. Our best was not very good, but it would have to be good enough. Chapman was in bare feet and I had my boots. It would be tough going for her, but I figured we might find a pair of shoes in her boyfriend's apartment.

We scaled the rocky shore and got up onto the road. Then started walking. Each of my steps was a noisy squelch, hers a soft, almost noiseless pad. That part of town was deserted. It was Port Morris,

Alaska. There would be action in a few bars and restaurants, but behind the closed curtains of residential houses, only the flicker of television screens betrayed the existence of metabolic life. One after the other, each house the same, but different.

We trudged up the road. Side by side. Chapman said, "We don't have the key."

I said, "We won't use a key."

The place was up the hill on the north side of town.

We came around the corner. The building took up a whole block and was painted in cream with turquoise window trim. Nothing moved in the street. Nobody walking, nobody in windows looking out. Everybody was home, maybe watching TV, or eating delivery pizza. A sign above the arched front door had 'Edna Bay Apartments' in gold curly letters. The front door was locked. There was a panel of buzzers to the right.

I was going to say something, but stopped myself. A man was walking down the sidewalk in our direction. A big guy, wearing a long coat and carrying a bag, like he'd just come from a convenience store. I couldn't see his face, but I saw the silhouette. He had a shaved head and pointy ears. When he got closer I saw the face, he was looking at me and smiling, then he looked away and kept on walking. I smelled tobacco. The bag bulged with the outline of a six pack and a bag of chips.

I got back to the task at hand. "You know which apartment?"

Chapman said, "Forty-six."

I figured forty-six would correspond to the fourth floor. I counted five stories. The buzzer panel was laid out in a grid. Each row corresponded to a floor, which made it easier to simultaneously depress buttons for the third, and fifth floors at once. I got some static through the intercom, and a couple of garbled words from various people all at the same time. Then there was a buzz and we were in.

The lobby was a spacious area with speckled cream tiles on the floor and a wall grid of mailboxes on one side. We took the stairs. Fourth floor was carpeted, a long colorless tongue laid out in the dark.

A black plastic square was glued to the door, with forty-six in white letters. I didn't have any kind of plan for picking the lock, just planned on getting into the apartment one way or another. I took a look at the door. But it wasn't any kind of Fort Knox lock either. The wood was old and cracked. The keyhole was embedded directly into the round brass handle. Which meant that the latch was inside.

I unclipped my knife and slid it through the gap between door and door jamb. There was enough play, but the knife came up against a security plate on the other side. The plate is supposed to prevent someone jimmying the lock, exactly what I was doing. But it was only as secure as the support was strong.

I was going to have to use force to push the screws out of the support surface. The plate was probably something decent, like steel, but it might be screwed into something softer, like sheet rock or soft wood. I was hoping it would work on the first try, so the neighbors don't get curious. In my experience, people generally want to stay on the sofa, or in bed, rather than go back out into the cold world investigating a noise. The rule of threes is usually correct. First time, it's a statistical accident. Second time, a coincidence. Third time, maybe something is going on.

I held the knife point inside the gap between door and jamb, tip pushed against the security plate. I gave it a good hammer with the heel of my hand. The plate moved slightly, but it wasn't enough.

I waited and listened. Nothing special was happening. Just me and Chapman breathing, and the regular noises from the hallway. A little buzzing sound from the exit light. Some TV sounds from individual units. That was it. I repeated the strike, trying to be accurate and focused. It took two more hits to get the plate screws loose enough for me to work on the lock. Three bangs.

One too many.

A door opened down the hall. Light spilled instantaneously onto the carpet, which was revealed to be blood-red. A woman in a housecoat stepped out and looked down the hall in our direction. I slipped behind Chapman. The lady down the hall was squinting. Her hand over her eyes like she was seeing far into the distance. I poked Chapman in the back. She took a couple of steps toward the lady and said, "Hi. Sorry for the noise. He had a few too many, know what I mean?"

The neighbor was standing stock-still in the light. She said, "What?"

Chapman got closer, she said, "We're sorry for the noise."

The woman said, "No problem with any noise, honey, I'm taking out the trash." The neighbor held up a garbage bag that had been hidden by her body. "You have a great night."

Chapman said, "You too," and came loping back. The neighbor walked away.

I returned to the task at hand. The knife blade went in at a diagonal angle and I slipped it behind the bolt. The blade compressed the bolt away from the jamb. I pushed, the door opened and I walked in.

The apartment was a corner unit, with windows looking out to sea. Even at night, the channel was all there, laid out with two islands offshore and the whole Pacific Ocean on the other side. The moon was coming up. We were standing in the entrance, which gave out on a living room to our right. I flipped the light switch. A corner sofa unit with coffee table. Nothing on it. Above the sofa was a large Japanese print of an ocean wave with a little wood boat caught in it. No television. A couple of paces away, a dining area nestled into the window corner. Off to the right was an open plan kitchen. Between the kitchen and the dining area was a counter. A pair of high stools were tucked beneath it.

There was mail on the dining table. Two envelopes slit open neatly. I pulled the contents. The first envelope contained a water bill, addressed to George Abrams. The second contained a marketing letter from a bank. Next to the mail was a yellow legal pad with a ball point pen beside it. The legal pad was half used up and the page on top was blank. From the dining nook I could see the lights of that cruise ship. Looking down steeply, I could see the street below with parked cars and the sidewalk on the other side.

Chapman was hovering over me biting her nails and looking very uncomfortable. I said, "Go find shoes, and something dry to wear." She nodded and went away. I took off my jacket and laid it over a dining room chair. The jacket was damp, but not soaking anymore. Gore-Tex. My other clothes were in worse shape. Particularly the jeans. I didn't care.

The kitchen was clean and neat and looked unused. Beside the bedroom, the living room and kitchen area, there was another small room. I flipped the light. It looked like an office. The desk and shelves were covered in boxes and loose paper. I didn't immediately see a computer or a phone. I yawned. The day had started early on the boat. There had been things to do, ropes to pull. The net had needed some mending. I was tired.

The bedroom was neat as the kitchen. Chapman was in there changing. She was naked, but I'd already seen that and she was not shy. The closet had a shirt rack, with five identical gray button-down shirts in it. Looked like George had a thing for preppy cardigans. Two of them hung up next to the shirts. They were fine quality wool, with discreet and expensive-looking logos. A shelf held four pairs of neatly pressed chinos in beige.

Chapman pulled a pair down and slipped them on. She chose one of the button-down shirts to go with it. I said, "Classy."

"Always." She started pulling through George's jacket collection, and stopped at a thin black leather zip-up. "There it is. I bought it for him last year and he never wore it. Now I'm taking it back." She pulled it on and admired herself in the mirror. "What do you think, Keeler?"

I looked at her. "Whatever. I don't think."

Truth was, if previously I had figured Chapman was not my type, now I was revising that thought, big time.

She let herself fall on the bed. "Holy shit. I think I might just pass out right here and now."

I said, "Bad idea. We go through the place and then we get out."

Chapman curled her knees up. "Are you always this much fun?"

"Oh, this isn't fun enough?"

She screwed her face up. "What are we looking for?"

"We're looking through everything, in case there is anything interesting. Included in everything and anything are computers and phones. Either of those will be considered interesting until proven otherwise."

She blew air up at the ceiling. "Got it."

I looked at her. The girl was exhausted and I was riding her hard. I said, "Half hour nap?"

"Hour."

"Forty-five minutes."

Chapman said, "Okay."

I suddenly felt the weight of the wet jeans against my legs. She looked at me, up and down. "You have to get out of that wet stuff."

I said, "I'm good thanks."

"No, you'll get the bed wet. Can't get the bed wet, Keeler. It isn't good manners. What will George think, when we find him?"

"Well if you put it like that."

I went back to George Abrams' closet and pulled down a pair of jeans. Too small. I picked up a pair of chinos, likewise. George was a skinny little guy. I was barrel-chested, my arms were all mass, and my legs were shaped like upside down bowling pins. Chapman was looking at me from the bed. She said, "Not going to work, Keeler. Just take it off and hang it up, then get your ass into the bed like a normal person."

"Never really did the normal person thing."

"You can fake it till you make it."

I stripped off the wet gear. It was like peeling rotten fruit. It wasn't just wet, it was wet with sea water and the salt had begun to crystallize. I hung my clothes over a chair. When I turned back, Chapman was under the covers. She pulled the comforter back like a marked page. She said, "Turn off the light."

I did so and got under the covers. Chapman had left me enough room and it felt amazing in there, almost instantly. Like a fluffy cocoon of pure comfort. Like being on the inside of a cloud. I realized right there and then that I hadn't been in a real bed for at least four months. Chapman couldn't have been more right. It was a whole lot better to be in the bed than out of it. Took me a minute to get warm and start feeling perfect. I set my internal alarm for one hour, then I closed my eyes.

Ten seconds later, I felt Chapman's shoulder against mine, skin to skin. Warm and getting warmer. Her hand came across my thigh and then further. Her hair brushed against my forehead. Then her voice in my ear. "Sorry, but there are a couple of things I like about you."

I took her hand and put it back. "I like you too, but no."

Chapman held still for a while, then she turned away. A phrase that she'd said echoed in my head: *You have to get out of that wet stuff.* The way she'd said the word 'have'. My mother had been French. She'd said words in a different way from other kid's parents growing up. Maybe Chapman had spent time in a European country as a kid. Maybe I'd remember to ask.

## CHAPTER FOURTEEN

An hour later we were lying side by side, still in bed.

I said, "What did Jane Abrams do?"

Chapman said, "Like what, you mean her job?"

"Yeah."

"I'm not sure. I think that she's rich."

I said, "Rich like how?"

Chapman shook her head. "I don't know. You think I should have asked?"

"I guess not."

George was an alarm clock user. According to the clock, the time was ten to midnight. By one a.m. we had taken turns in the shower. After that we got dressed. Her in clean clothes that smelled like laundry detergent. Me in damp salty jeans and my old t-shirt. At least George's socks fit. I got a clean pair from the dresser. His shoes were big on Chapman, but big is better than small in that department.

I started on the office. Stacks of papers and books were precariously placed on the desk and two shelves screwed to the wall opposite. Beside the desk was a filing cabinet. I sat at the desk and began to leaf through the papers. As far as I could make out, they were research papers related to George's academic work. There were diagrams and mathematical equations with lines and symbolic figures that I didn't understand. They were written in a secret language, that was for sure. There was a recurring phrase in the subtitle of many of the academic papers, 'Non-linear acoustics'.

Abrams had pinned three sheets of office paper on the wall above the desk. They were color printouts with abstract imagery. Waves of neon in bright orange, red, green, and blue. One color melting into another, and so on.

I reached down to my right and opened the filing cabinet. It was empty except for a laptop computer, tossed in with the power cord. I pulled it out and pushed a few stacks of paper back to make room. I called Chapman in. She came over and stood behind me. I pressed the power button. We waited for the computer to turn on, whirring and beeping and buzzing. Once it had settled down, the screen was blank except for a place in the middle where I was supposed to enter a password.

I looked at Chapman. She looked at me with a raised eyebrow. I said, "Password?"

She said, "Try *Abe and Louie*. No spaces, all lower case."

I said, "The steak house, Boston."

"George was crazy about their rib eye."

I said, "Spell that for me."

Chapman spelled it out and I typed it in. Then I hit return. The little box in the middle of the screen shook violently. A new message popped up above it, 'invalid password'. She said, "Try it all upper case." I did, and we got the same thing, an angry vibration. She said, "I don't know then, I guess George changed his password."

I straightened up and turned around to look at Chapman. She was biting her nails again and her blue eyes were looking right at me. I said, "Anything else to suggest?"

She shook her head. "Not that I can think of, no. We don't want to try too many, because it might do something bad."

"Like destroy the contents."

"I'm not sure, maybe. The rule of threes."

I thought about that for a second. Closed the laptop. I pointed to the color printouts on the wall.

"Any idea what those are?"

Chapman leaned in and looked at them. She hemmed and hawed. "Acoustic modeling stuff. I don't know exactly what, but they look like a shape that George probably wanted to memorize." She ran a long finger over one of the images, tracing a curving line that separated the neon red from the blue. "I think these are the same thing, an object that George would have wanted to be able to recognize in the field. When he didn't have his big computer."

"What would he have, out there in the field?"

She said, "Oh, he'd have a portable unit. You know, a pelican case with a field laptop and the hardware."

I said, "Hardware."

"Acoustic sensors that you can put in the water."

I left the laptop on the desk and tossed the rest of the office, looking for a phone mostly. Nothing there. Chapman was waiting in the living room. She looked at me when I came out. "Anything?"

I said, "No. Look for a backpack. We're taking the laptop. Also, we need to wipe this place down. Make sure we don't leave prints. And don't forget the bed. Sheets, towels, old clothes. We take them with us."

She said, "You serious?"

"Yes. We'll burn them."

Chapman went looking for a bag to carry the laptop in. I stripped the bed. Everything went inside the comforter cover. Then I tied the corners and had a large sack to sling over my shoulder. I threw that on the living room floor and took another look around.

Out the window, the view was the same, except the moon had come clear of the cloud. Its reflection made a line across Carolina Island, across the channel, and right up to the cruise ship.

I noticed the yellow legal pad again. Half the pages had been ripped out, half were still there. I carefully removed the top page and folded it into quarters. It went in my inside jacket pocket. There was something else. A glass bowl with a small key in it. It occurred to me that the key was for the mailbox in the lobby. I thumbed it into the coin pocket of my jeans. Chapman came out of the bedroom with a backpack. I put the laptop in it, zipped up, slung it over my shoulder.

We were ready to go.

I closed the door on the way out. The latch clicked into the bolt hole. The security plate was loose, but the lock still worked. We came out the way we had come in, down the stairwell and then down three steps to the lobby. I focused my attention on the grid of mailboxes. Each box was a small square in dull bronze with a keyhole in the center of each little door. I located number forty-six. Given that George hadn't been around to collect the mail, I wondered if there would be anything interesting inside. I pulled the small key out of the coin pocket and tried it. Bingo. The little box opened up and a month of mail sat there, which was exactly five envelopes. I unslung the backpack, unzipped it and shoveled the mail in.

I stood for a moment looking through a square window fit into the door. Parked cars and nobody walking in the darkness. No dogs. No bears. Not even a cat. I opened the door and stepped out to the sidewalk. I made it two steps, and a voice from my left said, "Nice and slow. Put the bundle down and get the hands up and out where I can see them."

I turned my head and saw a uniformed policeman. He was maybe thirty years old with a face like a burger bun. The cop stood six feet away, pointing a Glock at my face. There was another guy behind him, older, maybe fifty and change. No uniform. The older cop stepped out to get an angle, he swung his gun at my chest.

The younger cop said, "Is this the guy?"

The older cop said, "Yup. That's him."

I said nothing. But I was beginning to get pissed off.

## CHAPTER FIFTEEN

It was not just the two policemen outside of the Edna Bay Apartments, they had brought the whole crew. Must have moved in while we were on our way down the stairs. Across the street and to the right of the building entrance was an unmarked Ford Explorer. Two marked versions of that same vehicle had sealed off both ends of the block. I recalled my conversation with June at the SEAS office. Looked like Mister Lawrence had gotten a three-for-two deal from Ford, for the police vehicle upgrades.

I dropped the bundle and put my hands slowly in the air.

They turned me around against the wall and read me my rights. I was being arrested for murder. I looked over and saw Amber Chapman being taken away in handcuffs. We made eye contact in the brief moment before a cop's hand ducked her head and put her into one of the prowlers.

The older guy spoke to the younger cop. "Do the GSR on him."

The younger guy pushed me up against the unmarked Ford's hood. He said, "Stay here." A few moments later, he was back with a cardboard box. GSR stands for gunshot residue. The uniformed cop set up on the hood and tried to keep cool while fiddling around with the cheap-looking evidence testing kit. The older guy was leaning against the back of the car, sucking on a cigarette. When he was done, he flipped his butt and walked over.

"Make sure you do the lab test first, huh?"

"Yeah, Jim."

After the lab test, they swabbed me for presumptive. I knew this because I've done it myself. We had higher quality kits in the military. But they performed the same function. Presumptive tests are for the field. They can tell you if the guy discharged a firearm recently, but you need the lab tests to verify the presumptive. The lab tests are more thorough. We hadn't bothered with lab tests in Iraq or Afghanistan, nobody was going to have to prove anything in trial. Hadn't bothered testing at all in Syria.

The presumptive came out negative. Good news for me, but evidently not good news for the policemen. The younger guy packed his kit away in the worn cardboard box. They put me in the vehicle.

The uniformed cop drove. Next to him was the older guy. From his voice I figured him as the detective who had found Jane Abrams' body. Name of Jim, radio call sign thirteen. His sad eyes told me that he would rather be home in bed than in the police car. I was in the back separated by a wire grid. Both of them kept their eyes forward and their mouths shut. Which suited me fine, because I had no plans to engage in conversation.

The question on my mind was, how did they know I was their guy? One possibility was a security camera at Beaver Falls Lodge that I had missed. But if there had been a camera, they would know that I was not their guy, because they would have the shooter on video.

The other option was that someone had given the police my name.

Maybe it was Deckart.

Maybe he had discovered that I was not in fact working for Mister Lawrence.

Which would be easy to do, if he asked Mister Lawrence.

Then maybe Mister Lawrence had decided to take me out of the equation.

Drop the hammer on Jane Abrams and friends, set Keeler up for the fall. The only other person who both knew me and had a connection to the evening's events was Amber Chapman. I had been with her the whole time, so I shelved the possibility that it was her who had set it up.

The follow-up question was easier. What to do? The answer was nothing. In the United States, there is no escaping police custody. You can try. You can even be successful on a tactical level, for a period of time. Long or short, it does not matter. Because in the end they will get you. And the moment you cross state lines it becomes a federal situation. Once they get going, the FBI is very good at what it does.

The young cop parked in front of the police station. The detective got out of the vehicle and jogged across the street. I watched him get swallowed into the station.

I figured it was a good time to sleep. So, I closed my eyes and pictured a HALO jump at night. Throwing myself into the dark, then arching and relaxing and falling through the nothingness. It was not a realistic dream. I didn't land. There was no land. There was only air and nothing else. Nothing to break the spell of free fall. And no hundred and fifty pounds of gear on my back either. Somewhere in that free fall place, the older detective got back in the Ford. I registered that event. I even registered him speaking to the younger cop when he got back in. He said, "They've got a room in the barn for us." Registered, the way a CCTV camera records something that happened so that it can be played back later.

When the Ford pulled into a driveway up in the woods, I was awake and alert. The sign out front read 'Port Morris Correctional Facility'. It was a big sign planted into a flower bed. But it was a little late in the season for flowers, and too dark to appreciate them even if they had been in bloom. The Port Morris Correctional Facility was all corrugated cladding and painted red, which accounted for what the detective had called it, 'the barn'.

When the older guy opened the door for me, I got out. The detective was wearing a pancake holster clipped into a brown leather belt. It was a full-size Glock 22 in .40 caliber. No fancy grip, no tricked-out barrel modification. A plain vanilla standard law enforcement weapon. My hands were cuffed in front of me.

As I stepped out of the Ford, I visualized how I would take his weapon, kill him, and then the younger cop. Then I could take their vehicle. I estimated the task could be completed inside of a minute. Between fifteen and thirteen seconds, give or take. Closer to the upper estimate if I verified the kills, lower if I was content with a double tap and no verification.

But I was innocent, and innocent men don't pull those kinds of stunts. I stood outside of the car, looking down at the detective's puffy face. His hair was combed neatly in a side-part. He eyes were watery blue and his fleeting glance wanted desperately to stay out of trouble.

The detective said, "You'll spend the night here. We'll talk tomorrow."

If this had been Chicago, or LA, they would have put me in the box immediately, looking for that confession. But this was not Chicago, LA, or Detroit, it was Port Morris, Alaska, and the cops were tired. I said nothing. Just looked at him.

He looked away, coughed once and said, "Oh, so you're a tough guy huh?" He jerked his head to the red building. "Wait'll you try that with those fellas in there. You won't be so tough after that, buddy."

I said nothing.

The younger cop came around the vehicle. He verified that my hands were cuffed before daring to speak to his colleague. "Guy giving you a headache, Jim?"

The older guy shook his head. "Thousand-yard stare is all."

The younger guy looked at me. I looked at him and he looked away quickly, like he'd seen something forbidden. They walked me into the processing area, handed me over and left. Then I was alone with a room full of prison guards. I wondered if they were planning to make me breakfast. I was getting hungry.

## CHAPTER SIXTEEN

I COUNTED FOUR CORRECTIONS OFFICERS.

All four were staring at me. Not smiling. Not staring at me because they thought I was a famous actor. Two of them were young, two of them were not. None of them carried firearms, but each had a yellow Taser gun clipped alongside a radio to the front of a stab vest. Radio handset up high at the collar, opposite the dominant hand. Taser centered above the solar plexus, a chunk of yellow plastic, butt oriented to the same hand. The two young guys were clean cut and eager. One had black hair, the other was blond. Eager like they had a shot at going up the ranks, maybe competing to become warden one day. The other two looked faded and gray, like they'd given up on that idea a long time ago, like the concept of ambition was a distant memory.

The young black haired guy was in charge. He was preparing the paperwork at a clean white desk. He turned his arm to look at a wristwatch, scowled. Looked over at the blond young guy, who was standing there looking at me, hands crossed in front of him, with a fresh brush hair cut. The blond guy shook his head. The one in charge shook his head, it was contagious. Something was not right. I figured it was me.

I was wrong.

The door banged open and two more guards came into the processing room. New to the room, but not new. They were veterans, like the other two older guys. But these two looked worse. Worse in the sense that they looked like they'd never had any ambition to go up the ranks, because they had never intended to play by the rules. They looked like bad apples.

One of the bad apples was around forty and unnaturally jacked for his age. Which meant a diet of steroids with his Wheaties. His sleeves were rolled up, prominently displaying tattoos down the forearms. One side was a killer whale, the other a shark. Very original. I figured him for an ex-fisherman who either couldn't hack it anymore or had become *persona non grata* on the fleet for some reason. The other guy was slim with a goatee. He wore a uniform that was a couple of sizes too large.

The clean-cut young guy in charge looked up at them. "About time, don't you think, Gavin? Shift starts at one in the a.m." He looked at his watch demonstratively. "It is now two a.m. and two minutes."

The slim guy with the goatee must have been Gavin, and Gavin was the leader of the two. He said, "Sorry lieutenant, we got stuck in traffic."

This was such a ridiculous claim that the lieutenant kind of gagged at it. He was about to say something, but one look at the smirking officers was enough to stop him. The young lieutenant just shook his head and looked away. The slim, smirking guy smirked harder and looked at his friend.

The clean-cut guys walked me through processing. They put my jacket, loose change, wallet and the laptop backpack in a cardboard box. They took my finger prints and photograph, and put a bedroll in my hands. I was led into the prison through a series of security doors. I figured we had gone halfway deep into the place when the two guards stopped me in front of an open door. The cell was big enough. Bigger by far than I might have expected. But this was Alaska, and space wasn't an issue. The cell contained a bunk bed, a toilet with no seat, and a sink. All stainless steel.

The guard closed the door, a thick sound. Then his keys scraped and clanged for several moments.

Then I was alone, sitting on the lower bunk.

I ran through the sequence of events since that afternoon, beginning with the third bite of that burger, and ending with the prison cell door closing. When I was satisfied that I had it all straight and correct in my mind, I tipped myself over and lay down on the thin mattress. I didn't bother with the bed roll, which I had dumped on the floor. I closed my eyes and was instantly asleep.

I had been asleep for an hour and twenty minutes when I heard keys clicking and scraping again in the cell door. I swung myself up on the edge of the bed. Two silhouettes entered, backlit by the corridor fluorescents. The first guy was slapping a baton into his palm. The second guy slumped against the wall behind him. The two bad apples, the big guy in front slapped the stick into his palm again. He said, "Keeler, you're outta here. They're transporting you up to Juneau."

The older detective had said that we would talk in the morning. It was his investigation. I couldn't think of any reason why I would be transported to Juneau, about three hundred miles away. It was a trip that would involve several boats, wheeled vehicles, or an airplane. I wasn't buying it.

I said, "No, they're not. And no, you're not taking me."

The guy said, "Not your call, pal. Get up and ready, we're taking you now."

The guard behind him unclipped his Taser. He was the one named Gavin. He said, "Let's just Tase him. He's already resisting."

A Taser is a stun gun device that shoots two wired darts. Once both projectiles get into the skin, the device releases a 50,000 volt charge which connects up between the two steel darts through the muscle mass between them. The result is intense muscle spasm, pain, and momentary paralysis. I figured the Taser was the least of my problems. The big guy was standing in the way of the skinny guy with the Taser. I figured there was no time to lose.

I launched off the bunk, using my left leg to push out horizontally, like a catapult. At the same time, my right leg cocked and released into the big guy's left knee. I felt the knee give, and he grunted. I bumped up against him the moment his knee caved and he dropped. With my right hand I pulled the Taser from his stab vest. The big guy was slow to react. I pushed him off and aimed the Taser at the skinny guy. I pulled first, and the two darts shot out at 180 feet per second. One of the darts hit him in the neck and embedded. The other hit his stab vest, bouncing off uselessly. Those things need both darts to embed in skin, so I was out of luck. The skinny guy named Gavin had his Taser up. There was a pop as he pulled the trigger and the firing pin pierced a compressed air cartridge. Then, a whoosh as the darts came at me.

Next thing I knew I was thrashing like a fish out of water.

## CHAPTER SEVENTEEN

THE BIG GUY cuffed my hands behind my back while I was immobilized. Five seconds later I was raring to go. Gavin said, "Calm down, buddy. We're only taking you to the other holding cell for the transfer. It isn't our idea, orders from above."

I said, "Orders from whom?"

He said, "The prison warden. Just came through. They want you up at Juneau by end of day tomorrow. The transfer happens in the a.m."

"So why not leave me alone here?"

"Not our call. Maybe they got someone else for the room."

I said, "Not happening."

The big guy was massaging his knee. He blew air through his lips. "What a pain in the ass."

Gavin had his Taser up and reloaded. He said, "You want another load of this?"

I said, "Bring it on. Just makes me more likely to want to kill you."

"Last warning. I'm gonna juice you up good this time."

I shrugged. The slim guy discharged his Taser. The barbs hooked into my rib area and the muscles spasmed. It was unpleasant, but the second time I was ready. It was only pain, and pain can be overcome. I would have ripped the darts out with my hands had they not been cuffed behind me. There was too much slack in the line to use my body and tug them out. The guy sent the electricity down the line for a good ten seconds, more than enough to put most people down. I rode it out until the battery ran down. When he was done I felt bad, but not as bad as I'd have felt if I had capitulated.

The big guy said, "Had enough now? Ready to cooperate."

I said, "I don't think so. I won't be cooperating."

The slim guy pulled the wires sharply and the barbs tore out of my flesh. There were now four wet and bloody smudges on the shredded front of my shirt. Gavin looked at me with his mouth open, panting. He said, "Screw this guy. He can have the damn room. Right?"

The big guy said, "I guess so. Not our problem if he thinks this is fancy real estate."

The slim guy said, "Pal, you're going to realize that we were only ever trying to do you a favor by moving you. Now you'll have it the way you want it, the hard way."

I said, "Is that right, what was it going to be otherwise, the easy way?"

He said, "You got a point. It was always going to be the hard way, but you chose extra hard, with cheese."

As they left the cell, the big guy said, "So long."

The cell door closed. I was alone again, in the dark. I had a sense of impending doom mixed with the growing excitement that always precedes combat. The move to Juneau was a ruse. Those two had wanted me out of the cell for something else, which wasn't ever going to be a yoga session, or a group meditation, a tea making ceremony, a seminar on contemporary art, or anything else supposedly good for my health.

Fifteen minutes later there was the sound of someone fussing with the lock. The cell door opened once more, spilling light from the corridor. There was a pause, then three new men walked in, blocking the light, and ducking their heads as they entered the doorway. They came in one at a time, lining up. The silhouettes were considerably larger and taller than before, and the figures bumpy with accumulated prison muscle, like plastic action figures. After the third silhouette had ducked his head through the threshold, the cell door closed with a hard clang and keys scraped and clinked. The cell darkened.

So this was the extra hard way.

It came to me, why the guards had wanted to move me to a different room. It must have been for the view, so that they could watch what was about to go down. Here they had a very poor angle and dim lighting. Maybe they had another room, larger with a two-way mirror. Maybe they were supposed to film the whole thing. The three guys stood in a loose arc on one side of the cell.

I stood up from the lower bunk. My hands were still cuffed behind me.

All three were bare-chested, which was their way of showing off the severe tattoos inked into over-pumped muscle. I could see in the half light that it was all about the swastikas, the German crosses, and the number 1488. Given the swastikas and crosses, I figured 1488 was some kind of white supremacist code. The three hulking beasts were not speaking. They were just standing there watching me.

Like a story book definition of scary.

But not for me.

I wondered who these people thought they were dealing with. Maybe they thought it was going to be easy to beat me to death, like a Roman colosseum with three experienced gladiator slaves and a lion going up against a one-legged librarian and his pocket mouse. But it wasn't going to be like that.

The United States Joint Special Operations Command brings together rough boys from the various branches to form assault teams. They get them from Delta, and the top SEAL teams. But there is always a combat medic attached. Which is how I came to work with the brutes from SEAL team six. Those guys are smart, and like all of us, they receive the highest level of combat training known to humankind, ever, in the entire history of the species. But what really sets SEAL team six apart from the rest, is the fact that they are born killers with more than their share of natural aggression. Born killers smart enough to have made it into the top squad tasked with legalized and glorified murder. For them it was like Christmas every day.

And every day in SEAL team six begins before dawn with *fight club*.

Fight club is like the movie, bare knuckles brawling. But it isn't fake brawling with skinny Hollywood action stars, it's brawling with the most elite killers the world has ever seen, before breakfast. Since I had been attached to JSOC for around four years, I had more than a thousand fight clubs under my belt. We had all loved fight club, but then again we were all professional killers.

These small time prison losers didn't come close. But it would be better without handcuffs. So, I decided to bait them.

I said, "It isn't white of you to beat me down with my hands tied behind my back."

The guy in front looked around at his friends. He said, "What do you know about being white? You're what we call a race traitor. We aren't just going to beat you. We're going to beat you slow, from every angle, on every part of your body. Until the sun rises. That's how much time we got. Until dawn, which makes it how many hours?" He looked around, but white supremacist prisoners don't wear watches. "Whatever. We got enough time. I will personally push your button when I see the first ray of light. How's that for me being a nice guy?"

I said, "It's even worse than being a race traitor. You'll live the rest of your lives as race cowards. You won't deserve to call yourselves white people. Is it truly white to beat a man with his hands tied behind his back?"

The three guys shifted from foot to foot, rippling their gym muscles. They knew that I was baiting them, and they didn't like it. Three on one, the odds looked overwhelmingly good. But what if it got out, that they'd beaten a guy with his hands cuffed behind him? Maybe they'd be seen as brutal and remorseless. Maybe they'd be seen as cowards. Maybe one, maybe the other. Maybe all three would keep quiet about it, but maybe not. There were the prison guards to consider.

The guy in back spit against the wall. He rapped his knuckles five times on the cell door. A minute later the door was opened. He said, "Need to uncuff him."

I could see the slim guard's silhouette in the door. He said, "Need is a four-letter word."

The guy in back said, "Just do it."

Five seconds later, a key came skidding across the concrete. I put my boot heel down to stop it. The door clanged shut again. I sat on the floor and picked up the key, behind my back. I stood up and looked at the three guys.

The one in front was the biggest, and likely the more aggressive. He was grinding his teeth together and it was making a noise. I realized that they were all grinding their teeth, which probably meant that they were on some kind of speed. Amphetamines, the bread and butter of white supremacist gangs. It was weird to see three prison Nazis in the half light, grinding their teeth. The triple mouths glowed coldly in darkened faces.

We were getting closer to the moment of truth and they were nervous, as most people are before a violent encounter. Nervous with good reason, I thought. Behind my back I was unlocking the cuffs, quietly. When I had them off, I kept them behind my back, and put the four fingers of my right hand through the twin steel rings, like a set of brass knuckles. My thumb slid the key into my back pocket. I said "I can't get them off by myself. I need you to help me do it."

The guy in front said, "What do we got to do, kill you with kindness?"

I said, "Just get these things off me and I'll beat you down."

The guy grinned, his teeth flashing brighter in the dark. He stepped forward, arm extended. "Let me see that."

Which was exactly what I had been waiting for, some momentum. When a person gets his body into motion, it becomes really hard to change direction, or to adjust for leverage. Motion commits weight transfer, and the guy had committed. That is because one of the effects of crystal meth is to make the user physically over-reactive. The guy hadn't stepped forward so much as leapt ahead of himself.

Too fast out of the gate, too late.

I stepped out of his line, swiveled back at him and came in at a new angle. The guy tried to adjust his balance, get in the right place, at least to defend himself. He was wide open, like a rabbit caught in headlights. My hand was ringed in steel. My armored fist was pure kinetic energy, and slammed into the side of his head, just to the right of a swastika tattoo on his upper cheek. There was a cracking sound. Either his skull breaking, or the handcuffs clashing. I didn't care which.

The guy went down.

Another lesson from fight club, no pause, no let up, no delay. Only relentless aggression will save you from being beaten to a pulp by some protein powder-guzzling Navy Seal Green Team warrior. And like a good pool player, you have to always consider the next shot.

The next shot was the next guy in line. This one had a full-on illustration of Adolf Hitler tattooed from belly to neck. Hitler was snarling and holding up his arm in a *Sieg-Heil* Nazi salute. The guy was reacting defensively, throwing his hands in the air to block a face strike. No real experience. I was already in motion, allowing the strike on the first guy to spin me at the second guy.

I came in fast, got down below his raised arms and punched into his groin with my left elbow, throwing a hell of a lot of energy into him. I felt my elbow sink into soft flesh, stopped only by slamming into his pelvic bone. The guy screamed sharply, in a high-pitched voice. He curled over and jerked back. Hands dropped to protect his bruised genitals, which left his face open to whatever I wanted to do to it. I wanted to cave it in, to destroy it. I twisted as I came up, put my steel-cased fist straight into his mouth. The cuffs punched through his front teeth, which shattered into the back of his throat. He fell back against the wall, choking and coughing.

Two down, one to go.

Looked like the third guy was less of a coward than his friends. He was not panicking, yet. He was right in there, coming at me with his arm cocked back. The fist was coming in, a good shot, aimed straight at my nose. I turned away in time and took the punch on my cheek. The guy followed up with a knee aimed at my chin. It was an acrobatic move, requiring him to push off his left leg, throwing all of his momentum into the knee strike.

Which I blocked, grappling with his leg and taking control of it. He tottered, a look of surprise on his face. I tossed him back. The guy scrambled and lost his balance, slammed into the door. I was up on the balls of my feet. The hatch to the cell door window was open. I could make out a widened eye looking in.

The guy went for the door, he wanted out. I grabbed his belt and held him. I said, "Too late."

The third guy's head was shaved on the sides and the back, but long on top, in some kind of Neo-Nazi pony tail. It was like a ready-made handle. I gripped him by the hair and lifted his face so I could see it. The guy was grimacing, mouth in a clenched rictus from the fear and the speed.

He said, "Please."

I said, "No."

I smashed his face into the cell door window, right into the frightened eye of the watching guard. The guy slid off, leaving a bloody smear on the glass. But I had not let go of him. I did it again, this time using my full weight and leverage to bash his head against the stainless steel sink. He took the edge on the bridge of his nose, which made a crunching sound as the cartilage was pulverized. Then I did it again, three times more in quick succession. With each hit the sound was more wet, less solid, more like slamming a bag of fleshy bones into a boulder. Then I dropped him, letting the Nazi flop between the sink and the toilet.

Three down. Maybe twenty seconds.

I looked around. The first guy might have been dead, I wasn't totally sure, and since I didn't care, I didn't bother to check. Same with the third guy. Maybe alive, barely, but no guarantees. Number two was on his ass, against the wall. He was trying to spit out shattered teeth. Groaning and wriggling. I said, "Don't get up, don't make any noise and you might make it to daybreak. Then you can worry about teeth, and the future of eating."

He stopped moving.

One of the guards was peering in again, trying to see. I couldn't tell which one, skinny or big. The beam from a flashlight was playing along the floor, picking out the would-be killers in their various stages of bad shape. The light coming in the cell door window needed to pass through the blood smear, bathing the cell in a red ambience. It looked like a circle of hell. I guess the guard didn't like what he saw, but there was not much that he could do about it. The light went off, and the little hatch closed over the window.

I waited for something to happen, but nothing did. They were probably in some kind of panic. This had not gone according to Plan A. I doubted they had a Plan B. I guess sending in the boys from 1488 was usually effective for prison assassinations. For now, it looked as though they were going to leave me in there with the casualties.

Which suited me just fine.

I could hear the number two guy breathing. I said, "Are you planning on being a problem?" I saw his head shake, no. I stepped back to the bunk bed and stepped on something hard, the pair of handcuffs. I slipped them into my front pocket, I already had the key. Then I lay down on the bunk and closed my eyes. There was no way of knowing what the morning would bring, so I figured it was time to get some shut-eye.

## CHAPTER EIGHTEEN

A COUPLE of hours later I opened my eyes from an excellent sleep, well rested and feeling good. It was one of those waking moments when a vivid dream begins to recede almost immediately, leaving behind only a faint outline. The only thing I kept from the dream was the sensation of being underwater at night. When you do your first solo night dive, navigating at thirty meters all alone in the black, the saying is that you 'see the witches'. In this case it was not a witch, it was the pale figure of a white shark, swimming in the gloom alongside me.

I heard the scuffle of keys in the lock. The cell was a horrifying sight in the weak daylight. Two of the bodies lay motionless, in awkward positions. The guy whose face I had caved in was snoring through his brand new dental configuration. Heavy mouth breathing through the missing front teeth made a high pitched whistle. The jaw line looked bad. Puffy and bruised.

The cell door had opened quietly this time, with only the slightest jingle of keys and a minor scrape of steel on steel. They were coming in cautious and prepared. One guard entered, followed by two more. They wore full riot gear and carried Remington Breacher shotguns with the pistol grip. The face shields were dark, making the guards faceless. They moved in short crab-like steps. I stayed in the bunk. I figured they would have bird-shot loads, and I didn't want a face full of bird-shot. I figured they'd give me that if I gave them half a chance. So, I stayed quiet and pretended to be asleep, lying on my side with eyes opened just enough to see.

The first guy had his gun on me point blank. The Breacher is a dull-looking weapon on a good day. Up close like that, the hole in the barrel was cold and indifferent, utility gear for shredding flesh. Grim and efficient. The other two guards started dragging out the casualties. When the bodies were gone, the first guard in became the last one out. He crab-walked backward, never lowering his aim, until the last moment, when he stepped into the hallway. Another guard closed the door, and I was all alone again.

A good chance to get an extra hour of sleep. In the end, I got two.

A NEW GUARD came this time. Fresh on shift. He looked around the cell, at the various blood stains. He said, "What the fuck." Then he looked at me. "Let's go."

I said, "Where to?"

"Police came to get you."

I stood up. The guard cuffed me. Then we moved out of the cell.

The detective was waiting in an interview room. A table and two chairs faced each other. A window looked out to the corridor. The detective sat in one of them. The younger cop had called him Jim, radio call sign thirteen. He spoke to the guard. "Take the cuffs off."

The guard said, "Not sure that's a good idea, detective."

"Just do it."

The guard shrugged and removed my handcuffs. I sat down in the chair and put my hands on the table. The detective looked at me, then at the guard, who walked out the door and closed it. Then he looked at my hands. The right one was bruised on the knuckles. Using the handcuffs as brass knuckles had been a painful workaround. Particularly the part when I punched into the Nazi's head. Skulls are hard.

The detective said, "What happened there?"

I looked up at him. I said, "You know how it is. Breaking through flesh and bone is hard work."

He said, "I told you what would happen you play it tough."

I looked him in the eyes and said, "I didn't play it any way. They sent three guys to kill me. It didn't work. That's all."

The detective let out a small laugh. "You serious?"

I said nothing.

He gave me a dead-eyed look, then he turned away. "Shit." The detective's mouth was a horizontal line. He looked tired, which made sense. It was early. The guy had come out here first thing.

I said, "It was two of the guards who arranged it, if you want to know. One of them was a big guy with tattooed forearms, a whale and a shark. The other was his buddy, slim with an ill-fitting uniform, like he'd been fat once and lost weight suddenly."

He said, "A skinny fat man."

I said nothing.

The detective glanced at the guard, who watched us through the glass. He licked his lips. Then he said, "I'm Jim Smithson, Detective, Port Morris PD. I just need to ask the question, okay? Where you were last night, between five and six p.m."

I said, "Up on the old fire tower."

Smithson nodded as if a ritual exchange of passcodes had been accomplished. "Fine. That's all I needed you to say. Lucky for you that's what another person says, and she carries a lot more water around here than you do. Lucky for you, she came in. That and the GSR tests came back negative from the lab, confirming the presumptive. So, you're good to go, Mister Keeler. On behalf of the Port

Morris Police Department, I apologize for holding you. We are just doing our job."

"Who fingered me, was it an anonymous tip?"

His eyes closed and he looked away as he spoke. "I'm not at liberty to discuss an ongoing investigation."

I said, "What about the girl I was with?"

"Miss Chapman was released last night."

I wondered what Chapman had told the investigators. Had she admitted to being at the Beaver Lodge last night, or did she lie and tell them she was somewhere else? If so, where. Those were questions that I kept to myself. It occurred to me that they might not have even questioned her.

I said, "So you think that's it?"

"That's it." Smithson stood up. He looked like he could use a caffeine intravenous drip, and maybe that wouldn't be enough.

I said, "Sit back down. That's not it, detective."

He stood with his hand on the chair. "What?"

"Sit down. We're not done here."

Smithson wavered, but he sat back down.

I said, "Guy named Deckart. Has a sidekick name of Willets. At least those are the names they gave me. Do you know them?"

"Any reason I should?"

"Yesterday, those two were following Jane Abrams and her friends, and from what I understand, they were pursuing a campaign of intimidation against them."

He said, "Who is Jane Abrams?"

I said, "Don't be funny."

"I'm not being funny. Who is Jane Abrams?"

"The woman killed at Beaver Falls Lodge."

Smithson smiled, as if he'd managed to trick me. "And how would you know anything about Beaver Falls Lodge?"

I said, "I'm not playing. You're the cop, do your job. I didn't kill Abrams, you know that. So quit delaying. I'm giving you information that can help you find the people who did. Maybe you want to take notes and write this down, so I don't have to repeat myself."

Smithson rapped his fingers on the table between us. "Why would this guy intimidate her?"

I said, "I don't know. Fact is that they did. I said write it down."

"What?"

"What I've just told you. Write down the names, if you don't have them. So you can look into it. Do your job, Smithson."

"What do you know about my job?"

"Detective, you might get shot tomorrow, or wind up eaten by a killer whale, who knows. Shit happens. If you write down the pertinent facts in a case, I assume that the person coming after you might find them useful. If nothing else."

Smithson dropped his gaze and licked his lips. Patted his pockets and pulled out a small notebook and a cheap pen. He flipped open to the first page. I repeated the names, Deckart and Willets, Gavin the prison guard. He wrote them down dutifully, in the unschooled handwriting of a ten-year-old child. I said, "You got it now?"

"Yeah. I got it."

"Good. You've been forewarned."

Smithson met my gaze unsteadily. "Forewarned for what?"

"For whatever's going to happen."

The detective motioned to the guard, who opened the door. I waited with Smithson in the processing room while the duty officer hunted around in the back. After a minute or two she came out with a sealed cardboard box. She sliced through the tape with a utility knife. My jacket and the laptop bag were there, untouched, along with my wallet and change. I had wondered if the detective would be curious about the laptop, but he showed no interest.

The exterior siding of the building was faded red in the daylight. I squinted. Smithson tugged at my elbow, pointed over to the side of the driveway. A Ford F-150 pickup truck was parked, two tires off the road. Leaning against the hood was Lavinia Stone Chandler, Chief of Police, Chilkat Tribal Authority. Otherwise known as Ellie.

Ellie waved.

I turned to the detective. He was looking at her, then at me. "See you around, champ."

Smithson walked to the unmarked Explorer parked in a reserved diagonal slot. I walked over to Ellie. She had a thumb hooked into the belt hoop of her jeans. She looked well rested.

She said, "Just a guy, huh?"

## CHAPTER NINETEEN

The Ford rumbled hungrily. Alaska rolled by. Ellie glanced at me across the front bench. The glance turned into a searching examination which made me self-conscious. The t-shirt was torn and bloody. I had the jacket balled up on my lap. My hands rested on it, knuckles bruised, dried blood in the nails. The jeans were salt-encrusted with significant blood stains. It is no easy task to smell yourself, but even so, I could smell myself, and it smelled bad.

We made eye contact. I shrugged.

She said, "Let's go to my place, get you cleaned up. Then we can go to the New York cafe, if you like bagels."

They had not bothered feeding me at the Port Morris Correctional Facility. Not even a tray of prison food, with a boxed drink and a plastic spork. Yesterday's lunchtime burger seemed like the distant past. A long way off, in more ways than one. Made me glad that I hadn't stopped at the third bite.

Ellie's place was northeast of town, about a mile off the paved road. Not far from the fire tower.

The pickup truck bounced over the trail until a large cabin came into view around a turn. It was an old house, built in another century, from wood and stone. The tenons and mortice joins were roughhewn but precise, put together by experienced and knowledgeable hands. The house was set facing south, with a rise on the southwestern side. It backed into the woodland that I figured stretched up all the way to the fire tower.

When we came inside, Ellie made me take off my boots at the door. She showed me to the bathroom, tossed me a towel and shut me in. I was left with my dirty self, and there was nothing to do but clean up. I removed the few items in my pants pockets. My wallet, and the handcuffs and key I had ended up with at the prison. I laid all that up on a shelf above the sink. Then I removed the various layers of textile that had once been clothing. The t-shirt peeled off painfully, in three pieces. The shower was very hot, the water pressure strong.

Ellie had a large collection of bathroom products lined up on the tiled shelf inside the shower. The products came in many colors and odors, mostly in tubes and bottles. Like magic potions. I tried all of them, one after the other. Some had mysterious functions that escaped me, like *skin exfoliator*, and *body butter*. There were various shapes and sizes of ocean sponge. This all happened through a thick mist of steam. After the wet part, the towel was dry and absorbent. I figured that's what a five star spa experience must be like.

Ellie knocked at exactly the right moment, when I was wondering what to do next. I put the towel around my waist and opened the door. She carried a pile of clothing, neatly folded, one on top of the other. Jeans, button-down plaid shirt, socks, underwear. She said, "It's all clean. Bob's stuff. He won't mind if you take it."

I said, "I hope not. Wouldn't want to get on the wrong side of Bob."

She said, "Wrong, Bob's a pussy cat. It's his mom you have to worry about."

Ellie held out a black garbage bag. I looked at it, then at her. Then I understood. I said, "The old stuff?"

Ellie nodded and closed the door. I saw a pair of electric beard clippers on the shelf above the sink. I figured Ellie's son Bob wouldn't mind. It was time the beard came off.

I came out of the bathroom a new man. Clean shaven, wearing clean clothes. Felt pretty good. But I was a hungry man. Luckily Ellie had made the correct decision regarding the bagels. Better off going for bagels in the real New York City than in a Port Morris cafe. She was in the kitchen making an omelette. Coffee was hot and black in a pot on the counter.

It was as if the shattered world had suddenly repaired itself.

I told Ellie everything, starting from the beginning, holding almost nothing back. She didn't interrupt my telling of it, except to nod and grunt. Once in a while she got up to refill her cup, or my cup. The coffee was black and perfectly measured. Ellie had a police radio on the counter, tuned in at a low volume. Once in a while there was a squawk. She had made toast, and bacon to go with the eggs, butter and strawberry jam to go with the toast. When I was done talking, I sat back in the chair.

She said, "You want seconds?"

I said, "Does a bear shit in the woods?"

Ellie took my plate. While she was replenishing it, I could see her thinking, head down, knitted eyebrows. She set the plate in front of me again. Then she poured more coffee. She sat down across from me and started to ask questions.

"Two groups. One looking for the missing boy, the other trying to prevent them from doing so."

I grunted through a bite of toast, affirmative.

She said, "The girl, Chapman. Any idea where she is now?"

I shook my head, negative.

"So, the missing boy. George. Looks like he is the hinge. Whatever he got involved with. And, as far as you know, there are no demands. It is not a kidnapping."

I gulped down a mouthful of fresh and hot coffee. "Kid's missing. Mom comes looking for him, gets pushed around, then winds up killed along with the guys she came with."

Ellie said, "Pretty extreme response, if you ask me."

I said, "These people are not playing around."

She said, "The boy is supposed to be here in Port Morris. He's a fisherman, or a tour guide or something?"

I said, "From what Chapman and Abrams told me, George is a scientist. Some kind of fancy physics. I had a look at his papers, up in the Edna Bay Apartments. The term *non-linear acoustics* kept on coming back. I guess that's a field of research, although I have no idea what it is."

Ellie said, "Hold on." She picked up her phone and started tapping into it. I watched her get the results, a split second later. Her mouth opened in an oh shape as she read. Tough reading, the lips were moving slowly, hesitantly getting around difficult-to-pronounce words. Then she tapped a few more times and put the phone down. She said, "Something to do with sound, maybe the kind of sounds that don't travel in a straight line. But it sure looks a hell of a lot more complicated than that."

I said, "No doubt. The question is what was George the young physicist doing in Port Morris, Alaska?"

Ellie said, "Yes. That's the interesting part. Now you remember what I told you up on the fire tower, about the Navy research center."

I grunted affirmative. Noticed the backpack containing George Abram's laptop resting on a chair inside the door.

Ellie continued. "The proper name for it was the Naval Surface Warfare Center. I don't know much about what they did out on the island, but I have heard that it was all about the way they can hear things underwater, detection and stealth."

I said, "Submarines."

Ellie said, "Bingo. It wasn't a sub base, the big one is up north. It was a research outfit looking at ways to hide our submarines, and to find theirs. Maybe that has to do with acoustics."

I had seen several submarines during the salmon season, along with pods of humpback whales. The big boats were nuclear powered, Ohio class submarines. They were about five hundred and fifty feet long and looked awesome in the sunset. The stealth material sucked in the sound, but also the light. Kind of like a black hole in the ocean. You would see them suddenly sliding up out of the depths. Flat black forms, almost two football fields in length, slipping across the horizon.

I said, "But that's all closed now, you said."

"Yes. Closed for some years. I doubt this George kid would have been a researcher for the Navy. But it is a coincidence, don't you think?"

I grunted.

She said, "What does that mean, that sound you just made?"

I said, "No such thing as a coincidence."

Ellie tipped her head to one side and smiled. "I'm curious. How did the Jane Abrams people find you?"

I said, "One of their guys was a computer geek. They got a photograph of me and ran it. Found me in the Southeast Alaska Seiners Association database. Then they found my military record somewhere."

Ellie thought for a moment. She said, "The military record. Is that something that the Abrams people would find attractive, a reason to approach you?"

"I served in an Air Force special tactics unit, pararescue."

"How did they think to get a picture of you?"

I told her the story about Chapman and the bearded giant in the Porterhouse Bar.

Ellie said, "Makes some sense. No offense, but if they needed muscle, there you were. Efficient thinking, really. Membership in the SEAS is required for anyone working on a fishing boat. Your name would be in the data base with a picture. Standard operating procedures. Have you seen their offices?"

I said, "Yes, and often. Me and June go way back, all the way to July."

"So you know they wouldn't actually need a computer geek to gain access to the SEAS files. You could probably pay for it by feeding June donuts, or ice cream. But not the military record. So how did they find that?"

I said, "There are exactly a dozen ways to get authorized access to military records from outside. Each of those requires paperwork and time. So I figure that's the computer geek part. They must have hacked into a government database."

"I guess." She lifted her eyebrows. "That's quite impressive don't you think?"

"Yeah. It isn't bad."

Ellie was done eating and done drinking coffee. She had cleaned up her plate and was sitting with her legs crossed beneath her on the chair. It looked like a terribly uncomfortable position, like some kind of torture. But Ellie was serene, like someone had given her the secret to a happy life.

She said, "Okay, so it's about George, as far as you're concerned. And it's a missing persons case. According to what you know from the dead mother, Jane. But what about the people who you found following them?"

I said, "Deckart and Willets."

"Right. Deckart and Willets were actively harassing the mother. You like them for the murders?"

I said, "Possible but not probable, far as I can make out. I took a good look at the bodies. The hits were clean and precise. The shooter used a .22. Triple shots for each victim. I don't take Deckart and Willets for professionals. I think that they are more likely a lower species of hired freelance muscle."

Ellie said, "Then there is the Mister Lawrence link."

I said, "Deckart and Willets were convinced that I was one of Mister Lawrence's guys. I don't know exactly what that is supposed to mean, but I do know that they expressed that sentiment only after a tussle."

"A tussle?"

"A display of controlled violence."

Ellie said, "On your part. The display. Meaning it would make sense for Mister Lawrence to have a guy like you working for him."

"Something like that, yes."

I brought the plates to the sink and started cleaning the dishes. The sink was strategically located in front of a window, with a view. On the left side was the driveway, sloping down. On the right side, the hill continued into the forest, probably going endlessly out into wilderness. When I was finished, I turned and leaned back against the counter. Ellie was still in her complicated pose on the chair.

I said, "So what about all this interests the Chilkat Tribal Authority?"

She unfolded her legs and turned on the chair to face me. "The Tribal Authority is really just an office building in town with a vague jurisdiction. I've got two guys in one room working for me, two days out of five. What we mostly get involved with are disputed claims to tribal blood, hunting and fishing rights. The other areas of jurisdiction are tribal lands, largely wilderness, but there are some populated areas, small villages, and there are some business establishments here and there. We are tuned into the Port Morris Police Department radio frequencies. I heard your name over the radio, before the bodies were found. Actually, I heard your name about an hour after I saw you. Then there were the bodies found. I called Jim Smithson on the phone. He called me back when they had an estimated time of death. So, I knew for a fact that you had not been at Beaver Falls at that time."

"Smithson the detective."

"Yes."

I said, "When did they have a time of death?"

"Not until early this morning. Otherwise I would have gotten you out earlier."

"I appreciate you speaking up for me."

She said, "It was just the right thing to do is all."

"Even so."

"Well, it isn't just about you. I've taken a personal interest in the question of Mister Lawrence, you could call it a hobby."

"Because of the place up by the fire tower?"

Ellie nodded. "Yes." She had a strange look on her face, like she didn't know exactly how to express what was swimming around in her head. "The land is smack dab in the middle of tribal territory, like a black hole in my jurisdiction. That's one thing. Another thing I didn't tell you. Happened earlier this year, late March. We found a body up by the fence. Looked like it had been there all winter long and nobody had come by to find it."

"What fence?"

"Perimeter fence around the property." Ellie pointed through the kitchen window to the right. "Up there after the fire tower. Property starts about a hundred yards off. We found the body leaned against the fence. Some old toothless guy." She put her hand back on the table and curled it around her coffee cup, like it had gotten real cold all of a sudden. "At the time we figured it was some old drifter who froze to death, and that's probably what it is. But that was early April by the time we'd given up on identifying the body, and we still have no idea who that was because of the lack of dental information. Prints came up clean."

I said, "Which side of the fence?"

Ellie snapped her fingers. "Bingo. Our side of the fence, which is precisely why I was never able to go up there and ask any questions. So, truth is, we've never even been able to go look into that compound. No idea what he does." She took a sip from her coffee and swallowed elegantly. "It just rubs me up the wrong way is all. So, yeah. When you mentioned Mister Lawrence, and the trouble you've been having, let's just say that the entire situation gets my ears pricked up and alert."

I said, "So what are we doing here?"

She said, "We're going to team up, Keeler. You and me. I've told you how I see it, what about you?"

I said, "Way I see it, your Mister Lawrence mystery is a sideshow at the moment. From my point of view it's more simple than that. A mother comes up here looking for her missing son and gets killed. Doesn't look like anybody's picked up the trail, so I'll take it from here. No doubt it won't be pretty. I wouldn't mind finding Chapman either."

She said, "Oh yes, I'll bet. Apparently the Port Morris PD had a great time with the bed sheets."

I didn't rise to it. I continued. "Like I said, what are we doing here?"

"You mean, assuming the Port Morris PD isn't going to be doing effective work."

I said, "I've got a few reasons to believe that the Port Morris PD will not be sufficient. The first is that as far as they're concerned it's a murder, not a missing person's case. Abrams went to the police and got bounced, hard. Second, someone gave the local cops my name as Jane Abram's killer, which they accepted without enough critical reflection, far as I'm concerned. I'm operating under the assumption they are constitutionally unable to work in any acceptable manner."

She said, "Jim's a good guy, but he's one guy."

"Good guy meaning what?"

"Meaning not corrupt, and only drunk in the evenings and weekends." Ellie leaned back and looked at me coolly. "So where do we start, Keeler?"

I said, "You have to know something Ellie, before we get into it. There aren't two ways of doing this, and there aren't any moral equivocations, as far as I'm concerned. The ethical part of this is all wrapped up with a bow on it. My moral compass has only two settings, wrong and right. I'm not the philosophy department. People have done some very bad things, which they are currently getting away with scot-free. No reason why they'd shy away from doing more bad things. Now that I'm here, it's going to get straightened out. Simple as that."

She said, "You seem very confident. But things are never simple, Keeler."

I said, "Every problem looks impossibly complicated when you don't know the solution."

Ellie's eyes were smiling, her mouth too. She said, "You're like a poet, Keeler."

"That's what Deckart said. We'll see what happens to him. Dollars to donuts he doesn't last the week." I glanced at the backpack over by the door. I said, "Two things up top on my list. One, while you were telling me about the toothless old guy, I was thinking that it might be a good idea to get a look at that old Navy research base after all, tangential or not. Two, we need to find a computer geek of our own."

Ellie cocked her head to the side. "Why?"

"See that backpack over there?" I pointed to it, Ellie followed with her eyes. "George's laptop, from his apartment. Password protected, so maybe one try left before it triggers whatever security he's got set up."

She whistled. "Withholding that from the police?"

I got up and walked over to the backpack, parked on a chair by the door. "Are they investigating the disappearance of George Abrams?"

Ellie said, "No, not that I'm aware of."

"Right. I am."

I opened the bag and removed the envelopes that I had taken from George Abrams' mailbox. I brought them back to the kitchen table. Ellie was watching me carefully. I cleaned off a knife and started slitting the envelopes open. The first two were junk mail.

She said, "I may be able to find a geek. In fact, you met him briefly. At the old fire tower."

I said, "In regards to the first thing on the list, I borrowed a bike from Guilfoyle's boat. Need to get it back to him."

She raised her eyebrows. "Need is a four-letter word."

"So I hear. But the bike goes back to Guilfoyle. We need to find a boat anyway."

Ellie shrugged, "A dime a dozen around here."

I said, "The *Sea Foam* is a fishing boat. That gives us cover in case there is security at the island."

I had stopped opening the letters. Five envelopes, all open. Four of them inconsequential junk mail, one of them semi-interesting with potential but unknown consequences.

Ellie said, "What?"

I handed her the sheet of paper.

I said, "Speaking of boats. I took his mail, back at the apartment. Looks as if Abrams rented a boat and didn't bring it back."

"Oh."

The letter was from a boat rental place, Salty Charters. George Abrams had taken out a twenty-eight-foot fishing charter, a Bayliner named the *Katrina Flynne*. The cost was $175 for the one day, including fish finder, life jackets, GPS, and a CD player. But Abrams hadn't brought the boat back, so the letter was a warning, and a revised invoice of twenty days, plus the threat of legal action. They wanted $3,500 plus a $200 penalty fee. The date on the letter was fourteen days previous.

Ellie read the letter.

I said, "How long before they send a cop over to his apartment?"

She shrugged. "Depends when the charter company filed a complaint. How long would they give it before they reported the boat stolen. Once they did, it would take a while before the police got the investigation going."

I said, "Do you know the place?"

Ellie looked up at me. "Yes. It's on the way to Eagle Cove."

I looked at the clock above the breakfast table. The day had started early. It was only seven-thirty in the a.m. I might just get a second breakfast at the cannery.

## CHAPTER TWENTY

The boat rental guy was large, both ways. He had tousled blond hair and wore a long yellow rain slicker. Salty Charters was a one-man operation run out of an insulated and rain-proofed box set up on the docks out near the paper factory. The guy ran a repair facility along with the charter boat rentals. About a dozen boats were tied up out front. One boat was up on blocks. It looked like it had been there for a while. Maybe the guy would get to it, maybe he wouldn't.

The office was accessed by a steep wood deck with railings. When we arrived he had just flicked on the coffee machine. He came out to meet us after Ellie knocked. I figured that we'd caught him before the first cup of coffee.

The boat rental man's eyes were deep in their sockets, crusted from sleep. "Yeah?"

Ellie showed him her badge and the letter. I leaned back against the deck railing and observed. Despite the lack of coffee the man was paying attention. Ellie handed him the letter and he read it conscientiously before looking up at her, confused.

"The guy brought it back a week ago."

Ellie said, "And paid off the bill?"

"Yeah. Paid the bill. Why are you asking?"

"You have the boat here?"

He pointed to a modest white leisure vessel. Clean, and a new blue and white paint job. Chrome bars around the edge, and an enclosed cabin with a roof to protect against rain and cold. I walked down the dock until I could read the fancy curling script. Gold on deep blue. It read 'Katrina Flynne'.

I walked up to meet Ellie and the boat man. I said, "Same guy brought it back as rented it?"

"Same guy, different guy. How the fuck should I know? You think I remember?"

I said, "Guy rents a boat, what does he need in terms of ID?"

The man said, "Driver's license." He held up a finger and disappeared into the office. Which was a great excuse for him to harvest the initial offerings of the coffee machine, quietly dripping away in the background. After the man had collected the resuscitating hot beverage into a waiting cup, he found his way to the filing cabinet. A minute later he came out with a photocopied driver's license. The man held it in front of us with his left hand, with his right he sucked down the coffee.

Massachusetts driver's license featuring one George Abrams, a couple of years younger than the photo that his mother showed me.

The boat man said, "This isn't the guy who brought the boat back. What's the deal, they running drugs?"

Ellie said, "No."

I said, "You didn't ask why a different guy was returning the boat?"

"The boat came back, that was a relief. Like, one more hassle taken out of my goddamned life." He was remembering. "Guy who brought her back was apologetic. Paid the fee, plus the penalty, plus an extra hundred for the hassle."

I said, "What did he look like?"

The man jutted his chin at me. "Like you. A mid-thirties male who looked like he could complete fifty pull-ups and a hundred push-ups in under five minutes. Unlike me, who needs coffee just to start up the old neurons. Are we done here, fellas? I got shit to do."

I looked at Ellie. She shrugged. I said, "I guess that's it."

We walked up to the road.

Ellie said, "Not looking good for George Abrams."

When we came to Ellie's truck I leaned against it and looked out to the ocean. I said, "George Abrams takes a boat out, it comes back a couple of weeks later without him. Chapman told me that Abrams had a portable research kit in a pelican case. No mention of that coming back."

Ellie said, "Triangulation. George Abrams rents the boat. His mother comes up and is followed by a bunch of guys who are working for Mister Lawrence. He disappears, she is killed."

"Assumed to be working for Mister Lawrence."

"Mister Lawrence owns the property up past the fire tower, plus Bell Island, an abandoned military research facility."

I said, "Deduction. George Abrams took the boat out there to Bell Island with his pelican case full of research gear. Then he disappeared."

Ellie said, "Boat comes back with someone else, who's happy to pay the late fee, no questions asked. Avoid the escalation."

I looked at her hard. "Conclusion. Not looking good for George Abrams."

THE HORN behind the Eagle Cove cannery blows at eight o'clock in the morning, heralding a new day. Fish to be caught, fish to be processed. Packed into cans. Stacked up in room-sized ovens. Superheated in rows and stacks, like miniature coffins. Forklifted out to cool. There are two kinds of people who listen for that horn, the cannery workers asleep in their dormitory beds, and the fishermen asleep in their narrow berths.

The salmon season might have been closed, but work continued at Eagle Cove, at least for the next couple of weeks. Catching up on a successful salmon season. Prepping for the winter. Maybe switching over from salmon to crab, or halibut, or whatever else was next up for harvest. Which meant that breakfast rolls were still happening for the time being. Which was as good a reason as any to get out of a bunk. Ellie and I came through the cannery floor at nine. I was rolling the bike, retrieved from the place I'd left it the night before.

We found Guilfoyle sitting on a railway sleeper, looking out over the water. He held a hot breakfast roll in one hand and a cup of coffee in the other. Over by the oil dock, a bald eagle perched on a post looking for something to kill or scavenge.

Guilfoyle watched us coming over. I leaned the bike against the sleeper and made the introductions. "Guilfoyle, Ellie. Ellie, Guilfoyle." They shook hands. I said, "Sorry I couldn't get the bike back last night."

Guilfoyle was finishing up a bite of his breakfast roll. The cannery people have a counter with a window where a guy can get one for himself. Just walk on up and put out the hand. Someone will put a freshly baked hot package in it. A package of cheese, egg, and sausage with ketchup and hot sauce included inside some kind of dough.

Ellie saw me looking at Guilfoyle's roll. She was shocked. "You're still hungry?"

I shrugged. "Maybe." Looked at her. "Not you?"

"No, not me."

I said, "Give me a second."

Three minutes later, I was walking back with a breakfast roll of my own, hot and heavy in my right hand. A nutritious bundle of grease, protein, and carbohydrates. My motto is 'get it while you can'. A cup of coffee was balanced in my left hand. Black, no sugar. Guilfoyle was finishing his roll, the last corner disappearing into his beard. Ellie was talking. When I came up on them, they both turned to me.

I said, "So where were we?"

Guilfoyle said, "We're at the part where you ask me to take you out to Bell Island. You've moved from fisherman to private detective with a single shave."

I said, "It's an old Navy research base. Just want to take a look at it." I jerked a thumb at Ellie. "She tell you about the missing kid?"

Guilfoyle said, "Yes. She did. Naval Surface Warfare Center is what they called it officially, the base out on Bell Island. The research was secret, but not the existence of that base. A lot of stories flung around about that. I'd be happy to take a look, just for my own curiosity. I'm assuming this is connected to the murders over at Beaver Falls everyone is talking about."

I nodded. "It is." Ellie shot me a look, I looked away and sat down on the sleeper next to Guilfoyle.

He said, "I heard a boat got scuttled out in the passage last night."

"That right?"

"Apparently so."

Ellie looked at me again. I hadn't told her about the zodiac. I played it poker-faced. "They going to dive for it?"

He said, "Doubt it."

I blew on my breakfast roll; it was very hot. "They'd need a damn good reason to bring in a dive team, what is it, seventy meters? For the time it would take to figure out what happened. Engine go down?"

"Yup."

I said, "Well there you go. No chance of getting that working again, if the valves were open."

Guilfoyle said, "More like eighty-five meters in that part of the channel."

The sausage roll was exceptionally good. I finished off the last corner and washed it down with the end of the coffee. I stood up. "So let's do it."

Guilfoyle stayed seated. "Not right this minute, Keeler."

I said, "What's the problem?"

He said, "Bilge is getting pumped out this morning. Probably take until after lunch, knowing those guys. Let's say three thirty or four to be safe."

I looked at Ellie. She shrugged, said, "So, we'll come back."

We walked over to where the *Sea Foam* was docked alongside the other remaining boats in the fleet. I hauled the bike over the side and then fixed it back behind the smokestack. Guilfoyle had disappeared into the boat somewhere.

TEN MINUTES LATER, we were sitting in her truck. The keys were in Ellie's hand. The engine was still warm, windows were open, and I had an elbow up on the edge. Gulls were flying over the woods on Ellie's side. On my side the low cannery buildings stretched out below, and beyond that, the Pacific Ocean.

Ellie said, "What are you thinking, Keeler?"

I said, "Thinking about those two guys who were following Jane Abrams' crew yesterday."

She said, "Deckart and Willets."

"Maybe I should go pay them a visit, maybe break their heads if they don't talk to me nicely. What do you think?"

Ellie looked at me from behind the steering wheel. "Sounds exciting, but we need to do the boring stuff, Keeler. It always needs to be done."

I said, "I can feel it coming. A room, a chair, a desk. Computers and telephones. Bad posture. Bad skin. The modern world. What did you have in mind?"

She said, "The basics. Who, how, when, what, where. Four of the five W's give or take an H."

"Detective stuff."

Ellie said, "I need to make a call about the laptop you picked up. It would be a good idea to get some information on the missing kid, George. Then we should do background on the murder victims. I know that you're an army guy, Keeler, but there is a place in this world for the pencil-necked office dweeb making calls and typing out emails and messages."

I said, "Air Force actually. What do you think Detective Smithson is doing, right now?"

"My guess? Background on the victims. Other than that, he's waiting on forensics maybe." Ellie was looking over across the water to a paper factory nestled into the armpit of Eagle cove. She laughed to herself. "The question to ask of course is: what is Smithson *not* doing." The factory stack was spewing white smoke. She said, "Smithson cut his teeth as a State Trooper up around Fairbanks. Came down to Port Morris ten years ago. He's above board, but not very imaginative. I reckon he might help."

I was suddenly thinking about Ellie. Whatever I might have imagined a Chief of Police, Chilkat Tribal Authority to be like, it was not her. I said, "I'm guessing your background in law enforcement didn't begin here in Alaska, or in the Chilkat Tribal Territories. You're lower forty-eight."

She chuckled. "Certainly not here. You going to take a guess?"

I looked at her and chewed it over in my mind. What was I looking at? I ignored the exterior to some extent. Good-looking woman, so what? Outdoorsy type, could have been something she picked up later in life. There was a wariness about her, disguised by her outward appearance. Some wounds that she had recovered from, but the scars showed through. My assessment was a competent type of person, decent, and inherently suspicious.

I said, "Big city cop. Something didn't work out. You came out here. Chilkat tribal authority, not by being born here, but because you were able to claim the blood ties. Some kind of an escape."

Ellie had a twinkle in her eye. "Can you keep on going, or is that all you've got?"

I said, "You are in your forties. Got a kid, probably away in college or something. No husband. So, I'm guessing divorced, maybe collateral damage from your old job. You haven't been up here for that long. Maybe five years max. So, twenty-some odd years on the big city force. Fifteen shy of retirement. Five years in uniform, then some kind of anti-crime unit. Someone saw the potential in you. You used that to go up to Robbery Investigation and get your detective shield halfway through. But that's when it ended. Some kind of a problem happened. Could have been anything. Stopped cold. Game over."

Ellie smiled grimly. "Well done, and thanks for the flattery. Bob's not in college, he's a smokejumper with the National Park Service. Stationed down at Yellowstone. Far as my career goes, I put eighteen years in. Ended at the Homicide table but got caught up in something."

I said, "I've got experience in government bureaucracy. Back east or out west? Your accent isn't strong either way."

"Philly."

I looked out the window. The gulls were flying over the truck and out to sea now. "You said four of the five W's. Why not the fifth?"

Ellie said, "The fifth W is *why*. We don't give a shit about *why*. Cops looking for motive is bullshit. Cops look for convictions, which come from confessions, witnesses, and evidence. Motive gives you nothing. It's a narrative that plays for the movies, the press, and the public. Civilians want to know *why*, because they need to feel that bad things happen for a reason. Truth is, sometimes they do, sometimes they don't. Sometimes shit just happens."

We locked eyes. Hers were clear and glossy, confident and activated. They didn't show me a cynic, or a bitter person. They showed me a realistic and practical woman. A professional, stopped cold at the top of her game. She was someone who I could learn from.

I said, "You've been wasting your talents on this bullshit for five years, Ellie. Now it's time to make up for that."

"Yes."

"You know there's something not right up here. We're going to take them down."

She said, "Game on, brother."

## CHAPTER TWENTY-ONE

The Chilkat Tribal Authority was an office in a functional cement block across the street from the Port Morris town hall, itself a functional building with a grassy landscaped square out front.

We did the two-floor walk-up, then a pale tiled corridor lit by fluorescent tubes built into the white drop ceiling. The office was one of two on that floor. The other being a pair of shuttered double glass doors marked 'North Pacific Travel Industry Risk Assessment'.

Forty steps after that, we arrived. 'Chilkat Tribal Authority' was printed in gold letters on glass doors. Very official-looking. Inside was a waiting area. Sofas around a low coffee table offering magazines promising features on tribal life. Leaflets featuring the issues and problems of tribal life were fanned out for the taking. There were several photographs on the wall, well-spaced and neatly hung. There was a receptionist, big and young and wearing black-framed glasses. He was reading a paperback.

Ellie said, "Hi Dave."

Dave looked up and said, "Hey Ellie." He swiveled his eyes to me. Then Ellie was taking me through, past the reception desk, too far for Dave's eyes to follow without serious risk to his neck. The offices were clean and white and carpeted in beige. There was a big photocopier in the corridor. It looked immovable and set to do all kinds of mysterious things besides copying. There was an office on the left after the photocopier. Door open, two women inside sitting at facing desks. They looked up simultaneously as we passed.

Ellie opened the second door on the right. A big room, with a big table and several chairs gathered around it, a speaker phone gadget in the middle. She had a desk on the other side of the room, butted right up to a wall of windows looking out over the town hall green. There was desk space for two others in a corner area away from the door.

I said, "Where are the other two guys?"

Ellie gave me a sideways glance. "They run charter fishing trips for tourists when they aren't here, which is often." She looked around theatrically. "And it looks like they aren't here. So, they must be fishing. My guess would be up near Sitka."

Ellie dragged one of the chairs away from the conference table, set it alongside her office chair. She unclipped her badge and threw it on the desk. Then, reached around with her right hand, and unclipped the holster from her left hip. She slid her service weapon onto the desk, a Ruger SR9. We sat elbow to elbow. She depressed the power button on her computer. We watched it start up, like watching grass grow.

Ellie turned to me, I looked at her. I said, "Office work."

She said, "Yes, Keeler. Three vectors, think of each of them as a circle." Ellie stood up and walked to a white board hung on the wall. She took a marker and made a red circle. "Circle one, Jane Abrams and her people." Ellie wrote J. Abrams inside the circle. "Circle two, Deckart and whatever his name is that I keep forgetting." Ellie wrote, Deckart.

I said, "Willets."

"Willets." She drew a third circle. "Mister Lawrence." Ellie wrote Mr. L in the third circle.

I said, "Mister Lawrence is nothing more than two words out of Deckart's mouth. Besides that, no link, no nothing. No reality as far as I can make out. No form or substance in my imagination. Like the legend of Mullah Omar in Afghanistan, a Taliban leader, supposedly."

Ellie shifted in her seat, interested. "He wasn't a Taliban leader in reality?"

I said, "He was a short guy with one arm who had a beard that grew up past his nose. Like his nose was inside the beard. For the Taliban that was a special sign, like he was anointed. Omar had a good run with the Russians, but by the time we got there he was like the Wizard of Oz, just a little old guy behind a curtain."

"Words are things, Keeler. *Mister* and *Lawrence* are two words that could become important. We don't know which one of these circles will snowball and produce unexpected results. Like more people and more things involved."

"Fine, so what, we each take one of your circles and start looking into it?"

Ellie stood up slowly. "I'm going to do some human intelligence work, Keeler. I'll walk across to the Port Morris Police Department and take Smithson out for coffee. He's got a thing for apple crullers. We'll see if he's made any interesting headway. In the meantime, you could do background on the victims." She reached over and picked her gun up off the desk. Clipped it back with a practiced gesture.

I said, "I've only got one of the names. Jane Abrams. The others I know as Jason and Adam. No last name given. Maybe you could get those from Smithson. You going to tell him you're running a parallel investigation?"

She said, "I'm just going to buy him coffee. Cop to cop stuff. And it isn't a parallel investigation. I've got a legitimate and professional interest because of the Lawrence link. The property is smack dab in the middle of my jurisdiction and it's a disputed land situation."

I said, "George's boat is a possible hinge between Jane Abrams and Mister Lawrence. If he took the boat out to Bell Island. You should dangle that in front of the detective, see if he bites."

Ellie said, "I'll give Jim the boat link. If he goes for it, they might be able to extract navigation data from the GPS. I'll ask him about the victims, try and get the names of the other two. Hopefully he'll disclose without making a meal out of it."

The backpack with the laptop I had taken from George Abrams' apartment was sitting limp on the conference table. I said, "You were going to make a call about the laptop."

Ellie waved her mobile phone and left the office.

I got in the desk chair and started typing the words 'Jane Abrams' into the computer. I got back results. Lines of text on the screen, and grids of photos. Pictures of women mostly, a couple of other genders mixed in for good measure. There was an underwear model named Jane Abrams, she looked a little on the young side, and blonde. There was an Australian politician in her seventies, who had written a book on wild dogs and humans called 'The Way of the Dingo'. She had given interviews on television, so they had her on video. Too old, different continent, wrong eye color.

I tried combinations. Like, Jane Abrams Ultra High Net Worth Individual. Nothing came back. There was an entire world of people named Jane Abrams, but none of them were the woman I had spoken to at the airport.

On the other hand, George Abrams was real, according to the internet. I searched for *George Abrams, Physics*. Got back a half-dozen results. First up was his student profile at MIT. Abrams was a doctoral candidate. He had a PhD supervisor and was listed in a couple different research groups. His MIT profile had the same picture Jane Abrams had shown me.

Next up were the external engagements. George Abrams was listed as a speaker on the web pages of several academic conferences. All but one of them in the United States, the other in Estonia. He was a credited collaborator on two research papers. I was able to see the abstracts, not that I would have the patience to read the papers. To me they looked identical to the gobbledygook I had seen on his desk.

I eased back from the desk and stood. Sitting like that had made me get all hunched. I stretched and cracked my joints. The shoulders, the back, the knuckles. What I needed just then was a cup of strong black coffee. I emerged from the office and poked around. There was a common kitchen. On the counter sat a lonely looking coffee machine with a blinking green eye. Beside it was a bowl full of sealed capsules. Not a chance. Far as I'm concerned that stuff doesn't count as coffee.

Out of the office, down the hall. I nodded to Dave and rapped my knuckles on his desk as I passed. He was buried in his book. Out again to the corridor, down past the North Pacific Travel Industry Risk Assessment office. They were opening now. As I came through the hallway, a trim guy in a shirt and tie was pulling up the shutters. Behind him, I glimpsed a reception area. Sofas, coffee table, brochures stacked up and fanned out for the taking.

In the center of the town hall green, a bearded skinny guy with large hoop earrings had parked his coffee cart. The guy made excellent coffee. Cost more than a couple of bucks but it hit the spot. I put a small one down right there and then, short and bitter. Then I asked him for another. There were no customers competing for his attention, so the guy got right to it. He pulled the levers, machinery hissing and puffing as the pressure valves adjusted. After a small eternity, the pungent brown liquid emerged from the chrome spouts, collected by a fresh little paper cup.

The cup was hot, precious and fragrant in my hand as I came back up to Ellie's office. It was also precarious, filled to the brim and ready to spill right out. I carried the coffee carefully up the stairs, then down the corridor. I paused in front of the North Pacific Travel Industry Risk Assessment office. Someone had set out a brochure rack, right next to the door. The brochures were neatly stacked in purpose-built plastic cubbies. They stood upright, five or ten deep. Behind the cubbies, a sign read *Emerald Allure: Legendary Memories*. Behind the text was a photograph of the ocean, blue and green and perfect. Beyond that, a glacier and a white-capped mountain range. In the foreground, the white cruise ship. Like a floating mobile city, serene and geometrically refined. The photograph had been taken at a perfect three-quarter angle from high up, probably by a remotely controlled drone. The boat was supposed to look noble and refined.

I picked up a brochure and brought it into the Tribal Authority offices.

Ellie wasn't back yet. I put my feet up on her desk and flipped through the brochure while I nursed the coffee. I looked at the pictures, which were plentiful. Photos of bears catching salmon in rushing, sweet water swells. Well dressed older people with white teeth photographing whales. Dolphins playfully leaping in the *Emerald Allure's* wake. Fancy dimly lit restaurants with well dressed waiters. A roulette wheel surrounded by tuxedoed geriatrics holding fruity drinks with umbrellas and orange peels.

Then there were hero pictures of the *Emerald Allure* herself, overlaid with info-graphics, and data visualizations. The photos burst with statistics. The boat could house 3,329 passengers and 1,446 crew. It had seven restaurants and eight bars, including several karaoke salons. There were multiple spas, and various sporting facilities. A full-sized swimming pool, and five gyms. They had a helicopter landing pad just in case, which doubled as a dance floor when the weather was good.

Toward the back of the brochure was a two-page spread: *Meet the Crew*. A grid of photos with titles and names on the side. The captain came first. A grim-looking middle-aged woman, smiling desperately in an ill-fitting captain's hat and jacket with gold braiding on her shoulders. Then there were the department heads and their deputies. All of the important positions plus their backup, like Head of Entertainment, and the Head Chef. The Head of Customer Satisfaction was further down, alongside the Head of Excursions and her deputy. Competent-looking people in early middle age with a slightly younger second in command.

At the bottom of the spread was a photo of Deckart. He looked different. As if someone had taken his picture, put it into a computer, and worked hard on it, trying to make him respectable, strong, and kindly at the same time. Tough job, but they had done good work. Deckart was smiling broadly. He looked tough and confident, wearing a white crew hat and a white crew uniform with some gold braiding laced into it.

The bio read: Deputy Head of Security, Walter M. Deckart.

By the time I finished the espresso, I had already decided that the *Emerald Allure* deserved a visit. It wasn't far, and Ellie had not returned. Her police badge was gathering dust underneath her computer screen. I picked it up. Heavy and reassuring in the hand. Like a special object.

## CHAPTER TWENTY-TWO

I CAME DOWN the hill to the dock. The *Emerald Allure* was about a hundred yards away, towering over the adjacent buildings. The boat had two gangways. One closer to me, the other toward the stern. A fancy German mini-bus was parked up near the bow side gangway. It was the same one I had seen back at the airport. Green with the white logo that read, 'Green Gremlin Tours', with a smiling gremlin sitting on top of the word 'Green'.

A special lift delivered two wheelchair-bound passengers from the bus to the pavement. As I came up to the ship, the hydraulic platform was returning from the road back up to the door. More wheelchairs on their way down. The first set of chairs was already being pushed up the gangway by attendants, past a white-uniformed security guy at a podium with a clipboard.

I walked straight up and showed Ellie's badge. I had it clipped to my jeans, lifted my shirt just like I'd seen her do up at the fire tower. Flashing the badge gave me a little taste of cop power. The guard's attitude flipped instantly when he saw it.

I said, "I need to talk to the head of security."

"Give me a sec." The guy spoke into a handheld radio.

"Gretchen?" Gretchen was a crackle and a hiss. A human voice was hidden in there somewhere, riding the middle frequencies. I pictured Gretchen as a woman in a room surrounded by security camera monitors. On duty. Whatever she had said, the guy understood it. He said, "Need you to send someone down." Gretchen hissed and crackled again. The guy said, "Okay thanks." He turned back to me. "Someone will be down to get you in a minute."

I pushed past him. "Thanks. I'll meet them on the boat."

The guy said something, which I didn't catch, because I was already moving up the gangway. Which was a passenger tunnel, like those coming off an airplane. Airless, but thankfully short. The gangway thumped under my feet. I dodged one of the wheelchairs. It contained a man. At first glance, an old person. But closer in I saw that he wasn't old so much as sickly, paper-white skin and sunglasses. He was breathing through a gummy mouth, making quite an effort. The windows were Perspex and badly scratched. I looked up and over at the breadth of the boat. Going to the window and peering down below I could make out the short stretch of blue water between the dock and the ship.

Then I stepped into an entrance area. Like a fancy hotel lobby, but on a boat.

One side was taken up by a concierge desk. The colors were muted beige. A reassuring tone the shade of coffee with too much milk in it. Recessed lighting was built into contoured wall paneling. There were four or five stations manned by slickly outfitted men and women, busy with problems. Pecking into computer screens and speaking softly into phones. The passengers milled around waiting, heavy with logistical annoyances and preference issues. Off that was a space designed to impress. A vast hall that rose up almost as high as the *Emerald Allure* herself. The centerpiece was a gigantic chandelier, which looked less like a chandelier as I knew it, more like a projectile vomit of mirrored squares.

I pushed through and entered what looked like the sports area. There were two tennis courts on my left, and an indoor swimming pool on my right. The pool was generous. The windows were steamed up some, so I didn't have a clear view. But I could make out figures cavorting in the turquoise waters. And it didn't look like they were elderly people, or middle-aged mothers of adolescent children. Looked more like a half-dozen swimsuit models taking turns doing flips off the diving board.

The ceiling of the pool area was all glass panels. Sun loungers were lined up either side of the blue rectangle. At the back was a smoothie juice bar that took up the width of the space. A pale blonde woman stepped up and executed a perfect back double twist. Through the steamed glass she was a dead ringer for Amber Chapman. Tall, and slim, a body that I recognized. I froze at the window. The figure emerged from the water like someone born to it. The woman did five strokes freestyle, then smoothly bobbed under again.

There was no entrance door from the corridor where I stood, just the wall of foggy windows looking in. The entrance was on the other side. I kept my eye on the blonde as I walked around, trying to find a way in. She came out of the water, lifting smoothly off the tiles with toned arms. Definitely moved like Chapman. I came around as she was drying herself off, chatting with a slim dark-haired woman. The other three or four were gathering close, wrapping towels around themselves. I saw the entrance, tucked behind the bar at the far end. I would have to go all the way around.

There was no direct route into the swimming pool.

First there was a concierge to bypass. I flashed Ellie's badge and he let me through. Next I had to negotiate a maze of dressing rooms and foot-rinsing basins and body-rinsing showers. They wanted me to take my boots off. By the time I found the way into the pool, I was holding my boots and my socks in one hand and there were no more cavorting swimsuit models. Only a clutch of silver-haired and bald men belly-deep in the shallow end.

The entrance to the women's showers and changing room was through a tropical forest of potted palms. I put my shoes on and started moving through the fronds, when a hand gripped my elbow. I turned to face a small woman, maybe thirty years old. Maybe Filipina. She was in uniform with a badge. She said, "The arboretum on board contains half a football field of tropical plants and trees. It's called Paradise Valley and people find it very romantic."

The badge at her breast read, 'Hospitality Princess.'

I said, "I saw someone I knew, she went through there."

"I'm afraid that is the women's changing rooms and showers, sir, men are not allowed. You are the policeman?" I grunted, affirmative. She said, "Would you like to come with me, sir?"

The Hospitality Princess walked me back to the big area with the chandelier, and over to a bank of glass elevators. She pressed the button and stood patiently. Her hair was shiny, black, and straight, sculpted into a wave over her head. I said, "Where are we going?"

She glanced at me politely, eyes diverted to my chin. "I'm taking you down to the hospitality offices sir."

"I want to speak to the head of security."

"I'm afraid the chief officers have not yet boarded, sir. We pick them up in Juneau, the day after tomorrow, with the main body of passengers. You know that Juneau is the capital of Alaska, sir."

"You're running the boat without officers?"

She chuckled. "Of course not. We have approximately 1,300 personnel on board. A quarter of those are officers. Believe me, sir, there is plenty of expertise aboard the *Emerald Allure*." Then she whispered conspiratorially. "We could actually do just fine without the chief officers, but people like to see them. The boats are mostly computerized these days."

I said, "The deputy chief will do just fine."

She hesitated for a moment, looking at my shoes. Then she said, "I will see if he is available." The elevator was descending from up high. A glass-sided barrel with gold trim. "We will take the elevator in any case."

The doors opened and we stepped aside to make room for an elderly couple. The guy was pushing a walking frame. His wife shifted patiently behind him. He looked pissed off. Once we got into the elevator and were moving, I turned back to the woman. "So what's the point of the stop at Port Morris?"

She said, "It's our home port. Some customers choose to board here. About a quarter of our guests. Port Morris is a popular destination for viewing the salmon creeks. We run excursions to see the humpback whales on the other side of Carolina Island."

I said, "What's special about the *Emerald Allure*?"

She smiled. "Where do I start? We have 3,000 miles of electrical cable. A 100 megawatt electrical grid, which is enough power for 100,000 homes. We consume around a million gallons of fresh water per day. We make most of that water ourselves, with both evaporators and reverse osmosis production. We have the largest hospital facilities of any cruise ship on the seven seas."

"A lot of people get sick out here."

"Guests find our hospital facilities reassuring. A sign of the times. We had the clinical deck refurbished last year." She whispered. "It is possible that we will begin to offer elective procedures onboard, perhaps in a year or two."

"Plastic surgery."

"For example. But don't limit your imagination, sir. We deal in dreams."

The elevator stopped softly, no lurch. Only a purr from the brakes. The Hospitality Princess led me off the elevator and down an empty corridor. This time the interior cladding was oak or teak, lined with maritime brass trimmings. At the end of it was another lobby. The whole ship was some kind of a lobby. She indicated a sofa. "If you will just wait here for a moment, sir."

I sat and waited. She disappeared into the offices beyond. The sofa was comfortable, fresh, maybe new. It felt good sitting there. Alongside me was another collection of potted palms, in varying heights and widths. A couple of minutes later the woman came back out. Behind the smiling Hospitality Princess was Walter M. Deckart, dressed in white with gold braiding at his shoulders. He looked uneasy. Smiling for the woman.

Deckart said, "I'll take it from here, Emma. Thanks."

Emma nodded curtly and grinned at me once more. "Thank you, sir. It was a pleasure speaking with you."

Then she was gone and Deckart looked at me. He put a hand up to his mouth and coughed. Then he grumbled under his breath. "Where'd you steal the badge?"

## CHAPTER TWENTY-THREE

I SAID NOTHING. We stood together on the soft carpet. The waiting area surrounding us like a soft shell.

Deckart said, "You lied to me. About working for Mister Lawrence."

"I never said anything. It's what you wanted to believe is all. Psychologists call that confirmation bias."

He blinked slowly and passed fingers over his mustache. "Yeah. I wouldn't know about any of that bullshit. Tell you what I do know, you got a beating coming for what happened yesterday. I was you, I'd leave town."

I stepped into his personal space. I could see him resisting the urge to step back. I said, "Take me into your office, or whatever you've got. Or I could slap you around out here if you'd like that better."

Deckart stood for a moment, weighing up his options. He turned and started walking back. I followed. We didn't speak. I watched him walk. Deckart was a muscular man, stepping his bow legs wide to compensate for exaggerated quadriceps. Large airy offices were distributed either side of the corridor. Left side offices featured port holes punched into the walls, letting in soft ocean light. The right side offices had walls and extra lighting built into recessed grooves at the ceiling. Deckart entered a room on the left. He had a big mahogany desk with flat screens lined up in a row on one side. He pointed to a chair. "Sit."

I sank into the chair, which looked and felt expensive. The handcuffs I had taken from the Port Morris Correctional Facility were hard steel rings bulging in my front pocket. Deckart pointed at the ceiling. The opaque dome of a surveillance camera was fixed in a corner. He said, "Twelve hundred plus cameras on this ship. You ever act in something, like a school play?"

"I don't remember school. I'm not sure that I attended."

"Me either, to tell the truth. But I learned to act after school. I'm acting now, and so are you. Everything that happens on this boat is for the cameras. Thousands of actors on board."

"Audio?"

"No. But they'd be able to lip read if it ever got to that point."

"I see you've put some thought into this."

"Sure. It's my job."

"Where does the video feed to?"

He patted one of the screens lined up on the side of his desk. "Right here, buddy. Right in my office."

I said, "Those people you were following and intimidating. They got killed."

Deckart leaned back in his executive chair, spread his fingers and interlocked them behind his head. He leveled his eyes at me. "So that's who you're working for, those losers. No disrespect to the dead intended. They sure hired the wrong protection." He shook his head. "First off, I twisted the guy's goddamned finger *after* he came at me, not before. And that is it. I heard there was a murder at Beaver Falls, and I figured it was them, because how many other people get killed out at Beaver Falls? But I had nothing to do with that."

"I actually believe you, but I bet you know who did do it."

"Nope. Fact is, I don't." He leaned forward and the chair came with him, delivering both thick forearms to the wood desk. "Really, I don't."

"Your client changed his mind and took it up a notch. Leaves you in a tricky situation."

He blew air through his mouth, as if I had asked an impertinent question. "Nothing to do with me or my partner. We do freelance work, like anyone, but nobody gets killed. Nobody even gets very hurt. Nobody needs to go stay too long in the hospital, if you know what I mean. People scare easier than you might think."

"You need to go to the police and tell them about your involvement."

Deckart laughed nervously. "You don't know what you're talking about. You're an outsider. This is my town. The police here aren't like the cops in Beverly Hills or Chicago. That's the first thing. Second is client confidentiality. It's the backbone of the security industry. I go volunteering information to the police, even the Port Morris police, how do you think that's going to look to my clients? And the third thing is, why do you care anyway?"

I said, "*Why* I care doesn't enter into it. I care, simple as that."

He shook his head, as if something I had said was strange, or funny even.

Deckart said, "You're wasting your time, and mine. Go crawl back into whatever hole you came out of. I don't even know your name. Tell you something for free. If I have to learn your name, it isn't going to go good for you up here."

I smiled broadly, truly happy. "I think you've just threatened me. That right, Deckart?"

He laughed and opened his arms wide, hands up. "It is what it is."

I came out of the chair in a single smooth movement. Fast, maybe a quarter of a second from first muscle twitch. My hands pushed off the cushioned leather arms, and my legs used the floor to catapult me into the air, and right up on top of the wide mahogany desk, both feet landing balanced, like a world class acrobat. Deckart jerked back in his executive chair, but not fast enough. I only needed a short wind-up to kick him square in the face. The kick landed at the bridge of his nose. The steel toe crushed the cartilage inward, squeezing. Compressing the veins and channels. Nose blood sprayed down through Deckart's nostrils, staining his mustache and painting two expanding cones of deep red on the front of his immaculate white uniform. Deckart's overly groomed head whiplashed back, rebounding off the cushion.

I had a moment to examine his reaction. Condition black, wild panic. No control. Totally clueless.

By the time Deckart realized what was going on, I was on the other side of the desk, controlling his left wrist. I clicked one set of cuffs on. Pulled the right wrist around and clicked the other cuff. Now he was controlled, stretched across the wide back of his fancy office chair. The position looked like some kind of very advanced yoga move, in other words, torture.

I came around front and sat on his desk. He was sort of getting it back together. Breathing heavily through his mouth. Licking the blood dripping into it. I unclipped my folding knife.

"Listen, Deckart. You're out of your league. See what just happened? It's going to be like that for us. You'll never be able to protect yourself from me, and I won't stop coming at you. If I ask you a question, just answer it simply. There isn't any reason to make it complicated. I'm not in a patient mood. Plus, I've got to get back to something else."

Deckart was trying to control his breathing. It took him a minute, but he managed to speak finally.

"What's the question?"

I spoke patiently. "Mister Lawrence. Tell me what I need to know about him."

He shook his head. I pressed my thumb into his broken nose. He pushed back into the seat, but I didn't let him get away from the pain.

He said, "There is no Mister Lawrence. There is no 'him'."

"People talk about a Mister Lawrence. I spoke to someone who has seen him. You thought I was working for him. What is it I'm not understanding here, Deckart?"

Deckart was eyeing my knife, which I was twirling in my hand. It was a great knife. I'd had it all season. Bought it for around fifteen bucks soon as I got up to Alaska. The handle was an aluminum skeleton. Blade was half serrated and half not. Perfect for rope work, or fish work, or anything really. There had been plenty of time on the boat to keep that blade razor-sharp. I moved the tool slowly. Closing in on Deckart's shirt. "Let me help you out here." I sliced off a button with just the smallest amount of pressure. The little plastic disk flipped off onto the carpet.

He said, "You're on video, you know that."

I said, "I know. I'm pretty sure you'll erase it when we're done. If you still have fingers left to push the buttons. If not, you can dial with your nose. Call the hospitality princess, I'm sure she can help you out."

I sliced off another button.

Deckart spoke quickly, all of it coming out in a single breath. "Mister Lawrence isn't a person. It's a company name. It's a brand. They make desserts. Like cakes and shit. You ain't heard of them cause the company sells in Asian supermarkets. There's a picture of a bald white guy on the boxes. But his name ain't Mister Lawrence."

"What's his name?"

"I don't know what his name is. He's an actor."

"So a company named Mister Lawrence bought the place out of town here. Why would they do that?"

"I guess they're making cakes out there. How would I know different?"

I said, "Same company owns this boat?"

Deckart said, "Different company but, yeah, same in the end maybe."

"Help me understand that."

"Mister Lawrence is a shareholder in the company that owns this boat. But the boat company is different, technically speaking. From what I understand." He looked up at me. One of his eyes was already bloodshot, the other welling at the corner. "Like a shell company or something. Owns a bunch of shit but hides it."

I said, "And you know this how?"

He rotated his head against the high-backed leather chair. "When you're running security on a boat, you know what goes on. This is like a floating luxury hotel, okay? There are entertainment suites and facilities that those people use when the boat's docked here in Port Morris. The actor's probably at the casino right now. Spends half his life gambling, the other half doing even dumber shit."

I said, "Usually an actor gets hired for stuff and then goes back to wherever he's living. What is this guy, like a resident clown for the company?"

Deckart laughed bitterly. He had no way to wipe the blood from his lip, so he was forced to lick at it. His tongue returned into his mouth. "I don't really know, man, but yeah they keep him around. Like he's the face of the company or something. I guess it's why everyone around here thinks Mister Lawrence is a person. Maybe that's why they do it. I never had the opportunity to ask."

"And this Mister Lawrence company hired you to intimidate Jane Abrams and her friends. How did they even know about her?"

"The lady in the black Suburban, she started blabbing around, soon as she got up here from the outside. Like she was suicidal or something. The job was to encourage them to leave. That's it."

I said, "You aren't giving me enough detail, Deckart. I want you to concentrate deeply on organizing the information in your head, getting it to your mouth, and then into my head."

He said something unrepeatable, followed by, "I've already told you enough."

I grinned and pulled Deckart's shirt apart, like the pages of a book. I placed the tip of my knife to the left of his solar plexus, and about three inches below. He was gazing down past his nose, stunned and horrified. I said, "What you have there is your kidney, lying just in front of the small intestine." I shifted the knife blade up slightly.

"There, now it's only the small intestine." I placed my palm over the knife handle butt and tapped on it lightly. He flinched. I said, "I'm going to put this between your ribs here and puncture your small intestine. It won't kill you. You'll leak your own shit into your own body for a while before you start to feel bad. I were you, I'd go get medical advice as soon as you can, after I leave. But don't forget to erase that video, wouldn't be very good for your security business if folks saw you in such an insecure position."

I pressed the knife to Deckart's skin. Deckart was looking down. Sweat was beading up on his brow. I tapped the knife handle. Blood began to well up beneath the blade.

He said, "You're fucking crazy. I'll tell you anything you want. I'm not hiding anything from you."

"Start with how they approached you."

He licked his lip. "Everything's through the internet."

"Like what, you got an email?"

"Yeah, email. They knew about me working security on the boat. Knew about my freelance work."

"You keep all the emails?"

"There was only one, only the first step. After that, I had to sign up to a dating site for married people who want to have affairs. Smart shit. Now I've got a profile up there and everything is through the encrypted chat. That's part of the deal with that site, guaranteed chat encryption. Like the people that run the website can't even read the chats."

"How did they tell you about Jane Abrams?"

He licked more blood, tongue reaching up to his thin mustache. "Okay, so it isn't like I'm just doing the Abrams job. I've been working for these people on and off for a couple of years. With Abrams, they posted a photo of her on the site with a different name. That's how they do it, if I'm supposed to follow someone or something. They make a fake dating profile for the target so I get the picture and the details that way. Then the chat tells me where to meet them."

I said, "As if you're arranging a date."

He nodded. "Yeah. Like I said, smart."

"How do you know that you're working for Mister Lawrence?"

Deckart coughed. "I mean, I just know."

"Tell me how."

"The way I get paid. They pay me with gift cards." I pressed the knife in harder. Deckart grunted. "Cruise ships have gift cards, all of them do it. Customers can use them to buy stuff on the boat, like spa treatments, excursions, the casino, restaurant stuff, whatever."

"And you can cash them out. How do you do that?"

"Casino's the best place to cash out."

"The same casino where the bald guy actor likes to hang out."

Deckart said, "Exactly. And guess how that guy pays his bills."

"Gift cards. No credit card, no bank trace."

"You're a genius."

I switched it up. "What did they ask for specifically with Abrams?"

"They told me about her, where she was staying. Told me to make life hard for her and her friends. They wrote it in the message, like it was coming from her. Like she was a perv interested in getting hurt but within limits, like not hurt too bad. Know what I mean?"

I pictured Deckart getting orders through an extra-marital dating site. Cruising through the images of desperate housewives and robot scammers. I said, "You enjoyed the work."

He shook his head, trying to sound sincere. "No. We strong-armed the guy she was with, but only when he stepped to us first."

"Only the guy she was with. What about the girl, the blonde?"

He shook his head. "No. Nothing. I didn't do anything to her."

"Not you maybe, but your guys."

Deckart was adamant. "No. Not true. You can't pin that on me."

I said, "Tell me about George Abrams."

Deckart said, "Who's that?"

I pushed the knife in. It penetrated a millimeter and Deckart grunted. Blood ran freely. He was already sweating, but his face was now pale and his body rigid with fear. I said, "George Abrams. Blond kid in his twenties."

"I don't know who that is."

"Never got an invitation to date him, Deckart?"

Deckart grimaced. "You'd be surprised, man. Ain't only women on that site. But no, nothing about a George, only a Jane."

I pulled the knife away and wiped it on Deckart's shirt. I admired the object and clipped it shut. Deckart's head fell onto his chest and he began to pant. It was as if he'd given up on dignity. I removed the handcuffs and left him limp in his executive chair.

I said, "I hope you have a change of clothes, Deckart. Starting to smell bad in here."

He looked up at me. There was real hate in his bloodshot eyes. He said, "You're a dead man walking."

I said, "Ain't that the truth."

## CHAPTER TWENTY-FOUR

The elevator carried me back to the first deck. The reception desk had cleared up somewhat. The guy saw me coming and looked up. Then he shifted his eyes back to the computer. I figured I didn't look like a client. I rapped Ellie's badge on the desk in front of him. His gaze settled briefly on the bronze badge, then crawled up to find me looking right at him.

I said, "I was speaking to a woman in the pool, wonder if you know where I can find her again. Tall, blonde, in her twenties. She was with a bunch of others about the same age."

He didn't need to think too hard. "I know the group you're talking about. They're staff. You could go down to the staff quarters, minus three, but it isn't accessible to the public. Would you like me to call security?"

I shook my head. "Don't bother."

I turned and walked back in the direction of the elevator. Behind the elevator pod was a door to the stairs. I pushed through it and went down. Three flights to minus three. Out the door was another waiting area with an empty reception desk. Corridors led in all directions, but there was a map. Which manifested as a plaque mounted on the wall. A red dot marked my position. The staff quarters were located on the other side of the boat, past the medical zone and the laundry rooms.

The medical area was accessed through a door behind another reception desk. A man sat there and watched me approach. Which I did from far off, because the corridor was empty and very long. When I arrived, the guy was looking at me with frank curiosity.

"Help you, sir?"

"Staff quarters."

He pointed down the corridor. "Just keep going, sir. Past the laundry room."

It was another couple of minutes hike past the laundry room. No reception desk this time. Just a secure door with a fingerprint sensor and a square of toughened glass set into the middle of it. I peered through the glass. Corridors and rooms, like a high-class prison, or a hotel with no stars. I tried to imagine getting out of there in the event of an emergency. Like a ruptured hull and freezing arctic sea water pumping in under extreme pressure. I figured most people would probably drown. The ones that didn't would have to be fast and ruthless.

Staff quarters wasn't looking like any kind of good bet. If Chapman was on the boat, it was unlikely that I was going to run into her. The boat was just too big for that, and I wanted to get back to Ellie's office. There were things to discuss. On the way out I passed the guy at the medical desk again. I said, "Got a lot of customers in there?"

He didn't smile. "Never empty."

"How many beds you got in there."

The guy looked at me with lazy eyes. "Enough so you don't need to worry about it." He kept the eye contact for a little too long. The guy was a mind reader. He grinned. "Nah, I'm only messing with you. We have fifty beds. There's an old guy in there right now with a broken toe, but that's all."

I said, "Is fifty beds a lot?"

He shrugged. "I think fifty's enough."

IT FELT good to get off the ship. The *Emerald Allure* was like an enclosed world of its own, but not a world that I would choose, that's for damn sure. I came off the boat onto the dockside and took a deep breath of fresh air. I don't know how they circulate the air on those cruise ships, but it wasn't a satisfying simulation of real life, more like huffing a bag of someone else's used breath. The Green Gremlin mini-bus was gone.

I came up Bryant Street from the waterside. Exactly where I had first seen the blond guy with the well-trimmed beard. Yesterday. Today he was dead. I wondered if the floor beneath the pool table at the Beaver Falls Lodge was stained, or if the Lodge had already sent the cleaning crew in to set up for the next batch of rich tourists.

I took a right turn after the ice cream place. The town hall and green opened up in front of me like a small gift. The espresso guy was still working the machine, with the same hissing and huffing pipes and gauges. But this time he wasn't alone. Ellie and Smithson were waiting by the side of his cart, deep into some kind of a discussion. When I pulled up in front of them, both gave me the wary cop's eye. I figured it was more out of habit than malice, and I'm not one to hold grudges. Ellie raised her eyebrows to me. Smithson looked away, to the coffee dripping out into yet another fresh paper cup.

I said, "So, what's going on?"

Ellie shrugged. "Coffee time." She looked at me blankly and raised her eyebrows again. This was some kind of cop-to-cop protocol thing, like you don't discuss business in front of civilians. As a retired top-tier military operator, I'm not any kind of average civilian. When I saw Smithson and Ellie standing there looking back at me with attitude, I didn't see anything except glorified civilians. Smithson was going for some kind of look he must have learned as a State Trooper.

I was about a half-second away from ripping his nose off his face when he was saved by the coffee guy. Smithson lurched to the cart, and the guy handed two cups over the counter. Alongside the coffees were two apple crullers.

At least Ellie had manners. "Do you want something, Keeler?"

I shook my head. "I'm okay, thanks."

Smithson handed over a cup and a pastry to Ellie.

He saw me watching and stopped drinking coffee. "What?"

"You didn't answer my question?"

"What question?"

"I said, *so*. Which meant, so what have you done about the situation at hand?"

He said, "You're a pain in the ass, you know that?"

I said, "You don't like me or something. Maybe it's a trust issue."

"I trust you just as far as I can throw you." He looked at Ellie. "And no disrespect. Like I said, your choice, not mine."

I said, "Just help me out with one thing, so that I understand. Who was it tipped you off that I was the perpetrator out at Beaver Falls?"

"Like I said, I don't comment on ongoing investigations." I saw Smithson's eye crawling down my shirt to the hem, where shirt meets jeans. I looked down. Ellie's badge was poking out from under, bronze and official-looking in the weak Alaskan light. He looked back up at me, face turning red.

Ellie said, "He's deputized, Jim, relax."

She was looking at me sternly. Smithson said, "He's what?"

"Deputized. I've made him a deputy for the term of this investigation."

Smithson shook his head at her. "What is this, the Wild West?"

Ellie looked around, at the hills above town, a forest that extended a thousand of miles before it returned to some form of human civilization. She said, "Well, yes, Jim."

He snorted and sipped his coffee. When he came up for air he spoke. "Okay. So you want to know who called in. Answer is, I don't know. I didn't take the call. It was logged in at the switchboard and the caller left no name."

I stepped in. "And then you show up at the Edna Bay Apartments. Same tip off?"

He shrugged. "Same answer. Didn't take the call. Dispatch sent it out over the radio."

I looked over at Ellie. She shrugged. I thought about the Edna Bay Apartments. Besides Amber Chapman, there was the neighbor and the guy who'd walked by with the six-pack in a convenience store bag. Bald head, pointy ears.

The detective said, "So are we done here or what?"

I said, "One second."

Smithson was already turning to go. He swung to a halt on the ball of one foot. "What?"

There was no reason to make an enemy. Smithson could be useful.

I said, "We got off to a bad start detective. No harm, no foul. I don't think you've done anything particularly wrong, and I'm sorry if I caused you any offence."

Ellie raised her eyebrows and looked at the policeman. He looked at me.

"Okay."

Smithson extended a hand and I took it.

I said, "I'd like to get up to speed on your conversation." I lifted my shirt to show the badge. "As a deputized member of the Chilkat Tribal Authority's police force."

Ellie rolled her eyes. She looked at the detective. He nodded. She said, "So I got with Jim about the victim, Jane Abrams. Guess what."

I said, "Abrams doesn't exist."

She elbowed Smithson. "Told you he's smart." Then she turned to me. "You found the same thing on the internet. She ain't there. But all you got was the negative, the woman doesn't exist. But Jim got a positive, her real name, which is not Jane Abrams. Port Morris PD identified the vic as one Valerie Zarembina of Maryland, from the outside."

I said, "What's the outside?"

Smithson said, "What locals call the lower forty-eight states, the outside."

I said, "Zarembina. Isn't that something related to ice hockey?"

He said, "That's a *zamboni,* Keeler. The machine that cleans the ice on a hockey rink."

I said, "Identified how?"

Ellie said, "Prints came back from the FBI."

We locked eyes and I nodded at her. "Okay."

Smithson said, "I have to go." He looked at Ellie. "You need more help, you let me know, Ellie."

I looked at Ellie. "You tell him about the boat rental?"

"Yeah. Told him about the boat." She looked at Smithson.

He said, "It's tangential, but I'm having someone follow that up. Ellie gave me the paper."

I said, "Tangential."

Smithson sighed. "Keeler, you're impatient. I have limited manpower and I take orders from the chief. It takes time to properly investigate. We do it by the book, starting with the forensic evidence taken at Beaver Falls, the identification, and the known associations. From there we expand the investigation." He drank from his coffee cup. Wiped a shirt sleeve across his mouth. "Think about it from my point of view for a second. Ellie came up with this story about a mother and her son. Jane and George Abrams. I hear her out." He turned to Ellie. "Right, Ellie?"

Ellie nodded. "Right."

Smithson continued, earnest now, like he meant it. "What am I supposed to think? The mother, the son. That's bullshit right? The vic comes back as Valerie Zarembina. So, I look at you, I look at Ellie. I don't see the answer to my problems. The answer to my problems is the procedure. One step at a time. Police work. Working the scene, getting the book together. You see what I'm saying?"

I did.

But Smithson wasn't done. "Right now, we're at the first stage. It hasn't even been what, twenty-four hours? You and Ellie are taking it from a different angle, which is the tribal authority's prerogative. You're starting at a different place." He shrugged. "If we meet in the middle, I'll catch you there."

Smithson raised his coffee cup and walked away.

Ellie and I crossed the lawn to her building and neither of us spoke until after we had entered the offices and gone past Dave. Dave only barely looked up from his book. I followed Ellie along the corridor and into her office. Then I closed the door.

Ellie sat at her desk wiping her hands on a napkin. I walked over and leaned past her. Put a hand on the cruise ship brochure and slid it in front of her. "Back page, crew list."

She opened up the leaflet and studied it, found the relevant page and scanned. A few moments later she looked up at me and made eye contact. "Your man, Walter M. Deckart. Deputy Head of Security. Oh my. I wonder what the M stands for. You know who owns that boat?"

I said, "I just came from the *Emerald Allure*. Had a little talk with Mister Walter M. Deckart. Boat's partly owned by Mister Lawrence. And here's the kicker: Mister Lawrence isn't a person, it's a company."

Ellie raised her eyebrows. "I'm guessing that Mister Deckart didn't exactly volunteer the information you extracted."

"No, there was significant pressure applied."

"No shit. Thank you for not mentioning the visit in front of Smithson. I'm not sure how that would have gone down."

"I thought it would be best to keep it on a need-to-know basis."

"Indeed, so who's the little hairless bald guy everyone sees around town?"

I said, "Apparently he's an actor."

Ellie covered her mouth, suppressing a surprised smile. "Gosh."

She stood up and walked to the white board. I unclipped the

bronze police badge from my belt and slapped it on her desk. Ellie was writing the words 'Valerie Zarembina' next to the J. Abrams circle. She turned at the sound.

I said, "You really deputizing me?"

"No. There's no such thing anymore."

"But you're not angry that I took the badge."

"No. I think it's entrepreneurial, and that's what this country's all about." She turned back to the whiteboard. "The other thing we got from Smithson. Zarembina is an employee of the United States Federal Government, Department of Energy." She wrote 'Energy Department' on the board, and drew a line from Zarembina to it. Then she linked the Mr. L circle and the Deckart circle with the words *'Emerald Allure'*. She stood back and looked at the board. "They didn't say what Valerie Zarembina's job was at Energy."

I lowered myself into Ellie's desk chair and agitated the mouse, which had the effect of bringing the computer back to life again. I jabbed 'Valerie Zarembina, energy' into the keyboard with two stiff fingers. Then I punched the return key. A blink of an eye later the results populated the screen. Not too many women named Valerie Zarembina, just one. The photograph was correct. She was different. For one thing, she was alive, but also younger and smiling against a neutral gray background. Behind her right shoulder the stars and stripes were perfectly furled on a flag stand. I clicked deeper. No job title, no office number, no phone number, or any other contact details. Just the name, Valerie Zarembina, on a white web page with US Department of Energy logos above and links at the side to other sections and areas and features of the official web site.

Ellie said, "What does *that* mean?"

"Maybe she doesn't work there anymore."

"And they forgot to take her off the web site?"

I said, "United States Department of Energy. Imagine the size of it, how many people work there. How long would it take for HR to trickle that information down, all the way to the guy who updates the web site."

Ellie whistled. "Years. Decades. Who could know, maybe forever. It's like those people who die but remain alive on the internet because there's nobody to take them down. As if you can live forever electronically."

"Bureaucratic immortality."

Ellie was chewing on a knuckle. She dropped her hand and said, "Okay. If she wasn't working at Energy anymore, where was she?"

I said, "There is one way of finding out more, without going through the official channels."

She said, "Amber Chapman."

"Correct. I think I saw her on the cruise ship."

Ellie's eyes widened and her eyebrows went up a notch. "You think."

"Yes. In a swimsuit, with a bunch of other women at the pool. I said 'I think' because there was no clear view of her. The windows were steamed up." I looked at Ellie, she was looking at me, forehead creased.

She said, "Weird."

"Yeah."

"You didn't speak to her, didn't verify?"

"I was on my way to brace Deckart. I tried to verify after, but not hard enough."

"Hmmm."

I said, "Chapman told me that George Abrams was her boyfriend. Before he disappeared. Which means it's likely that she lied. Which puts things in an even more interesting light."

Ellie said, "Maybe she didn't lie. There is a way that she could have been in the dark about Zarembina. George tells Chapman that Zarembina is rich mommy Abrams. But if Chapman was in the dark, this goes deep."

I said, "There's another way in which Chapman doesn't lie. If the George guy disappears, and *then* Zarembina pops up as mom." I leaned back and cupped my head in two clasped hands. I had an idea. I sat up. "Valerie Zarembina showed me a photo of George. It matches what I found on the internet. Which means that George Abrams is a legitimate existing human being. We need to check that he's actually missing, and known to be in Port Morris, Alaska. For all we know George Abrams could be back east in Boston."

Ellie looked surprised. "Oh god, you're right. Why didn't I think of that?"

I brought my hands once again to the keyboard and mouse. I had George Abrams' MIT profile page open on the computer. I clicked on the name of his PhD supervisor. A new web page appeared with a picture of a guy in his late thirties. There was an office phone number.

I said, "What's the time difference?"

She drifted over to the desk. "Boston is going to be four hours ahead of us." Ellie looked at the computer clock. "It's 10:30 a.m., which makes it 2:30 p.m. in the afternoon back east." She looked down at me sitting in her chair.

I said, "That works."

Ellie perched on the desk, reached out and swung the phone around to face her. I reeled off the number and she punched the buttons. Dial tone came out of the handset. Ellie punched another button and the dial tone switched to speaker. There was a crackle as the call was answered on the other side. But it was voice mail. The professor was not in his office at the moment. We were invited to leave a message, which Ellie did. She left it vague, identified herself, and asked that the professor call back on her mobile phone.

I typed 'Amber Chapman' into the computer. Ellie pulled a chair from the conference table and rolled herself next to me. Amber Chapman was a very popular name. Hundreds of results. Grids of images, each image a woman, or a girl. Older or younger, darker or lighter, thin and thick. The varieties were endless. None of them were the Amber Chapman I was looking for. Which didn't mean anything, because there were so many of them. I typed in 'Amber Chapman Physics', and got her.

It was a photograph in a grid of search results. I clicked the picture and it opened up larger. Amber Chapman perched on the edge of a circular fountain. She was dressed in black. Stylish, with her straw-colored hair up in a complicated-looking braided crown. She wore sunglasses and a pair of white sneakers. Behind her was an imposing building. It looked like a palace. The word 'baroque' floated from the inner recesses of my mind. The palace was constructed from some kind of sand-colored material, but the ornate facade was detailed in ochre paint.

One thing for sure, it wasn't in America. Not Alaska, and not the outside as they called it. I figured the photograph was from Europe.

Ellie said, "That her?" I grunted. She said, "Click in."

Below the photograph was a link. I clicked it. The page blanked and then redrew itself from top to bottom, line by line. Ellie leaned in. She said, "It's a blog. Someone's journal."

There were several images besides the one we'd just seen. All of them had been taken in the old town of some European city. Cathedrals and that kind of thing. Old bridges and ornately decorated stone structures that had become tourist locations, like an even more expensive version of Disneyland.

The photographs all had young people in the foreground, posing against the grand backdrops of the old world. Students, I figured. The type of young person who does not go into the military. Then there was a group picture in a restaurant. They were seated around a large oval table with a white tablecloth. The shot had been taken after dinner. Faces were flushed from the beer and wine. Empty glasses littered the surface. Ellie pointed to Amber Chapman on one side. My eyes flicked over the faces and I caught George Abrams on the other side of the table, face slightly averted, concentrating on something off-camera.

I scrolled up and started reading the author's comments. The city was Tallinn, capital of Estonia. My mind made the jump to the physics conference that had been listed on George Abram's MIT profile page. I got that up in another computer window. I flicked between the two. Ellie had her chin grasped in her hand. She looked at me. I looked at her.

"Interesting. Maybe they met there."

Ellie said, "Maybe they did. I bet a lot of scientists meet in academic conferences. Where else would they meet?"

I said, "I don't know, I guess they meet places that other people meet, like bars and dinner parties and church."

Ellie looked at me. "You ever meet anyone at church?"

I said nothing.

She said, "What?"

"I'm thinking about Chapman and that boat, the *Emerald Allure*. I want to know if she gets off the boat, so I can find her. Either that, or I'll have to go there again. What do you do here, when you need to keep an eye on something?"

Ellie said, "Usually, I get Dave to do it."

"The guy out front?"

"Yes, that Dave."

"You deputize him?"

"Don't need to."

Which is what happened. Ellie called Dave into the office. It wasn't complicated. The *Emerald Allure* had two ways on or off, both visible from multiple spots on Water Street. Dave listened and agreed. We showed him the photograph of Chapman. He said that he could recognize her even if she was dressed differently. Dave was eager. I was skeptical. I questioned him on technique. Turned out that Dave liked to read detective novels and knew all about stakeouts. He would secure donuts and coffee. He would piss into an empty milk jug. He had a car and a phone, and he had Ellie's number programmed into the phone. Which was one extra point for phones. Too bad the minuses outweigh the pluses.

Dave was gone two minutes when Ellie's phone buzzed in her pocket. She was at the computer and had to push back her chair and stand up. Ellie pulled the vibrating thing from the front pocket of her jeans and pressed a button. Which stopped the buzz, but lit up the screen. Ellie looked into it, read something to herself. Her lips moved as she did so.

I said, "Can't be Dave already."

She looked up at me. "No. The computer geek. He says he can look at George Abrams' laptop right now." She turned to the conference table and hooked the straps of Abrams' laptop bag. "You want to go?"

## CHAPTER TWENTY-FIVE

The computer geek lived in the Chilkat tribal territory with his mother, who lived in a trailer. Which would have been a terrible cliche, if it wasn't for the mother and the trailer. The mother, because she was a kind of geek herself, and the trailer because it wasn't a trailer, but the weird result of a marriage between a double wide mobile home and a log cabin with a boulder stuck in the side.

The house looked absurd. The left side consisted of the double wide, and the right side was a log cabin. At the ball of the joint was an enormous boulder where the log cabin and trailer homes collided in a mesh of logs and aluminum siding. An old Toyota Land Cruiser was parked off to the side.

It took a while to get there, and when we did, Ellie switched off the Ford truck and we sat there looking at the place.

I said, "That's a hell of an oddity."

She agreed. "We could get Helen together with Mister Lawrence and win all kinds of architectural prizes." Ellie took the keys out of the ignition and twirled them on a finger. A feather hung from the rear-view mirror. She fisted her keys and popped the latch on the driver's side door. I did the same on my side and came down off the truck onto gravel and dirt.

Helen was the woman whom I had met at the fire tower, with her son, Hank. The front door was glass, and gave directly on to the kitchen, which in turn opened to the living room. There were multi-colored crystals arranged in several areas of the house, like small shrines to Alaskan's mineral heritage. A tie-dyed peace sign was framed above the kitchen sink. So far, so good. Helen offered us her own lemonade. I tried to be polite and show interest. Helen said that she worked on the internet as something called a Mechanical Turk. I asked what that was, and she said, "Anything really, particularly things that a robot cannot do."

I said, "Give me an example."

"Sure, what I was working on right now. They gave me a bunch of pictures, like three thousand of them, all dogs. My job was to mark out the ones I thought were cute."

"A highly subjective task," I said. "I'm guessing that the least threatening dogs are the cutest."

She smiled. "That's right. Highly subjective, so it depends. The other day I had to take a survey on things I like to do on the weekend."

Ellie said, "Do robots have weekends?"

Helen's son Hank walked in. He was wearing a t-shirt, jeans, and a pair of sheepskin house shoes. Hank was the computer geek. He looked tired but smiled when he saw me. Hank looked out of the big square glass set into the front door. The sky was gray. He said, "Crappy weather, means it's a good day to stay inside and do computer stuff."

Helen said, "Nothing illegal, I hope."

Hank said, "Ellie's the police."

Helen said, "Kind of." She looked at Ellie. "No offense, Ellie."

"None taken."

Hank's room was like a computer dungeon. Machines on every available surface. And noisy, not only with the buzzing and cackling of electricity, but the loud whirring hum of cooling fans. If Hank had been a little limp out of the room, in it he gained a whole new aura of confidence. I produced George Abrams' laptop.

"We tried twice on the password. I figure maybe there's one more try left."

Hank spoke with authority. "Forget the password. I'm going to get it into recovery mode. Bypass the front end."

I said, "You already lost me there, Hank."

He said, "I'm trying the back door. No big thing. I do it all the time."

Ellie said, "Okay, whatever."

Hank placed the laptop on a purpose-built stand fitted to a clean wood board serving as a desk. He examined the accessory ports on the laptop and plugged in the power cable. A tiny green light blinked on to prove the thing had juice. The screen remained blank, like a robot poker player. Maybe it was on, maybe not, it wasn't saying.

Hank removed a fist-sized black box from a drawer and connected a cable between the box and the laptop.

I said, "What's that?"

"Like a brain, but not exactly intelligent, more like an idiot savant."

Ellie said, "That's real helpful, Hank."

Hank rolled his eyes. "The box goes between the laptop and my other machines. Like a circuit breaker in case there's something malicious in there."

I said, "Malicious how?"

"You are trying to break into some guy's computer, right?"

"Right."

"So, the next assumption is that the computer might have belonged to someone engaged in criminal activity." He looked at Ellie. "I mean, after all, Ellie's kind of police."

"Okay."

Hank said, "So the tertiary assumption is that the possible criminal might have installed code that guards against intrusion, right?"

I said, "Like having a guard dog in a house."

"That's correct. Only that in my world, if you disturb the guard dog, he doesn't necessarily stay in his house when the intruder runs out of it and shut the door. In my world, the guard dog comes over to your house, burns it down, and kills your family."

Ellie said, "So you're protecting your own stuff with that black box."

Hank said, "You done asking questions? Want me to get on with it? I've got other boxes that I plan to connect, and if you ask me about each one we'll be here for a long time."

Ellie said, "Go on, Hank, we won't bother you anymore."

Hank turned back to the machines. He connected other boxes to the Abrams laptop, then he connected his own laptop to two of the boxes. Then he flicked a switch and sat back. Hank's laptop came to life in the form of lines of white text on the black background. Abrams' laptop remained a blank. Over on Hank's machine, lines of text began to scroll. Hank was peering closely, surveying the unfolding situation. He seemed pleased.

He said, "I'm in."

I said, "Back door?"

"Back door. Easy. Now I'll be able to get the files off of this computer, and onto one of my external drives. Then we'll have them in quarantine."

"In case they are infected with something?"

"Yup. They'll be all locked away and harmless."

Hank manipulated his laptop, a flurry of fingers flying, clicking and dragging and scrolling and entering codes and commands. He sat back and watched for a minute. The cursor on his laptop was blinking in place, a small vertical yellow rectangle. We were watching Hank's screen. I looked closer. Lines of text were writing themselves, then moving up a line while a new line was written below. The text was computer gobbledygook.

I said, "What's it doing?"

Hank pointed at the lines of text as they formed. He said, "It's just copying locations on this laptop, and replicating the file structure on the drive. That way, we have an exact copy."

"Will that take a long time?"

Hank shrugged. "Might take some time, depending on the speed of your drive." He pushed his chair back and swiveled to get up out of it. Walked over to a two-seater couch and picked up a guitar. I stood up and looked around his room, which despite the computers was still the room of a teenager. There were black light posters of women with panthers, stuff like that. Hank noticed me looking.

"Want to see it in the black light?"

"Sure, why not."

Hank stretched out for a remote control. He pushed a button and the room lights went off. Another button activated ultraviolet tubes secreted into the edges of the ceiling. Hank's computer cave was suddenly some kind of rock and roll fantasy land. He strummed enthusiastically.

Then Ellie said, "Hey."

I said, "What?"

She said, "This red light is on. I don't know if it's been on the whole time, or if it just started now."

Hank dropped the guitar and came over. The screen on Abrams' laptop was still blank, but now a tiny red light was pulsating, hidden in some recessed area of the plastic bezel frame. For a moment, none of us moved or said anything. And then Hank reached over and slammed the laptop shut, cutting off the red light. "Shit!" He quickly ripped cables from Abrams' computer.

I said, "What?"

"Hold on." Hank typed furiously on his laptop. "Fuck." He looked at me, then to Ellie. "Oh shit. Turn the light on."

I walked over to the remote control and reset the lights.

Ellie spoke slowly. "Hank? What's going on?"

Hank ignored her and looked at his own screen, scrolled around, clicked and tapped for maybe two minutes without speaking. Shook his head and cursed again. He turned to us. His face had gone even more pale yellow than it had been.

"That red light was the laptop camera. I think it was recording us."

Ellie said, "Why was it doing that?"

Hank said, "I don't know why, Ellie. I think it was sending out."

I said, "I thought everything was quarantined by your black box? How did it send out?"

Hank was scrutinizing his own laptop, clicking around rapidly. He pulled a phone from of his jeans pocket and examined it for a minute, tapping and swiping with fingers and two thumbs. "I think it spoofed the Wi-Fi." He looked at George Abrams' laptop, sitting on the desk. No longer just a slab of expensive plastic and silicone, more like a menacing object heralding an invasion. Hank glanced at Ellie. "What the fuck is this?"

Ellie was cool. She said, "I have no idea what's going on. Take it slow, Hank, and explain simply."

Hank ignored her and re-opened George Abrams' laptop. The red light was now off. Hank leapt up and scurried to a work bench, retrieving a tiny screwdriver and a roll of electric tape. When he had returned to the laptop, Hank ripped off a piece of tape and stuck it over the pinhead-sized camera. He unscrewed the top plate where the keyboard sat. The keys came up, connected to a thin multi-colored ribbon. Hank lay that against the screen. A rectangular hole now gave access to the internal components of George Abrams' laptop. Hank examined the contents. To me, it looked like the inside of any computer, all wires and computer chip boards, but not so to Hank. To him it looked special. He pointed at a tiny gray box, attached to the circuit board by a couple of dozen nano-sized legs, like an evil insect.

"It's got its own sat link." I saw that Hank was sweating. He looked at me, then at Ellie, eyes wild. "You guys brought me a Trojan horse."

Hank hunted around inside the laptop. Found something else

and tapped on it with the screwdriver. It was another tiny computer chip, blue and brown. He retrieved a pair of needle-nose pliers from the work bench, clamped the blue and brown chip between the two steel mandibles and pulled and twisted until the tiny thing popped out of Abrams' laptop. He gently laid the chip onto the desk. Then did the same thing with the gray box. Afterwards, he sat back gasping for breath.

I put a hand on Hank's shoulder, squeezed firmly. I said, "Slow it down, kid. Explain this calmly. Assume that we don't know what you know. Like we're dumb and ignorant old people, like we are your mom."

Hank took a deep breath. "I would never try and explain this to my mom." He picked up the jewelers' screwdriver. Tapped the gray box resting on the desk. "The little box there. It communicates to satellite. Which means it connects to its own internet network, doesn't need mine. Doesn't need anyone else's." Then he pointed the screwdriver at the blue and brown chip he had removed. "This is a Wi-Fi spoofer. Neither of them have power now because I removed them from the motherboard."

Ellie said, "I can guess about the satellite link. But what is a Wi-Fi spoofer, Hank?"

Hank took another deep breath. "I have Wi-Fi in the house, like a normal person, right?"

I said, "Right."

"All of my devices and computers connect to my home Wi-Fi, and that's how I get online."

I said, "Yup, still with you."

Hank tapped the little blue and brown chip. "This thing identified my home Wi-Fi, learned all about it, and then *pretended to be it*. So all the other things that connect to my Wi-Fi, like my computers and my phones and my mom's stuff, maybe even the TV, they connected to this little box here because they thought it was kosher."

Ellie said, "But it's not kosher, Hank, is it?"

"No. It isn't."

I said, "What did it do?"

He said, "Remember the little red light that was on?" We nodded. "Well, that was taking our picture and sending it to someone."

Ellie's eyes were wide. "Let me guess, we don't know who?"

"No."

I said, "And the Wi-Fi spoofer, what did that do?"

"I don't know." He looked at his laptop screen, blinking blankly. "It was operational for what, a minute, thirty seconds? Maybe even two or three minutes. I guess it could have done a lot, could have sucked out all kinds of information from me and my mom's stuff."

I said, "And sent them to that same someone, right?"

Hank looked very scared. "Right."

Helen came into Hank's room then. She said, "Honey, the internet is out. Do you need to reboot it or something?" Hank looked at me, I looked at Ellie, Ellie looked at Helen. Ellie looked back at me. Helen said, "What's going on?"

I said nothing.

WE STOOD next to Ellie's pickup truck.

She was nervous. "What the hell was that, Keeler?"

I shrugged. "I guess it was a trap."

"What do you mean by a trap?"

"The laptop was left in George Abrams' apartment in case someone came snooping around. Then, they would know who was looking. Open the laptop and get it to turn on, thing takes a picture of you and they suck down your location and whatever other information it can get."

Ellie said, "Jesus. Who are *they*?"

"Same people who did Valerie Zarembina and her friends out at Beaver Falls Lodge," I said coolly.

Ellie looked into the gravel of the driveway. She said, "We can't know that, Keeler. It's conjecture."

I locked my eyes on to hers. "No. It's not conjecture. There aren't two things going on here, Ellie, there's one. We just haven't connected the dots yet."

She pursed her lips and scratched her ear. Like a tell. Then she looked at me and gestured to the trailer. "I don't think we can leave them here alone. What do you think?"

I said, "Do you have anywhere you can put them?"

"How much time do you think we have?"

"None. We need to go, right now."

"Let's take them to my place."

I shook my head. "Bad idea, Ellie. Somewhere else."

"Shit, Keeler. I can't put them in my office either. Maybe the police station and I'll ask Smithson what he thinks."

I agreed.

## CHAPTER TWENTY-SIX

But Helen didn't agree. She didn't want to leave. Not just yet, she wasn't done with her work.

Ellie tried to explain it to her, that there was danger, without the details. But Helen wasn't listening. The situation alarmed her, but so did her work. And Helen was an optimist who believed in the healing power of crystals. Plus, her online reputation was at stake. As a Mechanical Turk she received reviews from her clients, for each task. Apparently that was important.

Hank got the Wi-Fi working, and Helen wanted to finish up her computer tasks. She was stubborn, and Ellie relented. I agreed to stay with Helen and Hank while Ellie ran into town to confer with Smithson. Ellie was hoping that the Port Morris police would come on board and offer protection to Helen and Hank, at least for a couple of days. Her going back to town was my idea. After what had happened with the laptop, I didn't figure that phones were safe. Not that I had thought they were safe before. Ellie would come back in a few hours and we could drop those two off somewhere before heading over to Guilfoyle's boat as planned.

Helen closed herself in her study, worried and eager to get to work. Hank came into the kitchen where I was drinking a glass of water. He was sullen and withdrawn. I figured he blamed me for what had happened, which I thought was unreasonable. Sometimes the chain of causality is tough to call, too far gone to assign responsibility to any individual person or thing. At that point it's in the 'shit happens' category.

Hank wanted to make a sandwich. He put two slices of bread in the toaster, then went to the small bathroom off the living room. I walked over to look at the tribal artifacts hanging above the sofa. Two carvings, like a short totem pole sliced vertically in half. Each half hung next to the other. The carvings were distorted faces, one on top of the other. Like a stack of cartoon ghosts, or gods. I smelled burnt toast. Smoke curled out of the kitchen into the living room. Hank came out of the bathroom and went into the kitchen. He called out to me. "Can you open the window?"

I opened the window. It swung in on noiseless hinges. The rainforest was quiet, not much wind. The temperature was chilly but comfortable. Crisp. I lay down on the sofa and closed my eyes.

An hour later, my eyes clicked open all by themselves. They were catching up with my ears, which had been awake longer, communicating with the back of my mind. The ears had caught on to something far away, and tracked it as it came in, even as I slept. The ears were hearing a buzzing sound like a mosquito, but getting louder than that. From where I lay on the sofa I was looking out the open window into the white nothingness of an autumnal Alaskan sky. The thing appeared as a speck at first. Just a tiny black dot, barely moving in one corner of the window, like a far away gnat.

But the gnat was getting bigger. Not really big, but bigger than it had been, and bigger than a gnat, definitely. And I realized that it was not a gnat or a mosquito, it was a drone.

When it was still far away, I could see from its profile that the drone was a consumer model, the kind that can be purchased in stores or online. Not the cheapest model, but a high-end drone. Exactly what the enemy in Syria had been using when I was there. In

Syria the ISIS drones had often been strapped with a load of explosives, like remote-controlled flying IEDs. Or sometimes they had just dropped grenades from really high up. Those drones had terrorized the Syrians we worked with.

In places like Mosul, the front lines were close. ISIS fighters were dug into the ruins of destroyed cities. Bombed out neighborhoods where progress was measured in buildings taken, tunnels destroyed. The problem for them was that the drones didn't have any kind of long range. The flying part wasn't a problem, the video part was. Those ISIS drones were not flown from a hundred miles away, not even five. The video signal stopped working after less than a mile.

I watched the incoming drone. I was thinking about the people operating it. The drone would arrive in a few seconds. If the range was a mile or less, the corollary was that those people were less than a mile way. Trouble was already here. Faster than expected.

Hank came into the room. He said, "Keeler, you see the drone?"

I said, "Not a neighbor?"

"We don't have neighbors."

I had already moved off the sofa, in a crab like scuttle. I was crouched against the wall under the window. I said, "Don't talk to me, do something normal."

Hank was standing there in the middle of the room looking confused. He had a glass of milk in his hand. His upper lip was coated with the white liquid, caught in the fuzzy hairs of a hopeful attempt at a mustache. "Normal like what?"

"Like standing normally at the window looking at it."

I swung the window inward a tad, so that I could see the reflection. I only saw a brief blur, but I heard it well enough. The drone came in close, buzzing past in a loud high-pitched whine. It veered off above the trees, then came in again, slower. Hank stood at the window looking at it. The drone hovered over the driveway, oriented at him, the rotors screaming. I could see the reflection well. The thing was silhouette against the sky. Quad rotors, a wedge-shaped brain, and something hanging pendulously below the main brain. Maybe it was armed somehow. After half a minute, the thing veered away and went over the house. We heard it on the other side, scanning laterally across the pitch of the structure, looking in windows. It was doing reconnaissance. The pilot was unconcerned about being obvious.

In the back of my mind I was thinking about weapons and sensors. Maybe it had infrared. Maybe not. Maybe it was wired to explode, like a kamikaze. Maybe not. I was leaning on the side of not.

Hank was still standing there, looking highly uncertain.

I said, "Now's the time to tell me about any weapons you might have in the house, Hank."

"Oh." He said, "I've got the bear gun and the squirrel gun. Mom's got the Glock."

I said, "Bear gun and the Glock, Hank. With whatever ammo you've got."

Hank left the room wordlessly. The drone on the other side of the house suddenly whizzed up over the roof again, careened into the front yard and spun around to look into the living room once more. I stayed down, glancing hopefully in the window reflection, but unable to see the drone. Then it was closer, buzzing madly, right in front of the open window.

I realized that the drone was coming inside.

I stayed very still. The noise of the quad rotors was intense and getting louder. The drone was inching in through the window, directly over my head. I could feel the rotor wash. Like standing under four madly rotating fans. I slowly tilted my head up. The thing was right over me, moving forward in jerky increments. One tiny twitch at a time, as the controller flicked the joystick. The thing hanging from the main brain was a high end camera unit. The camera had its own motor, and probably its own controller. It was swiveling on a gimbal, tiny servo motors wheezing. A modular system of interchangeable lenses, like what they use for movies. I revised my estimate up to fifteen or twenty grand, maybe more.

What I also revised was my image of the operators, the people behind it. There were two of them. One for the drone, the other for the camera. They'd be sitting somewhere relatively safe and secluded. Maybe a car, parked off road. It would be somewhere close, that was for damn sure. They would be discussing what they saw, calculating their approach, figuring out what they'd need to get the job done.

The drone drifted further in. Soon it was going to be too far for me to reach. All the controller would need to do was swivel the camera around and see me, crouched under the window. So I did the only thing that there was to do, reached up to take hold of it.

But the drone suddenly buzzed back the way it had come, a straight path out of the window. I managed to remove my hand in time, hoping that the roving camera unit hadn't caught it. The drone was buzzing away from the house and up into the sky. Ten seconds later it was out of sight. A minute later, the sounds of the forest returned.

Hank was not back yet. I counted two minutes. Nothing happened. I stood up and went toward the back of the house, where I figured Hank was looking for his weapons. I ran into him coming the other way. He said, "Sorry, I forgot the combination and had to ask Mom."

I said, "No problem. Did you get her Glock?"

"Shit." He started to backtrack toward Helen's office.

I stopped him. "Just focus on the bear gun, Hank. I'll go see your mom. Show me where her office is."

Hank pointed down the corridor. "It's there. She went to the bathroom. Maybe she's back at her desk now."

I went to Helen's door and knocked. No response. I opened the door. Nobody in there. An empty office chair facing a large computer screen filled with information. The other side of the room looked like an art studio. Paint brushes and paints, charcoal sticks and foam implements. The wall was covered in sketches and paintings. I walked out of there and back toward the living room. A toilet flushed behind me, and down the corridor. Helen, no doubt.

The window was still open, I walked toward it. I was a couple of feet away when I heard the sound of gravel crunching under boots. Four boots. Two guys coming up the drive. I ducked down under the window again.

A voice shouted out, "Hello, anyone home?"

The footsteps came closer. Then one set of feet departed from the first. The second set crunched gravel toward me, then directly outside the window under which I was crouched. The second set of feet kept on going to the right of the window. The first set took up again left of the window, near the kitchen door.

The same voice shouted again. "Hello, anyone home? It's Alaskan Broadband."

I was calculating the distance between myself and the kitchen, on the other side of the living room from me. There would be knives, hopefully big and sharp ones. Maybe a hammer if I was lucky. I figured, hammer in one hand, carving knife in the other. I'd be invincible. I was also thinking that I didn't have much time to find out. Maybe ten seconds. But then Helen came into the living room, wiping wet hands on her jeans. She glanced at me innocently and shouted out, "Hello. Yes, we're home. We got it working now."

Then she looked at me strangely, because I was crouched under the window. She mouthed, "What are you doing?" I was waving at her madly, trying to get her to stop walking in that direction. But she was already moving. Helen turned and looked at me, puzzled. Then she turned again, framed in the open doorway, seeing someone who I couldn't see.

I was going to explain it to her, the danger and the issues at hand. But before I could say anything, I heard the double cough of a silenced, small caliber semi-automatic weapon being triggered twice in quick succession. Both of Helen's eyes were shot out and she collapsed soundlessly to the ground, like a tea cloth fluttering off the hook. It was like a trick shot, a show off gag. She fell at about the same time as the glass from the kitchen door window. A tinkling on to the doorstep and the gravel. The weapon coughed again, once. I figured the third shot would be between her eyes, to keep things symmetrical. The shooter was showing off his skill, making a joke, which made me very angry. I couldn't see Helen's body at that point, but I knew that the shooter could see it through the door.

Which meant that I knew where the shooter was.

It was the shooter from the Beaver Falls Lodge, where the killings had also been done with morbid panache. No doubt whatsoever in my mind. But I also remembered how over at Beaver Falls, there had been no shell casings to find. Which meant that the shooter was hunting down brass right now.

So, it was my turn. Right now.

The first two shots had come from outside. The third, I didn't know. I hadn't heard the door opening, but then again, I didn't know if it would have made any noise if it *had* been opened. In the back of my mind I thought the shooter was still outside, because it was how I would have done it. Outside there was less chance of the brass being lost in some nook and cranny of the house. Maybe in a shoe, or in a plant pot, you never know. Outside, the rounds would eject right there on the gravel, easier to find.

If I was lucky, there would be fractions of seconds to play with, perhaps no margin at all. I rolled over the window sill, out into the chill air. Boots hit the ground and I was sprinting. The shooter was crouched, both knees bent, head down and looking the other direction. He was reaching for a brass casing with his right hand. The left hand was flattened on top of a pistol, balanced between the palm of his hand, and his knee. The way I read the situation, he was a right-handed shooter who had shifted the weapon to his left in order to pick up the shell casings with his dominant hand.

Which was one point in my favor. Another was that the pistol was pointing the other direction, across his body, away from me. The guy's head swiveled to me. He was a man in his fifties. Close-cropped silver hair with a solid hairline above experienced blue eyes that watched me as I came in. I registered the green tattoo lines coming up from the collar line and crawling around the ears. His hands were also covered in ink, and busy doing the complicated shuffle that would be necessary to stop me.

He was some kind of murder artist, but the question this time was about speed and efficiency more than aim. He had made a big mistake when he decided to switch over the gun from right to left. Now his left hand was trying to spin the gun around and present the butt to the right hand, like an old friend. The shooting hand was delicate, like the hands of a pianist. I could see the slender trigger finger seeking out the trigger guard, eager to get in there. I could see special tattooed symbols on the fingers, but I wasn't interpreting them just yet. Guys like that shy away from the experimental. They don't really want to get off a shot with the wrong hand, because their right hand is so perfect.

Which was one advantage I had at that moment.

The man was looking at me blankly while his hands were busy. But then, the busy hands got confused. The left hand was spinning the gun for the right hand to take, but I was coming at him fast and the mental pressure was piling up. In Air Force special tactics training we had learned about decision-making loops. Observe, Orient, Decide, Act. The OODA doctrine is straight out of fighter plane dog fights in the Korean War.

The point is to get inside the other guy's OODA loop. I had already observed, oriented, and decided. Now I was in the middle of the last phase, action, already at the end of my loop by the time the guy started his up. He made a deadly error by switching tactics suddenly and abandoned the plan of getting his good shooting hand inside that trigger guard. The shooter picked up the gun clumsily with his left hand and tried to get the barrel up.

I was way ahead of him. Already deep inside a second decision-making loop, cognizant of the other guy who had come with him, probably around the side of the house, creeping in the back. Maybe already in the house. What I didn't want was this shooter to make a sound. So, I came at him full speed and put a knee into the side of his head.

Something came loose in there, like a clicking sound and a soft thunk as his skull whipped sideways with the impact. The killer crumpled and the pistol fell with him, clinking onto the gravel. I spun around and was controlling him before he had a chance to regain his bearings. I took his head in my hands from behind. Chin grasped in my left palm, my fingers dug into the side of his mouth. My right arm was wrapped around his crown gripping his left ear between fingers and thumb. My forefinger was embedded in his ear canal for a better grip. I twisted hard and fast and in a slight diagonal, pulling up. His neck broke with a sharp crack and that was it.

By the time the guy hit the gravel and started convulsing, I had his pistol in my hand and was moving into the kitchen. The door hinges squeaked. Helen's body lay at an awkward angle, her face made blank with holes where the eyes should have been. The third shot had entered under her nose, above the mouth. Like a third nostril.

# CHAPTER TWENTY-SEVEN

I MOVED from the kitchen into the living room. The gun was a Browning Buck Mark .22 caliber. Semi-automatic. The gasses released by the third shot into Helen had chambered a round, sitting there waiting to be fired. Small and unassuming, but deadly in the right hands.

Which got me thinking about Hank. I was not sure which room he was in. And there was another shooter at large, possibly in the house now. I was in the hallway, going toward Hank's room on the other side of the house. There was a bedroom off to the right, which I figured would have been Helen's bedroom. The door was open, and on the other side of a neatly made bed was a double window looking out to the woods in back.

I moved inside the room, around the bed to the side of the window. I peered one way. Ducked under the window, peered the other way. Nothing and nobody. I went back out to the hallway. Dark and unlit. Another room up ahead to the right again, this time the door was closed. I toed the door open.

A utility room, tools and cleaning items neatly organized on shelves. To the right side, a worktable with a grinder and a clamp.

The left side, a gun cabinet with Hank standing looking into it. He didn't notice me. He was leaning inside, fiddling with the combination lock of a safe. I figured he was trying to get to the ammunition, kept sensibly locked away. Sensibly that is, if you didn't expect to actually need a weapon to defend against a home invasion.

On the other side of Hank was the window. Hank sensed me entering the room. He took a step backward, framing himself perfectly in the window. At the same time, I saw movement outside, behind him. He looked at me and started to speak. But I spoke first. I said, "Step to your right. Now."

Hank swallowed and stepped to his right, my left, and back to the gun cabinet. The second guy was outside, behind Hank, with a pistol up obscuring his face. I didn't know why he hadn't fired yet. I suppose he was caught in a decision loop.

I fired through the window and the glass splintered around a tiny hole, which had the effect of disturbing the transparency of the glass for a fraction of a second before it spidered. I saw a dark blur of movement from the guy. I was not sure if I had hit him or not. But he was moving, so I got moving.

The back of my mind had registered the ammunition capacity of the Buck Mark .22, four rounds fired, six or seven left.

I went through the window after him, exploding through the remaining glass. I felt something sting my left cheek. Thought, maybe a shot, maybe the glass. Whatever, I was through and out behind the house. I heard something crashing loudly through the woods—the guy was trying to get away. Wrong move again. Bad decision, he should have gone to ground immediately and picked me off when I cowboyed out the window. I went after him, fast. I ran hard for about twenty seconds and saw the guy as he broke out of the trees. Running as fast as he could, but not fast enough.

He was a good runner. Younger than his buddy, and in shape. He had long blond hair tied back in a pony tail. Maybe not a murder artist, maybe just backup. The guy had entered a clearing in the woods, with a little pond right in the middle of it. So, he was forced to carve around the pond, like an athlete around the track. As fast as he was, and as slow as a .22 caliber bullet is relative to say, a .45, he wasn't going to outrun the bullet.

The disadvantages of using a .22 caliber round are equal and opposite to the advantages. On the plus side it's a small round, not much kick, so you can be accurate enough without putting in too many hours on the range. The bullet tends to stay inside the body, which is useful when you don't want to blow something to a pulp. Like if you are squirrel hunting, or assassinating people discreetly. On the other hand, the .22 caliber is slow, and not very powerful. It doesn't have much stopping power. The guy wasn't going to fall down unless I put a bullet into exactly the right spot. Which could be one of his vital organs, or his head. Most vital organs are contained in the thorax, so a body shot would do it. But hitting the right internal target would be a throw of the dice. The wrong part, and he's out of the clearing and into the woods on the other side, maybe with a broken rib, or maybe just a flesh wound. On the other hand, a head shot would knock him down and probably kill him right off the bat, but the head is a smaller target than the body.

I braced my shooting arm against the trunk of a spruce tree. Slowed my breathing down and tracked him over the sights, leading only slightly. The gun had a suppressor screwed into the barrel. It coughed loudly, twice. The first shot missed completely. After the second, I saw a tiny impact at the top of the guy's head and he went down.

When I got to him, he was face-down in the dirt, alive. The bullet had nicked his skull and might have concussed him. I rolled him over with my boot. He was confused, disoriented. I said, "You need a minute?"

The guy's eyes focused and he brought his hands up defensively. He said, "No, don't."

"Why not?" He didn't have an answer. I said, "Who sent you?"

He said, "Fuck you."

I shot him twice more in the face. One of the rounds went under his eye, another into his forehead. He had three tattooed tears under the edge of his left eye. The .22 round had made a small hole right beside them, like a fourth teardrop. His expression didn't change in death, it remained exactly as frightened and sour as it had been in life.

## CHAPTER TWENTY-EIGHT

THE GUY HAD no ID on him, or anything else for that matter, except for a Glock 19 in his hand and an extra magazine in his pocket. I pried the Glock from his death grip. The gun had a full magazine, plus one in the chamber. I slipped it into my waistband at the back. The extra magazine went into my front pocket.

When I returned to the house, Hank was in the kitchen with his dead mother. I had come around and was standing over the murder artist's body. The boy was sitting at the little breakfast table, his eyes wet with tears, face red as a plum tomato. A Mossberg 500 was on the table. I figured that was the bear gun. Helen's body was slumped on the floor between the kitchen and living room. Her face blank with the eyes shot out. I stepped over the dead guy, came through the kitchen door and Hank looked at me without malice.

He said, "Why did they do this?"

I said, "I don't know exactly. I guess they thought they could get away with it."

I pulled a light blanket from the sofa and covered Helen's body.

Hank said, "Who are they?"

I walked to the corpse of Helen's killer. The body was laid out on the dirt and already looked unhealthy, like a magnet for insects and worms. I searched the dead guy and confirmed what I already knew, nothing. No ID, empty pockets. Same as his younger friend up in the woods. And just like the friend, covered in Neo-Nazi tattoos.

I figured that even members of the 1488 gang got out of jail once in a while.

I looked up at Hank, he was sobbing into his hands.

I said, "Hank, help me move this body inside. The drone might come back."

Hank didn't respond, he wept onto the table, tugging his hair with both hands. He was moaning in anguish. I came back into the kitchen and looked at him for exactly a second and a half. On any other occasion I would leave the kid alone, but we weren't safe, so I wasn't going to let him wallow in despair just yet.

"Hank." No response. I stepped over to him and pulled his head up by the hair. Forced him to look at me. "Hank." He didn't struggle or avert his eyes. He looked at me, mute and flush, cheeks wet with tears. I said, "Mom's dead, Hank. I liked her, even though I only knew her for five minutes. She didn't suffer, didn't get too old. You just got an advanced start on your own life as an independent person, like a second birth. You went from teenage dependent to grown up man in about fifteen minutes. You can either take that badly or take it well. If you take it well you'll be more of a help getting back at the people who sent these assassins to kill you and your mom. If you take it badly, you'll be less helpful. That's pretty much it. You want to help me move that body now?"

Hank nodded.

Together, we carried the body into the house and put it on the living room floor. Hank stood over the dead guy, looking down at him. There was something slack about the killer's face. I was thinking about other matters. I looked at Hank. "You good?"

He shook his head, not quite sure that he was good, but getting there. He said, "I'm a long way from being good."

I was aware of ruthlessly shoving the kid into the fast lane, but I figured there was no choice really. He'd have the rest of his life to play with his computer once this was over. I made the Browning safe, wiped it with my shirt and put my pinkie finger through the trigger guard, the gun hanging down. I held it out to Hank. "Kid, it's probably best if you took the credit for this guy and his friend."

He looked at the gun I was offering to him, then at me. "What?"

"You killed them, it's just self defense. Like a no-brainer. Your house, your mom. Me, it's more complicated. I'm trying to avoid complications, Hank. Not having much success, so I'll take any help I can get."

"So what do you want me to do?"

"Take the gun, give it to Ellie when she gets here."

Hank took the gun and tossed it on the corpse. He said, "Don't the bodies stiffen up?"

I said, "Yes, but not quite yet."

He said, "How long does it take?"

"Couple of hours, Hank."

"Oh."

I said, "They must have parked closer than a mile, but probably not exactly your driveway. Can you think where?"

Hank didn't have to think for long. He said, "There's a trailhead by the river, just over the hill. You can get there from the road."

I pointed at the Mossberg on the kitchen table. "You know how to use that thing without accidentally shooting me?"

"Yeah I guess."

"It's one or the other, Hank. Yes or no, no guessing."

"Yes."

I said, "Good. Let's go."

Hank led the way through the woods, to a footpath leading down to a river bank. He held the shotgun like a kid who had grown up in the Alaskan outback. That is to say, he held the gun correctly and I felt safe around him. More than I could say for most people. A shiny green Jeep was parked by the river. It was a new model. Front end like a recognizable Jeep, but the back end was extended, like an SUV.

The trail wound away from the house to an unpaved road. I figured it was the same road that we had used to get to the house. I approached the vehicle cautiously with the Glock ready. Hank stood back. But I already knew the Jeep would be empty. In the back seat was a Pelican case. It contained the drone, packed neatly into bespoke compartments. The Jeep's keys were under the driver seat.

I drove back up to the house. Hank sat next to me, silent for the two-minute ride. When we stepped out of the vehicle, Ellie's pickup truck was pulling into the driveway after us. She jerked to a stop. Came out of her truck looking worried. She said, "What happened?"

I said, "They came faster than we expected, Ellie."

She looked at Hank, then at the house, then at me. "Where's Helen?"

I shook my head. "Didn't make it."

Ellie took a step forward, shock on her face, reddening suddenly. The world of violent death that she had been a part of her previous life as a big city homicide detective had furiously returned in remote Alaska.

She got over it fast. "Bastards."

I said, "Dead bastards. She didn't make it, but neither did the guys they sent."

Ellie's face had hardened, old habits die hard. "How many, Keeler?" I held up two fingers. She said, "Show me."

"One in the living room, the other's out back in the woods. Helen's right there in the kitchen."

Ellie looked at the dead man. "He died here?"

"No. Outside."

"Why did you move the guy into the living room?"

I said, "They sent a drone first. I had half an idea that it would come back. But it didn't. Turns out the drone's in the back seat of the Jeep we found."

Ellie nodded and walked into the kitchen. She hitched her jeans, bent down over Helen's body, pulled back the blanket and examined the wounds without disturbing the scene, like the pro that she was. I came after her. Ellie was shaking her head. "Scumbag shooter was having fun with her, huh? Like a damned game."

I said nothing.

Ellie glanced at Hank, not dealing with him yet, stepped into the living room and stood over the shooter's body. She was looking for wounds, but there weren't any. Ellie felt around his neck and then looked at me. "You broke his neck?"

I said, "Not me, it was Hank."

She looked up at Hank, standing limp in the doorway. Ellie wasn't buying it and wasn't happy. "Quit pretending to be a damned comedian, Keeler!" She returned to the body, feeling with her fingers around the spinal cord and then up the jaw line. Ellie whistled respectfully. She pulled down the guy's shirt collar and exposed a chest tattoo. "1488."

I said, "Same guys who had come at me in the prison."

Ellie said, "You know what it means, 1488?"

"I figured it was a date."

"Well, Keeler, here's a little Alaskan education for you. Fourteen words in the slogan: 'We must secure the existence of our people and a future for white children.' Eighth letter in the alphabet is H. So, two eights equal HH, which stands for Heil Hitler."

I said, "Like a secret society of morons."

"Yeah. Pretty dedicated morons."

I didn't say it, but I was feeling pretty good about taking these two out of circulation. Ellie walked to Hank and put her hands on his shoulder, pulled his head to her breast. "Hank, I'm so sorry about your mom. She was a good person."

Hank pulled away after a few seconds. "Thanks Ellie, I appreciate it." Then he looked at me.

Ellie said to me, "What do you think?"

I said, "These are the same two who did the job at Beaver Falls. Same MO from the shooter. Same caliber bullet. Second guy was backup. You'll confirm it with forensics I'm sure."

She nodded. "I have to call it in. We have a liaison with Port Morris for the wagon and the technical part."

I said, "It's your jurisdiction now, Ellie. Your investigation. You call the shots."

She said, "True. Port Morris PD will consider this case closed if the forensics add up as you say. Jim Smithson will clear and forget, even if we don't end up identifying these two." Ellie stood looking at the body. She said, "I have to deal with this. But more importantly, how am I going to explain *you*, Keeler?"

I said, "You aren't going to explain me. It was Hank who took out the bad guys. I wasn't even here."

She gave me a look, turned to Hank. "That right, Hank?"

He nodded mutely.

In Ellie's green eyes, I saw the computations happening in both the front, and the back of her mind. Like troubled water swirling in little pools and eddies. Outwardly, she shook her head, shoulders hunched and tense. This was the disbelief phase. Turned back to me, pupils dilating, verification that I was not joking. Looked at Hank and squinted, calculated the extent that he would play along. Turned back to me and blinked, relaxed her shoulders, accepted the entire thing.

Then Ellie got back to business. "You said there was a drone. Is there video?"

Which was another good question.

We got the drone out of the case and up on the dining room table. Hank was pretty good at the technology part. The drone had a memory card, like the kind of thing that goes into a phone. He hooked it up to his laptop and we could see the video files stacked up on the screen. The first one we opened was the video from just now. We saw the drone's point of view, flying over the forest from the spot by the river. Coming to the house. It was an alien viewpoint, flying over the trees. The house grew larger in the screen, until we saw Hank standing at the window looking out. He looked anxious. Then the drone flew low over the house, skimming the roof and breaking to the other side. The drone banked then, and Helen was visible in a window, working at her computer. She hadn't noticed the flying camera. It then came up and over the house once more, returning to the front. The living room was empty, and the drone moved into it, poking into the window. Ellie and Hank were mesmerized by the video. I made eye contact with Ellie and she grunted something about it being good that the video hadn't had me in it.

The other file was a night shoot. Video from the drone flying over water, then approaching Beaver Falls Lodge, lit up nice and warm by the fire in the chimney and the soft luxurious lamp light. We saw the two guys playing pool. No sign of Amber Chapman, who I figured was in the sauna. We saw Jane Abrams, AKA Valerie Zarembina, sitting with the guys in the games room, a glass held in one hand, a phone held in the other. None of them seemed to notice the drone outside. The music must have masked it.

Ellie said, "Got them. This will be a wrap for the Port Morris Police. Definite clearance for Jim Smithson, and believe me, he'll take it and be happy about it." She looked at her phone, held it up. The screen read 3:32 p.m. "The boat, Keeler. Your guy is waiting. We said three-thirty. I'm going to be here until late. I need to make calls. You should go."

I nodded.

She said, "Take my truck. I'll get a ride back."

I said, "Keep the truck, I'll take the Jeep."

"Can't do that, Keeler. That's the perp's vehicle. We need to keep that here."

Hank said, "I'm coming with you. We can take my mom's truck." He picked up a set of keys from the kitchen counter and tossed them to me.

Ellie said, "Can't go, Hank. I need you here."

I spun the key ring around my finger and stepped between them. "Hank's coming, Ellie. You can interview him later."

She looked at me, alarmed. "He's just a kid, Keeler."

I said, "Not any more he isn't."

We locked eyes. She was the first to break contact. Ellie swiveled to look at Hank. Hank nodded to her. Ellie stepped toward me and put her hand to my cheek. "You got scratched." Her hand brushed my skin. I was looking into her eyes, green and clear.

She said, "Go get them. I'll cover this end. Catch you on the rebound."

I was going to say something in return, but Ellie's phone began to vibrate and buzz in her hand. She looked down at the screen briefly, then held it up for me to see. The incoming phone number began with 978. Hank proved his nerd-hood then. He said, "Boston area code."

I said, "It's the guy from MIT."

Ellie tapped the green button and put the phone up to her ear. "Ellie Chandler."

## CHAPTER TWENTY-NINE

Ellie glanced at me as she listened to the voice coming from across the North American continent.

Her expression changed and she turned toward the house. Then spoke quietly for a while, strolling slowly away, meandering in a circle. After a minute her chin raised and she turned to me, making eye contact. She nodded meaningfully, confirmation. It was the professor from MIT. He knew George Abrams. She spoke a few sentences in a laconic tone. I figured it was her way of being precise. Then, once again, she was listening.

It took a while, more back and forth. More of Ellie listening and the other guy talking. Mostly him talking. But eventually the guy had said all he needed to say, at least for the moment. Ellie signed off professionally. The phone screen returned to standby, and her hand slipped to her side.

She came back to where I was standing with Hank. "Well, that was something." She looked at Hank, then to me. "Should we go inside for a minute?"

Hank was standing and staring into the woods. His eyes were red-rimmed. He looked bitter and hard hit. Understandable, given what he was going through. When he heard Ellie's suggestion he turned angrily. "I don't think I can go in there, Ellie. I mean, my mom's dead body is like, on the floor."

Ellie put her hand on his arm. "I'm sorry, Hank, I wasn't thinking."

Hank wiped his nose with a shirt sleeve. He looked at me morosely. I looked back at Ellie.

I said, "Spit it out."

"It was the doctoral supervisor. He confirmed that George Abrams is one of his students. He confirmed the trip out here. There was a bunch of malarky that I couldn't understand, but there was interesting stuff. He told me that Abrams was not out here working on his PhD project. He was working on something else."

"Like what exactly?"

"According to the professor, Abrams was working as a consultant for an outfit called the USNRC. Ever heard of it?"

I said nothing.

Ellie said, "No shit, you haven't. I don't know if anyone has. USNRC stands for United States Nuclear Regulatory Commission."

"What's a physicist who specializes in non-linear acoustics doing as a consultant to the nuclear regulatory commission?"

Ellie did a thing with her hair. Pulled out the elastic holding it all up, and then shook it all out. "Right, good question. Short answer is, the professor wasn't sure. Said it wasn't any part of Abrams' doctoral research. The most he could say was speculation that this USNRC outfit required Abrams' particular skill set. So, it wouldn't necessarily be his doctoral research, but it would be something related to his scientific expertise."

Hank stepped forward. "What does this crap have to do with what happened here, with my mom getting shot?"

I said, "We're trying to figure that out, Hank."

"Why aren't the real cops figuring that out?"

Ellie gave me a look. "Hank, the police aren't looking there yet, because there isn't enough evidence to convince them of where to look. That's what we're trying to piece together."

Hank said, "Piece together what exactly?"

Ellie pursed her lips and kept quiet. She looked at me, like she didn't know what or how much to say. I figured the kid was smart enough and old enough to know.

I said, "Some people were killed the other day, Hank. Then they tried to have me killed. Now they've killed your mom. The bad guys are getting away with murder, and we're trying to stop that. The guy we've been talking about, George Abrams, seems like he's a lynchpin in this. He's a young scientist who's gone missing. Ellie just spoke to his academic supervisor over at MIT in Boston. You heard what she said. We're trying to figure out what's at stake here."

Hank said, "If we need to know more about this Nuclear Commission, why don't we go do that?"

Ellie said, "What do you mean, Hank?"

I said, "He means on his computer."

I started to walk back to the house. Hank followed directly, no longer concerned about running into the corpse of his dead mother. It took Ellie more of a moment. She said, "Got to make this fast, guys. I need to make some calls."

Back at the house, Hank helped me move his mom's body onto the couch and covered her with a blanket. I figured that might be a cathartic moment for him, contact with the object that used to be his mother. Ellie wasn't too thrilled about that. I figured it was no big deal since the cause of death was not a mystery. Hank and Ellie went back into the computer geek cave. I stayed in the kitchen and made coffee.

I found the coffee and filter for the drip machine. When I reached up for the box of filters I felt the rustling of paper in my inside jacket pocket. And then I remembered the yellow pad and the top sheet that I had torn out of it in Abrams' apartment. I set the coffee to brew. Then I removed the sheet I'd taken from the apartment, which was now a small folded square. I unfolded it on the kitchen counter.

A blank sheet of lined yellow paper, like others. I had removed it from the pad for a reason. I went to Helen's office and found a stick of charcoal among her art materials. Back in the kitchen I lightly rubbed it across the yellow sheet. Once the page was covered, I lowered my face and blew gently across the paper. The charcoal powder was swept away from the surface but remained within the indentations made when the sheet above this one had been marked by the pen. That sheet had been torn off and thrown away. But now I could see what had been written there.

TGN8462.

It would be something modern. Like a password, the serial number of a manufactured object, or maybe the identifying number of a vehicle. I memorized the number. Then I burned the sheet of paper over the stove. The ashes got flushed down the drain and the coffee was ready.

I brought three mugs back. It was quite a balancing act, but neither Ellie or Hank paid any attention to my talents. They were glued to Hank's big computer screen and accepted the coffee without comment.

I pulled a chair over. I said, "What do you have?"

Hank said, "We don't have the new, but we've got the old."

Ellie shifted over to make room for me. "Hank couldn't get into the Nuclear Regulatory Commission computers, so I suggested that he go for the Department of Energy. Looks like he got it."

Hank said, "It's no big deal. These are old web pages that have been cached. Like, backups. It's not top secret or anything. All I needed to do was guess about the directory structure."

I said, "Whatever that means. Can you just spell it out for me?"

Hank flipped to the website we had already seen. Zarembina's photograph with the flag and the Department of Energy logo, but nothing else. Then, like a magic trick he flipped to the same web page, but this time with a whole lot more information.

He said, "See what I mean? They changed the page, just taking off all the information, but the old one still exists on the server."

Ellie said, "Zarembina was an investigator with Energy." She pointed at the screen. It showed the same photograph I'd seen of Zarembina, but this time showing her as a Special Agent with the Office of Investigations.

I said, "What do they investigate at the Department of Energy?"

Ellie said, "We looked it up. They mostly go after fraud and abuse. The Department of Energy contracts work out to private enterprise, so they look for bad guys trying to rip off the taxpayer."

Hank said, "Their yearly budget is like forty billion bucks, so that's a shit load of cash ready to leak."

Ellie was looking into space, a thousand-yard stare.

I said, "What if Zarembina was still doing the same job, but now with the Nuclear Regulatory Commission. It's what you're thinking already, Ellie."

Hank looked from me to Ellie, not entirely following. She leaned back in the chair and nodded. "Yeah. That's exactly what I'm thinking."

I said, "Zarembina moves on from energy to become an investigator with the USNRC, where she meets George Abrams. Then this. Doesn't entirely explain the situation, but it's the best theory so far."

Ellie looked at me. We both knew that there was more, but that this was a pretty good start. Hank was hunched over the keyboard still, not moving but staring into the screen. I said, "Hank, let's get you away from here. Fresh air and ocean spray will do wonders for you."

He nodded vaguely. "You think?"

"We can keep going on this later." I gave a significant look to Ellie.

She said, "Get going. I'll deal with this, and Hank, I'll see you later about making a statement."

Hank shut down his machines reluctantly. He was way too comfortable with his computers. By the time we got outside I could tell he was restless. I shouldered him hard and Hank wobbled, but grinned despite everything. The kid needed to do something physical, to get himself worn out and ready to sleep it all off and wake up a new person. He needed an ordeal to get his mind off what had just happened.

I said, "Good to go?"

"Yeah, I guess."

"Let's do it."

Hank followed me around the front of the trailer to his mom's Toyota Land Cruiser and I threw him the keys. "You drive, Hank."

He looked at me, like a doe speaking to a leopard. "I don't have my license yet."

I shrugged. "So what? This is Alaska."

## CHAPTER THIRTY

THE BOY WAS quiet on the ride out to Eagle Cove. He gripped the steering wheel with white-knuckled hands and chewed his lip. Otherwise, Hank's eyes were fixated on a spot somewhere over the horizon. Not a good look for a driver, but I was fairly confident that this wasn't his first trip behind the wheel. They start early up in Alaska.

In my hand, I still had the Glock pried out of the dead fingers of the assassin. I popped the glove compartment in front of me and put the gun in there with the extra magazine. The scenery from the passenger seat blurred by like an out of focus movie. Dull and faded homes were set into hillsides bursting with an almost uncontrollable vegetation. Once we arrived, Hank put the Land Cruiser into park and turned to me.

His face was deathly white. He looked rough. "Keeler, what we are doing here? What's the connection? I don't get it."

I was patient with him. "We think the guys who killed your mom were working for people who own some property up past the old fire tower."

"You mean Mister Lawrence."

"That's right, Hank. We don't know exactly what they're up to, but it isn't any good. They're prepared to kill people, and your mom isn't the first, and might not be the last. Reason we're out here is because the property they own comes with a private island. It's their island now, but it used to belong to the government, who loaned it to the navy to use as a research base. I want to take a look at the island. So that's why we are here, Hank."

He said, "And what happens when we find out what we want to know? We just give the information to the police and hope that they'll catch whoever killed mom?"

Which was Hank's real question, and it was one that I respected. Ultimately, he wanted to know about getting revenge. I said, "No. I won't settle for that. I'm not a cop. When I find the people who are responsible, I'm going to take them out, Hank. Big time."

He nodded, his gritted teeth showing through chapped lips. "Yes, I want to be part of that. I have the right."

I shook my head. "Rights are for lawyers and the legal system, and we're drifting from those shores, buddy. Out here there are no rights. If you want rights you're better off keeping out of it. Live to fight another day."

Hank said, "I can shoot, Keeler, and you'll need someone who can shoot."

I thought for maybe three seconds. I figured there wasn't any better rehabilitation therapy than righteous revenge. An eye for an eye sounds good, but not when it's both of your mom's eyes. Then you'd be better off tearing out ten or twenty of theirs. I said, "You do what I tell you, when I tell you. No more, no less. You just do your part. You'll get your revenge, even if I'm the one doing the taking. It'll be yours as well. Hear what I'm saying?"

Hank nodded once and turned the ignition key to off. The engine stopped running.

I led the boy through the cannery, and out to the docks. He followed a few steps back, alert and curious. About half of the boats had shipped out by then. Joe Guilfoyle was up in the wheel house. When he saw me he made no gesture of recognition. Just put down the book he was reading and stood up from the chair. I stepped on board. Hank followed and a minute later the diesel engine kicked over. Two minutes after that, we were chugging away from the cannery dock.

I brought Hank up to the wheelhouse and introduced him to Guilfoyle.

The *Sea Foam* was a fully equipped working boat. Which meant that the quarter-mile-long net was piled up on the flat stern with an aluminum skiff trailing behind, attached by a tow rope. The way it works is the skiff and the boat each get one end of the net. They pull in opposite directions, making a big semi-circle. Then after waiting awhile, they meet up, completing the circle. The skiff driver hands off the rope to someone on the mother ship. At that point the big boat has control of the net, which gets hooked into the winch. When the net is winched in, it gets tighter and narrower. The circle closes, collecting all of the fish into the middle. In the end, the fish are hauled up in a part of the net called 'the sock'. They get dumped into a hatch filled with ice chips and sea water.

Game over for the fish caught in the sock.

Guilfoyle maneuvered the *Sea Foam* into the channel between the mainland and Carolina Island. Hank was looking at the rippling wake formed by the boat. I was looking out to sea. Presently the view was over to the cove on Carolina, where I had stopped the zodiac with Chapman the night before. Carolina Island receded and a half-hour later I heard the motor drop. I tapped Hank on the arm. He looked away from the water and I motioned up to the wheelhouse.

Guilfoyle was kicking back in his chair looking east through a pair of binoculars. He heard us coming up the ladder, dropped the binoculars to his chest. "Here we are, like you wanted. A mile out. What now?"

I held out a hand and he put the binoculars in it. I looked toward the mainland. Bell Island was a lump of green a mile off. I could make out some low buildings, not much more. I said, "Spotting scope?"

Guilfoyle said, "Roger that." He eased out of the chair and slipped into the captain's quarters behind the wheelhouse. When he came back he was carrying a long tan padded rifle case. He unzipped the case and pulled out a Remington 700 with a glossy walnut stock. Up on the rail was a Leupold scope. I noticed Hank eyeing the gear up in the wheelhouse. Guilfoyle had a fancy large screen unit that did fish finding and GPS navigation, all in one, and of course, the gun.

Guilfoyle flicked off the lens caps on the scope and handed me the rifle. I opened the side window. He passed me a clean microfiber cloth. I set the hand guard on the folded cloth and sighted through the scope. Bell Island got a lot closer all of a sudden.

I could make out three single-story buildings, a fenced-in area, and a pebble beach. Behind the buildings was a tall communications tower. About two hundred yards in front of the beach was a very long dock. A horizontal platform in the middle of the water. No movement, no people, nothing happening. I focused again on the dock for a moment.

I said, "Looks deserted from here."

Hank said, "Should we get closer, maybe go around it?"

I said, "Good idea." I glanced at Guilfoyle and inclined my chin. "What are we supposed to be doing, in case someone is watching?"

Guilfoyle said, "Well Keeler, I reckon we are prepping the net for dry dock storage."

I said, "Let the net go and bring her in, do a full round?" He nodded.

I took Hank down and we got the wet gear on. Bib pants and hooded jacket. All yellow and orange. I took an old SEAS hat off the hook and handed it to him. He declined. I said, "A lot of people end up wearing these, Hank. We'll be bringing the net in from the water, over the winch."

He said, "That's okay, I don't wear baseball hats all that much."

"People tend to wear them, working on a boat."

"Thanks, but no thanks."

I shrugged and adjusted mine. "It's here if you need it."

Meanwhile, Guilfoyle raised the anchor and turned the boat toward Bell Island. It had become a beautiful day, clearing up a little from earlier. The cool breeze and salt spray coming off the Pacific felt great. I looked down over the rail at the wake. A pair of porpoises was playing in the troubled water.

## CHAPTER THIRTY-ONE

Hank and I stood behind Guilfoyle in the wheelhouse. We were coming up on half a mile away from the island. I put my hand on the captain's shoulder.

"Pass close in, see what we can eyeball. Maybe draw security if they've got it."

Guilfoyle cut the throttle. He bobbed his head twice. "Roger that. Why don't both of you get on the net? Look like you're working the boat, in case they have anyone watching."

I motioned Hank to come down out of the wheelhouse. I brought Guilfoyle's binoculars with me. We got to the back of the boat and sat on the netting piled up in an organized mess.

Hank made himself comfortable on a spiral of webbing. "What's going on?"

I said, "We'll go in close to the island, and Guilfoyle's going to bank us past real slow. If there are no issues, I'm thinking we might take the skiff in and land it. Then we get to look around."

He said, "Sounds good to me. Why all the gear?"

I said, "In case there are issues. We're a fishing crew. It's standard practice to do a last run with the net before putting it up in the loft for the winter. We do that, check out the condition of the webbing and see if anything needs to be repaired right away. In fact, we already did that three days ago."

Guilfoyle had the throttle pushed all the way forward, the diesel engine gurgled like a healthy and energetic beast. I watched the island through the binoculars as we got closer. There was nothing remarkable about it. The compound of buildings was visible to the naked eye now. Three low structures, fenced area, beach, skeleton communication tower tucked back in the bushes. None of it in use, abandoned for years. Then there was the long dock in the middle of the water, about two hundred yards out. I put the binoculars up to get another look. Scanning from left to right I saw nondescript, functional structures. I figured there would be desks and chairs, and in the past, computers and calculating equipment. Maybe a kitchen. One of the buildings was likely to be reserved as quarters. Single rooms for the officers, doubles or more if there had been enlisted men. I could see the reason for the fenced area. A round dome was smack dab in the center of the square of dirt. The dome was white, its surface not quite round, but speckled with flat geometric tiles. Like a die with a thousand faces. That would be a satellite communications rig.

Then I heard a sharp intake of breath from Hank. At the same time, Guilfoyle eased up on the throttle. The engine sound went from hell-bent to idle in less than three seconds. Once the *Sea Foam's* throttle cut back, I heard the other boat.

Hank said, "Keeler."

I put down the binoculars. A powerful zodiac had come around the north side of the island. It was cruising on an interception trajectory. I could make out two men. One of them was at the wheel in back. The second man was standing at the bow, legs wide apart. He was looking at us through a pair of binoculars.

I said, "The guy standing at the bow, did he see me looking?"

Hank said, "I don't think so. He just got the glass up a second ago."

"Alright, so take it easy. Let Guilfoyle handle it. They'll speak to the captain, not us."

Guilfoyle brought the boat to idle and drift-turned so that he was port side to the incoming zodiac. Hank and I sat on the net like hired help taking a break before the hard work begins. The zodiac was alongside us in a half minute. I raised a hand at the two crew members, who didn't reciprocate. They were guys in their thirties wearing good practical marine gear.

Guilfoyle came out of the wheelhouse onto the little platform above the ladder. He called out, "Howdy."

The guy at the wheel cut back on the throttle so that the zodiac remained in place. The other guy standing on the bow called out to Guilfoyle. "Government property. Got to ask you to keep your distance. Three hundred yards is the limit. Be happier if you kept off four hundred."

Guilfoyle nodded vigorously. "No problem. Didn't know it was still government property. What am I, five hundred yards out now, thereabouts?"

The guy didn't respond. Guilfoyle said, "We're gonna set for two and we'll be out of here. I need the depth so I want to come in about a hundred yards more. Give or take. We'll stay clear of your perimeter."

The guy didn't say anything but eyeballed the boat hard. Then he nodded briefly, almost imperceptibly. The zodiac driver got the signal. He gunned past us and banked around in a tight U-turn. They came roaring by again, skimming the water. The zodiac drifted into an idle at two hundred yards. The men both turned to watch, waiting for us to change tack.

Guilfoyle came down the ladder, walked out on to the stern, and stood with one foot on a pile of webbing, like he was briefing us on the work. He said, "So we've got issues."

I said, "What did you mean by needing the depth?"

"There is a reason the Navy chose Bell Island. It's got an unusually deep approach."

Hank said, "I wonder how they spotted us coming in? Kind of touchy, if you ask me."

I said, "Very touchy. Either a lookout, or electronic sensors."

Hank said, "How would they do that?"

Guilfoyle said, "Buoys beneath the surface. Seeded a couple of miles around the base."

I said, "Which makes me curious, Hank. I want to go up on that island, that's for damn sure."

He said, "But how are you going to do that now?"

"You know how to drive a boat?"

He said, "Basics, yes."

"You're driving the skiff." I looked at Guilfoyle. "Can you handle the net by yourself?"

He shrugged. "Not my favorite thing to do, but in a pinch, yes."

I said, "I'm going to need to borrow your dive gear."

A ripple of worry passed over Guilfoyle's face. Like every fishing boat, the *Sea Foam* carried basic diving equipment. This was in case of any tangles with the net and propeller, or other problems beneath the surface. But it was rarely used.

Guilfoyle said, "To be honest, Keeler, I'm embarrassed to say that I'm not entirely sure the dive gear is in order."

"It's in order, Guilfoyle."

"How do you know?"

"I know because I checked and made sure it was. The weight belt clamp was cracked, but I changed it out."

"When did you do that?"

"Back in Seattle."

After four months, Guilfoyle knew significant parts of my biography. So he kept quiet. He had nothing more to add to the conversation.

I turned to Hank. "Once we're set up, I'm going to lie down in the skiff so they don't see me. Guilfoyle, you'll screen us with the big boat when we board the skiff. Hank's going to drive it and tow the net." Hank was just looking at me, open mouth. I said, "You'll be fine. Just get me as close as possible to the island. The less swimming I need to do, the better. Then I'm going over for a look around. I want to see what's out there."

Hank said, "Shit, you sure that's safe?"

I ignored that and lifted my chin to Guilfoyle. "What's with the floating dock?"

Guilfoyle said, "Submarine dock."

I nodded. "What I thought. Is that because of the depth here?"

Guilfoyle nodded. "That's right. Trench runs parallel to the beach there. Starts a hundred yards out, ends about where we are now."

"So a sub can cruise up, enter the trench and dock. But why the need for that depth?"

He shrugged. "Maybe wanted to run tests at depth. Usually subs dock at the surface."

Hank said, "How long will you be gone?"

I said, "An hour and a half, two hours? Guilfoyle, think you can putz around that long?"

"Why not. Where are you thinking to land?"

I shrugged. "Zodiac came from the north side. So I figure there's either a dock installation on the other side of the island, or they came out from the mainland. I'll go around to the south. Find a spot to come out of the water."

The sea was flat and only a slight breeze troubled the surface. Guilfoyle got the boat around. I went down into the engine room where the dive gear was stored.

The wet suit was tight, but it just about fit. The weight belt went around my waist. The mask went around my neck. The booties were the right size. Guilfoyle's dive knife strapped to my right leg, above the ankle. I pulled the other gear up the ladder. Guilfoyle had maneuvered the *Sea Foam* so that the stern was out of sight. I loaded the skiff with flippers, regulator, vest, and the double air tanks. Then I whistled to Hank. When he came over and boarded, I lay flat on my back. The skiff was deep enough that there was no chance of the men on the zodiac eyeballing me.

I felt Guilfoyle increase the throttle and bring the big boat around. Then he drove it straight in toward the island. I was looking at the blue sky. Not a single cloud. When Guilfoyle banked again, I spoke to Hank. "Okay, start her up."

He depressed the starter button and the skiff engine roared to life. Hank had his eyes on Guilfoyle. From where I lay, I could strain my neck and see the *Sea Foam* once in a while, when the waves lifted the skiff. I watched Guilfoyle come out to the stern, in front of the net pile. He raised his hand, thumb up, then he yelled out, "Let her go!"

Hank got it just right. He hit the throttle, gunned the skiff away from the mothership. The last thing I saw was Guilfoyle pulling on the release rope, setting the net free from the big boat's mast. Then there was the vibration of the big skiff engine, and the thump, thump, thumping of the floaters coming off the *Sea Foam* with the net.

I had to shout to be heard over the noise. "You see them?"

Hank shouted back from a couple feet away. "Yes. They are watching us."

"Okay. So I'll need you to screen me with your body when it's time. I'll need maybe three seconds."

He said, "Right now?"

I couldn't see where we were. I said, "Your call. After the net is all out and you see the tension in the line. Then just get me close."

Hank said, "And then?"

"When I'm gone, you go back to the boat, hand off to Guilfoyle. Do the whole thing one more time, then I'll be back here. Same spot."

Hank got back to business and gunned the boat, hauling the net for about three minutes. Then he cut the engine to idle and shuffled to the middle of the skiff, where I lay. He had a rope length with him and began to attach it to an eyelet on the skiff side. He wasn't actually doing anything but looking busy for the watchers. Now was the time.

He said, "How will you know the spot?"

I had already peeked over the side of the skiff, looking for a fix.

The communications tower on the island was high enough that it visually crossed one of the mountains in the background. Like all mountains in Alaska, Skinner Mountain has a white peak, year-round. Looking to my right, I could see another white-peaked mountain further south. I memorized the relative positions, like memorizing a face. Two objects in the background, relative to one in the foreground. Simple triangulation by eye.

I said, "Just be here."

I had already attached the tank to the vest and inflated it enough to be buoyant. I dropped that over the side and held on by a strap. Then I slipped over, flippers in the other hand. The water was cold at first, as it usually is. There was no current to speak of. I was now screened by the skiff. No problem.

The flippers went over the booties, straps tightened. I spit in the mask and rubbed it around, rinsed and pulled it over my eyes. Then the vest and tanks got strapped on. I had trained hard and operated long enough so that maneuvering the various tubes and straps was like a second nature. I had it straightened out in a minute. I looked up at Hank. He was at the stern with the engine.

"Good to go." He nodded. I said, "Keep the net away from the big boat. That's the only thing to do. If you're late, don't sweat it."

Then I released air from the vest, bit down on the mouthpiece, and let the weight belt take me under.

## CHAPTER THIRTY-TWO

The ocean was a thousand shades of blue. Dark to the depths, lighter to the surface.

I let myself descend to fifteen meters, before allowing some air into the vest and neutralizing the buoyancy. I pictured the geography. To get over to the south side of the island, I would be swimming broadly toward the edge of that floating dock. I would cut to the south and east of it maybe a hundred meters. My goal was to stay under until I came around the south side. I planned to surface and find a good place to land. The island was mostly forest and boulders. I didn't expect to have any issues hiding the gear.

Once I was neutral, and neither rose, nor sank, I was flying through the water. I swam hard, kicking at a steady rate. I focused on swimming straight. Visibility was good, maybe fifty meters. Which is why I was able to see the barrier before I ran into it.

I saw it from fifteen meters out. A massive underwater net blocking access to the island, difficult to notice against the big blue. I swam closer and began to see details. It was some kind of steel, or compound material. More like a very flexible fence than a net, finished in dull matte gray, but the inside of each link shone. The dive knife would not be effective against it. The net was hung from gunmetal blue floaters at the surface. I couldn't see the bottom of it. I stopped swimming forward and descended to thirty meters. The underwater fence continued down into the depths, until there was nothing to see but the darkness. Installing that thing had been a major project.

I was not going to get under it, but figured I could go over it.

I swam hard south, parallel to the security net. After five minutes of swimming, I came up to three meters. I slowly surfaced, careful to maintain neutral buoyancy. I wanted only the top of my head and my eyes above the water. I was broadly on target. Coming up on the south side of the island, but approximately two hundred and fifty yards out. I could hardly see the zodiac, anchored about five hundred yards away. The Sea Foam and the skiff were working the net.

I took hold of the thick steel cable at the surface and hauled myself over it and then under again. No way they could notice that at five hundred yards. Back under, I swam hard for the south side of the island, descending at the same time to fifteen meters. I figured it would be a five-minute swim. I relaxed my body and settled into the rhythm, kicking, and breathing.

A minute later, I saw a form in the depths. A shape in the darkness, darker even than the ocean below it. The only thing that could be darker than the deep blue was deep black. The thing had the shape of a thick torpedo, and I knew immediately what I was looking at, a nuclear submarine, two football fields long. I stopped swimming and released air from my lungs and from the vest. I began to descend.

As I got closer, the submarine became clearer.

It was inert and lifeless, and approximately sixty meters down. I got to thirty meters and could see pretty clearly. The cladding had originally been black, but was now covered in barnacles, like the skin of an ancient whale. No shine, nothing coming back but dark malevolence and decades of neglect. It was a salvaged wreck.

I swam along the sub's axis, from south to north, looking down at the beast. The old submarine was held in place by two enormous arms ending in gigantic clamps that made a C shape around it. The other end of the C clamps were embedded in the rocky edge of the marine trench.

When I had swum up to the middle of it, I could see over to the other side.

The sub and the clamp were encrusted with barnacles and mussels. They looked like they had been submerged for decades. I checked the tank dial. I had used up more than half of my air, a combination of the depth I was at, and the unexpected swim along the submarine. I was not going to make it to the island, but I wanted to see if I could get eyes on the submarine's markings. Which was not going to be easy given the depth and the age of the thing. I estimated the top of the sub at sixty meters, but to properly read the markings I would need to get down to fifty at least.

I went into a kind of physical trance, barely breathing, my body inert and limp. At the same time, I depressed the buoyancy of my vest and began to sink. I kept an eye on my depth meter. After thirty-five meters, nitrogen compresses enough to pass through the cell walls and enter the blood stream. I felt it hit me at forty meters. Euphoria. On the other hand, oxygen can become toxic after sixty meters. I had to explore efficiently. I needed to swim to the sub's bow, where the markings would be.

By the time I got there, I was low on air, high on nitrous, and sucking down poisonous oxygen. I was a little light-headed, which was pretty enjoyable. The old submarine came into view more clearly. Green tendrils of algae had attached to the sides along with layers of assorted crustaceans. I could see indentations that I figured were places where the sub had been crushed by the sheer pressure of all the water above it. In the Pacific Ocean, that sub might have been submerged under a mile of water or more.

I saw the residual white traces of the submarine's identification markings. The identification code was K-349. There was nothing else. I scanned for another minute. Then I broke off and swam due west. The only thing that mattered now was getting over that security net before I ran out of air.

When I hit the net, I was sucking the end of the twin air tanks. I decompressed at ten meters for five minutes, holding on to the net with fingers. I needed to get those nitrogen bubbles out of my blood stream. Five minutes is a long time to hang out when you've just found a salvaged nuclear submarine. I was buzzing.

I thought about what Ellie had said about mysteries versus puzzles. With a puzzle you know exactly what you're missing, with a mystery you don't even know if there's a puzzle out there to solve.

Now we had a puzzle inside of a mystery.

Valerie Zarembina, aka Jane Abrams, had worked for the Department of Energy as an investigator, but she wasn't with Energy anymore. George Abrams had been called in by the United States Nuclear Regulatory Commission to consult. Triangulate that with the salvaged nuclear submarine lying in a deep water trench up here. There was even more reason to believe that Zarembina had moved from Energy to Nuclear, and that her and George Abrams had been investigating what I had just found. Add to that the boat that George had rented, which came back without him. They were pieces of a puzzle, that was for damn sure.

There are no coincidences.

And there was literally nothing left in the tank when I surfaced.

I took a look around. No sign of the zodiac. I flipped myself over the cable. The *Sea Foam* was four hundred yards out. I was not wearing a watch, so I didn't know how long I had been gone. When the skiff came, I waited until it was pulling the net at full tension. I detached from the security fence and swam out. I saw Hank looking at me, then looking away, concentrating on the task at hand. I dropped my gear into the skiff. Then hauled myself in and landed on my back like a beached shark. Hank glanced at me. He looked tired and wet. He was wearing a baseball cap and his face was red, which is how I knew he'd been helping Guilfoyle with the net.

When we got back to the boat, Hank handed off the net to Guilfoyle, who snapped the connector into the winch. We came around and tied up to the stern. Down in the engine room, I stripped out of the dive gear and back into the fishing rubbers. The winch motor came on and the diesel smell was strong.

Up top, Hank and Guilfoyle were stacking the net, coming over the top of the winch wheel above. Pulverized chunks of Cordova-red jelly fish were raining down on their covered heads. Each molecule of Cordova-red contains a tiny protein spring that literally embeds into skin. The constant rain of poisonous jelly fish bits is like having a thousand little wasp stings per minute. After you experience that for the first time, you tend to cover up.

I took my place on the stern and looked over at Hank. His face was a rash of red. But now he was wearing that old SEAS baseball hat.

I yelled at him over the noise from the winch. "Told you people end up wearing baseball hats out here." Hank grimaced in response. He concentrated on his work. I watched him for a moment, the kid was tougher than he looked.

## CHAPTER THIRTY-THREE

By the time we were motoring back to Eagle Cove, the sun was kissing the horizon. The water was calm, and golden light pierced through the gaps made by dozens of islands that dot the inside passage. Guilfoyle piloted the boat while I cleaned up with Hank. The deck had to be thoroughly hosed down and all the equipment cleaned and put away in the right place, in the right order. The work is never done on a fishing boat, and when we finally got out of the wet gear, Hank slumped on to the net pile, exhausted.

I said, "Go lie down, buddy. You look like shit."

Hank went in and lay down on the galley bench. He was sleeping five minutes later.

I climbed up to the wheelhouse. Guilfoyle waited for me to sit down. I took a seat on the bench behind him. He said, "So, what happened out there?"

"Never made it to the island. They have a security net blocking off access." Guilfoyle whistled. I continued, "I went over that, and then I saw what they had at the floating dock."

"What, a sub?"

"Yes, an old one. A salvage."

"That's interesting. You see markings?"

"Just the identification number. K-349."

Guilfoyle's eyes almost popped out of his head. "Holy shit, that's not ours. It's theirs." He jerked his thumb over his shoulder, across the Pacific to the Asian continent.

"Russian?"

"Hell yes. Ours are all USS prefix and theirs are K. So they've got a salvaged Russian submarine out there on Bell Island. I'll be damned. Was it big?"

I told him what I had seen. The size, big, the apparent age, old, and the fact that the hull had looked crushed in some places from the depth. Guilfoyle nodded. He said that after a certain depth the water pressure will crush any structure, so subs are always rated to what they call a 'crush-depth'.

He looked over at me, appraising. "Given the size, it's likely the sub is nuclear."

"Which means what?"

Guilfoyle looked through the wheelhouse window. We were approaching Port Morris. The town's lights were a cloud of pin points in the dark. He said, "I don't know. Could mean a couple of things I guess. You have to check out if there's any information around on that hull identification. K whatever."

I said, "K-349."

"K-349." Guilfoyle glanced at me. "You want to tell me what's going on, Keeler, give me the big picture?"

"Sometimes Guilfoyle, what you don't know can't hurt you."

He was looking at me, and now his eyes dropped and settled on the steering wheel under his hand. Polished mahogany, a classic and timeless object. Connected to the rudder, steering true through the Pacific waters. A stable and unchanging object in a chaotic world. He was captain of the *Sea Foam*, and I had served under him as a guy working the boat. But we weren't working the boat anymore.

He said, "You got a point there."

I said, "Keep it simple, captain."

He chewed his beard for a moment, looking out again at the diminishing daylight. "You just let me know what I can do to help."

"Will do."

He said, "I think I'll kick off tomorrow, after breakfast. You know, get one more of those breakfast rolls in me before I end the season. If you get this wrapped up by then, you might think of joining me for the trip down."

I nodded. "Copy that."

Guilfoyle looked at me, unsmiling. "Good, because I'm not going to say it again."

I smiled for us both. Up in the North Pacific I had noticed that many people like to keep their conversation minimal. As if in a perfect world all you had to do was say something once and folks would pay attention. For the remainder of the journey I told Guilfoyle about Hank and his mom. How he'd become an orphan today. Guilfoyle nodded through the story, whistling here, glancing at me there. When I had finished telling it, the *Sea Foam* was pulling into the dock at the Glen Cove Cannery and the sun had gone over the horizon.

Ellie was walking out to meet the boat.

Guilfoyle brought her in easy. Hank set the bumpers and I jumped off with the rope. I glanced at Ellie. She looked tired and serious, as if things were piling up on her, weighing her down. I noticed the shoulders, tight and high. She was hugging herself. First thing she said was, "Dave called. He's got eyes on Chapman."

"Where are they?"

"It was only ten minutes ago. He said that she was in a group. They got into a vehicle and he was following."

I said, "Dave keeping you updated?"

"Yes, but I think we should be positioned close. We need to speak with her."

I said, "Come on board."

"We need to get going."

I said, "We need to eat, and then we need to talk. Lack of nutrition is responsible for a whole lot of bad decision-making. Millions have died due to lack of the right minerals, vitamins, all the right fats. Brain food, Ellie. If Dave's got eyes on them, we should let them roll. Maybe we'll learn something new."

She looked at me strangely but stepped onto the boat regardless.

By then Guilfoyle was on the barbecue, seasoning the steel before the fish hit the grill.

He threw me a couple of beer cans from the refrigerator. Two cans, arcing high through the air, one on the left, one on my right. I caught the cold and dense projectiles, underhanded one to Ellie. She held the cold can to her forehead. Hank was awake and Guilfoyle pushed a beer can across the table to him. I popped the tab and took a sip. Heavy on the hops.

While we had not been looking to catch fish, fish had nonetheless found their way into the net. Among them, a King Salmon. The King is the biggest species of Pacific salmon. Protected by law, with no commercial harvesting permitted. Guilfoyle said that he allowed one accidentally caught King to end up on his grill every season, and tonight was the night.

I watched Hank watching Guilfoyle as he filleted the big fish. Hank was gnawing at the beer can's edge. I figured he wasn't really seeing the knife slipping over bones and slicing off flesh, he was probably reflecting abstractly on the momentous day so far. The course of his life changed forever in a couple of seconds. Pretty much a random occurrence. Hard to get your mind around that. Hank caught me looking at him, held the gaze, and then looked out to sea. Ellie was staring into the darkness, unresponsive. I figured her brain chemistry needed replenishment. Luckily, that was coming right up.

Guilfoyle put the two sides of the salmon down on the grill and the pale flesh sizzled. Ellie raised her head, eyes narrowed. She said, "Oh my god, I'm starving."

Guilfoyle said, "Five minutes on the meat side, five on the skin side. Then we eat."

That's how Guilfoyle did it. Freshest fish possible, squeeze of lemon, sprinkle of sea salt. Damn good. When we were done and satisfied, he came over and clapped a weathered hand on Hank's shoulder. He said, "Hank, you were green as the hills when you came on board, but now you're a real fisherman."

Hank smiled weakly. "Thanks, captain."

Guilfoyle put a pot of coffee on. He nodded to me and spoke to the boy. "Come on up to the wheelhouse with me, Hank. I have something to show you."

When they had climbed the ladder, I looked at Ellie. She was fully alert, all systems refilled and replenished, raring to go. I was sitting in the galley. She swung her legs off the bench, came over and slid into the booth across from me.

"They're going to clear the Beaver Falls murders. Zarembina and the two males. They're expecting forensics to confirm."

I said, "The same gun?"

"Yes, certainly not the teeth or the fingerprints."

She placed both of her hands in front of her, flat down on the Formica surface. She looked at me and there was no sadness in her eyes, only a kind of burning anger. Ellie was tired, that was for sure. But it was the indignation that hurt. She said, "Tell me what you've got, Keeler."

I told her all about the trip out to Bell Island. The men in the zodiac, and then the salvaged Russian submarine. She listened attentively. By the time I was finished, the coffee was ready. I got up and poured two cups. I slid back into the galley bench. Linked a couple of fingers through the cup handle and took a sip. The coffee was hot and strong and black.

Ellie said, "This confirms what we were thinking, that Zarembina was an investigator for the USNRC, just like she had been over at Energy."

I said, "What isn't clear is why she had to come up under a fake name, with a bunch of amateurs. The fact that nobody from any alphabet soup of a governmental agency has come forward for Zarembina, or to recover her body."

"Are the Port Morris police making contact?"

She looked at me and nodded. "That'll only take a few million years."

Ellie looked at me for a while. Like an unseeing thousand-yard stare. She was thinking. Then she broke out of it. "People tend to rise to their level of incompetence. Zarembina was killed what, yesterday?" Ellie drum-rolled her fingers on the table. "Let's talk this through a little more. I want to establish the basics."

"Sure."

Ellie said, "That submarine you found links Zarembina and Abrams to Bell Island, and by extension the mysterious Mister Lawrence."

"Because Mister Lawrence owns the island now."

"Correct."

I said, "Zarembina, Abrams and Bell Island. Orbiting around them we've got Deckart and Willets, Amber Chapman, and those two Neo-Nazi assassins."

We were both silent for a while, looking over across the ocean. The image of Amber Chapman came into my mind, front and center.

I said, "It's going to flip if we keep pushing. It will start to shape up and make sense." Ellie was looking at me intensely, I held her gaze. "This is going to be pretty big, Ellie. If you think about the property up there. The house and outbuildings, plus the installation on Bell Island. The fact we're dealing with a company not just an individual. There's something going on up there and we're going to end up taking it down. We need to go hard, relentless."

I saw Ellie contemplating, and I knew she was thinking about scale, about what and who might be out there. She said, "Jesus, I need to tell this to Smithson, the stuff about the submarine. We need to get help. We can't do this on our own."

I agreed. "Smithson's not going to be enough. You'll have to get the FBI involved, what's the process?"

Ellie chewed that for a moment. "I'm not sure really. Some deep bureaucratic shit storm, that's for certain. Let's go see Smithson right now."

I said nothing.

She said, "You got a better idea, Keeler?"

I said, "I have a few. Not all of them are collaborative. There are two things that you need to do now, Ellie. One of them is talking to the police here about bringing in the FBI. But we both know that that's Plan B. In case we get taken out of the game. The other thing you need to do for both Plan A and Plan B is to get your hands on the building plans for the property up there."

Ellie looked away for a long moment. Then she looked back. "What's Plan A? I thought you just said we'd need to bring in the FBI because it's too big for us to handle."

I said, "Two layers of contingency, Ellie. We need both. Get the wheels turning with Smithson, then get your hands on information about the property. Push comes to shove it'll be useful for us, and for the feds if and when they materialize. You're best placed to do both. Whatever they call it. There will be a place somewhere in town with filing cabinets, a coffee machine and a photocopier. They'll have building plans, septic plans, fire inspection certificates, and stuff like land use change records."

She said, "Code enforcement office."

"Sounds good to me. Get in there and get us some useable intelligence on whatever the hell is up there."

"What, so you can invade?"

"Yes. But not right away."

"Jesus, Keeler. What are you going to do right now, after this?"

"While you start on that, I'm going to join Dave."

Ellie brought out her phone and tapped in a message to Dave. She said, "He'll text me his location." She appraised me. "You don't have a phone do you?"

I shook my head.

She said, "That's convenient."

I said, "What's your phone number. Case I need to call you."

"With what?"

"There's no shortage of phones, the world's full of them, like cockroaches, rats, and bureaucrats."

"You're going to borrow someone else's phone?"

I said, "That usually works."

She reeled off her number. I memorized it.

Ellie said, "Smithson's going to be at home. I'll drop Hank off at my place on the way up. Then I'll go and see about the other thing." She slid out of the booth and came past me through the door and stepped out onto the stern. I stood up and stretched, slapping my hands on the doorway.

I said, "I'll stay in touch."

"With someone else's phone."

I shrugged. "Whatever."

Hank came down from the wheelhouse ladder and leaned out, holding one of the rungs. He swung around. He said, "Hey Keeler." I looked up in time to see Guilfoyle throw the Remington rifle case down at me from up top. I caught it. He leaned against the railing looking down at me. "Me and Hank just cleaned it for you. You're good to go, buddy."

I slung the padded case over my right shoulder. "Appreciate it, Guilfoyle."

He nodded at me, then disappeared back into the wheelhouse. Ellie put a protective arm around Hank's shoulders. He smiled shyly. Hank was holding a cardboard box with a hundred rounds of ammunition. The box was red and had the words 'Federal Premium' in white lettering. Hank said, "Sierra Match King loads, 175 grains. Guilfoyle's not playing."

I took the box from Hank. "He was a marine."

Hank leaned against the galley. "You were military too?"

"Air Force."

"How was it?"

I said, "I only remember the good parts, but there was a lot of bullshit, that's for sure."

Hank said, "What were the good parts like?"

"They were good, Hank. But like I said, there was a lot of bullshit that went with it." Which Hank didn't want to know about, because nobody wants to be bored by bullshit.

We left Guilfoyle on the boat. Walked through the cannery and out to the parking lot. Ellie's truck was parked alongside Helen's Land Cruiser. Before we split up, Hank held his phone out to me. He said, "Keeler, why don't you take my phone?"

"Okay, Hank." I reached over and took the offered phone. It was a small one, with just a number pad and a little screen.

Hank said, "Ellie's number is already in it. Password is 'helloworld', one word no spaces."

I looked at the phone. Each of the numbers had a couple of letters printed small in the corner of an already tiny button. Hello World with no spaces would be 4355696753. I figured using a phrase was a mnemonic device for Hank. As a computer geek I might have expected him to prefer numbers. Ellie took the phone from me and entered Dave's number into the little device.

I got into the Land Cruiser, Ellie and Hank got into her truck. I watched them leave the parking lot. Ellie's F-150 made a low chugging sound. It was a sound I liked. When they were gone I called Dave. Who was parked elsewhere, out front of the best Chinese restaurant in Port Morris.

I took the road toward town, and then cut into the trails before the first residential neighborhood began. It was dark up there. No streetlights. Nothing but the rainforest either side of the old Toyota Land Cruiser, pushing through the night. I preferred to come at the downtown area at an oblique angle, rather than straight on. Just in case anyone was watching the main roads.

While I drove, I thought about what we had not mentioned, the cruise ship.

*Emerald Allure* they called it. Nice name. Sounded about as phony as you could get. That enormous boat floated up there in the front of my mind. At the same time, in the back of my mind was the salvaged submarine. Except it wasn't a salvage anymore. In my waking dream the sub was new and sleek. Cutting through the murky depths of the Pacific, powered by a nuclear reactor. I didn't know much about how a nuclear reactor worked, but I figured it involved atoms being split and sparking off barely contained chain reactions. Fueled by a fissile material, like plutonium.

And swimming from the back of my mind to the front was Amber Chapman, like a pale mermaid moving through the dark waters.

## CHAPTER THIRTY-FOUR

The Land Cruiser was a comfortable vehicle. A big wide bench up front, same thing behind. I had the Remington long gun laid in the back seat. I removed the Glock from the glove box and put it up front with me, like an ugly but competent passenger tucked under my right thigh. The dashboard had a clock, which read a couple of minutes after eight.

It took about five more minutes to come down through the residential areas into town. I cruised past the Golden Lights Wok, not too fast, not too slow. The street was three or four back from the waterfront. At this time of night things were winding down. I didn't see anyone walking. Nowhere to go. Stores were blank, nothing was happening. Nothing except the Chinese food being prepared in the Golden Lights Wok.

I clocked Dave slumped into the driver's seat of a faded red Ford hatchback. I turned the corner and parked two blocks away. It took a minute to double back on foot. I came at the Ford from its blind spot. The model was Fiesta. There was a bumper sticker with the Alaskan flag, the Big Dipper in yellow against blue. Next to that was another sticker, older and just as faded as the car. It read 'Proud Mother of a

U.S. Soldier'. I figured Dave or a sibling had served, and he was driving his mother's car.

When I slipped into the passenger seat Dave jerked upright from his huddled position. He glanced at me in panic. I looked at him and he settled down. Dave had parked with a clear view of the entrance through the driver's side window, good view of the street through the windshield, and an acceptable view behind him through the mirrors. Not perfect, but workable.

He had been finishing up a donut when I came in. Dave wiped a leather jacket sleeve across his mouth and said, "See the Hummer?"

I had already seen the Hummer across the street, same side as the restaurant. A squat and ugly machine in matte black.

I said, "You sure it was Chapman?"

"Based on your description, yes. Four girls and two guys driving. Look two cars back from the Hummer and check out the Subaru."

Two cars back a Subaru was parked facing the same direction. It was the vehicle I'd seen Willets driving the other day, when all of this had begun. In the dark, the car didn't look teal, it had a murky color, like old seaweed on a beach.

I said, "Who's in that one, cruise ship security?"

Dave turned to me. "How'd you guess?"

I said nothing.

He said, "One guy in the Subaru, uniformed. He came off the boat with the girls. Girls got into the Hummer with the other two, Subaru followed them here."

"Recognize the other people from around town?"

"No, they don't look like they're from around here."

"What do they look like?"

He said, "No beards." Dave shrugged. He was wearing a parka, and his chin and upper lip were fuzzy with a very limited growth. It might have been limited, but it was all he had. He looked at me and I became conscious of the fact that I'd only just shaved my beard.

I said, "Did you do a walk by?"

"I did actually, but there's no way of seeing inside. The front does take-out and the back has the seating. I didn't want to go into the restaurant itself."

I looked at the facade. The Golden Lights Wok had three windows that gave into a waiting area with a fancy counter. The counter was decorated with strategically arranged orchids, which I figured must be fake. Behind the counter, a paneled screen blocked off the rear part of the restaurant. The panels were painted in a calligraphy style. Chinese mountains with the odd heron flying up high, and oriental boats coming down winding rivers. The woman behind the counter was dressed in a pink sweater. It looked soft. She was concentrating on something right in front of her, maybe her phone.

I said, "I'll go in."

Dave moved his head incrementally to look at me. I flipped open the door handle but stopped short of pulling the door and activating the interior light. I had seen movement. A man was coming out through a break in the panels, from the back of the restaurant to the front. He was wearing a white uniform, with gold braiding on the shoulders and a hat. It was Willets. The uniform made him look even more untrustworthy. Like he'd stolen someone's Halloween costume. It was in the angle of his hat, and the slight sloppy way that he'd tucked in his shirt. Willets had a Chinese food take-out bag in each hand.

Dave said, "That's the guy. Watch him go to the Subaru."

I said, "That's a lot of Chinese food, Dave."

Dave spread two fingers to brush across his faint mustache. "True. They make good egg rolls in there."

"You're suggesting the bag is full of egg rolls, Dave?"

He looked over without moving his head. "No. I don't know how many egg rolls are in there, Keeler. But if there *are* egg rolls, they will be good."

We tracked Willets as he moved to the car and handled the take-out bags. He settled them safely in the passenger side floor, racking the seat forward to hold them steady. Then he went back around and got into the driver's side. We watched Willets put his seatbelt on. I said, "Like a normal citizen, Dave."

Dave said, "Yeah. It's amazing how normal people look when you watch them for a little while. And then sometimes they go and do all kinds of crazy shit."

I said, "You see a lot of crazy shit?"

Dave shrugged. "Not that much. But you do get your crazies up here, that's for sure."

We watched Willets take off. Part of me wanted to follow him. Another part of me wanted to get eyeballs on Amber Chapman. That's the part that won out in the end. Wasn't much of a competition. I got out of Dave's car and walked back until I was directly across the road from the Golden Lights Wok. Through the big window I could see the space between panels that fed back into the seating area. I crossed over to get a closer look. There were two round tables visible. Large tables, filled with people eating and drinking. None of them were blonde, none of them were young, and none of them were Amber Chapman.

I opened the door and walked into the Golden Lights Wok.

# CHAPTER THIRTY-FIVE

The woman at the counter looked up at me and didn't smile, not even a little bit. Her pink sweater was cashmere. It looked like somewhere you could crawl into and hide away until the winter was over. Which was a long, long time in Alaska. I'd only tried wearing cashmere once, and it tore to shreds in less than forty-eight hours. Too delicate for me. The woman looked about as delicate as a Mossberg 12 gauge. Her voice had a hard high-pitched edge to it, like something that could break glass.

"Take-out?"

I said, "No thanks. My friends are already here. I'll just go back and find them."

I took my eyes off her and moved. I knew that she was not happy, that she didn't like my attitude, or my face, or the fact that I was now completely ignoring her and walking through the opening in the panel screen.

I felt the weight of the Glock 19 in my jacket pocket. I had no plan to speak of, just the feeling that Chapman was in there and I needed to get eyes on her. Dave had seen a tall blonde, but was she Amber Chapman?

I moved into the back. More spacious than I would have imagined from the empty street out front. A large room with big round tables, each big enough to seat ten comfortably. And the place was jammed. I counted forty-two people. Noisy and boisterous and in other circumstances would have looked like a really good time. But these were special circumstances and I wasn't looking for a good time, just a blonde woman named Chapman.

But she was not among them.

By the time I'd done the full scan I was about to butt up against the back of the room when I bumped into a short and rotund woman with dark brown hair in a pony tail. It was June from the SEAS office. She didn't recognize me immediately. I managed to pivot out of the way and June stepped back. Then she looked up. It took her a moment to get past the clean shaved face and see me.

"Keeler. You came! Who told you?"

I was lost for a second. Then I remembered that it was June's birthday.

I said, "Tell the truth, I didn't remember. I'm looking for a friend. But happy birthday just the same."

"Whatever, you're going have a drink with me right now. You look different without a beard."

June had taken my arm and was pulling me toward one of the tables. I had scanned the room when I'd come in but missed her because she had been in the bathroom. A waiter was busy collecting dishes from a table across the room. The woman in pink cashmere had returned to face front again. June had seven or eight friends around the table. Young locals, red-faced with drink. As we moved up I could see a large collection of shot glasses gathered on a tray in the middle. When the friends saw us coming a chair materialized next to June's. By the time my ass hit the seat there was a shot in front of me.

June turned to me, then the others, "North to the future everyone!"

It was the Alaskan state motto. The drunk friends yelled it out in unison and the shots went down. Vodka, not nearly cold enough.

June flushed and said, "You see your friends?"

"No. But they came in here."

"They have private rooms downstairs. I was just down there in the bathroom. Definitely saw some people hanging out. What's your friend look like?"

"Tall woman in her twenties, blonde and pale."

"Tall blonde? Yeah I think I've seen her. You should go down there."

I thanked June and wished her happy birthday again. Then I started over to where she had emerged from the bathroom, the corner of the main room. Alongside the kitchen was a narrow entrance giving onto a stairwell. One direction, down. The kitchen doors swung open and I was hit by a wave of garlic and oil. I ducked into the stairwell and everything got a lot darker and a lot quieter. Down at the first landing was a switchback to the next flight of stairs.

At the bottom the landing went three directions. Straight ahead to the bathroom, left into a broom closet, or right down a hallway to another door. There were two guys outside that door, silhouettes backlit by a brightly glowing exit sign. One of the guys had pointy ears and a shaved head, the smooth lines were perfectly recognizable. The same silhouette I had seen outside the Edna Bay apartments. A foot soldier for Mister Lawrence. He was speaking into the other one's ear, not looking at me.

It clicked, another piece in the puzzle. They'd been watching George Abrams' apartment. Seen me going in with Chapman and called the police. They must have thought that was a clever way to get rid of us. It had not worked out that way.

I had my right hand in my jacket pocket, resting there casually on the pistol grip. The Glock has no real safety mechanism, so if I needed to rock and roll I'd just pull the gun and squeeze the trigger. But the pointy-eared guy had not seen me. The guy he was speaking to had, but there was no recognition there.

I pushed through across the hallway to the bathroom.

# CHAPTER THIRTY-SIX

THE BATHROOM WAS a dark corridor with one stall on the left and another on the right. In the middle at the end was a shared sink area with a mirror. I wondered how June had been able to see into the private area down there. Then I noticed an entrance to the right of the sink. I looked in on a coat room. No counter, no service. Just a small room filled with rails and hangars and around fifteen or twenty coats. On one side of the room were spare chairs and on the other, a makeup station with a round mirror framed in light bulbs.

I heard music. Through the coat room was another doorway, this time with an actual door. I figured this was one way of getting into the private room, the other being past the bald guy with the pointy ears. I liked this one better. I brushed aside the coats and arrived at the closed door. It wasn't shut all the way, so I put my eye to the crack.

The room beyond was dimly lit. The crack in the door was tiny, and my field of vision confined to a slim cone extending and widening uselessly at the end of the room. On the wall opposite I could make out a neon sign. Not exactly a sign, more like the illustrative electric outline of a golden wok in orange and a pair of hot pink chopsticks stuck in it. They were going for the nightclub vibe. A woman began to sing, but I couldn't see her. I could see the backs of four people. Two male, two female, and the shoulder of a third guy. They were oriented toward the singing, and I figured there was a stage there. I figured this was a room dedicated to karaoke. The voice was low and smooth. The singer made an abrupt movement, like a dance move. A part of her became visible for a fraction of a second. I saw no face, no fully formed figure, only a flash of blonde hair. I carefully pushed the door open another inch.

Then the phone rang in my pocket.

Hank's phone. An old school mobile phone with real buttons. Thankfully, also a phone with a low buzz and a physical vibration instead of a high-pitched beeping ring. I stepped back through the hanging coats and pulled it out of my pocket. I pressed the green button to accept the call. Put it to my ear without saying anything.

Dave's voice. "Keeler?"

I spoke softly. "Yes, Dave."

"Keeler, can you hear me?"

I said, "Speak."

The connection was bad. Dave's voice came through like it'd been squeezed down into pure sound with none of the essential elements of conversation. No voice or meaning except for the obvious urgency of his cadence. I moved closer to the bathroom and the voice cleared up some. But, by then he was done.

I said, "Say that all again, Dave. I got nothing."

There was a pause. Then Dave's voice came rushing. "Keeler, they've just come in. Do you see them? I couldn't call you before because they were watching me."

"Slow down. Who's coming in where, the restaurant?"

He said, "The Golden Lights Wok, yes, the restaurant. Four guys. I just wanted to tell you. I think they're the same people. Another Hummer."

Then I heard voices from the bathroom and hung up on Dave.

I knew what was going on. Whoever had just arrived was coming into the coat room. I had about ten seconds. I removed my jacket and fit it on a coat hangar. Then I got under the makeup station and hung the jacket in front of me. I stayed in an upright seated position under the table, the jacket just in front of me. It swung slightly in and out, I held my hand against it until it stopped moving. The pistol was in the jacket pocket. If it came to that, I'd have to fumble for it.

A couple of people walked into the room. I only had a view of legs. There was one big guy with a pair of steel-toed hiking boots, and a smaller guy with pair of penny loafers. Another big guy with another pair of steel-toed hiking boots came after them. All three walked through the door and into the adjacent karaoke room. When the door opened, the music and laughter came in loud and clear. Male laughter, female singing. The singing didn't stop.

There were a couple of excited shouts and the growls and grumbles of conversation. I heard a man speak clearly.

He said, "Alright the cavalry's arrived. Let's get the hell out of here."

The door closed with a bang and the music was muffled once more. There were voices, conversation. I heard furniture shuffling. A single female laugh. I stayed there under the table and counted three minutes. By then, the song had ended. Which produced a moment of silence before the next one started. In that silence I heard voices from the karaoke room. Not many. Two people speaking in normal tones. I got up from under the table and put my jacket on. The music started back up, then a man's voice singing. I walked to the door and pushed it open.

A large man was on the stage reading lyrics from a flat screen on the wall. He was middle-aged and balding, and swaying drunkenly in front of the neon wok. In the foreground a man and a woman stood with their backs to me. The woman was blonde, slim, and wore a blue dress. The man wore a plaid flannel shirt and had a hand at the small of the woman's back making tiny circles. He was speaking into her ear. The guy on the stage stopped singing and stared at me. I noticed another woman, a tall and thin brunette sitting on the stage and staring into a phone in her hand. She didn't notice anything.

The two in front turned around.

Not Chapman. The woman in blue had Asian features and wore heavy eyeliner to match the dress. The blonde hair was a wig.

I said, "Sorry, wrong door."

I turned right and took three steps through the karaoke room to the corridor. The stairwell was up ahead and to my left. The guy with the pointy ears was no longer there. I took the stairs two at a time up to the restaurant.

# CHAPTER THIRTY-SEVEN

THE ENERGY HAD GONE up a couple of gears in the restaurant. Someone had changed the music. Before, it had been a generic playlist with moaning strings. Now there was rhythm. A thumping close to that of the human heart, but slightly faster. The alcohol had helped take it up a notch. June was laughing with her friends. Faces were red. Good times.

June noticed me a few seconds after I stepped into the main room. As if she had been waiting for me. Which she had, because she'd seen Chapman and couldn't wait to tell me about it. She came scampering across the room to me, holding a long-necked bottle of Coors in one hand. The other clutched at my arm.

"I saw her. Tall blonde with pale skin. She looks like a goddamned model. Is that the one?"

"More than likely."

June had her eyes wide. She understood the importance of this black swan event. I didn't know if it was important to her because of Chapman's looks, or the fact that she'd been in special company. June said, "Well, she left a couple of minutes ago with Mister Lawrence and a bunch of other guys. Did you see him?"

"I must have been in the bathroom."

June stepped back and smiled at me. She was done with that conversation. She twirled happily. "It's my birthday."

I said, "Have a good one, June." And walked out of the restaurant.

Out front of the Golden Lights Wok, it was once again Port Morris, Alaska. The street was empty, damp, and dark and getting chilly. I looked across at Dave's Ford. It was still there, and still faded red. But I didn't see Dave. No silhouette in the car. The driver's side window was down. Nothing in there but empty space and hardware, like the steering wheel and the rear-view mirror. I stepped across the road. Four paces and I was looking in. Nobody in the driver's seat. But the passenger door was open and a body was spilled onto the sidewalk.

I went around the car. It was Dave. I could tell by his endomorphic shape and by his brown leather jacket. I crouched down beside him and observed. Dave's legs were inside the car, but the rest of him had fallen out. His face was turned to the ground. I could see him breathing, so Dave was alive. No blood pooling under his head. So far so good. I stepped away and grabbed him by the armpits. Then I tugged him away, pulling his legs out of the car. I turned him over so that he was laid out on his back. The face was the issue. Broken nose and a nasty bruise on the side of his forehead. When Dave's nose had been busted, a jet of blood had sluiced out over his mouth and onto his shirt. I touched the blood on his lip. By now it was congealing.

I played out the scene. Someone had punched him in the face through the driver's side window. Another guy had dragged him out from the passenger side door. Then the first guy had walloped him again on the head, knocking him out. The Mister Lawrence people had not enjoyed Dave's amateur surveillance operation.

I slapped his cheek.

Dave mumbled something. I gave him a minute and he went back into a stupor. I slapped again, almost hard enough to break something, but not quite.

Dave's eyes opened wide. He was in pain. "What the fuck." The eyes focused, pinwheel pupils expanding like twin apertures on a mechanical camera. "Keeler."

I said, "How many?" He was confused. "How many guys?"

Dave rubbed his head. "I feel terrible."

"I bet you do. How many guys?"

Dave rolled onto his side and drew his legs up so that he was sitting on the curb, feet under the car. He said, "Two of them. They saw me. Then one of them came over and asked me to roll down the window. When I did, he just punched me in the face. I didn't see the second guy. He came from behind me and pulled me out. Then I don't know. Just this, now."

"You're alright. Just a broken nose." I cocked my head and examined his nose. It was crooked, turning to the left at the tip. I figured I'd save him getting gouged by private hospital expenses. "Hold still a second." I reached over and grasped his nose in my fist. Like holding onto a doorknob. Then I pulled it quickly out and straight. The cartilage cracked.

Dave howled loudly.

I said, "Relax, it's over. I just saved you a couple of grand. You should be thanking me." I looked up and over the other side of the street. No more Humvee. They were gone. "Did you see the girl?"

Dave had his hand up to his nose. Feeling it tenderly. He nodded. "Four girls in, then two came out. Blonde girl, like you said in the beginning. Tall and looks like a model." He looked ashamed of himself. "I didn't get to see which Hummer she went in."

I said, "It probably won't matter. You think you can drive?"

Dave looked around, then back into the car. The keys were still in the ignition. He nodded. "Yeah. Guess I'll go home now if that's alright with you."

I stood up straight and extended a hand. Dave reached his to mine and I jerked him to his feet, pretty much taking all the weight. I put a friendly hand on his shoulder. "You did good, Dave. You got jumped by guys with more training and experience than you. Next time you'll watch your six a fraction better. That's what experience does, long as you survive it."

He smiled gratefully through the cracked and dried blood that had formed rivulets on his face. "Thanks, Keeler."

"Don't mention it." I held onto his shoulder. Dave looked at me weakly, as if he was now uncertain. The weight of my hand weighing on his fragility. I said, "You sure you want to go home now, Dave?"

He was very confused. "Is there something else?"

"Be good if you could go back to the dock and just kind of hang around there. See if anyone else comes or goes out of the *Emerald Allure*."

Dave touched his nose. "But what about the face? I mean, I think I might have been knocked out, Keeler."

I took his head in my large, callused hands, turned it this way and that way, examining him carefully. Then I locked my eyes on his, pinning him like a plucked butterfly. "I think you'll live, buddy. Get your ass down to the boat and call me if anything interesting happens. There's plenty of time to lie in bed after this is all over. Once we're done here, the winter will be very cozy."

Dave nodded and I took my hand off his shoulder. He was grateful.

"Okay. I'll do that."

Dave walked around to the driver's side. I closed the passenger door. He fired up the car and pulled away. I stood watching until he was out of sight, wondering where Willets had gone with all that Chinese take-out. I was willing to bet the farm it was going to be back to the house. I strolled the few blocks to where I'd parked the Toyota.

Guilfoyle's rifle case was resting along the back seat. Time to pay another visit to Deckart and Willets.

# CHAPTER THIRTY-EIGHT

It didn't take much more than five minutes to drive up to where the streets were sparse, and the residential housing gave way once more to the Alaskan rainforest. I spotted the gravel driveway leading up to the house where I had first met Deckart and Willets. But this time I wasn't going to come in the same way. I drove around slowly until I found a parallel street that was higher up the hill. I parked the Land Cruiser in a secluded spot.

I stood outside the truck and leaned into the back seat. The long gun case unzipped and I was able to look at it in the weak yellow ceiling light. The 700 is a famous gun, like some kind of gold standard for a rifle. It comes in all kinds of flavors, but Guilfoyle had chosen a classic model in glossy wood, with an olive canvas strap. He hadn't skimped on the scope. I pulled a handful of rounds from the cardboard box, let them fall into my left jacket pocket. They didn't quite balance out the reassuring weight of the Glock in my right pocket.

I slipped into the woods with the Remington over my shoulder. It took maybe ten minutes to get to a good spot above the house, about four hundred yards off. Even so, I had to climb into the lower branches of a big spruce tree. Because of the incline, the perch gave me a good view of the house at a three-quarter angle. Two sides of the building presented themselves to me. Once I was nestled up there and relatively comfortable, I raised the gun and uncapped the scope.

Lights were on in the house. The big window faced out to the smoke shack. The scope was excellent. I could see in there like a kid looking into a doll house. The television was showing a basketball game. I could see all of the details, some more relevant than others. Atlanta Hawks versus the Brooklyn Nets. I had no opinion on that. But I could also see the dark-haired thin guy on the couch, his name had been Jerry. He was lying on the sofa scratching himself idly. No sign of Deckart or Willets.

The three-quarter angle provided me an additional perspective on the other side. I saw movement in the window of another room. A silhouette moving behind the screen of the roller shade. It was easy to see who that was, the bearded giant. A few moments after the silhouette moved through, the lights went out in that room.

I swiveled back to Jerry stretched out on the sofa. I focused to the right of the television, into the kitchen. The lights were off, but residual light entered in through the doorway to reveal the sink counter, a mess of beer bottles and Chinese food containers. I could read the label on the box. Golden Lights Wok.

Looked like they'd torn through that take-out and left no prisoners.

Two guys verified, neither of them Deckart or Willets. Empty kitchen. Maybe others were home, reclining on beds. Maybe watching other screens. Which meant a measure of uncertainty, which meant I wasn't going in through the front door just yet. Last time I had been here seemed like a long time ago. Before the killing had started.

My assumption now was hostile intent. Even if Deckart and Willets had not pulled the trigger themselves, I was sure that they were involved in the arrangement.

I considered clemency for a moment. The guy named Jerry might be innocent of any wrongdoing. He might just be a roommate. But I'm not a judge, and the law I lay down is different from that of the courts. One way to look at life is as a bunch of choices. Not everything is a choice, but every choice is important. And Jerry had made choices, now he was going to have to face up to the consequences.

I climbed down. Made it to the yard and stayed behind another big spruce, about fifteen feet back in the woods. I hung the Remington by the strap from a branch on the forest side of the tree. I went into the smokehouse looking for supplies. I found what I needed.

In Alaska, TV doesn't come from cables buried underground by a guy with a shovel. It comes from satellite dishes attached to rooftops and linked into electricity from the main supply. I found the link box around the back of the house and pulled out the cable. I stepped back into a dark spot. Jerry would need a minute to track the issue to the outside, which would be moving out of his comfort zone on the couch. He'd probably rather stay in there. But I figured he'd come out, eventually.

It had looked like a good game.

Three minutes later the kitchen door opened with a squeak. The screen door bounced back on the spring and rattled against the frame. Soon after that, Jerry came around the corner with a flashlight. He had the beam scanning along where the aluminum siding meets the concrete foundation. Looked like he didn't know where the box was, and there wasn't any good reason why he should have.

When he found the box, Jerry froze up, an understandable reaction. It isn't as if a cable gets ripped out of a junction box by accident. Of course, by then it was too late. I had the point of my knife blade at the base of his skull. I spoke very quietly, but clearly, so he could understand the words and follow the instructions. My mouth was just behind his left ear. His shoulders hunched up tight.

I took the flashlight out of Jerry's hand and turned it off and stuck it in my pocket. Otherwise, he was unarmed. I said, "We are going to talk, Jerry. Quietly. It won't be pleasant, but you will survive if you are honest."

Jerry's head dropped down on his chest. His voice contained a quiver of fear. He knew that I was not going to be very nice with him. "I have nothing to do with this, with any of it."

"With what exactly, Jerry?"

He didn't answer. I walked Jerry over to the edge of the woods. "Where are you taking me, man?"

I said nothing. I needed to know a couple of things, and I didn't have the patience to say please.

## CHAPTER THIRTY-NINE

THE WIRE SPOOL I had taken from the smokehouse rested at the base of the tree. The gauge had been good enough for the job of hanging fish to cure. The wire was thin steel and strong, and I figured it would be enough for another kind of job, similar, but different. Jerry saw it there, and I could see his head rotating on his thin neck, moving so that his eyeballs could trace the wire up to where it was looped over a branch, and back down again to where I had fashioned a noose. The Remington was hung close by, and Jerry's eyes settled on that for a moment.

He started to rattle with fear. When I wrapped the wire twice around his neck Jerry went inert, total paralysis. My foot went into the little noose at ground level, stabilizing the rig. I said, "Jerry, get up on your toes, like a ballerina."

He shivered. "What?"

I said nothing. He had heard me. Since he wasn't doing it, I did it for him. I grabbed him one-handed by the neck and lifted him about four inches. I looked down and saw his toes just about brushing the ground. I stepped down on the wire wrapped around my foot, like the gas pedal in a car. It had the effect of tightening the steel wire around Jerry's neck. Now, he was forced onto his toes. I split the balance between Jerry's neck and my foot. Forty percent Jerry, sixty percent foot. The wire went taut and his head jerked up.

I said, "I stomp hard enough, your head might come off, no guarantees." He couldn't speak, so I released the bite a touch. He was swinging around a little too freely. I steadied Jerry's body and turned him to face me. He flinched seeing me for the first time. I realized that I must have looked frightening to him, all big and malevolent.

He was shivering. "So now tell me about you and your friends. Tell it like a story that I can easily understand."

"What did I do, man? I have nothing to do with them."

I said, "Treat me like a child and start from the beginning. I need to get a feeling for your basic existence, simple as that may be."

He looked at me wildly, not comprehending. He couldn't move his head, so his eyeballs roamed freely in their sockets. I saw something like conscious thought going on in there. Then he tried to express himself. He said, "You mean like what we're doing here, in this house, like who I am?"

I said, "Good place to start, Jerry."

He said, "We're waiting for the boat to leave. What do you think we're doing?"

"Slowly. Take me through it."

"The *Emerald Allure*. The cruise ship. We work security on the boat. Deckart's the boss. Technically deputy boss, but he runs the show there. Ship's leaving tomorrow."

"Just the boat, Jerry?"

"What do you mean?"

I said, "Tell me about the freelancing. What you and your friends are up to here."

He shook his head. "I'm not involved. Deckart and Willets are tight year round. I'm up here for the job is all."

"Hard to believe you're uninvolved, Jerry."

"Just let me know what I need to do to prove it, man."

I said, "What about tonight? Who bought the food, who ate it? Where did they go?"

Jerry gulped. The wire biting into his throat made it hard and slow to do that. He said, "Willets brought the Chinese. I bought the beer."

"Where is everyone?"

I had stepped pretty far down on the wire noose, and Jerry was struggling to maintain his balance. He could barely speak, so I eased off a little. Redressed the balance in favor of the foot, seventy-thirty. Jerry managed to croak. "Deckart and Willets are out. They always go out together. I have no idea where. I'm alone in the house with the Viking."

I said, "The Viking."

"The new guy. We call him the Viking. I don't even know his real name. He's Icelandic or something."

"You know, Jerry, that if I find out that any of what you are telling me is in any way invented, I will come back and I will kill you."

He said, "I don't doubt you. I'm telling the truth."

"Deckart and Willets go out a lot?"

"Yeah. They go out."

"What time do they usually come back?"

He shrugged. "Man, they go out to the bars. Get back here, I'm already asleep. I guess they get back late, very late."

"And why not you?"

"I'm married, with kids. I'm a family guy. We have a house down in Fresno, California. Lower forty-eight. I'm only up here for the work, man."

I said, "Tell me more about Deckart and Willets."

He tried to shrug. "Not much to tell that I know of. They were together in the army, served in the same unit."

"Which unit?"

"Military police. Probably dirty cops, if you ask me."

I said, "That is a serious allegation. I'm asking you, Jerry. What makes you say that?"

It isn't easy to shrug with a wire noose around your neck. But Jerry managed to do it, with his eyebrows. He said, "Just a feeling. I've only been working boats with them for three years. You ask me, they'd do anything for money."

"Such as?"

"I don't know. Like shaking people down, intimidation. That kind of stuff. But they didn't get me involved."

"Why not?"

"I don't think they trust me."

I said, "Which bar do I find them in?"

He didn't respond quickly enough, so I jerked the wire. Jerry spluttered and I loosened it to allow him enough wind to speak. "The Rendezvous maybe."

"What do I find, if I pay a visit to the Rendezvous?"

"Pool table. Juke box. Live music sometimes. Like one or two girls, and one and a half out of two are hookers. Deckart and Willets getting into a fight maybe. Sometimes you can find crazy shit up there. Depends. Who the fuck knows what happens out there?"

I said, "Your friends like to fight?"

"They're both psychos. And they aren't my friends. I just work with them. A lot of guys work up here with psychos, doesn't make us like them."

I said, "Where's the Rendezvous?"

"Up past the airport, out of town. You know that road?" I nodded. "You keep going until you get to the end of it."

I said, "Then what?"

"Then you're there. But you should watch out."

"Why's that?"

"Cause you won't be in America anymore."

I wondered why that was supposed to make me scared.

I took Jerry back to the house. Holding him like a dog, bent over with the wire noose tight around his neck. He didn't struggle. I let him go first into the kitchen. In the living room, I hog-tied him on the couch. I pulled a wallet from his jeans. Two hundred and forty dollars in twenty-dollar bills. California driver's license. Jeremiah Delano Murphy. thirty-two years old. The word 'Veteran' was printed in capital letters with a red stripe above, and a blue stripe below.

I said, "Veteran of what?"

He said, "Marine Corps."

There was loud hearty laugh from one of the back rooms. He looked up at me. I tossed his wallet on to the couch, put my hand on the Glock and slipped it out of my pocket. Jerry cowered into the cushions. He said, "Come on, man."

I said, "Marines. Always got to go the hard way." One step to the couch and I nailed him in the side of the head with the gun. Jerry went out like a light.

I made sure a round was chambered and started back. Another laugh, same guy. Loud and innocent, but deep and rough. A large male, amused. The Viking. There was a hallway off the living room. Bathroom on the left, which was dark and smelled like mold. Straight ahead was an open door to a bedroom. Also dark. To the right was a closed door. Crack under the door was dark, but then I heard another amused snort.

I toed the door open and flicked the light switch.

The room was small. Barely space for a single bed and a dresser. The dresser had a mirror on it. The bed had the bearded giant on it. It couldn't contain him, and the giant spilled out on three sides, and was leaned up against the fourth side, the wall. His massive head was propped against several pillows. He wore a pair of improbably nerdy glasses, round and perched on his nose. Fancy headphones were wrapped around the giant's ears. Hair was loose. Falling over his shoulders and bare chest. He was startled. A laptop computer balanced on his hard belly. Open like a clam shell.

He slowly raised his hands where I could see them, which was the right thing to do. I said, "You hear me?"

He saw my mouth moving and moved one finger to touch the headphones.

He nodded. "Easy. I hear you now."

I said, "Let the computer fall off." He shrugged the laptop off and let it tip to the floor. I saw the screen, in motion. A crowd of Vikings were running across a glacier.

"Weapon?" He nodded. I said, "Where?"

He said, "I'm sitting on it."

I said, "Sit up slowly on the bed and let me see."

The giant swung his legs over to the side of the bed. He was wearing a pair of boxers and nothing else. The gun was lying there on the sheet. It was a Smith & Wesson special .357 magnum with a fancy blue grip. I kept the Glock on him and reached for the S&W. His eyes were dull, locked on mine. I stood back and put the weapon in my jacket pocket, right in there with the Remington rounds. The big guy made a sound, like kissing teeth. He said, "My uncle gave me that gun."

Nice gun. Five round capacity. Air-weight revolver with punch.

I said, "Sorry pal, I'm concerned about your welfare. If you got tempted to use this on me, I might have to take you down. Wouldn't that be a shame?"

He said, "I had nothing to do with Deckart and Willets yesterday. Those aren't my people."

"Why the gun?"

"Because I'm living with psychopaths is why."

I said, "Who's the psychopath?"

He said, "Alaska. People like you. You know how it is up here. Constitutional carry state. No registration or permit required, and no background check. Everyone can open carry and nobody gives a shit. Which makes me feel like it'd be a good idea to carry a gun. Okay?"

I said, "The girl the other night. What were you doing to her?"

The giant had long eyelashes, lined up in a horizontal half moon behind the reading glasses. Good-looking guy. He said, "What about the girl?"

I said, "What were you planning on doing to her, before I put you to sleep?"

I expected him to blink, to be surprised that it was me who had put him down. But he was not surprised, didn't blink. He said, "Shit. That was you? I wasn't doing anything. It was a warning was all. I was bluffing her, trying to get her scared."

"I guess that wouldn't be too difficult for you."

He shook his head again. "Not my fault I was born like this."

I said, "Tonight. What happened?"

"No idea what you're talking about. I've been watching movies all night. Half naked in bed. Before you came in and started ripping and robbing that is."

"Chinese food?"

"I don't eat that shit."

I said, "Healthy living?"

He said, "I'm a pescatarian."

"What's that?"

"I only eat vegetables and fish."

I said, "Watch the game?"

The giant shook his head. "That's Jerry, I don't like sports."

I said, "If you don't like sports, what do you like?"

He said, "I was watching Norwegian TV just now. Before you came in. There's a series about Vikings. You wouldn't understand, it's in Norwegian."

"You're Norwegian."

"That's right."

I found his wallet on the dresser. California driver license. Not a veteran. Name of Jakob Hagen. I studied the picture. No glasses. He looked frightening. But speaking to him was different. I tried it out. "Jakob Hagen." Hagen looked at me. He nodded. I said, "You don't look like a Jakob."

He said, "You'd get used to it."

I said, "Where are the others?"

"Out getting drunk, like a bunch of idiots."

"Tell me about your crew."

He said, "Hardly a crew. We're stuck here for the last week waiting for the damn boat to leave."

I said, "Security work."

"Cruise ship gigs pay good."

"Who asked you to scare the girl?"

"Deckart." He looked down at his knees. "I didn't know she'd get so offended."

"What did Deckart tell you?"

"He said the girl pissed him off. Wanted her to shit her pants. Whatever, I guess I'm sorry."

"That's not what Deckart said. He said he didn't know anything about that."

The big guy shrugged.

I looked at him carefully. He was hiding something. It wasn't quite so straight forward. All that overt confidence was masking something else, but I couldn't put my finger on what it was. I looked again at his driver license. I put it back in the wallet. Then I put the wallet back on the dresser. On my way out of the room I said, "I'm keeping the gun."

Hagen made no response. He looked like he wanted to say something.

I stepped back in. "What is it?"

He shook his head and blinked. "Nothing."

I took another look at him. Top to bottom. Big and muscular guy with almost no clothes on. Something was bothering me, and then I realized what it was. No tattoos. In every other way Hagen looked like a guy who would have tattoos, but he didn't. I looked at him for a long moment, before figuring that a lack of tattoos was not exactly a capital offense.

Back in the living room, the couch didn't contain a hog-tied ex-marine. It contained nothing but the wire, unraveled and untwisted. The kitchen door was wide open. I figured Jerry had managed to get loose and was gone. Maybe back to Fresno. That would be the right call, as far as Jerry's health and well being was concerned.

I went out and stood on the deck looking across the yard at the dark woods. Nothing moving. Nothing happening. Just animals staying silent and alert until they could relax once again. I came down the skeleton staircase to the yard, then walked around the side of the house and looked out front. Willets' Subaru was gone. There was an old pickup truck parked nose-in. Maybe a Ford. On the other side of it was a second vehicle. Not a truck, a recent model Nissan. A practical car, white and very dirty. The vehicles would belong to Jerry and the Viking. Except for the tourists and the hikers, people in Alaska don't tend to walk very much. I couldn't see the front of the vehicles because the drive was blocked by a line of low bushes.

## CHAPTER FORTY

I CROSSED the yard and retrieved the Remington. I got about forty feet deep into the woods and worked my way over through the forest so that I had a good view of the house from another position. The same but different. Another three-quarter angle, but this time the front and the side. The new position had a straight-on view of Hagen's window.

Because of the elevation on this side, there was no need to climb a tree. I set up behind a rocky outcrop which made a clearing in the woods above the house. I put my eye to the scope and scanned. Nothing much was going on. The roller shades were still down and Hagen hadn't turned off the light. There was a possibility that he might be too lazy to get up out of bed. Maybe he had returned to his Viking show with the fancy headphones back over his ears.

Maybe not.

I waited patiently to find out. The end of the rifle barrel was resting on rock. I was in a prone position, belly-down on the dirt and stones. Unmoving and watchful, an alpha predator with the advantage of height.

I thought about where Willets might have gone. Maybe to the bar up past the airport, like Jerry had said. Maybe not. I pulled out Hank's phone from my pocket and took my eye off the scope long enough to dial Dave. He picked up after three rings.

I said, "What's happening?"

He said, "Nothing. There's a boat the size of a neighborhood and water lapping at the dock. I've got the window down, so I can hear that. Besides the sound of water, I've got Fred Granson a hundred yards from the car, drunk as usual. I can hear his hiccups, one every thirty-two seconds, on average."

I said, "Fred Granson?"

"Local drunk guy. One of many."

"How do you know he's drunk?"

Dave paused. "Fred comes down to the water almost every night. Once in a while, his girlfriend and his mom come down and get him."

"Okay." I hung up the phone.

Twenty minutes later, Hagen's silhouette crossed the window. Ten minutes after that, the front door opened and out came the bearded giant.

He walked straight to the white Nissan. Hagen had left his glasses at home. I figured he knew he looked scarier without them. He got in on the driver's side. The car started up. The engine was modern and quiet, making an efficient hum. I tracked the big guy in the sights. He looked unconcerned, going through the motions of backing out his car. Hagen steered his vehicle down the drive, away from me.

Only then did I see the Alaskan plates, yellow with dark blue characters and numbers. Seven characters separated by a small Alaskan state flag, furling dark blue with eight yellow stars. TGN on the left, 8462 on the right. Which was precisely the combination that I had found revealed on George Abrams' yellow legal pad.

Hagen's vehicle disappeared around the curve at the bottom of the driveway. I took my eye off the scope and watched the taillights through the trees until they were gone. Red brake lights used prudently. The bearded giant's driving was reasonable and cautious.

The consequences were interesting. I pictured George Abrams in his apartment and went through some of the scenarios in which that license plate number might have been noted down on the pad, and the top sheet torn off.

The first scenario was Abrams returning home. He gets in the door and walks to the dining nook. There, he writes down the number on that yellow legal pad. It was a number he'd seen somewhere, heard from someone, something he wanted to check or pass on. Maybe.

A second scenario had someone else writing that number down. A mystery person, probably an adversary. It could be whoever had placed that laptop in Abrams' office. An intruder searches Abrams' apartment, plants the laptop as a trap for anyone else coming around. Gets a call from the boss. Reaches for whatever he can find and notes down the number. Then he rips out the page and pockets it.

A third scenario occurred to me. The dining nook in Abrams' apartment was tucked into a corner with large windows. I remembered seeing the cruise ship from the window, which was impressive. Less impressive was the view of the street. I mentally walked over to Abrams' dining table. The yellow legal pad was sitting right there, a ball point pen keeping it company. I visualized looking down through the window to the street below. In that third option, George Abrams gazes down the street, and sees Hagen sitting in the white Nissan. Maybe not for the first time. He notes down the plate number.

I was in no position to follow Hagen. The Land Cruiser was through the woods a ways. It was time for a rendezvous.

BACK AT THE VEHICLE, I laid the long gun into the case and zipped it shut. I removed the Match King rounds from my pocket and returned them to the box. I placed Hagen's Smith & Wesson into the glove compartment. Nice little gun, but not accurate enough to be useful. More like the kind of thing you'd use if you wanted to blow someone's head off at point blank range. More than ten yards from the target, I'd consider the gun useless.

The truck started and I rocked the lever south to drive. There was no way of getting straight out to the airport from that neighborhood. I would have to go back through town, and then up the airport road. And I wasn't in a patient mood. So I decided to wing it and get into the logging trails to avoid the paved roads. By then it was wet out, not exactly raining, but not far from it. Even so, moonlight trickled through the thin cloud cover. A light mist had blown in from the Pacific and was filtering through the rainforest. I didn't know the trails but navigating by intuition always worked for me. Maybe it is related to my sense of time, as if I have a special connection to the spinning of the planet on its axis.

Or maybe not.

The airport was a flat runway viewed through the fence, with the low mist crawling all over it. The logging trail ran alongside and pulled in after the fence. The Land Cruiser rumbled along the gravel, tires crunching. Past the fence I hit the asphalt with a lurching bump and turned left. Then it got nice and smooth. After a minute the airport was behind me, and the road just one more shade of gray making a hole in the darker shades of enveloping forest.

Until the road ended.

Abruptly, without a warning. A horizontal line of asphalt advanced under me as the Toyota sped through the night. Suddenly I was off the asphalt and onto dirt again. I stopped the vehicle, put it in reverse, and backed up quick. There had been a sign on the side of the road when the asphalt had ended. I backtracked to look at it. With the Toyota Land Cruiser's headlights I read two lines. On top it said, 'Leaving America'. Below that was written, 'Entering Tribal Lands.'

Another three miles of dirt road in the dark. Then the road widened to a parking lot, and I was there at the Rendezvous. The lot was big and flush with parked vehicles. I backed the Toyota into a spot with a good view of the place. Then I sat and watched for a while. The roadhouse was a one-story building. The roof was corrugated iron and the rest of the structure was clad in worn wood siding. There were colored lights and a porch. Music was coming out of it at a low, mellow volume. Roadhouse music.

I examined each vehicle. No silhouettes, no nothing. Just boxes on wheels with closed windows and the dead air inside of them. I waited two minutes. Nothing moved except the drizzle, the mist, and the leaves on the trees. A raccoon scuttled in from the right side of the lot. Three others came after it. The leader led the troop back to the side of the building and all four disappeared around it.

Then I smelled the barbecue.

The question was, go in armed, or not. I thought about it, for about a fifth of a second and decided to leave the firearms in the truck. I locked the vehicle, walked over and pulled open the screen door.

The room was large. A plain wood plank floor littered with cigarette butts and peanut shells, like something out of another time. Lighting design was courtesy of the Miller High Life sign taking up one side of the room, and the Coors Light sign on the other. In between were wood trestle tables, wood stand up tables, and a pool table with a worn green felt-covered slate top. Left of the door, the bar took up the whole wall. The juke box was on the right side, pushed against the wall. A woman was leaning into it, trying to feed the machine a five dollar bill, which it kept on rejecting. Straight ahead, across the room, was a double wide door. In front of it a guy sat at a table. Other than him and the lady at the jukebox, there were three other people in the room, one of them worked the bar, the other one was me.

I looked back outside at the parking lot. At least two dozen vehicles, maybe more.

The bartender was as far as you could possibly get from the door. I started walking to the bar, and he slid himself over so that we met in the middle. I leaned my arms on it, he mirrored the gesture.

I said, "What do you have?"

He said, "We've got Alaskan. You can take your choice of Alaskan Amber or Alaskan IPA, either one works."

"You choose."

"Okay."

I said, "I'm hungry."

The guy jerked his thumb to the double wide door in the back. "Ten bucks gets you in and gets you barbecue. Just pay Jimmy over there and he'll give you a stamp."

Jimmy didn't look up until I was standing right there in front of him. Jimmy opened his eyes and looked at me. I had a ten-dollar bill ready. He took the money with one hand, and the other stamped the back of my hand as soon as the bill was in his. It was a complex operation that looked simple.

I went through the double wide door.

## CHAPTER FORTY-ONE

THE ROOM WAS BARELY LIT, so at first I couldn't see a thing. Then the contours of the cinder block walls became clearer. Two short sides, two long sides, a rectangle. I stood smack in the middle of one of the short sides. In front of me was a wall of backs, specifically, the backs of men, and many of them bearded. Behind those backs were more backs, each one attached to a person. They were facing the far side of the room, the other short side. There was something going on up there. Some kind of a show.

A young guy leaned against the wall just inside the door.

He was clean shaven with short, cropped hair. Clean shaven was an anomaly here. It made him look out of place, and I figured it was the same for me. The guy was in the shadows, so I couldn't see his eyes. But I could tell that they had fastened on to me. I saw the silhouette of a curly earpiece cord against the light grey wall. It wasn't a phone cord, it was a coil tube earpiece for a two-way radio system. Which meant two things. A professional security detail, and someone to listen to through the earpiece. The guy wouldn't be alone.

I moved up the long axis of the room, against the wall. People made way for me. Mostly grudgingly, sometimes unwillingly. I got some looks, I gave some looks. I got some shoulder blocks. I pushed through them, hard. Mostly, people were letting me through because they were occupied with the activity in front of them. Whatever that was. I couldn't see up there because the room was ridiculously sloped in the wrong direction, up toward the front. No matter how tall you were, the guy in front of you was taller. Which was why people were locked in position, peering through any angle they could get. I wondered if it was worth it.

They were fixated on the front. Fixated and fascinated, or horrified. They weren't smiling, that's for damn sure. No music, no talking. Only a soft patter-patter coming from up front, like a couple of dripping faucets. Every ten drips punctuated by a soft slap. Then there was labored breathing. Like someone struggling but multiplied. Like two people struggling. I slid my way up the wall some more, until I could see properly.

A single light bulb hung from a long cord. Two men were hunched over, legs splayed for balance. At first, I thought they were staring each other down. But then one of them moved in a jerky way, an exhausted twitch toward the other guy, who absorbed it, steadied himself, then twitched in return.

They were playing a game of bloody knuckles. Each one took a turn hitting the other guy in the knuckles with a clenched fist. That was what the slapping sound had been, two fists hitting together. I didn't know how long they'd been going, but it must have been a long time. They were slow, clearly exhausted. Both fists were bloody knobs of raw flesh. Between them was a puddle of blood on the unvarnished wood flooring. That was the patter-patter sound. The steady drip of blood from inflamed, exposed, and bleeding muscle and bone. Each time they smacked fists, the blood splashed out in thicker spurts, increasing the growing puddle under their feet.

One of the men had long blond hair hanging to his shoulders, moist and sweaty from exertions. His face was specked with blood.

The other guy looked like a wrestler. No shirt, tribal tattoos, shaved head. The tribal tattoo guy was wide and solid. A lot of flesh on his body, but maybe that didn't work so well for the task at hand. The other guy was emaciated, like a tapeworm was stealing his nourishment, leaving him all bony and hard edged. I figured his punches might hurt more.

The guy with the tattoos landed a solid punch into the thin guy's right fist. It sounded like a tomato hitting a cement wall. Neither of them flinched, but the lanky guy sagged a little. Then he punched the tattooed guy's fist. It was a jerky punch from no distance. The wide guy absorbed the blow, his face expressionless. Deep pain, deep fatigue. Both of those guys were going to be permanently damaged.

I whispered to the guy next to me. "How long have they been going?"

He cupped his hand to his mouth and said, "Good hour. At least."

To win at bloody knuckles, all you have to do is keep going. The loser is the guy who stops. By now, neither of the two was able to open their hands. Fists were glued closed by the hemorrhaging blood and inflamed tendons and muscle. It was all about endurance and legs. I figured the wide guy had the legs, but he also carried the weight.

"What're the stakes?"

The guy indicated across the room. He said, "Ten grand to the winner. Zero to the loser."

I glanced in the direction my neighbor had indicated. There were a couple of cocktail tables, over on the other side of the stage, like a VIP area. I didn't have a clear view of who was sitting over there, because there were men standing in the way. Not in the way of the VIP's view, in the way of my view of the VIPs. But I was able to get a glimpse of legs and shoes. Specifically, female legs, and women's shoes. Legs that were presumably coming out of skirts or dresses. Two women on either side of one man. I examined the shoes. Two sets of heels on either side of a pair of penny loafers. Neither of the women were petite, that was for sure. Big healthy feet scrunched into sizable high heels. On the other hand, the man was not large, or at least his feet weren't. The penny loafers were child-sized, the feet barely touching the ground.

I recognized the penny loafers from the Chinese restaurant. Same guy who had walked through the coat room. Mister Lawrence, I assumed.

But then I was also noticing the security detail. Strategically seeded into the crowd were plainclothes guys like the one with the curly cord ear-piece at the door. They weren't big guys. No gym bunnies. These were guys in perfect physical condition. Lean and ready. It wasn't hard to pick them out of the crowd, because they weren't watching the show, they were watching me. So I turned to watch the show, figuring they'd get bored of the new guy. I had counted six men in the security detail, plus the guy at the back by the door. Seven guys, probably armed. Made me wish I'd brought the Glock.

On the other side of the VIP area was an opening. Maybe another area, or maybe just the bathrooms.

I saw movement among the legs. One set of female legs was moving, uncrossing, finding purchase on the floor and taking the weight of a woman's body. The small guy's legs were moving also, like he was shifting in his seat, paying attention to the woman. There was some shuffling of the men standing around in proximity. I figured they were glancing at the woman as she stood. An anomaly in a place heavy on the toxic masculinity. I saw blonde hair above shoulder height, the blonde was turning, making her way around legs and chairs and tables. Moving back to the bathrooms, or whatever was through there. I put the untouched beer bottle down and started to move through the crowd in that direction.

It took maybe half a minute to elbow and shoulder my way through. Not too fast so that I drew attention. Not too slow that I'd be blocked by a bunch of intransigent bearded men. Just fast enough to cut through quietly to the other side. Once clear, I looked over to the opening. I was in time to see a flash of blonde turning the corner. A guy was following her, coil tube earpiece curling from his ear to his collar.

The blonde woman had Amber Chapman's distinctive profile.

## CHAPTER FORTY-TWO

CHAPMAN LOOKED different all dressed up. She had makeup on and was wearing a deep blue satin dress that hugged her figure, making the most of slim curves. Her hair was combed and shiny and pleated into layers, different than the last time I had seen her being ducked into a Port Morris police department cruiser.

I came around the corner and there were two options. One was a hole in the concrete wall leading to an outdoor area, smelling of barbecue. The other was the bathroom. No men's room, no women's room, just one room. A large enclosure with stalls on either side. The guy who had followed Chapman was standing at the door. A steady flow of bearded customers moved in and out of the stalls, beer soaked bodies either relieved or in need of relief, either hustling in with short steps on tight legs, or coming out, loose limbed and ready for more Alaskan.

I entered just in time to see Chapman closing the door to a stall halfway down the left side of the room. The guy at the door was openly examining everyone coming through it. I blanked him and went straight in. I tried the door next to Chapman's but it was locked.

A guy came out of the one just over, two stalls down from Chapman. I slipped in behind him, closed and latched the door.

The stall was thick plywood, sturdy and tall. But not quite tall enough to reach all the way. A three-foot gap remained between the top of the wall and the ceiling. I didn't waste time contemplating my action, I guess I had already done that in the back of my mind. I stepped up on the toilet. From there it was only a short hop to get my hands gripping the top edge of the partition. I pulled myself up and over. Only took a second. Then I was rolling over the edge, high up. Gripping the partition with my knee and my arm and hand. Balanced up there like an acrobat. I could see down into the next stall, but not over into the room. Which was a good thing, because it meant the hard guy at the door couldn't see me either.

The guy sitting on the toilet had a good-sized bald patch on the top of his head. I could see a beard below a reddened drinker's nose. His remaining hair was thin and long, the strands pulled back into an aspirational pony tail. I swung down so that my legs were right above him, hands gripping either side of the stall. He had his pants around his ankles and wore a biker's leather vest over a blue and white flannel shirt. The leather vest made a perfect landing spot for my feet. I said, "Don't freak out, but I'm going to use your shoulders as a trampoline."

The guy jerked and looked up at me. But, by then I had both boots on his shoulder. I said, "Hold strong and keep your mouth shut." He sat up straight, on command. A real trooper. I used the guy's shoulders to bounce up again, gripping the other side of the stall. Like before, I gripped the top edge and rolled over so that I was balanced up there, peering down into the next stall.

Chapman was below me, unaware. She was crouched in front of the toilet, fiddling with something. It was a piece of white paper, and she was folding it over into a tiny little package, pressing it with her fingers. She slipped the wadded paper into the narrow gap where flush tank meets wall.

Like a secret message.

And the first thought I had was that it might be for me. But the thought after that discarded the first and found it naïve and ridiculous, of course it was not a message for me. For all Chapman knew I was still in jail. I watched her finish the job of hiding her little message. She pulled her hand back and turned around.

I wanted to think about what I had just seen, but it wasn't the proper time for thinking.

I leapt down, like some kind of jungle predator. Aiming to land just in front of her, clear of the door. Chapman was startled, which was not surprising. Anyone would have been startled, unless they were blind and deaf and even then, the vibrations might have freaked them out.

But most people would have been startled to the point of blind panic, what we call condition black, like a deer in the headlights. Shivering and shaking and recoiling. Maybe climbing up on the toilet in fear, like she had done way back in the Porterhouse Bar, when the bearded giant had attacked her. But not this time. This time, Chapman jerked up from a crouched position. But not innocently, like a surprised civilian in condition black. It was a practiced move. Meaning practiced in heels, not in combat boots. She came up with intent and aggression, like a trained fighter in condition orange, full awareness and knowledge, body reacting from repetition and drill.

Chapman hinged at the waist, transferring weight from her right heel up through her lithe body until the fist was coming at my throat with enough snap to take down a sumo wrestler. I couldn't tell if she was going for the trachea or the carotid. Either way, Chapman was acting with intent, hair swinging into her face, obscuring her vision. The fist was moving accurately and quickly. I hadn't really expected her to react in that way, but I was condition orange myself.

I stepped in and blocked the attacking arm out. Her fist snapped wickedly in the air next to my left ear. Chapman's face was flushed red and focused, but she was alert and then she recognized me. She didn't say anything, but there was an adjustment in her pupils, from pin-sized cold dots to welcoming orbs. Her right arm made a transition. She was able to soften the strike, and move her arm forward, over my shoulder, while her left came up around the other side. I was already near her, physically speaking, and then the gap was closed entirely.

Her arms went fully around my neck and her body fit perfectly against mine, like that was a natural way of things, like the way clouds are white and sky is blue. Her nose nuzzled into my neck. "You shaved. I didn't recognize you. I thought..."

I said nothing.

She spoke softly, lips close to my ear. "I had no idea. How did you get out of that?"

I said, "Long story." I pulled away. "What's going on here?"

Chapman gazed at me evenly. "I got in through the cruise ship." She bit her lip. "I didn't know what had happened to you. You understand. I didn't like leaving you there, but I had no idea what else to do. We had already connected the boat and the people George was mixed up with. Jane had." She looked at me, as if gauging my level of belief.

I said nothing. I neither acknowledged the fake name *Jane*, nor disavowed it. I was unsure what to think about Amber Chapman. Hostile or friendly, I was leaning towards benevolent and mysterious, if not necessarily friendly. Maybe undercover law enforcement, which would account for her need to lie to me. I decided to go with whatever bluff she was pulling.

She said, "There's a guy. An older man who is some kind of liability to them. Like some kind of evil clown. Bald, but not in the normal way. Zero hair on him, like a birth defect. They keep him distracted with girls and drugs. I got in that way, by getting close to him at the casino on the cruise ship." She came back to me, close in. I could feel the heat of her breath caressing my skin. And the heat of her body everywhere else. It was nothing that I had issues with, pretty much the opposite. She said, "I think they're going to take me inside, Keeler. Tonight. And I'm goddamned scared."

The fingers of her left hand dropped down the back of my neck and moved gently. My right hand came up and wrapped around her waist, fingers gripping at the small of her back. I know scared, and she wasn't. She was excited.

I said, "What's inside the property?"

Chapman said, "I'm not sure. Nothing good. The evil clown guy says it's the big night. Maybe I'll be able to find out what happened to George."

I thought of the rental boat coming back without George. I decided not to mention it to Chapman.

I said, "What's your plan?"

"I'm improvising. No plan."

"Do you have a phone?"

Chapman said, "No phone, they took it away." She laughed sharply. "When I agreed to hang out with the clown off the boat." Chapman looked past me at the door. "I have to go, or they might come looking for me. How are you going to get out of here without them seeing you?"

I said, "I'll take my chances. If the guy sees me, I'll just kill him."

She blinked. "Can't kill him, Keeler. I need to get in there, into the property. If you kill him, they'll lock down."

I took Hank's phone from my pocket, pressed it into her hand. Told her the password. Told her to use Ellie's number.

She said, "Who's Ellie?"

I said, "Police. If you want to get hold of me, call her."

"Port Morris police are incapable of tying their own shoes, Keeler."

"Not Port Morris. Ellie's Tribal police, and she's one of the good people."

Chapman's eyes narrowed. Then she pulled at my jacket. I saw again, in her eyes, a flat placidity. It was a confirmation that she was not freaking out. She was calm and excited, all at the same time. Not like a brave civilian going into the unknown, more like a veteran warrior going into combat.

I decided to push her some. I said, "You aren't going to tell me, are you?"

Chapman's tone switched immediately. "No. I'm not." She put a hand on my chest. She said, "I'm happy to see you, Keeler, but I hope you never figured that you were more important than the mission. Glad to see that they cleared you of charges. Makes sense, since you didn't do it. But hey, you never really know right?"

The woman was in control, which was obviously her preference. I liked that. There was an incredible energy between us. Like some kind of chemistry experiment. Anything could have happened, but what did happen was the phone buzzed in Chapman's hand that wasn't touching me. The hand that was felt warm and the fingers relaxed and pressed gently. She held the phone out and I took it.

I pressed the green button.

Silence. Then Dave's voice, low and conspiratorial. "Keeler."

I said nothing.

He said, "Okay. Notable event. Just watched a guy come walking down from town and give Fred something. I guess it was money."

"Why is that notable, don't people give him money sometimes?"

"People do. I've seen him take charity on multiple occasions tonight. It's notable because Fred gave him something back, change I'm assuming. Like the guy gave him a twenty or something and Fred gives him a five back."

"Anything else?"

Dave said, "The guy himself was notable. Huge guy."

I said, "Bearded?"

"Bearded. Came walking down, went over to Fred Granson and did the little exchange. Then walked back up into town."

I looked at Chapman. She was looking at me. Our faces were about ten inches apart. I looked away. "You sure they exchanged money?"

Dave said. "I couldn't see exactly. I think it was cash, yes."

"That it?"

"Yeah."

I hung up.

I looked up at Chapman. Our eyes locked and we were back in the bubble.

I said, "Shit happens."

"Way of the world. But now here you are." Chapman leaned in and kissed me quick. A dexterous and athletic movement. A light and delicate kiss. Which became less light, but even more delicate and complex, and eventually resulted in our bodies coming together again, like opposite poles of a magnet. Her hands went up to the nape of my neck once more, and mine went in different places. Then she pushed herself away, squeezed past me, and went out the door. Opening it just wide enough for her slender frame to pass through.

I locked the toilet door, counted off a long two minutes.

I considered two things. Hagen at the cruise ship, Chapman in here. One making an exchange with a drunk bum, the other stuffing something behind a toilet. Collecting, depositing. One deposits, the other collects. That's how I saw it.

I squatted down and removed the folded paper from behind the toilet tank. It was a white cocktail napkin. Not a thick and fluffy napkin to wipe dirty hands on, but a thin and elegant serviette that belongs under a martini glass. I unfolded it. In the middle of the white square was an eight-pointed star drawn in blue ink by a felt tipped pen. I folded the paper and slid it back behind the tank. Then I left the toilet.

The symbol was a message. I didn't have any idea what it meant, but I had a pretty good idea who it was for.

Out of the bathroom, I was facing the other hole in the wall. From which the smell of barbecue emanated. The other hole in the wall went back to a small outdoor area surrounded by cheap fencing. There was no grass, only dusty rock and a couple of picnic tables. The entrance fee had included barbecue, so I got barbecue and another beer. The big man at the grill handed me a plate of ribs on a slice of white bread. No fork, no napkin. I balanced the plate and the beer in two hands and went over to a picnic table. The other guy at the table grunted between fistfuls of pork and white bread.

I took a bite of mine. Spicy, which is what the white bread was for, in addition to being something you could wipe your fingers on. The food was good, great even. Barbecue ribs are not a complicated thing to eat, provided you don't mind using your hands. These had been cooked slow and long, so there wasn't much work to do. But patience would be important, and not easy under the circumstances. Barbecue ribs are not like burgers. You don't need three bites to get to the heart of the matter.

But it was three bites before I came up for air.

Which is when I saw Deckart and Willets. They were sitting at the other picnic table. Willets was grinning with a beer in his hand. Deckart's face was red, as if he was concentrating on something. He held a Bowie knife in his right hand. His left was splayed, palm down on the picnic table. His knife hand was stabbing the point into the wood, between his own fingers. Stabbing fast. Willets was counting the hits. While Willets counted, Deckart was softly speaking to himself.

Then Willets looked up, saw me, and stopped counting.

# CHAPTER FORTY-THREE

When Willets stopped counting, Deckart lost concentration. Not a good thing if you're playing the knife game.

And Deckart was good at it. The tip of that Bowie knife was flying fast and furiously from the number one position to the number six and back, not necessarily in that order. The first position is back of the thumb, off to the side of the hand. The six position is the other side of the pinkie. In between you've got the spaces separating each finger. The basic game is played in a 1-2-3-4-5-6-5-4-3-2 sequence. Start off back of the thumb, work your way up past the pinkie, then back again. But Deckart wasn't doing the simple version. He was showing off with the Australian version, 1-2-1-3-1-4-1-5-1-6. Alternating between the first position and the others.

I had seen this game played quite a few times, in all kinds of weather and altitudes. Sometimes it ended well, sometimes it did not.

Deckart was moving fast, and he was singing. That didn't surprise me. The best knife game players perform a chant, like a knife mantra. The words are chanted counterpoint to the hitting of pointy steel on wood. One syllable, one knife hit. Fast as you can.

*I have all five fingers.*
*The blade goes chop chop chop*
*If I miss the spaces in-between my fingers will come off*
*And if I hit my fingers*
*The blood will soon come out*
*But all the same I play this game cause that's what it's all about*
*Oh, chop chop chop chop chop chop*
*I'm picking up the speed*
*And if I hit my fingers then my hand will start to bleed*

Each time Deckart started the chant again, he got faster. The concentration was so intense that when Willets stopped counting the hits, Deckart didn't notice at first and kept on working the knife. But then he noticed the missing link in his rhythm. The knife was flashing in the weak outdoor lighting. The movement of the blade through the fingers was complicated by the shadow cast from the bare bulb. All of this was mesmerizing. And then the Bowie knife stabbed straight through Deckart's ring finger.

He grunted in surprise and looked up, saw me, then looked down. The top of his finger was separated from the rest of it. I was getting to the end of the barbecue plate. Mopping up the red sauce with the remaining white bread. Willets and Deckart huddled over the severed finger tip.

At that moment, a great roar came from inside.

It was the sound of a pent-up crowd releasing their tension. I figured the game of bloody knuckles was over. There was a whole lot of movement. People from outside going back inside, to see what had happened. People from inside going outside to get barbecue. One of the contestants had won ten grand. Both of them had lost the full use of their dominant hand. Was it worth it? I figured it wasn't up to me to decide that.

Deckart was cursing. I walked over and sat down at their table. I said, "Super glue. That's what you need buddy. Just glue that thing back on and it might heal. I'd say you have a five-minute window."

But Deckart was not happy with me. Neither was Willets. Deckart was holding the tip of his finger on, as if it would stay there by itself. Willets was distracted, alternating between me and his injured friend. Deckart looked up at me, and I saw murder in his eyes.

Deckart said, "I'd as soon look at you as kill you."

I said, "Why not both?"

Deckart was barely managing to hold his anger in check. I looked at Willets, who was looking at me under hooded eyes. I saw calculation in them, but not necessarily the intelligent kind.

I said, "What?"

Then Willets launched himself at me, which is what I had been expecting. He came up out of the seat and over the top of the picnic table. His boot gripped the edge and then he was flailing for my neck, trying to get a height advantage. But I was already gone, slipped under the table and out the side again. When I came up, Willets was spinning around looking for me. He came at me another time. A flurry of fists and elbows, like he'd been watching videos of highly paid fighters. I deflected a right-handed head strike, stepped inside and took control of his arm. I used his own movement to leverage him over my shoulder, heaved, and threw him through the fence surrounding the barbecue area.

The guy serving barbecue nodded to me in approval. He said, "What happens outside the perimeter doesn't happen."

I stepped through the broken fence. Willets was getting up and dusting himself off. I surged into his space and open-hand slapped him hard on the ear. The strike put him back down. He coughed and spat.

Willets opened his hands wide. He said, "Alright. You win. Calm down."

But I had already seen him glancing over my shoulder. He was trying to lure me into dropping my guard. I had a pretty good idea of what it was that he'd seen behind me. I side-stepped, lowered into a crouch and swiveled on the balls of my feet. Deckart was coming with the Bowie knife.

A Bowie knife isn't a normal knife. For one thing, it is bigger. I needed to even the odds. So I put a right hook into Willets' jaw. He dropped straight down. No hands out to stop the fall, he tumbled like a plank, flat on his face.

Then I turned to Deckart. Just in time. He was bleeding from the left hand. The knife was in his right, held in the Filipino style. Thumb on the blade's spine. Deckart came low and fast, leading with his right foot, in line with the blade. Better for the reach. Good form.

Attack was the only way out.

As he came at me, I went at him. Which confused him at first. Usually people run away from a dangerous guy holding a Bowie knife, or they stick their hands up in self-defense. I came right at him and gave him no choice except to strike. Deckart's knife came hissing in low, going for the inguinal artery on the inside of my leg. I blocked him with a forearm deflection, then stepped in for an uppercut to the jaw.

He jerked his head back and my fist brushed his chin. No stubble. Deckart was already slashing at my neck arteries, going for the bleeders. I pushed his wrist wide and head-butted him hard. I was going for the nose but made contact with his cheekbone. The impact sent Deckart tumbling. Before he could react further, I stepped in and kicked him in the face for the second time that day. His head whipped back and bounced off the dirt. I crouched down and pulled a phone out of his jeans pocket. It was a cheap burner.

I said, "Going to need your phone, buddy." I thumbed through the buttons. All working fine with decent battery life left and a fine connection to the local cellular networks. "Appreciate it." I pushed the phone into my pocket. Deckart's nose was a bloody mess, twice squashed. He sprawled limp and defeated. I stood over him. Loose and ready for whatever he wanted to do. But he wasn't going to do anything, even if he had wanted to.

A little crowd had drawn into a circle around the fight. A loud wolf whistle cut through them. The onlookers moved back to reveal a late model gold Hummer. The driver's door was open and the short bald guy who everyone thought was Mister Lawrence sat behind the wheel looking at me. He was a guy in his fifties with the kind of face that stops evolving at puberty. His look was flat and bored. With overly generous lips around a half-opened mouth. No hair of any kind in sight.

Amber Chapman was in the back, window closed. Two guys from the security detail approached Deckart. One of them lifted him to his feet. The other faced off with me, looking straight into my eyes and holding two hands up, palms out. It was my friend with the pointy ears and the shaved head. The first guy spoke softly to Deckart. I didn't hear what was said. The guy's t-shirt rippled with muscle.

The pointy-eared guy staring at me was about thirty. Like the others, he was lean and fit and looked dangerous. Like a poster child for Special Forces. The other one was just like him. Like they grew them in a lab. The guy dealing with Deckart gave him a quick and violent shove. A short sharp rebuke. Then he turned and looked at me. His eyes closed sleepily for a fraction of a second. Not a blink, more like a kind of acknowledgement. Of what, I wasn't sure. Then he said something harsh to his pointy-eared colleague. Harsh and fast and completely incomprehensible to me, because he wasn't speaking English or whatever language they speak up in the tribal territories, he was speaking Russian.

The Russians cut through the crowd and into a matte black Hummer, idling behind Mister Lawrence's gold one. Chapman was still looking at me through the window, expressionless. As I looked at her, I thought of the eight-pointed star she'd drawn on the paper napkin. I was going to get to find out who that was for very soon, and hopefully what it meant. Because one thing was for sure, it wasn't meant for me. The vehicles moved out and her look went with them. Out of the parking lot and onto the road back toward the airport.

By the time they were gone, the mist was crawling in from the rainforest. A touch thicker than it had been on the way up. The crowd had dissipated and Deckart and Willets were gone. I took a tour around The Rendezvous to see where the Humvees had come from, and if there was another access road that I had missed. There wasn't. The vehicles had been parked alongside the building, butting up against the woods.

I used Deckart's phone to call Ellie while I walked back to the Toyota.

She picked up on the first ring. "Yeah?"

"Keeler."

Ellie exhaled, like she was relieved. She said, "I spoke to Dave. We shouldn't say anything on the phone. My place, one hour."

I said, "No, I need you up here at the Rendezvous. Immediately. How long will it take?"

She was silent for a moment, weighing it up. Down the line I could feel something like the tension in her cognitive functions. She wanted to ask why the Rendezvous, but knew that the discussion was a bad idea over the cellular line.

Ellie said, "The Rendezvous, huh? Ten minutes."

I said, "Parking lot, immediate left. Find me."

I thumbed the disconnect button. Climbed into the Toyota's cab and closed the door. The parking spot gave me a good view. The place was far from empty. I took brief stock of my feelings. I was calm and alert, enjoying myself. The minor ruckus hadn't even remotely dented the evening. On the contrary, the touch of violence had only elevated the experience.

And I could still taste Amber Chapman.

The mystery and the puzzle, all wrapped up in a tall blonde package. I thought about her and allowed my thinking to associate freely, and move from Amber Chapman over to Hagen, then to George Abrams and Valerie Zarembina. The mental threads were hooking up and locking into place gracefully, like they had meant to tie in all along. My thinking even extended out from those people to the United States Nuclear Regulatory Commission. I thought I had it pretty much figured out, but confirmation was going to happen real soon.

I reached over to the glove compartment and removed the Smith & Wesson special and the Glock 19. The S&W was a pretty gun with that comfortable blue rubberized grip. There were five rounds chambered in the rotating cylinder. But each .357 round packed a punch, so they'd be made to count. The Glock held a full magazine, plus one in the chamber. Which made sixteen rounds. Add the extra mag from the Nazi assassin and the total was thirty-one.

I laid the weapons down on the passenger side seat. One beside the other, with the spare magazine between them, like a little collection. I climbed into the rear and racked back the bench as far as it would go, sunk down and settled in to wait and watch.

# CHAPTER FORTY-FOUR

ONCE THE WARM air hanging over the water strikes cold land, it forms a mist and starts to roll. Then, it has two choices. Either to double down and thicken into fog, or dissipate, becoming nothing more than wet ground. At the moment, the stuff hadn't decided one way or the other. It was okay remaining as a rolling mist. I sat in the back of the Toyota, waiting for Ellie, and considered from which direction the recipient of Amber Chapman's message would most likely approach.

The roadhouse front door faced south east. Which meant it was facing town. Port Morris is a couple of hundred miles from the nearest inhabited place with a population over five hundred, but that's as the crow flies. You can't just drive from Port Morris to anywhere else. You'd need to throw together some kind of travel cocktail. A boat and a car would do it, but it would take around ten hours. A plane and a boat and a car would cut that down to eight.

I was pretty confident that whoever was coming was traveling up from Port Morris, just like I had. Which reduced the question to a binary choice. Direct or indirect. I thought of what I would do in that position. And the answer was always going to be the indirect approach.

If it was me, I would drive up via one of the logging trails. Then I'd come in on foot through the woods. Slowly and silently. That would give me the option of not showing up, if I thought there were issues. I would choose my route on the basis of tactical and strategic factors. Strategic in the sense of my exfiltration. Tactical with respect to local features, like the direction of the wind and the topography. But there was no wind. Just the low hanging mist inching up from the creeks and channels. Ellie was taking her time. My breath began fogging up the inside of the windshield, so I reached over and rolled the windows down.

Maybe it was the mist, maybe not. But the smell of salmon hung heavy in the air. Which wasn't surprising, given that we were bang in the middle of their spawning season. The creeks and rivers were brimming with fish expending their last energy. Each one a story of success and struggle and maybe ultimate frustration. Each one spawned by an elder fish upstream. And each one coming of age in the great Pacific Ocean. The wild salmon is a predator, hunting smaller creatures. Once mature, the hunter returns to the sweet water creeks to spawn and die. Which is not as simple as it sounds. Each of them has to fight its way upstream, against the flow, against the wishes of the bears and eagles and fishermen who harness all their guile in an effort to prevent the fish from its purpose. In the end, what did the salmon get for the effort? Death and reincarnation as another nameless fish, just like the first.

The same but different.

Ellie's pickup truck pulled into the lot. She swept it around in front of me with a satisfying rolling crunch of large tires on gravel, coming to a stop twenty yards away. A minute later she was in the backseat of the Toyota with me. Ellie came with a scent of soap. I stole a glance at her. She looked good. Fresh and ready. I turned back to the view.

I said, "You look well rested."

"Hardly. Sorry it took me longer than I thought. Some kind of a wildlife incident on the road from town. What have you got?"

I was looking out the window, at the parking lot. Scanning the tree line on the other side.

"Chapman was in there. We had words. Not many because she is in a situation." I looked at Ellie. I had her attention. I said, "She's a player Ellie, not some kind of accidental victim. She's managed to get in with the Mister Lawrence crew, and it looks like they're taking her onto the property."

Ellie snorted. "Why would they do that?"

I said, "According to her, the guy everyone thinks is Mister Lawrence is some kind of an *evil clown*, her words. She seems to have exploited the clown and she's in there with them, wearing a dress and everything. You know how it is."

I caught Ellie nodding in my peripheral vision.

"Playing the femme fatale."

I nodded.

"When I was in there, I saw her leaving a message for someone. Someone who isn't me. Like what they call a dead drop in the spying business. Which is what I think we're dealing with here. She didn't see me seeing her. I've got some ideas about what's going on with Chapman. I think I've got a pretty clear picture in fact. But there isn't much reason for me to explain the ideas to you because we're about to find out who she left that message for. And when we do, we'll be hearing about a whole lot of other things as well."

Ellie was staring at me. "Are we now."

"Yes. I think so. And I wanted you to be with me so I wouldn't have to repeat it to you later. Save me the effort."

"Plus you missed me."

"Plus what else were you going to do tonight?"

"True, watching TV with young Hank wasn't as fun as this."

I said, "You're kidding, right?"

"Yes, I don't have a TV."

"What about you? Smithson and the building plans. Any of it work out?"

Ellie sank into the seat. I figured the tops of our heads were just about visible from outside, if you were looking hard and had very good night vision. She said, "First Smithson. I interrupted his favorite TV show, which wasn't something that he took very well. But he got over it and we had a conversation. The upshot is that he has agreed to get in touch with the FBI if he can get that past his boss. He said that he will let me know as soon as he knows."

I said, "Which is something he's going to get concerned with right away, or is he waiting for the show to be over?"

She shrugged. "I pushed him hard as I could. I said tonight. We shall see."

I wasn't surprised. "Luck with the building plans?"

"Luck didn't play much of a part in it, Keeler. Code Enforcement. I got the key from the chief enforcement officer. You know how it is, small town, no big deal."

I said, "We've got time, give me the details."

Ellie glanced at me and smiled. "The guy even delivered the key to me, Keeler. That's what I'm talking about. In his pajamas, wearing a pair of construction boots."

"Nice."

"Right, so I went into the office, flicked on the lights. Couple of rows of filing cabinets, cream-colored, steel boxes filled with papers in folders. All organized by geography."

"Coffee machine working?"

"I didn't stick around long enough to need coffee. Plus, I'm particular about my coffee. I like dark roasted."

"What did you find?"

"I took the whole folder. They filed plans for the build seven years ago. I didn't have any time to examine what it amounts to. Not like I'm a trained architect either."

I said, "Sounds good. You bring that with you?"

"No. Back at the house."

I nodded to myself. "Okay. Well done. After this we'll go back to your place and take a look. Make some of that dark roast coffee."

While we talked, my eye had been drawn to the edge of the lot where I'd seen the raccoons emerge earlier. A narrow gulley running along a slight incline to the east of the Rendezvous. At first there was nothing but stillness and the mist slowly crawling up. But I hung in there, because I trust my intuition. Which paid off when there was movement. A flicker before absolute stillness.

I stopped talking and Ellie said, "What is it?"

I said nothing. I held my breath and concentrated upon what I was looking at. For a while, nothing happened. Maybe a minute or longer. Then the bearded giant, Jakob Hagen, walked out of the woods and strode purposefully toward The Rendezvous.

Ellie and I watched him stroll. It wasn't like the guy had any other way of moving. He was ripped and ready, like a one-man bulldozer. But I'd seen an intelligence there that belied the menace. Too smart to be a simple thug. Maybe a complicated thug.

Once Hagen was inside, I collected the pistols from the passenger seat and put them in my jacket pockets. Smith & Wesson on the left, Glock on the right. The spare magazine went in the back pocket of my jeans and I was ready to roll.

I said, "You follow me."

We didn't walk across the lot. Instead, we moved back from the Toyota into the woods, and worked our way painstakingly around to that gulley. I led the way laterally, avoiding a descent to the trail I figured Hagen had taken. That way, when he came back out he wouldn't see any disturbed twigs or rocks that might alert him. The mist helped.

After about a half mile, the gulley resolved in a boulder-filled creek, pregnant with water boiling down from the hills. On the other side of the creek was a steep incline. I had a hunch that Hagen had parked his car on the other side of it. I figured I had at least a couple of minutes, so I carefully scanned the area. Five minutes later I discovered a faint boot print on one of the stepping stones that poked out of the rolling water. A big boot, which had crossed the creek toward the Rendezvous.

I showed it to Ellie and she nodded. I pointed her to a spot behind boulders a half-dozen yards from the crossing point. I came close and spoke softly. "You stay there and watch for my lead. If he crosses at the same spot, we won't have to worry about lines of fire, if it comes to that."

Ellie removed the Ruger from her holster and chambered a round. The action snicked softly, a different set of frequencies from the rushing water. She moved off in the darkness.

I concealed myself between two truck-sized boulders that Hagen would have to pass through if he was taking that path. The moving water was loud. There was no way I'd hear him coming. I could see the way up the gulley, but I figured it was too dark to be seen.

I leaned back against the damp stone and made myself calm and silent, allowed my pulse and breathing to slow down. It felt nice to be there. Peaceful with the sound of rushing water.

Fifteen minutes later there was movement up the trail. Hagen was picking his way down the gulley, keeping an eye on his footing. Which meant he wasn't looking ahead. I let him get over the creek, making his way one foot at a time over the stones. When he stepped over that last stretch of water, he entered the range of his own gun.

Hagen must have sensed my presence because he looked up from the ground then, and we locked eyes. I stepped forward.

I said, "What does it mean?"

The Smith & Wesson special was pointed directly at his head. With five of his own bullets in the cylinder, Hagen knew the likely outcome if he made a wrong move. He tensed up at first and looked very concerned, and rightly so. My finger was already teasing back the trigger, finding the sweet spot. I was prepared to pull at the slightest opportunity. I wouldn't have been surprised if he tried something, I would have put him down and moved on.

But Hagen did exactly the right thing. He relaxed and shrugged, moved his hands away from his body. He said, "You mean the symbol. The eight-pointed star."

I said, "Yes."

"It means a high-level thief. Usually it's a tattoo. A prison tattoo."

"A Russian prison tattoo."

He nodded. "That's right."

"So given the context, right here and now, what does that eight-pointed star tell you?"

"It's a confirmation, Mr Keeler. We are dealing with the theft of nuclear materials at a high level."

## CHAPTER FORTY-FIVE

I said, "How would Chapman know that, if she hasn't yet entered the compound?"

Hagen had his hands raised, palms up and out. He said, "May I reach into my jacket pocket to show you something?"

"Open the jacket first."

Hagen opened the black leather jacket. There was something rectangular held by the inside pocket.

I said, "Take it out."

He removed a burner phone. "It isn't just a phone, it's a radiation detector. Measures different kinds of emission. Chapman has one concealed in a lipstick case. If she sent this message it means that she's detected sufficient trace radiation to make that assessment."

"You mean radiation from the people she's been with?"

He said nothing.

I said, "Show me."

Hagen thumbed buttons on the phone, a combination of dialer numbers and side buttons. He held it up for me to see. I was looking at a little green screen with numbers on it. Low numbers, with decimal points that made them even smaller. Hagen looked around and pointed to a crop of craggy boulders in the creek.

He said, "Those boulders are Alaskan white granite. Which is a stone containing trace elements of radioactive stuff. Like uranium, and thorium. This should get a reading. You want me to show you?"

I gestured for Hagen to continue. I said, "What are you, a nuclear scientist or something?"

Hagen kept his hands up and walked to the stones. He looked the epitome of a Hell's Angel, but he was speaking like a college professor. He said, "Actually yes, I am."

When he arrived at the granite stone, the device in Hagen's hand began to click. First slow, then more rapid. Until it was clicking along steadily like a pacemaker on a rabbit.

Hagen read off the screen. "Zero point four one BQ, which stands for Becquerel. A very low trace, but fine to demonstrate. The device is sensitive."

I said, "Geiger counter?"

Hagen shook his head, "Geiger counter is too crude, it's fine for Gamma rays. This can detect those and others, like alpha particles. It's a Scintillation Counter, if you want the technical term."

I said, "Why the fancy dead drop with an eight-pointed star instead of a simple phone message?"

Hagen said, "We don't communicate interesting information over the phone."

I said, "I figure there must be a whole bunch of you out there, graduating in nuclear physics. What is that, a growth industry now?"

He stood up. Turned to me and shrugged again. "How do we end up doing what we do? I think a lot of it has to do with luck and coincidence, don't you agree, Keeler?"

Ellie had kept back. She was listening and she was armed. I lowered the Smith & Wesson, easing off the trigger. "I'm curious about the Porterhouse Bar, where you and Chapman put on that grand performance. That was staged for my benefit alone. You wanted me involved, but how did you know who I was?"

"We wanted you involved because we needed you. It was Chapman who found you among the fishermen. You were her idea. I just followed her orders."

I straddled a large boulder at the water's edge. Facing Hagen, keeping him between me and Ellie.

"Okay Hagen, let me take a stab at straightening this out."

Hagen looked at me with a little smile on his face, visible in the ambient moonlight coming off the mist.

I said, "You and Chapman are Russians. I'm guessing that you work for some unit of the Federal Security Service, investigating what my own government has refused or neglected to look into." Hagen hadn't moved or changed expressions. The same little smile was stuck inside of that beard. "Correct me if I get anything wrong."

He nodded.

I said, "For you people, this is all about the nuclear submarine. K-349. You must be working for a branch of the FSB that does non-proliferation. I figure you got up here because your people had gotten wind of a black market salvage job."

Hagen nodded. "K-349 went down twelve years ago. We picked up chatter about a successful salvage attempt two years ago. It wasn't any kind of good information, nothing actionable. But it was believable. So, the office developed a team to make computer models."

I said, "Like a map of possible places to store a stolen nuclear submarine."

"Correct. Believe it or not, there aren't very many. Not thousands anyway. Distance to the salvage site, depth at port, you get the picture. Port Morris was one of them."

"Okay. So far so good. You get wind of the salvaged nuclear sub. It's Russian, so you people feel a sense of responsibility about it. You lost it, and you failed to find it. Now you've got to do something about it."

Hagen was picking up pebbles and lobbing them into the water. "Well, in the beginning it was only chatter. Rumors and stuff coming in from the various listening stations."

I said, "But you people are devious and careful, and I mean that in a good way. Instead of committing resources yourselves, you decide to move through us. Chapman gets in early, gets her hooks into the United States Nuclear Regulatory Commission via a romantic affair with this kid, George Abrams. You people had identified him as a consultant for the USNRC's Office of Investigations. Being a consultant, he was easier to latch on to because you figured, rightly, that there would be less security around him. Chapman makes the initial approach to George Abrams at the conference in Estonia."

I was watching Hagen. He gave an almost imperceptible nod. "Go on."

I continued. "Chapman hooks into Abrams the consultant. She feeds him the K-349 story, in some subtle way that makes him think it was his own idea. He feeds it to his boss, Valerie Zarembina. So far, so good. It's the next part that I have trouble with."

Hagen scooped up a handful of pebbles and started grinding them in his hand. He said, "Yes to all of what you just said. But of course, none of that mattered because Zarembina's own people at the USNRC didn't believe her about K-349." He chuckled, shook his head and looked at me with a smile. "The bosses didn't think there was enough evidence and they refused to commit resources to it."

"But George Abrams managed to make Zarembina into a believer."

Hagen said, "Yes. Ultimately, yes."

"Zarembina sends Abrams up on a freelance mission, because she's sure it's real."

He nodded.

I said, "And that's why we don't have a thousand federal officers swarming over town right this moment."

Hagen said, "That's correct. I'm sure they'll come eventually, when it's too late."

I said, "But we aren't dealing in eventually, we are the ones right here, right now. Let's go back to you, Hagen. The team is you and Chapman. She's the senior officer. I figure she's got a degree in physics, but you're the real scientist. You look like a guy who kills bears with his hands but you're more of a geek. She's the real soldier. You come up here before Chapman, preparing the ground. You join up with Deckart via the security job at the cruise ship. You look the part, and no doubt you've got some faked credentials to prove it."

Hagen said, "You don't need much for that job, Keeler. Once we'd found a probable location for K-349, we did a lot of research. We found this Mister Lawrence group. Tried everything we could to get in with their organization, but they run a tight ship. The next thing was to look around at their contractors. Sort of the same thing we did with the USNRC. Found Deckart and took it from there."

"Not bad work."

He shrugged. "Well, it wasn't quite enough actually. We didn't expect the resistance we got from the Mister Lawrence people, or how deep they'd dug themselves in here." He laughed once. "Felt like we were back home in Russia or something."

I said, "And then what, figured you needed a little extra help?"

We were about ten feet from Ellie's position. Hagen emptied the handful of stones into the creek. "Something like that. It was Chapman's call. We were stuck. Going nowhere fast. She decided that we needed to insert a little chaos into the equation. Boris Spassky's got a famous chess proverb. Something about when you're stuck in a stalemate position, the best thing to do is to make a completely unpredictable move and see what possibilities open up. You were Chapman's move, Keeler."

I said, "I was the element of chaos you needed. Smart choice. Smart how Chapman allowed Zarembina to think she'd made the call herself."

Hagen said nothing. I said, "What?"

He said, "Arrogance. That's what made her easy to control. To be honest." He looked up from the creek.

I said, "What was Abrams supposed to do up here?"

Hagen said, "Abrams works on non-linear acoustics. Which is a complicated and dry topic. The important thing to know is that he's the kind of guy who figures out how to either find something underwater or hide something underwater."

"Give me the cliff notes version."

"The simple version is that you can't use regular vision to find things underwater. It isn't practical, and there's a far better way to detect stuff because of how sound waves travel through liquid."

"Sonar. Like a beeping version of radar."

Hagen said, "Correct. You throw a sound wave at something, measure the way it comes back. Seems simple, but it isn't. You need the academic minds in there to figure it out."

I said, "So Abrams was like the Seal Team Six of underwater detection, but what about hiding stuff?"

"Abrams' research was all about figuring out how to make sounds that can hide an underwater asset, rather than finding it. He was able to construct precise noise fields built from frequencies that were designed to absorb the sonar pings."

"Like a composer or something. A counter-surveillance sound artist."

Hagen snorted. "Something like that, although nothing that can be detected by the human ear."

I said, "But you never found out what he discovered up here in Alaska."

"From what George Abrams told Chapman," Hagen said, "His job here was to listen for exactly the kind of sound fields that he would have used to hide something like K-349. But the kid disappeared. It hasn't worked out very well in the end."

I shook my head. "You're wrong there, Hagen. It's working out fine, far as I can see. The kid disappeared. He took one for the team, which is a message all by itself. It says that he found something. It's like he was putting a gift in a box, but didn't have time to finish the job. Now we're going to wrap this all up and tie a bow on it."

Hagen said, "I wish I were as optimistic as you."

"You would be, if you were an American. But you're not. What we've got here is a situation gone FUBAR. It isn't looking good for George Abrams. Best case scenario, the whole thing just ends."

He said, "And what's your proposition for ending it?"

"I'm working on it. The only thing I'm quite sure of is that it's going to happen tonight."

Hagen said, "So you agree that we're on the same side, with the same intentions?"

I said, "More or less. Who are the Russian boys working for Mister Lawrence?"

Hagen nodded. "That's the other complication, and one of the reasons we needed to go in with a low profile. Mister Lawrence was smart enough to hire Russian mercenaries. Maybe they knew that we would be the most interested in tracing our missing property. The mercenaries are known as the Wagner Group. Very efficient, and very dangerous. All veterans of the war in Syria."

I nodded. "I know them. Killed a few, happy to kill more. Slightly weird, Russians going up against Russians."

Hagen shrugged. "Internal competition, same everywhere. Wagner group is run-out of our military intelligence agency, the GRU, we're the FSB. They won't hesitate to kill us all."

Ellie's boots crunched gravel. We both looked at her. The Ruger was down at her side. I said, "All good?"

Ellie said, "I've got a question."

I spoke to Hagen, "This is Ellie."

He looked at her and nodded. "Shoot." He smiled, like he'd made a joke.

She said, "How did you know that Chapman was going to be at the Rendezvous? She had no phone."

Hagen broadened the smile and looked at me with raised eyebrows.

I said, "Give me your wallet, Hagen." He pulled the wallet out of his jeans pocket, tossed it at me. I caught the tight leather package in my left hand and flipped it open. About a hundred and twenty in cash. Including one ten and a five. I hesitated and chose the five. I handed the bill to Ellie. "See if you can find a message on there."

Ellie used the light from her phone to scan the five-dollar bill. She found what I had expected her to find. She said, "RDV dash 5. Written right on Abe Lincoln's forehead in ballpoint pen."

Ellie handed the five back to Hagen. "What's RDV?"

I spoke to Ellie. "RDV is the French contraction for the word Rendezvous. The other part is what, fifth toilet counting clockwise?" Hagen nodded. "Chapman gives the bum a five-dollar bill, and then you show up and offer him a twenty in exchange for five in change."

Ellie said, "Did the drunk guy even know what he was doing?"

Hagen said, "I don't think he did, no."

I said, "That's a nuclear scientist for you. Smart." I looked at Hagen. "How did you know he wouldn't spend it?"

Hagen smiled very slightly. "No such thing as zero risk, right Keeler?"

I turned the Smith & Wesson around and handed it to him. He took the gun and inspected it. "Thanks."

I said, "Your uncle really gave that to you?"

"Some kind of an uncle, yes."

"Tell me something Hagen, how does it end. I mean as far as you and Chapman are concerned. What's a satisfactory outcome from your point of view."

Hagen shrugged. "We need to get the nuclear materials out of the hands of the thieves and into the hands of a responsible party."

"Such as the government of the United States of America."

Hagen nodded. "Yes."

With my other hand, I removed the Glock from my jacket pocket. I saw his expression change, from friendly to cautious. I said, "There's one more thing I need to tell you."

Hagen watched me. "What's that?"

I said, "Once it's done, I'll need you on a boat back to Russia. Either that or I'll bury you here."

For a while Hagen said nothing, remained motionless as if his pause button had been depressed. He said, "You would bury me, personally with your own hands?"

"I meant that proverbially."

He nodded. "I understand, yes. That's how it is going to be."

He held out a massive hand and I brought mine up to meet it. Hagen said something in Russian which I didn't understand. He said it again in English. "Russian proverb: Better to have a hundred friends than a hundred rubles."

"Amen brother."

# CHAPTER FORTY-SIX

We split from Hagen at the creek.

I wanted to look at the plans Ellie had retrieved from the code enforcement office. She and Hagen discussed the details of how to get to her house. Hagen climbed past the boulders and up the bank to his vehicle. Ellie and I returned the way we had come, stepping across the creek over stones. Now that I wasn't focused on Hagen, I noticed other sounds. There was the wind and the water, and there was something else. Which made me look to my left. Several forms moved in the mist, animal shapes. The shapes came with sounds and smell. The sounds were low and guttural, the smell was heavy and pungent. I realized that we were sharing the creek with other creatures. I looked at Ellie.

She turned to me with a grin. "Bears drinking. Isn't that cute?"

When we emerged from the woods back to the roadhouse, old-school country music was seeping out of the Rendezvous. A couple of men were sitting on the porch drinking from tall beer bottles. As I crossed the lot, a woman came out the front door, banging it loudly and shouting.

When we arrived back at the vehicles, Ellie turned to me. "Let's summarize."

I leaned back against the Land Cruiser. "You want to go first or want me to go first?"

"You were closer to him, so you heard it better. I'm a little fuzzy on the details."

"I thought you wanted the summary."

"Okay I'll go first. You fill in anything I'm missing." She leaned against the truck next to me.

I said, "Shoot."

Ellie was looking up at the place where dark sky ran into the treetops.

"The big guy and Chapman are Russian spies with an anti-proliferation unit of the FSB. The Russians figured out where the stolen submarine is located but they wanted proof before committing." She looked at me. I nodded.

"So far so good."

"So rather than send in a bigger team, they figured they'd get the Americans to do the heavy lifting for them. Chapman has an in with the USNRC via the hook up with George Abrams as an unwitting agent. She feeds him information that he feeds to Zarembina. That leads to George Abrams getting sent up here to investigate. But I don't get why he came alone."

"You missed an important step Ellie. Valerie Zarembina wanted to investigate. I met her. She was smart and tough, maybe fearless even. The kind of woman who would go all the way if she had a strong intuition. Zarembina felt that whatever Abrams had was good enough, but someone further up the ladder in the USNRC didn't agree. So, at that point the investigation is blocked. My guess is that Chapman slipped Abrams something extra, enough to push Zarembina over the edge and send young George up here alone. Probably she wanted to gather irrefutable proof."

Ellie was nodding. "Right. Which is why we're here now. George stopped responding. I guess Zarembina freaked out and came up here to try and clean up the mess, hoping to extract her agent."

"And behind all that is Chapman and Hagen, quietly scheming."

She said, "Yeah but we're talking about stolen nuclear materials. There's more at stake than George Abrams or any other individual person. Like you said, Abrams took one for the team. Am I supposed to blame the Russians here?"

"I don't. They had a major problem and needed it solved. Institutional failure both ways. Their people lost the sub, ours lost the opportunity to get the hint from Zarembina. Or worse, the Mister Lawrence people go deep and somebody's bank account got a bump."

Ellie said, "And now Chapman's put herself in the middle of it. Woman's got courage."

"Damn right she does."

Ellie looked at me. I shrugged. "You straight now?"

She said, "Enough for now. What about Dave? Can we let him go home?"

Dave had worked out as a useful appendage to the operation. "Yes. You should bring him a donut. It's the least he deserves."

Ellie nodded and brought out her phone. She tapped a couple of times on the screen and then held it up to her ear. Nothing. She looked at me. "Not answering. Goes straight to voice mail."

I said, "Dave's had an eventful evening. I bet he's asleep. You want me to go check on him?"

Ellie shook her head. "I'll cruise by on my way home. Maybe bring him that donut." She walked away from the Land Cruiser. Turned back and said, "See you when I see you."

Ellie got into her Ford pickup truck. The engine growled and then she was gone. Taillights receded into the dark. I pulled out after her.

About a mile from the roadhouse, the Land Cruiser hit the asphalt again. Tires that had been rocking over gravel now began to hum. I was back in America, whatever that was supposed to mean. I blew past the airport with the fence on my right. The runway was a strange field of mist, like a soft and flat surface that went on as far as the eye could see. Which wasn't far, given the reduced visibility. I had come in from a logging trail alongside the southern fence. Past that was another length of straight asphalt before a T-junction.

When I arrived at the junction there were three choices. But only two of them were viable. Left and right were official roads, straight ahead was a logging trail. Ellie would have taken the left turn, back to town and Dave. To get to Ellie's I would take a right turn. Problem was, it was blocked off by pylons and a big temporary Alaska Department of Fish and Game sign. The sign had the departmental logo on top, a circle divided into three horizontal areas: a goose above, a moose in the middle, and a Coho salmon on the bottom. The sign read 'Road Closure: Accident Ahead'.

I remembered Ellie saying that she had been delayed by a 'wildlife situation', I figured this was it. Who knows what had gotten hit by a truck up here. The logging trail was my best option.

The trail was wide for several miles, before pinching in and getting rough. I put the pedal to the metal and maxed out the four-wheel-drive, taking the turns hard and rollicking over bumps. I had the windows down and felt a surge of exuberant energy, which made me lean my head out the window and holler into the night.

The trail descended and the headlight beams got sucked into mist before they could project more than a yard or two. Making it only a touch better than driving with a blindfold. I flipped up the high beams. When the road dipped again, I was flashed in the eyes by another set of high beams reflecting in the rear-view mirror. Another vehicle was following close. I punched the gas and got some separation. But the mist was tough to penetrate. Which only made me want to push the Toyota harder. The vehicle behind maintained its distance, set back a couple of hundred yards.

After a couple of minutes the lights behind me were gone. But there hadn't been any other roads for it to go on. Maybe the car behind had turned off their lights to follow me in the dark.

I smiled to myself in the darkness of the Land Cruiser's cab, which must have looked wicked in the dim light from the dashboard. I was enjoying the thought of Deckart attempting to use his brains. The guy had put together some kind of a plan.

Bring it on.

# CHAPTER FORTY-SEVEN

I WAS CRUISING down the track at a considerable speed when I saw the thing, about three seconds before crashing right into it. A grey hump emerged from the low hanging gloom, right in front of the Toyota. A mound almost as wide as the trail itself. Three seconds was enough to hit the brakes and turn three into six. The big old Land Cruiser fishtailed like an angry rattlesnake until it came to a stop right up against the thing.

Which, in the strong light from the vehicle, was obviously a very large animal.

I looked in the rear-view. No more lights following. I came down from the Toyota and approached. The animal musk was there. Similar to what I'd sensed at the creek with the bears, but stronger. A close and thick stench. The thing was not dead, it was agitated and moaning and grunting.

And then I saw the distinctive antlers and knew that it was a moose. A moose isn't some kind of overgrown deer. It is another kind of thing altogether. Not on the level of an elephant, but maybe halfway there.

This one looked to be about ten feet long, which made it an adult male of the species. Standing, he would come up about six, seven feet at the shoulders. The moose was struggling, he was definitely not having a good day. My initial thought was that he had been hit by a car and come down through the woods from the main road, wounded and spooked. I looked for signs of damage by the light of the Land Cruiser's high beams.

But then I got up close and saw two things. One was the bright pink feathering of a tranquilizing dart in his neck, which had been hidden from view by the antlers. The other was the moose's enormous front leg, and the blood spilling all over the gravel trail. But the bright blood told only one part of the story and didn't attract my attention so much as the cut from which it spilled. Which was clean and vivid in the hard light, splitting the flesh unnaturally. I was able to see the cross-section of muscle, and the white tendon, severed too perfectly. The moose was floundering in a pool of his own blood, heaving and shifting on the gravel, unable to stand, but trying desperately to do so. The blood didn't come from a single cut, but four. Each of his limbs had been cleanly scored by a razor sharp blade wielded by a human hand. This intentionally cruel person had severed tendons to hamstring the moose, leaving him alive but incapable of getting up or moving.

I could think of only two reasons why someone might want to do that. One was to block my path and prevent me from continuing down the trail, and the other was for the pure psychopathic enjoyment of cruelty to another living being. Those cognitive processes took about a half second, and during that half second I detected another sound. Another, because it wasn't the humming car engine or the moose, who was making enough noise all by himself, grunting and groaning and heaving. It was a distinctly human sound, that of a foot stepping on gravel. Specifically a booted foot. And then there was a flicker in the murky dark beyond the headlights, as the high beams from the Toyota glinted off dull metal.

There was no time, so I lurched to my left and dropped. I allowed my body to relax and let gravity do its work, tucking my head under. I heard the abrupt and brutal sound of a shotgun cartridge firing. At about the same time, give or take a millisecond, I was hit. The shooter was using lightweight bird-shot, which would have been a good thing, if it wasn't for all the negative implications. Good because number nine shot won't kill you from twenty feet. Bad because it meant they wanted me alive. Very bad because, given what he'd been prepared to do to the moose, I wasn't optimistic about his plans for me.

The initial blast had propelled something like 600 pellets out of the 12 gauge barrel. They'd shot out in a tight pattern, but seeing as the pellets were light, they'd spread quickly. About ten or twenty of them struck me in the neck and the side of my face, the other five hundred and eighty odd pellets swooshed past and shattered the Toyota's left headlight. So, first thing I did when I hit the ground was raise the Glock and take out the other light.

One shot.

Which left me lying in the dark alongside a sedated and hamstrung moose with bird-shot embedded in my face and neck. But at least it was now dark, but not impossibly so. There's always going to be some ambient light coming down through the break in tree cover over a trail. The moose went still, maybe trying to understand what was going on, which might have been tough in normal circumstances, but incredibly difficult under the influence of a tranquilizer. That was one confused moose. I heard the shuffle of booted feet, two sets. What I didn't see or hear was the vehicle that'd been following me.

Which made me think of two sets of adversaries, the ones following, and the ones setting the trap. The ones who had set the trap were right up there with me on the other side of the moose. The ones following were sitting back and waiting. No way to kill two birds with one stone.

Many people finding themselves in a position like that would get up and run for the trees. I did the opposite and rolled closer to the moose. I figured he was so big that I could hide in the black shadow of his mass.

I backed right up to the animal, warm and bristly. I got perfectly still. Around me the moose was becoming agitated. He was trying to raise himself, wounded, incoherent, and double spooked by the gunfire. But there was no way he was going to get up. I was worried about being crushed if he lurched in the wrong way. I could feel my face burning with shot, dripping blood. I resisted the urge to wipe the blood away.

I heard an excited voice from the other side of the wounded animal, speaking low. "You get him?"

Another voice. "Yeah, but I can't see."

I recognized those voices, but couldn't place them. It was not Deckart or Willets.

The first voice spoke again, this time I detected slurring of the speech. He had been drinking. He said, "Fucking moose. What am I, a lucky genius or what?"

The other man said, "Shut up, Gavin."

I placed the voices. Gavin. The skinny prison guard who had set me up with the 1488 goons.

I saw a dark upright humanoid form creeping around the side of the stricken animal. I put up the Glock and pulled the trigger on two rounds, bang-bang. Directly into the figure's center mass. Then it was time to move.

I rolled out from under the moose and came up behind the first tree I happened to bump into. There was a sudden flurry of movement to my left, so I put two rounds in that direction and rolled off the tree. A second shotgun blast barked. The tree protected me. Shredded wood shot past and tinkled into the undergrowth. By now I was counting my ammunition. Five rounds fired, one that had already been in the chamber, plus the four pushed up from the fifteen round mag. Eleven rounds waiting.

Someone coughed near the moose. There was a sound of grunting from the animal. Then a whole lot of shuffling and shifting and heavy breathing.

I stopped behind another tree and stayed absolutely still and silent. Quiet enough to hear stealthy movement from the woods, across the trail from my position. Like someone tip-toeing through the forest. I stayed still another couple of seconds. More movement, this time further away. The second guy was trying to get away. Trying to do it quietly. The one I'd shot was wounded, and no longer on two feet. There were guttural noises coming from there and a muffled cry. Like moose and man combined in one flailing package of misery. I crossed the trail and entered the trees.

I moved fast and quiet. My aim was to flank the guy who was trying to get away. I came around without making any effort to get a visual on him. Concentrating on moving fast enough to get ahead of the guy. I cut inside his line. In front of him, and in his path. I stuck myself against a large tree.

A moment later, I heard loud panting, and heavy footsteps approaching. The guy didn't know how to walk quietly in the woods. He came level with me and I saw his silhouette. A heavily built guy. The other prison guard, the one with the tattooed arms. I had the Glock up. Problem was the other people, the ones who had been following me in the car. I had no location on them, no idea where they might be.

It was best if they felt the same way about me. I slid the Glock into the waistband at my back. My knife thumbed open with a soft click.

I considered throwing the knife at the guy. The salmon season on a purse seiner is interesting and tough work. But there is downtime. In such times, the fisherman will occupy himself with knife work. Many guys carve things into wood. Like pretty maritime pictures, or the initials of their girlfriend's name. I used the time to practice my throwing technique. Which was good. I could nail a target at six feet, no problem. Hard. I could get that point buried into soft wood. I knew the weight of that knife like an extra limb of my own body. Like what the scientists call proprioception.

But that would not be necessary here. Which was too bad, I'd never taken down an enemy that way.

I could see the dark hulking form against the darker background. I was close enough to the tree that he didn't see me there. The guy was breathing heavily. I could hear his teeth chattering. He was condition black, panicking, not seeing anything clearly. I was condition orange. On the spectrum of combat awareness, the precise opposites.

Condition black, the world converges into an impenetrable morass of chaos and fear.

Condition orange, the world divides into discrete and intelligible elements, harmony.

I was able to weigh and judge with care. I stayed patient and let him come. The knife was up and out. My thumb on the butt for added force. Once he was close enough that I could recognize his face, I stepped forward and stabbed down diagonally through his left clavicle, otherwise known as the collarbone.

It's the only horizontal bone in the body, and it takes a slim and long blade to get in there. But once you do, there's nothing left but quick death from the internal bleeding of severed arteries right up close to the heart. I wasn't completely sure that the fishing knife was going to do the job. So, I used extra force. The collarbone snapped under my fist. I felt the collapse and the extra penetration, gaining maybe two inches or more. The knife went right past the clavicle and did its work in there.

I took his weight down and lowered him into the undergrowth nice and easy. My other hand covered his mouth and I kept it there until he was well into his death rattle. Up close I recognized the prison guard's face, eyes bulging and staring at me. With what he'd done to the moose, I figured the guy deserved to enjoy the rest of his death alone.

I picked up his fallen gun. The contours and shape were familiar, a Remington Breacher.

I slipped back through the woods to the trail. The moose wasn't any happier. I'd have to take care of that and ease his suffering. But first the human threat. I walked around the struggling animal and looked for the guy I'd shot, the one named Gavin.

For a moment I couldn't find him. Then I did. He was pinned under the moose. Only a leg and an arm stuck out. The phantom limbs looked permanently out of commission. Gavin must have slumped after I'd shot him, slid under there and been finished off by the restless beast. If he wasn't already dead, the weight of the animal would have been enough to suffocate him. I waited for the moose to shift. When he did, I pulled the body out by the arm and leg. It was Gavin alright. He had a surprised expression on his face. But he wasn't surprised anymore. He was dead.

I was focusing my mind on the others. Safe in their vehicle, up the trail. I was angry. Not in any unfocused way, and not because they wanted to kill me. Fair game. I was pissed off because of the moose, who hadn't asked for any kind of trouble, he'd just been minding his own business. Or worse, he'd been hit by a car and then used to try and trap me. The more I thought about it, the angrier I got.

The moose looked at me, eyeballs pale in the moonlight. I put a hand on his head. The eyes blinked. I said, "Give me a minute, buddy." I hoped that the tranquilizer was still working.

## CHAPTER FORTY-EIGHT

I FIGURED it was Deckart and Willets up there, and that they deserved a terrible and surprising end.

The Toyota's engine was still going, had never stopped running. I pulled the vehicle around on the narrow trail, carefully performing a K-turn. My mind was firing off orders to my driving hands and foot. At the same time, it was making other calculations. They'd have heard the two shotgun blasts, and the four little popping sounds from the Glock. So, they'd be thinking about what might have happened. I wondered how they were judging it. Two shotguns, one shot off each. One handgun, two sequences of two shots. Bang-bang twice. That would be hard to call.

I drove slow at first, not wanting to make any more noise than the Toyota had already been making. The noisiest part of a vehicle is the tires on the road. Engine hum pales in comparison. My goal was to reduce the sound of tires on the trail.

I crept up the track for a sixty-second count. I estimated that they would have stopped close by, no more than a half mile. The Toyota had no working headlights, and I didn't want to use the brakes because the taillights would give away my position. I wanted nothing but darkness. After that first sixty count, I stopped trying to navigate consciously and went on pure instinct. I counted another thirty seconds slow creeping. Then it was time to make the magic happen.

I hit the accelerator and shot the Toyota up the trail.

I had a dim memory of that part being pretty straight. I must have hit sixty going up the small gradient. The engine was whining maniacally and the Toyota was definitely making noise from all aspects of its locomotion. Which is why they did exactly what I figured they might do. They flipped on their headlights to see what was coming at them.

I saw the Subaru in a blinding flash of white. Much closer than I had estimated. I was really right on top of them. I almost drove right by them. But I used the fraction of a second to twist the wheel and home in on target. As I closed in, their headlight beams reflected off my Land Cruiser and I saw Deckart and Willet's faces congealed in a single ghastly white-strobed impression of terror, a millisecond before the end.

The Toyota was an older model with a steel body. A heavy utility vehicle designed to withstand anything that man and nature could throw at it. Three and a half tons of military grade steel exploded into the Subaru's fiberglass shell.

No contest.

The front end of the Subaru shattered into thousands of pieces as I drove the vehicle in. The block exploded right through the Subaru's smaller engine, dislodging it from the shell and thrusting it through the dashboard and into the cab, crushing everything in its path.

The crash took less than a quarter of a second. That quarter-second absorbed all movement and it was suddenly deathly still. Only the sound of hissing from severed tubes and crushed electrical work remained. The impact happened at an angle, so the majority of force punched through into the passenger side. I came out of the Toyota with the Glock ready.

In the passenger seat, Willets was a pulverized mess. Like someone had introduced a strawberry pie to a stump grinder. Around the other side, Deckart was alive, but not doing well. I came up to his window, shattered into half a million pieces all over him. His head was lolling on a broken neck. The mustache had somehow remained connected to his upper lip.

I said, "Did you do that to the moose?"

He was just about alive enough to look at me with one eye. The other eye didn't seem to be working, but this one worked just fine. He was shocked and fatally damaged, but he might have had an hour of life left in him. Who knows, these days medical know-how can perform wonders.

I said, "Answer my question. The moose."

He looked at me again with that one eye, confused, but largely coherent. I realized that he couldn't speak. Maybe his brain was attempting to make words, but the rest of him just couldn't understand what the brain wanted, couldn't get the message because the wires were cut. Which meant that Deckart wasn't going to answer my question, so I put a 9mm bullet through his head. Not a fancy shot, just a single round into the forehead.

I recalled mentioning to Ellie that Deckart wouldn't last the week. Sometimes you just know things about a person.

A phone rang from somewhere in the destroyed car.

I looked at Deckart. Wasn't coming from him because I'd taken his phone. I looked at Willets. There wasn't much to look at, more like some kind of birthday party accident. But the ringing was coming from over there. I went around to the passenger's side, caved in and collapsed into what used to be a human form. The phone rang, insistent and annoying. Not to mention loud. I looked in. There it was, a rectangular plastic thing, somehow intact. I guess whatever had been around it was softer than the phone, which had survived. I reached into the gore and plucked it out.

I pressed the button. When Willets had been alive and breathing and talking, he'd had a whiney voice, the few times I'd heard it. I tried to do an impression.

"Yeah."

A woman said, "You're on speaker. The board is here. We wanted to get a status report."

A man's voice cut in. "Is it done?"

I said nothing. I was listening. Two people so far, but I had the impression there were more.

The woman said, "Can you hear us?"

A third male voice. "They might be out of reach in the woods. Maybe we should hang up and call again, get a better connection."

I said, "It's done. Now I'm coming for you."

Silence on the other side. Then the woman speaking urgently and quietly. "That's not Deckart. Not the other one either."

There was a frantic round of whispering that I couldn't understand. Then the woman's voice once again, not fussed to whisper. "It's the guy. Keeler. That right?"

I said nothing.

A fourth male voice spoke quietly in the back. "Means the others are dead, so don't finalize the gift card credits."

The woman sighed. She said, "Keeler. We admire your work. It doesn't need to go any further. Will a cash payment do? We can probably reach six figures."

I said, "There is no price. I'm going to drink your blood and then spit it out so the sharks can feed."

Silence. The third guy's voice came, quiet in the background. "Does that mean he's near the water?"

The woman said, "You're making a mistake, Keeler. We're very well protected here. Really. You can't buy better protection than what we have."

The second guy said, "You won't last the hour, Keeler. Just take the money. Cash, wire, crypto. You name it and we can handle it. Otherwise, it's just a shame. One more body to add to all the rest. Unnecessary, unfortunate."

I said, "You can't buy protection from me. Nobody can. If I were you, I'd consider some kind of collective suicide. I hear there's euphoria before communal death, except for the last guy or girl left standing. They get lonely. Maybe you'd be best off drawing straws or rock paper scissors. I don't know for sure if suicide is the answer, maybe there is no answer to your problem."

The woman said. "That's bullshit. You won't make it past the first perimeter. But let me ask you something, Keeler. What is it all for? Why the useless crusade?"

I said, "That's a good question. I'll ask myself that once it's over. But right now it's game on and I'm starting to enjoy myself."

The fourth guy spoke to the others. "So, he's just insane."

There was silence and the phone line crackling. I pictured a conference table, oak or maybe teak. Four executives gathered around. Maybe they had a tray of sandwiches and a coffee machine, bottled spring water and chocolate chip cookies. And then I pictured a package of Mister Lawrence cookies. I hadn't ever seen them, but I could guess what they might look like.

I said, "I've never tried your product. Any good?"

The woman said, "Come on over and try some of our new cakes, right off the production line. You'll like them, Keeler."

The woman addressed me again, voice clearer. "Alright Keeler. Last chance. Six figures, in a suitcase or on a keychain. We don't care. Take it or leave it."

I said nothing. There was a long pause, devoid of any possibility. Then the line was cut as someone pressed the disconnect button on the speaker phone.

The front end of the Toyota was a heavy metal wreck that wouldn't be going places tonight, that's for sure. The doors worked fine. I took Guilfoyle's Remington out of the back seat and slung it over my shoulder. Then I hiked back to take care of the moose. The animal would recover from the tranquilizer, but not from four severed tendons. The moose would be picked to pieces by morning. The only question would be wolves or bears.

On the way back I found the vehicle the prison guards had used. An old GMC Sierra truck. I was happy about that. Another steel body to potentially use as a weapon. The more the merrier. I found some interesting gifts in the cab behind the seat. Six boxes of 12 gauge ammo. Two boxes of Brenneke slugs, two boxes of buckshot, two of bird shot.

The sight of all that good stuff produced a warm fuzzy feeling in my heart.

I retrieved both Breachers. I opened up the tailgate of the truck and laid the shotguns side by side. A winch was installed into the back of the bed, which is how they'd maneuvered the big animal. The guns were beautiful and brutally ugly, all at the same time. Both were tricked out with side saddles for an extra six cartridges each, mounted on the outside of the stock. The guns were from the correctional facility, with inventory stickers on the stocks. They were loaded with light bird-shot, because that's what they use in prisons. But bird-shot wasn't going to cut it out here. I pumped out all four lightweight shells from one Breacher, and four from the other. They hit the dirt and I didn't give them another look.

I loaded both Breachers with a happy new combination. One Brenneke slug, one buckshot cartridge, Brenneke slug, buckshot, repeat. Five rounds in each mag, one in the chamber. Six rounds clipped into the side saddles. Which combined was enough firepower to stop a herd of moose, or elephants, or pretty much anything. I figured I could line up the board members of Mister Lawrence and take them all out with a single Brenneke slug.

The first chambered slug was for the wounded moose, even less happy than before, the tranquilizer was wearing off big time. I walked around the animal and found what I was looking for. He'd been hit by a car up on the main road. The impact had broken one of his hind legs. The prison guards must have brought him down here in a fit of alcohol-inspired sadism. They had gotten their just deserts in the end.

I caressed the moose's neck again and whispered into his ear. He was calm and ready.

I set up about ten yards out and aimed above his front leg, a third of the way up his body, looking to penetrate the big heart through both lungs. The chunk of heavy metal punched into the beast at around one thousand miles per hour. A perfect shot. Instantaneous and painless. The noble moose shuddered and slumped into eternal rest.

## CHAPTER FORTY-NINE

THE PHONE RETRIEVED from inside the mess that had once been Willets lay on the passenger seat. When the truck rolled onto smooth asphalt, I picked it up and wiped it on my pant leg. The jeans were no longer clean in any case. I dialed Ellie's number with my thumbnail.

"Chandler."

"Keeler."

"Where are you?"

I said, "Change of plans."

"What do you mean?"

I looked in the rear-view mirror. Dashboard glow lit up the side of my face, peppered with shot. I knew that if I slowed up now and stopped moving, the stiffness would come on fast. I'd lose the ability to smile, which would be tragic. I needed the adrenaline to keep flowing.

I said, "I'm on a roll. Tell me what I need to know from the plans you found."

There was a pause on the other end. I heard Hagen's voice asking what was up. Ellie ignored him. I pictured her moving from the kitchen to the dining room. I pictured the plans laid out on the table, her standing over them.

She said, "I'll give you the salient features. The lot is 700 acres, most of it woodland. The house has two floors. The other built structures on the property are marked as test production facilities for the Mister Lawrence product. Two 5,000 square foot one story buildings, lined up next to each other, about five hundred yards west of the house. Each of them has an annex. One is marked as an office, the other as a lab."

"That's it?"

"Yeah, just about."

"Nothing on the Bell Island facility?"

"Nothing. What do you want me to do?"

I said, "You should call the morgue, tell them to figure out some extra capacity. Tell them it's urgent."

There was silence down the line.

I said, "How's Hank?"

Ellie said, "He's sleeping, Keeler."

"Good."

She said, "Do I need to be worried about you?"

"No."

I heard Hagen's voice in the background.

I waited a moment. Listening down the phone line while keeping the truck straight on the road ahead. There was a fumbling on the other side, Ellie passing the phone off. Hagen taking it and putting it to his ear.

Then his voice came through. "Keeler. I got a call from Chapman. She's in the house with them. She wasn't able to speak but I got the message to her that I had spoken with you, and that you are an ally. You copy that?"

I said, "She wasn't able to speak. What does that mean, Hagen?"

He said, "Sorry. I wasn't clear. Chapman used the phone keys to communicate in code. The beeps. She was in the room with somebody, I assume. Perhaps she gained control of a phone without being seen, such as hiding it under covers or beneath clothing, or in a pocket. We are trained for this kind of communication."

"Using the phone keys without looking."

"Yes."

I said, "Okay, thanks."

I thumbed the button and hung up the phone.

I was cruising fast, on the road toward Ellie's house. A minute later I passed the turn-off. I thought of her, Hank, and Hagen. Sitting around her kitchen, hopefully safe and sound. Kind of like a happy family. The Mister Lawrence property was three or four miles west, off the Tongass highway. When I was a mile out, I flicked off the headlights. By now the moon was up and the road was straight. I could run dark without any issues. Half a mile from the property's front gate, I pulled the truck off road and killed the ignition.

I sat in the cab, windows down. It was quiet out there. The air was still and smelled like ocean algae. Dark Alaskan rainforest all around, in a 360 degree circle. I felt centered, in the palm of a gigantic living hand. Things died in the wilderness and were born again. Trees and plants, animals and fish. A vast and barely comprehensible web of life operating in a cosmic cycle, or so they say. But not for us, humans don't get to be born again. We just die once and that's it.

I climbed out of the cab and walked around back. The two Breachers lay side by side next to Guilfoyle's Remington. I filled my jacket pockets with ammunition. Shotgun shells in my left pocket, .308 Sierra Match King rounds in my right. Glock tucked into the waist band. Extra mag in the back pocket. Knife in my front pants pocket. I hoisted the rifle over my back, picked up a Breacher in each hand. Like a one-man assault team.

Good to go.

I knew that the property was north and east of my position. The entrance would be over the hills on my right. I hiked for ten minutes until I was just below the wooded rise. I came up the incline, slow and soft. Walking with the heel first, then lowering the ball of my foot. Silent, or near to it. I reached the crest and brought Guilfoyle's rifle up to look through the Leupold scope at the driveway below. The track snaked north. At the end I could see a gate. In front of it was a parked pickup truck with a double cab. Nothing moving, everything dark and misty. The mist caught the moonlight and held it, making the whole landscape glow weirdly.

I retreated below the ridge and walked another five minutes before cresting again. I laid the Breachers on the ground and got into a prone position with the Remington. I flipped the lens caps on the scope.

First the gate. It wasn't special. No fortified entrance. Any special precautions that Mister Lawrence had taken were confined to Human Resources. Specifically, the Wagner Group mercenaries. Up here at the entrance they had one truck parked in front of the gate, and another inside the gate. I examined the vehicles. Identical Toyota Hilux models. Each contained two men in the front cab. Warm and protected by the elements.

Two trucks, two comfortable guys. One gate.

Which was shut, maybe even locked. Which meant that an attacker would have to go through it or over it. But half the guard force had the same problem. I grinned to myself. Take out the guys inside the gate, then worry about the ones outside.

I considered the Human Resources issue. My guess was the Mister Lawrence people would not be able to afford a full-strength squad of Russian mercenaries. A Spetsnaz reconnaissance squad is organized into five teams, each with five or six men. My ball park guess was two six-man teams. A dozen qualified opponents. I did a second round of mental math. One team would be close protection for the Mister Lawrence people, the other would be assigned to the perimeter. They had four guys right here at the fence, which meant that another two mercenaries were positioned deeper in. Defense in depth, a decent concept.

The first target was going to be the truck inside the fence.

I reached into my jacket pocket and fingered the Match King

.308 rounds. Nice number. It has a ring to it, appealing to a certain mathematical asymmetry. The three and the eight are strangers, but the zero holds them together, like a middle sibling or something. I slipped a round into the chamber and pushed it into the internal magazine. Did the same for another four. The sixth round went into the chamber and I drove the bolt home, guiding the bullet with my finger as I did so. I was looking into the cab of the second truck, the one inside the property. The two guys in there were talking. The guy in the driver's seat was smoking a cigarette. He was flicking the ash out the window. The passenger was eating from a plastic bag. Looked like potato chips. From that distance I couldn't hear them.

I switched back to the first guy with the cigarette.

He wasn't there anymore.

## CHAPTER FIFTY

I took my eye off the scope and got the big picture view.

The guy had stepped out of the truck, leaving the door open. Looked like he was going to take a leak. I let him do it. Not for any sentimental reasons, only that shifting the sights from him pissing against a tree, back to the cab of the truck was going to be sub-optimal. I watched him flick his cigarette against a tree, littering. Another karma point against him. I noticed that it was an apple tree. I let the scope wander. Beyond the fence the land was an orchard. The trees were mature and dispersed in rows. The guy was taking his time. I wasn't in a rush. He had maybe one more minute to live. I wasn't going to hesitate.

I read somewhere that seventy-five percent of American servicemen never fired a shot during World War Two. Luckily, the other twenty-five percent did.

The man got back into the truck. I saw the door close before the sound of it reached me. The interior cab light went off.

I put my eye back to the scope. The gun was live. I took a breath. The guy was talking again, looking at the other guy. I put the cross on his face. Right in the middle of it. Hank had told me that he and

Guilfoyle had cleaned the gun. Nobody said anything about checking the sights. I estimated a three point five pound trigger pull. I inhaled deeply and closed my eyes. I let the breath out slowly and did it again. The second time I was very relaxed. My finger pulled and the Remington barked.

I switched to the other guy and eased the bolt back at the same time. Let the brass eject. No pause, no looking at the result. I worked the bolt in and used my middle finger to guide the next round into the chamber. The weapon was live. I held the next guy's blank face in the sights. Fired.

I didn't look. Not a single wasted thought or movement. I ejected the round. Fingered the safety back on, pocketed both cartridges and slung the rifle on my back. I picked up the Breachers with my free hands. Three seconds after the second shot I was moving back from the ridge and shuffling laterally. Once I was about forty feet away from the shooting position, I cut over the hilltop and worked my way quickly down the hillside to the driveway.

Silence, and then the sound of a wounded man.

Which is never a good sound to hear. But it's better to hear it from the enemy than from one of your own guys. In fact, wounding an enemy is often better than killing him. Makes his friends scared, saps their morale and makes them want to take care of him. Meanwhile I could take care of them.

But maybe the two guys on my side of the fence would think about themselves instead of their friend. Who had turned into one very wounded and unhappy individual, bellowing and moaning for help. Maybe the windshield had gotten misshapen on the first shot, so that by the second round the deflection was extreme. In which case the round would have deflected low, into the guy's belly or chest.

I listened to the noise he was making. A chest wound would have been accompanied by some kind of wheezing, so I figured he'd taken it in the belly. Terrible for him and those of his friends still alive, okay for me. The surviving mercenaries finally reacted. It was exactly as I pictured it. One option they had was to open the gate and drive to their friend, or back to the house. But to do that, one of them would have to get out of the truck and work the lock. I didn't figure that would happen, and it didn't. They did the other thing, which was to drive the truck away from the property, to get the hell out of there. After all, who wants to die?

I was waiting in the brush at the side of the track. The truck started up. I could see the passenger looking toward the ridge top where I'd fired. I wasn't there anymore. The driver was bringing the vehicle around in a tight semi-circle. I got one of the Breachers up and in a decent firing position. The other rested at my feet. I was screened by heavy brush. I could see through it, but they couldn't see me. The driver hit the gas, eager to escape. He could probably taste it, maybe ten seconds off. If he managed to get that truck thirty yards he'd be free. The truck came by me on the driver's side. When it was a hair away from being parallel to my position, I let the Breacher rip.

Buckshot tore through the driver's side door like it was a sheet of printer paper. There might have been a slight reduction in force, maybe two percent. The driver got the other ninety-eight. A tight pattern of steel shot at approximately chest height. Which was game over for the driver. The guy next to him got nothing but a face full of his friend. The driver's grip must have been affected, because the truck veered to the right and buried itself into the dirt bank.

Two seconds later the passenger door flung open. By then I was striding across the road. Both Breachers up. I saw the survivor extricating himself from the cab. He was hopping on one leg, trying to get out from the bent metal. The door was catching on his clothing. With his other hand he was trying to get an assault rifle up. By the time he got free of the truck I was all over his decision loop.

I squeezed the trigger on the other Breacher. Another roll of the dice. This time it was a Brenneke slug, a very large and ugly chunk of shaped lead alloy. There is no mental preparation for the violence of gunfire. It's always a lot more violent than most people expect. I had aimed for center mass. The slug impacted as planned and blew the guy into two parts, along with the assorted pieces and fluids that came off and sprayed back. His bottom half tipped over and fell on the spot, the torso and head were thrown onto the dirt bank a couple of feet away.

There was silence in the surrounding woods. I walked toward the fence. The quiet was pierced by an agonized bellow. The wounded guy moaned. A couple of feet away from the gate, I raised one of the Breachers and blew the lock off. I kicked through it. The pickup truck was off to the side and about twenty feet from the fence. The windshield was starred by the two rifle rounds and buckled inward. I pulled the driver's side door open. The driver had no face. I pulled the corpse out of the truck and threw it to the ground.

The passenger was making shallow breaths and humming to himself, like a mantra. Maybe he was a religious person. He had an assault rifle across his knees, a Tavor bullpup. His hands were nowhere near it. And even if they were, so what? The guy was gut-shot. His torso was one dark wet stain from the chest down through the groin. The human gut is lined with nerve cells, like a second brain. You get shredded metal up in there and you're not going to be thinking about much else. Maybe in the movies a gut-shot man can keep on fighting, in reality he can't. He can keep on dying, is all. The guy looked at me and mouthed words, but I couldn't understand what he was saying. It all sounded like moaning to me. I stacked the Breachers over his knees. Then I unslung the Remington and stacked that on top.

I said, "Hold those for me."

He moaned again, a sorrowful sound. In the middle of the moan were words. I finally made them out. "Finish me." It had been the Russian accent.

I ignored him. A wounded enemy was worth more than a dead one at this stage. I had been making a plan on the walk over from the fence. Ellie had said that there were two outbuildings, then the main house. My plan wasn't complicated. Take the outbuildings first, then the main house. That way, the important people would have more time to get scared and come together in one place.

The truck was new. I thought of the mercenaries out there waiting. Defense in depth. They would not be far away. The guy next to me had a radio ear-piece. But he wasn't in any condition to be communicating. Looked like he couldn't even move his hands. Which meant that his living team members didn't know what the deal was.

They'd find out soon enough. I turned the ignition key. The engine kicked over nicely.

## CHAPTER FIFTY-ONE

THE SKY WAS CLEAR, black and speckled with stars. Residual mist hung low, on the way to disappearing. This was high ground. The ocean looked clean and black in the moonlight. The orchard was a beautiful spot. I turned the truck around, so that it faced toward the house and shifted the gear box into park. The guy next to me had found a position where it hurt less, and he was trying to keep it. I lifted the Remington off his legs and he moaned. I got the rifle pointed out the window and looked through the scope.

The driveway curved up through the apple trees. It was hard to see anything up ahead. A couple of hundred yards away the orchard ended in a thicket. There were boulders in and around the heavy growth. The driveway punched through all of that, presumably to the house. I liked what I was seeing. It fit right in with my plans. There was risk, but there's always risk. The rifle went back on the pile. I flipped the high beams up. Fed the engine gas and the tires bit into dirt and launched us up the track.

Not too fast, not too slow.

I figured a ninety percent chance there were guys out there in the brush watching. Fifty-fifty chance of a bullet. The men out there would be uncertain. Waiting to see what was going on. They couldn't know for sure who was driving, if it was their friend or their enemy. If there were two of them out there waiting, maybe one of them thought they should fire on the truck immediately, the other felt differently. Maybe they'd align. Maybe not. The compromise was most likely. They would wait until the truck got closer.

The truck was getting closer.

I steered with my knees, picked up the Remington and looped the strap over my shoulder. We were about two hundred yards from the tree line. I had the truck moving at around twenty miles per hour. Nice and easy. I took one of the Breachers and fit it between the seat and the gas pedal. There was too much room, so I had to ease the seat forward in little jerking intervals. The guy screamed like someone was stirring his intestines with a knife. I ignored him and adjusted position so that the Breacher was feeding the right amount of gas into the engine. The needle stayed at twenty.

One hundred yards from the tree line I grabbed the second Breacher from the guy's legs. He was looking pretty bad, definitely delirious. His moaning had turned into a high keening, like an unhappy ghost.

Jumping out of a moving vehicle isn't a recommended activity. If you're going to do it, you should make sure there is a soft landing. You'd also want to keep an eye out for rocks and tree stumps. Two types of hard object a guy wouldn't want to meet when landing.

I looked ahead as much as that was possible. Picked my moment and flipped the door latch. One hand clutched the Breacher and the Remington's strap. The other hand opened the door. I had my feet out on the running board. Pushed off with the legs, while at the same time flipping the door shut again with the strength of my fingers. I was hoping the high beams would be blinding enough to mask my movement.

I landed on my ass, skidded through the dirt and weeds for about ten feet and bumped right into a rock at the end of it. If there were guys out there watching, they were keeping discipline. I dropped to a prone position. The truck ambled off the track, wobbled over dirt and rocks, then plowed into the base of a boulder.

The impact must have displaced the Breacher from between the pedal and the seat. The truck stopped dead against the rock face. At first there was a great silence. Then the wounded man began to howl. He'd been lurched out of a relative comfort zone. His bellowing cries were worse than ever. Which was the way I'd intended it to be. He was the most miserable person in the universe. If he were a friend of mine, I don't think I'd be able to stop myself from putting a round into his head.

Which is how one of his friends must have felt. A single shot cracked out from the woods, followed closely by the tinkle of the windshield being penetrated once more. Silence. I homed in on the muzzle flash. The Remington was up and hot. It was dark in there. The distance and angle didn't help any. I was watching a section of the woods, maybe ten feet up among the rocks. Nothing moving. The guy had taken his shot and was doing his best to be invisible. Through the scope everything looked gray and uniform and murky.

Then I saw him. One moment it was all grainy indistinguishable monochrome. The next moment I was looking at the shape of a hand. The hand moved slightly, and I saw that it was connected to a weapon. I shifted the scope higher and found the guy's head. I couldn't make out the features in the gloom. I moved down to center mass and put a round into his chest.

I hit the dirt and rolled. The response was almost instant. A triple burst came at me from the other side of the driveway, east of the first guy's position. The muzzle flash was white. The rounds came over my head. I didn't wait for the shooter to adjust. I rolled to an apple tree and waited. The shooter's own muzzle flash might impair his night vision for a couple of seconds. He might not have seen where I'd moved. I got the Remington up and braced against the tree trunk. Through the scope my eye sought any and all movement. I was hungry for the shot, but not starving.

The guy fired first, he had seen me. Another triple burst out of his assault rifle. Three rounds, thudding into the tree. Almost perfectly on target, maybe three inches too far to the right. An impressive shot in the dark. At the range he would have been a hero. I zeroed in on the muzzle flash and found center mass. A millisecond too late. The guy rolled off as I dropped the pin on a .308 round, which spun into the thicket, sparked on the rocks, and ricocheted up into the ether with a loud ping. I pulled back behind the tree again. Another meticulously aimed triple splintered wood chips off the tree, spraying me with shredded wood. He was a very good shooter.

My brain started doing mental math. I'd jumped out of the truck at around seventy yards and eventually rolled up against the tree. Call it fifty yards from the target. Well within rifle range, but not buckshot. Thing is, with buckshot you don't need to worry so much about accuracy. At forty yards the spread would be effective. Ten yards to go. Like a football game, I needed to get back to first down.

I pushed out and ran like a maniac for the next apple tree. I saw muzzle flash spitting lead in my direction. Heard the whirring whizz of hot rounds tearing the air. But none of it tore into me. I racked a shell into the Breacher's chamber. Buckshot or slug? I was hoping for buckshot. The guy fired another burst. The rounds slapped into the tree trunk like a snare roll. I brought the shotgun around and fired in the direction of the muzzle flash. Boom. A slug.

The heavy metal tore into the trees, but not into the guy.

Disappointing, but not for long. Two mental events occurred then. The first event happened in the guy's head. He now knew that I was armed with a weapon designed for close-quarters combat. Which meant that I was unafraid to come at him, a thought that made him panic. The second cognitive event happened in my head. I made a mental note that after the slug, the next shell up was buckshot. The guy wasn't completely wrong to break cover. He might have been in a bad position for close-quarters, exposed and vulnerable. You can't know what's in someone else's mind. Whatever the reason, he broke and dashed to get behind one of the big boulders. I raised the Breacher and put buckshot into him inside of forty yards.

I saw the pellets hit. The guy was running hard. When the shot reached him, his body was slapped weirdly off its intended line, as if pushed by an invisible hand.

I got up and walked the forty yards. The shooter was alive, breathing heavily. His weapon was in the dirt, ten yards away. The buckshot had struck him in the hip and the groin. I racked the next round into the chamber. A slug. We made eye contact. He didn't stoop to begging, so I gave it to him clean.

## CHAPTER FIFTY-TWO

STRANGE NOISES CAME from the pickup truck. The engine was still turning over, the gear shift in the drive position. The noise was a looping banging on top of the engine sound. There wasn't pressure on the gas pedal, but the low idle was pushing the vehicle forward into the boulder like an autonomous robot gone bad.

I crossed the driveway to the truck and killed the ignition. The Breacher was lying on the floor, dislodged from where it had been wedged against the pedal. I crouched in the lee of a boulder and fed ammo into the shotguns. Same as before, one slug, one buckshot. I liked the combination. Recharged the internal magazines. Same for the Remington. A gentle breeze had come up from the ocean. The water was glowing. I was calm and centered. I sniffed the clean air. The briny smell was the calm part, the sour hint of gunfire and earthy blood were the exciting part.

There was nowhere I would rather be.

I was quietly slipping the bolt on the last .308 round when I heard the sound.

Someone moving in the thicket. I kept still. If they hadn't shot me yet, it was only because they didn't know I was there. Both Breachers were at my feet. I slung the Remington over my shoulder and picked up one of the shotguns. Then I saw movement in the brush. I got the Breacher up and hot. My finger brushed the trigger back and tightened up the slack.

I saw the face first, a pale oval outlined in shadow. A woman. She was standing in the thicket, looking at me with wide eyes. Not an enemy. The woman looked bad, like she'd missed breakfast, lunch, and dinner for weeks, if not months. She was coming through the branches and she wasn't alone. A cluster of figures followed in her wake. They looked like something out of a news report on refugees from an industrial disaster or a civil war.

I said, "Come through. I'm not going to hurt you."

They were dressed in loose, dull clothing. As if they had been wearing the same outfit for so long the colors had come out. They were a mix of young and old, male and female. The flesh was wasted and unnaturally pale, almost glowing in the dim moonlight. Like they'd been kept underground. I counted six of them, unarmed. They didn't look like they had enough strength to hold a weapon.

It was impossible to tell the woman's age. Old and young, all at the same time. Or perhaps a young person who had grown old real fast. The skin was loose, hanging off desiccated flesh in folds.

Her voice was cracked and hoarse. "Please. There are more of us up at the property. They wanted to take us out on the bus. Everyone's scared."

When she spoke, I saw the inside of her mouth. The fine hairs rose on the back of my neck. Because when she opened her mouth, the only thing I saw were toothless pink gums gleaming wet in the moonlight.

I stepped to the next one, an older man.

"Open your mouth."

He was embarrassed, looking away from me, but opened up just the same. Pink toothless gums.

I said, "The radiation."

The man nodded. He shifted his eyes back at me, like he was

going to have to trust me now. I figured these were people who had been made to handle nuclear materials. The man's sad eyes stuck on me, hungry for something. As if continuing to hold me in his gaze would guarantee deliverance, or at the minimum, understanding. He began to say something. His mouth opened. Wet and pink. But nothing came out except a few droplets of saliva on the lip. He licked them away, eyes never leaving mine. The group was staring at me. An endangered organism with twelve eyes, each one full of sorrow. I didn't know how long these people had to live, but it wasn't going to be years or decades, more like weeks or days.

I looked at them, taking my time, examining the faces looking back at me like the living dead. Radiation poisoning. None of them had teeth. Just like the body Ellie had found at the fence this spring. She had said he had no teeth.

It occurred to me that we had been misreading the situation. This was not some kind of master criminal enterprise. It was a failed project. The corporate people were bailing out right now, cutting their losses.

I was looking at losses.

A triple burst of gunfire rapped out from the direction of the house and outbuildings. It was followed by another. Two snare drum rolls, filtered and slightly dampened by the trees. The little sad cluster of victims flinched and ducked their heads. Those were NATO rounds from one of the assault rifles these mercenaries carried, another Tavor bullpup. I ignored it for the moment.

I addressed the woman, the leader. "You said something about a bus."

She nodded. "Yes, the green bus."

The entire situation finally clicked into place in my mind. The mystery became a puzzle. The mini-bus at the cruise ship. Green Gremlin. The cruise ship's special hospital facilities. They were moving out the casualties to the *Emerald Allure*, cutting their losses. There was no way of guessing what the Mister Lawrence people planned to do with them. Maybe dump them in the Arctic, make them disappear somewhere. The whole concept was insane, which had not prevented them from committing to it. I didn't know what country was being used for the flag state, but I did know that if the *Emerald Allure* got to international waters there might not be an easy way of stopping them.

I got out Willets' phone and dialed Ellie. She answered on the first ring. Her voice was hot and heavy, rushed and anxious.

"Keeler."

I said, "Two things. One, you need to get the Port Morris cops to the *Emerald Allure* cruise ship. Make sure the boat doesn't leave the dock. Second, you need to get to the front gate of the property. I've got people here. I'm sending them up to the gate, they'll need help. Copy?"

Ellie didn't answer immediately. I looked at the phantom faces, watching me watching them. Ellie's voice finally crackled down the line. "Copy that. We'll be there."

"Any news from Chapman?"

"No. But Smithson got FBI cooperation, there's a team from Fairbanks landing at the airport in half an hour."

The tinkle of another triple burst filtered through the trees. I hung up the phone.

The woman in front of me looked back over her shoulder and shuddered.

I said, "You need to get to the front gate. Think you can make it there?"

She nodded, fatigued but resilient. "We'll get there."

"How many more of you back at the property?"

"There are five more. Too weak to get up and go when the lady came for us."

I said, "The lady, blonde and tall?"

She nodded. I smiled inside. Chapman wasn't stuck in the house anymore. She had gotten loose and was causing a ruckus. The shooting was her. Which made me feel warm and fuzzy. First, I had to get this group on their way.

Two of them could barely stand, but they were able to count on those who could. The column trooped mournfully in a single file behind their leader, each holding on to the shoulder in front, like something out of an old Dutch painting, the blind leading the blind. Except they weren't blind, just dying.

When they were safely across the orchard, I turned away. It was quiet again. The shooting had stopped up at the house. The islands below were dull green spots in a black surface. I stayed there for a moment, planning the sequence. Chapman was loose. I'd give her the benefit of the doubt and stick to my plan. Outside in. Clear the external buildings, then arrive at the main house to attend my first board meeting.

## CHAPTER FIFTY-THREE

I CAME THROUGH THE WOODS, west side of the property, avoiding the driveway.

It was dark and crisp and clear. Any residual mist had been pushed away by the wind. The back of the first building was blunt and windowless. I went to the rear exit and waited. No sound coming from inside, no light filtering out through the door cracks. Nothing moving, no more gunfire. Just calm silence. The knob turned without resistance. The door opened and I stepped inside.

It took a moment for my eyes to adjust. Compared to the interior, the moonlit landscape had been bright. I counted off sixty seconds. By the end of that minute, my pupils had dilated sufficiently to use the light from electrical fixtures set into the walls and machinery. The place was filled with machines, none of them working. Nothing moving. Only a hum from the electricity surging through circuits, fueling the immobile hardware with potential energy. Once I could see, I started to make sense of what I was looking at. Which was a cake factory.

The place ran like the instructions in a recipe book, multiplied by a thousand, and automated. Each machine had a little sign on it indicating the function. First came the mixing tubs where dough was put together. Next came the giant ovens. After that were stations that pumped filling into the cakes through plastic tubes. Once that was finished there was a dipping station. I plunged a finger in. The vat was filled with chocolate, still warm. The cooling machines came next. Finally there was a long zig-zagging route to the packing stations, where the product was siloed into plastic wrap and cardboard boxes. All automatic. All of it connected by wide conveyor belts. Thousands of cakes rested silently on the motionless conveyor belt, in various stages of completion. At the end, boxes of Mister Lawrence product were stacked in piles that went above my head.

The boxes were white with a picture of a cake, a logo, and a smiling bald guy above it. Mister Lawrence.

Someone had hit pause, then turned off the lights.

At the far side of the packaging area was a loading dock. Two forklifts were parked side by side. Then there were the doors. One large rolling cargo door, one normal person-sized door. I pulled the handle. Unlocked. I pushed it open a couple of inches with my foot. Through the crack I could see the house, about fifty yards to the east. The connecting areas were clear of brush and trees.

Halfway to the house was a dark shadowed form, a human figure who had been stopped and put down. Didn't look like he'd be getting up again.

I stayed there watching. After the gunfire there was too much silence. The shadows had eyes.

I counted five minutes. The patience paid off.

A figure broke from the trees to my right and crossed the dirt yard. Huddled tight, gripping an assault rifle. There was a brief moment when he was exposed, but the operator knew to keep to the shadows. Below the door was a steel staircase. Five steps down to the ground. The guy crept along the edge of the building and under the staircase. I could hear his breathing and the soft padding of his boots on dirt. He tucked himself below me and to my left. I heard him speaking softly into a radio. Russian.

Chapman was out there and the hunt was on.

My ballpark guess was six enemy remaining. She had taken out the one that I could see, which left four plus this guy. He wasn't going to last long. The question was how best to kill him. I figured I would be most useful to Chapman as a silent accomplice. I pulled further back into the factory and set down the weapons. First the Breachers, then the Remington. Once I had lightened the load, I crept back to the door.

All that separated me from the guy were the twin railings of the steel staircase and a three-foot drop. I figured I'd vault the railings and come down on the guy's back. I could grip him with my legs and my left arm and stab him a dozen times in the chest. I brought my knife out once again and locked the blade.

The door made no noise. I eased it open slowly. My eyes didn't leave my prey, maybe seven feet away. Once I made the move, I'd be committed. There was no going back because the guy would react to movement. His weapon was ready but pointed down across his chest. He was staring into the shadows made by the growth across the yard. I figured he was waiting for something, maybe a friend. I got the door open wide enough so that I could move out freely. I took a long breath and went for it.

Total commitment. Like an athlete, except getting it wrong wasn't going to be try and fail, it was going to be try and die.

One fast stride onto the platform, one step up onto the first railing. Boot planted firmly. I pushed off hard and sprung into the air. The guy was still clueless, looking deeply into the trees. Trying to draw meaning from the wind in the branches. Or maybe he was thinking, reflecting on life. In either case he was condition white. Unaware.

I went over the other side of the railing and up, a panther coming down from a jungle tree. The guy was slow to notice the movement above and behind him. He was still fixated on the spot across the yard. I was a quarter-second away from landing when my peripheral vision was disturbed. I whipped my head back to the staircase I had just launched from and caught a blur of black clad movement. Another guy, coming right behind me. I got eyes on him just as he was grabbing at my foot in mid-air. I tried to pull the boot back. At that point my target grunted in surprise, noticing what was happening for the first time. I felt the new guy's hand scramble to grip my boot but I managed to twist it free of his grip. I lost balance. I wasn't going to land as intended, that was for damn sure.

I landed on the guy below, bringing us both to the ground. He scrambled clear of me.

At that point I was dealing with two enemies. My only instinct was to prioritize the threat. The guy I'd landed on was recovering his wits. He'd been thinking about something, which had kept him condition white. Now he was moving out of that and transitioning to another mental state, gearing up for a decision. But he wasn't there yet.

The second guy was condition black, fully alert and combat ready. I moved the first guy to my peripheral vision and brought my full attention to the guy who had come at me from behind. One thing I registered instantly, the smoothly shaved head and pointy ears. This was our fourth encounter.

One too many.

He was putting up his weapon and smiling. I had landed badly, rolling my ankle and coming down hard on my ass. I saw muzzle flash as the guy fired twice, in quick succession. I was hit once on my left side. The impact came like a glancing blow from a sledge hammer.

I'd been hit before. When it happens, it happens fast. No time to understand what's going on, only time to react.

My hand still gripped the knife. I had practiced throwing it so many times that doing so now was only a muscle reaction, not even a conscious thought. The pointy-eared guy was sucking in air. I figured he'd been winded by the lurching and grabbing and had forgotten to take a breath before letting off two rounds. Whatever. I guess I saw the target and just went for it. By the time my thoughts caught up, I had flicked the knife backhanded. It spun in the air a couple of times and went straight through into his open mouth.

Which was one move in a fast-moving sequence. The guy I had landed on was backing up and raising his weapon. Maybe the knife play had caught his attention. Maybe he was a thinking person, which didn't bode well for his chances of surviving. By the time he'd paused his philosophical reflections I had the Glock out of my waistband and had squeezed two rounds into his chest. He fell back, his breath coming out quick and hard, the way a balloon deflates. I pulled the trigger on a head shot and nothing happened. The slide was jammed. I dropped the weapon and turned back to the guy with the pointy ears and my knife in his mouth.

He was on his knees trying to deal with a serious situation. My blade had buried itself in the back of his throat. Which caused him to clutch and gag and generally bug out. That might have been enough, after a while, if time had been allowed to play out. He might have choked on the thing or bled out. Or maybe the blade had gone into key areas in the neck, areas that are necessary for the continued viability of the human organism.

I'll never know.

What I do know is that I moved at him very quickly, with neither mercy or delay. I vaulted the stairs, seized his head and ripped it the wrong way, with maximum prejudice. I felt the vertebrae pop as they separated unnaturally, tearing out and shredding vital elements of the pointy-eared guy's nervous system. In the darkness I saw the whites of his eyes film over as he ceased to be a living being and became an inanimate object. Black magic. It was as obvious as shades being lowered on a window. I eased the body to the steel platform. He was dead weight, all slack and nothing holding it together anymore.

His mouth closed with a sharp snap, like some kind of involuntary muscular contraction. A final, jealous reach from the nervous system. For a moment I hesitated. That knife had become an important souvenir of my time in Alaska. Now it was locked up in the guy's head. I released the object from my mind. After all, it was just a knife.

I stepped into the factory again. Picked up the Breachers. I knew at least two things to be true and meaningful. I had been hit, and the only thing keeping me going was the adrenaline of combat. No time to lose, no reason to stop. Two more enemy down. I stepped off the stairs and crouched against the wall. Waiting and watching.

From across the yard came a low wolf whistle.

The whistle came from the spot that the first guy had been staring into, which had drawn his attention. I couldn't see anything in there. A figure emerged from the darkened brush. Slim, tall, blonde hair. Chapman moved slow and cautious to the edge of the woods and crouched low. She was wearing a blue dress beneath a black tactical jacket that she must have looted from one of the Wagner mercenaries. I loped across the dirt and pushed into the growth. Chapman had also taken one of the Tavor assault rifles and her feet were bare against the soil.

Just like old times.

## CHAPTER FIFTY-FOUR

CHAPMAN STEPPED BACK into the trees. I followed. Once we were away from the open yard, she stopped and examined me. The cold moonlight filtered in through leafless branches. I could see her very clearly. Her sharp profile and large, wide-set eyes, blue, and cutting.

She said, "That was really quite something, Keeler. I knew you had game, but I never expected anything like that."

I said nothing.

She said, "I was stuck here waiting for the guy to stop staring in my direction. I was hiding in the shadow and I think he couldn't quite see me. I didn't want to shoot him because of the other one. I knew the second one was out there, but I didn't know he was coming through the factory. Well, first I thought you were him when you came out."

"But then you noticed my style."

"You were like a berserker, Keeler." Chapman said this in an admiring tone, like being a controlled psychopath was the best thing you could hope for, which made her part of my world.

I said, "What are we looking at?"

She said, "I sent people up to the gate. I guess you met them."

"I did, and I called it in. There's a welcome committee coming."

"There are more here. People who couldn't walk so good."

I looked around. It was deadly silent. I said, "Pretty quiet here."

She said, "The opposition has gone to ground. When I got out of the house, they were in the middle of an operation. Moving those people out on the bus. I took down two of them over there. Then another guy coming out of the house. Now there are at least a couple more inside the house protecting the VIPs."

"I figure they're cutting losses. You get that impression?"

"Big time. The clown was nervous. He said that the bosses had flown in and were cleaning up. Seemed to me that he was getting ready for the chop."

"Like they'd kill him?"

Chapman was nodding. "The guy was a creep, but an intelligent one. Like he knew the score but didn't know how to face it. He was going hard tonight, like it was the last night."

I said, "How did you get out?"

Chapman was crouched close to me. The blue dress was thin for the temperature, but her metabolism was going hard. I could feel her warmth.

She said, "Second floor, back side of the house. I was in there with another girl and the bald clown guy. Some kind of bachelor pad fantasy room. Guard outside the door. The clown spiked our drinks with Rohypnol. She was drinking, I was faking it, pouring it into a potted plant."

"And?"

She shrugged. "The clown tried to do his thing and I did mine."

I looked at Chapman. She didn't look away. Her bright eyes were clear and uncomplicated by doubt.

I said, "Where did that happen?"

"What?"

"You, doing your thing."

"The bathroom. You want the full picture. Marble tiled floor.

Right next to the shower. Guy was wearing a kimono, like he was a samurai or something."

"And?"

She said, "And I broke his neck."

"In that dress."

Chapman looked down. There was a tear in the dress. She looked up at me and shrugged. "Yes."

I pictured the scene. The Mister Lawrence guy on the floor by a shower in a very uncomfortable-looking position. Dead and half naked in a silk kimono that had come undone. I pictured his neck, black and blue and misshapen. An image populated my mind of Chapman's powerful swimmer's thighs wrapped around the guy's neck, squeezing patiently, pulsing with muscle. I could see the guy trapped, red-faced and flailing. He would have been in a state of disbelief, wondering how this could have happened to him? Like an over-confident rat who find himself in the embrace of a constricting snake. No need to wait, Chapman would have gone in for the kill, a quick shake of the hips and a twist of the knees.

I said, "Good work. Let's go."

She looked at me, and her eyes travelled to my torso. "You got hit."

I lifted up my jacket and shirt. Nothing but blood and shredded flesh. Chapman bit her lip and moved closer. She felt around with her fingers, probing. It hurt. But I knew that the loss of blood was minimal.

I said, "Flesh wound. I got lucky. Let's get this over with so I can put a Band-Aid on it."

Chapman was now very close. Her hair brushing my neck as she moved. She explored my wound with expert fingers. It was painful and pleasant, stimulating. Until she pressed hard into my side and made me pull away involuntarily.

She made a shushing sound. "Keeler, you are a lucky man. A graze. One centimeter closer and I would be so sad."

"Yeah, just don't make me laugh okay?" I pulled down my shirt and the jacket. Felt better that I was wrapped in clothing. The pain made me impatient.

"Let's do it."

She shook her head. "There's something you have to see first."

Chapman didn't wait for me to agree. She took off through the woods. Barefoot and silent. Assault rifle up and ready. I followed. We arrived around the back of the second production facility building. Identical to the first. Another back door. Chapman paused at the side of the door. She removed a chrome cylinder from her pocket and held it up for me to see.

I said, "Hagen told me about your hidden Geiger counter."

"Good. But it isn't a Geiger counter." Chapman flipped the top off on hinges and twisted the cylinder once. It popped up from the middle to reveal a digital readout. She waved it around me and then moved to the building. She lowered the device and scanned the closed doorway. She turned and showed me the reading. There were numbers, they didn't mean anything to me.

I said, "So what?"

"Normal reading. Baseline gamma radiation, okay?"

"Okay."

Chapman twisted the lipstick case one more turn and it clicked. She showed me the readout. The numbers had gone way higher.

She said, "Now I've switched the selector to find alpha particles."

"Whatever you say."

"There is an elevated concentration, but we are still outside the building."

Chapman teased open the door and we went in. Darkness until our eyes could adjust. Then I could see. No machinery like in the first building. I thought I was looking at an empty space, but then I saw what was in the middle of it. A cube the size of a large room. It looked solid. Like you couldn't move it with a tank. Chapman ushered me to a round door, like a submarine hatch. She held up the lipstick device and showed me the reading. More numbers, higher than before.

She said, "Right now, standing here, we're being exposed to about the same amount of gamma radiation as we'd get from a full body CT scan."

"Is that a lot?"

"Not too bad, but you wouldn't want to stick around long. That's out here. Inside that we'd be toast in an hour. Look at that door. It's a military grade seal. You open that and step inside, you got a fifty percent chance of dying within a month." She looked at me critically. "Personally, I think you'd survive, Keeler. You seem like a resistant organism."

I said, "I'll take that as a compliment. What is it in there, a storage facility?"

She shook her head. "They've extracted the reactor from the submarine. From the descriptions I gathered from those people, I'm willing to bet that they've managed to create a high neutron flux reactor in there."

I said nothing.

Chapman turned the selector on her radiation detector once more. She got down low to the ground and waved it over the floor. Then she stood up and showed me the reading. I had no idea what the numbers meant, but they were high.

She said, "Alpha particles. Extreme concentration."

"What does that mean?"

"It's a radioactive substance, mostly comes off of decaying radioactive materials, uranium for example. It isn't dangerous to us, being on the floor. That's because alpha particles don't travel well. But if it gets inside of you it is dangerous. If it gets *in* you, then dangerous is an understatement."

I said, "So?"

"So, this is not just the traffic in nuclear materials anymore. I think they've been using the salvaged reactor to produce Polonium-210. You know what that is?"

"Assassination weapon used by your countrymen. Killed some guys in London. But the assassins got caught. Polonium has killer stats, 250 billion times more toxic than hydrochloric acid, if I remember correctly."

Chapman said, "Your recall is fine. Technically, one gram can kill fifty million people. If you can get it in them, because the other thing about Polonium-210, it needs to be put into a body. Like I just said. The particles can't penetrate skin."

I said, "As far as I know, it's only produced in Russia."

Chapman said, "Yeah, until now that is."

I was thinking about the sick people I had seen, and the ones who remained. The cube had rust build up from the humidity of ocean air. This was not a recently installed facility.

I said, "They got the reactor out of the sub a while ago. This looks well established."

"They told me it was finished a year ago. Which means they've had a year to harvest polonium."

"How much of it could they make in a year?"

She shrugged. "Maybe half a gram. They would have it stored in here. Something like a tiny vial in an extremely secure case. Once in a while they get to add a milligram. One milligram, enough to kill 50,000 people."

"How much can they sell a gram of that stuff for?"

She shrugged. "Priceless. Thing about Polonium is that it is virtually undetectable. That case in London was the exception, and they wanted the British to know about it. Like a warning. But other incidents go undetected. Very few people will have the interest or ability to look for alpha particles when a dead guy turns up, unless he's an oligarch or a known spy in some major city like London."

"How much could they get for that stuff?"

She smiled. "How much is it worth to kill your enemies without anyone being able to prove it was murder?"

I said nothing.

Chapman said, "Legitimate polonium for research labs goes for five grand per micro-curie, which is one millionth of a gram. Non-legit stuff would go for five times that at least."

I did the mental math. "Which makes it 25K per millionth of a gram. You're talking billions."

Chapman nodded. "The perfect assassination tool, Keeler. Accessible only to the nuclear powers, and they aren't selling. How much would everyone else pay for it? Billions."

I thought aloud. "This has been completed for a year, which means that nobody needs to handle nuclear materials anymore. It's all safely tucked away inside that new thing they built."

Chapman said, "High neutron flux reactor"

"Whatever." I was thinking about the group of toothless people, the radiation sickness. "A year is a long time. Those people couldn't have gotten radiation sickness from handling the nuclear materials. They'd be long dead."

Chapman looked at me, surprised. "Who said that they got sick from handling materials?"

"It's what I figured."

She shook her head slowly, her eyes fixed on mine. "Oh no. These people got sick because they've been used as human guinea pigs to test the product. They were drifter types picked up by a team of recruiters. People who could just be disappeared without issues. Some of them were used to demonstrate it to clients."

I said nothing for a while.

She nodded. "They used it on George too, as a demonstration to a buyer. I asked about him and it's what the sick people said."

I said nothing.

Chapman was nodding at me. We were on the same page, as usual.

I said, "Time for that board meeting."

WE CAME at the house from an oblique angle.

We approached through the trees on the opposite side of the yard. As I got closer, I could see the building well. It was a modern design which had been all about the windows. These were massive glass panels, flattened out like black ice. It wouldn't be easy to put a bullet through that glass. You could see by the way it absorbed the light rather than reflecting it. There were micro particles in there—it wasn't the same material as regular window glass. That was for damn sure.

I spoke into Chapman's ear. "Special glass."

She nodded.

Through the windows, corridors could be seen running the width of the building on each of the two floors. The steel structure was black. The interior walls were dark wood. Wall sconces glowed, dim and discreet. Bottom floor, a guy stood guard next to the steel staircase. Top floor, a guy stood next to a door. Two guards, both in tactical black, both holding assault rifles, both with trigger fingers along the trigger guard, rifles up and ready. Both men were sweeping their eyes left and then right. Slow and regular, like automated lawn sprinklers. Sweep left, sweep right. One covered the stairs, the other the second floor door. Which meant that something important was happening inside that door.

Which made it the primary target.

I spoke softly. "Tell me how you got out of there."

Chapman turned her head so that her mouth was close to my ear. "I was in the back. Second floor, like I said. I climbed through an air conditioning duct from the attic to the roof. Shimmied down the corner. Same as you see there."

I was looking at the corner. A single steel beam painted in black. I was thinking that we might go in the way she'd come. But then I started to feel a stiffness building up where the bullet had grazed me in the side, which was wet with blood. Chapman was looking at me. My face was feeling the birdshot. She must have been reading my mind because she reached her slender fingers to pick out a pellet and flicked it into the dirt. "Too many to take out now. We'll have to wait."

I grunted.

Being wounded made me prone to a short temper. The idea of climbing up that building was aggravating me.

I said, "Where's the bus?"

## CHAPTER FIFTY-FIVE

The Green Gremlin mini-bus was parked two hundred yards away in a half-circle cul-de-sac. It was the same vehicle I'd seen over at the cruise ship. It had been transporting sick people on wheel chairs. Now I knew where they'd come from. Here, the mini-bus had been ready to do the same thing again, transport the remaining group to the cruise ship. My best guess was that the Mister Lawrence people had planned to ditch them in international waters, presumably the colder and more remote the better. They'd probably planned a special excursion.

Chapman had put a stop to that plan. Which made her a hero in my eyes.

When we arrived at the bus I could see one of the mercenaries was slumped in the driver's seat, his head distorted by a single gunshot wound high on the temple. The driver's side window was starred around the bullet hole. Good shot. The passenger door was open. Another gunman's body lay sprawled across the steps leading to the interior. Chapman hadn't been fooling around. I counted two entry wounds in the body.

The Gremlin grinned broadly above the tour bus logo.

Which reminded me of the first time I had seen it, back at the airport. The passengers coming off the silver Lear jet. I realized that they had been the board members. Arriving to finalize the project, no doubt.

A weak voice spoke from inside the bus. "Don't shoot. We're in here."

I stepped over the corpse and boarded the vehicle. It was very hard to see anything, but I made out dim figures sprawled over luxury seats. If I hadn't been able to hear them breathing I would have assumed that they were corpses. They would be dead soon enough, so they'd have an interest in the time that remained.

One of the walking dead men had looted a Tavor assault rifle from the mercenary's corpse. He sat up front with it. His face was slick with sweat and glowed like an irradiated clock dial. Chapman stepped forward and waved her lipstick cylinder above the seats. She moved slowly and carefully. Then she stepped back outside and motioned for me to follow.

Chapman spoke softly. "Don't go in the back with them for long. It isn't safe. They are soaked in it."

"The big guy said that you don't need product, or the submarine returned. That right Chapman?"

Her voice came clipped and precise. "We need to end it. That's all. Just a guarantee that the product and the reactor are taken care of and made safe by a reputable authority, like the United States of America."

I said, "Okay, Alaska *is* American now. You sold it to us, remember that."

Chapman smiled. "No doubt. What's the plan?"

I said, "The plan is simple. Bullet-proof glass works both ways. They won't be able to fire out. We're going to ram it with the bus."

"Then what?"

"We'll take it from there. Nobody expects to be rammed by a

Green Gremlin mini-bus. It's blue sky thinking. Innovation in action. We'll break the box open, then we'll see. Surprise is on our side. The remaining enemy will be tired and fearful. We've delivered all of their friends to the other world. Never underestimate chaos and fear."

Chapman grinned. "Why I wanted you here in the first place."

"You did the right thing. That was out-of-the-box thinking."

She said, "Good. I have high expectations of the future. I'm full of hope."

I said, "So am I."

I pulled the dead guy off the driver's seat and onto the grass strip bordering the driveway. Then I did the same with the other corpse. The coming dawn was visible on the higher tree branches, the blue hues of impending sunlight, distant but making an initial announcement.

I turned to the passenger area. The doomed sat back, watching me. I said, "We're taking a ride. It's going to be dangerous. There is a serious risk of injury or death. Maybe both. If you want to get off the bus, now's the time. Otherwise, welcome on board."

Nobody moved, nobody spoke. Not even a whisper or a grumble. I hadn't expected them to. They had skin in the game. For them, it was the only game in town. Plus, the extra weight wouldn't hurt.

The bus fired up. A strong German engine under the hood. As powerful a battering ram as a guy might hope for. I tucked the two Breachers behind my back and kept the headlights off. I made the turn in the cul-de-sac. The house was straight ahead, two hundred yards. No hesitation, no pause. The end was in sight, right there in front of me. My foot pressed steadily down on the pedal. Nice and easy, but relentless.

The engine began to growl hungrily. Momentum was building up.

I hollered to the back, "Assume a brace position, folks."

Chapman was in the passenger seat. She glanced at me sharply before lowering her head to her knees.

The driveway tore by. We were picking up speed. I could see the building approaching rapidly. The mercenaries on guard were noticing. The familiar form of the Green Gremlin bus, approaching in the half light, rapidly building up momentum.

The guy on the bottom fully realized what was about to happen. He moved indecisively, left, then right, then left again. It was like watching insects in a glass-walled ant colony. Scurrying this way and that way, alarmed but helpless.

The guy up top started agitating in the same way. But he was oscillating between the door behind him and the railing looking out front of the house. He finally turned and opened the door. I figured he was asking a question. It was too late for a satisfactory response. We arrived.

The bus hit the glass-fronted building. We were doing around sixty miles per hour.

The impact made a noise like a giant thunderclap. The whole facade cracked as the vehicle shot through. Like the sheet ice on a frozen lake hit by a meteor. I raised my head. We had come parallel to the guy who had been guarding the bottom stairs. The bullet-proof glass fell in sheets, like guillotine blades.

The guy had ducked for cover and fallen short. He was trying to get under the stairs. He would have made it if he hadn't slipped on the marble floor. His weapon had come out of his hands and he scrambled for it. I was pulling a Breacher out from behind me. The sheet glass swayed from the steel framing and came loose. The whole thing took maybe two seconds. The guy was scrambling for a weapon. I watched, fascinated. He wasn't doing badly, a focused operator in condition black. Verifying his weapon, about to be legitimately shot. Like a hero. I had the Breacher up and ready, resting on the driver's side window frame. The sheet of thick glass came off in one piece, about the size of a small car. It fell off at an oblique angle and sliced him in half from the shoulder down through the groin.

One down. One to go.

I came off the bus with the two Breachers held ready. Chapman was right behind me. I bounded up the stairs. The guy up there fired at me, a triple burst from his Tavor that pinged off the steel beam, like knuckles rapping impatiently on a bar counter. I ducked down and a second burst buried itself in the wall. Chapman raised and fired two bursts in the guy's direction. I used her fire as cover to vault up the stairs.

The second floor had a little lobby area which fed into a conference room. I could see people in there, at a big wood table. The guy protecting them was down on a knee taking cover from Chapman's suppressing fire. He came up and we made eye contact. I saw the Tavor muzzle rise. He was doing well. In a second or two he'd be in position to take me out.

The Breacher spoke first.

A slug this time. It caught him below the shoulder and punched a hole through him, showering his viscera and blood in through the open door. I came into the board room. There were six members of the Mister Lawrence executive board. Four men and two women. All of them looking like they'd been roused from bed, wearing pajamas or robes. Like a perfect picture of privileged comfort. The board members sat glumly around the big table with their hands in the air, as if I were going to read them their rights.

The woman spoke first. Same commanding voice as before. She was in her early forties with well-preserved hair. She was examining me with a jaundiced eye. It didn't surprise me that she'd had the gumption to fix her hair during the emergency. Her face was streaked with blood from the guy I'd shot through the door. She didn't seem to mind.

The woman said, "Sir, I must inform you that this is an illegal intrusion. The governor is on the way down from Juneau. We are in telephone contact with the mayor, who is at this moment dealing with the federal officers at the front gate. There is no jurisdiction for the FBI here. This is private property, and private property remains sacred, at least in the state of Alaska. That said, we intend to cooperate fully with the authorities."

I said, "You're wasting your breath. Save it for God."

"What?"

"I advised you to commit collective suicide. You didn't listen."

She looked up at me. "You must be Keeler. Did you actually imagine that we haven't planned for this possibility? What do you think is going to happen to us in the hands of law enforcement? Do I look to you like a woman who is destined for prison?"

Chapman said, "You think your lawyers and lobbyists can help you?"

A guy spoke up from the back of the table. I recognized the voice. The woman had called him Frank on the phone. He said, "We own the state, bitch. So just shut your trap and let the cops come. The FBI has no jurisdiction here." He addressed the woman in front. "Jill, Cory's on the line. Cory, are you there?"

A voice crackled from the telephonic device built into the middle of the table. "I'm here."

I raised the Breacher and put a load of buckshot into the speaker. Which shattered into a thousand pieces and ceased to exist as a discrete object. Most of it went into the face of a small man across the table. His face had been surrounded by a white beard, with a magnificent head of white hair. All of that disappeared fast when the blast ejected him violently from the comfortable chair and sent him across the floor. I didn't bother to check if he was alive or dead, or if he still had a face.

Instead, I turned to look at Chapman. "Think they'll get off like they say?" Chapman said, "They've got the lawyer, the mayor, the governor. Sounds like they've got it all covered. In my country, for sure, they would be covered one hundred percent. In my country we wouldn't even think about legal proceedings, we'd go right to torture, interrogation, and then secret execution. All in a quick succession, maybe on the same night. Then we'd bury the bodies in a forest. Here, I don't know. But I generally take a realistic approach to things Keeler. Why would it be any different here?"

Frank started to speak. The word coming out of his mouth was 'democracy', but he didn't get it all the way out. The woman cut him off. Her face had drained of color. "Shut up, Frank."

She was looking at something behind me. I turned to see what it was.

The first toothless sick guy was coming in the door slowly. His eyes were red-rimmed and wet, weak and rheumy. They were rotating hungrily in their sockets, absorbing the visual data. I could see that the desire for revenge was burning in him. He looked famished for it. The others started to crowd through behind him, like a shambolic mob of the living dead. They were intense, chewing and sucking on lips with toothless gums. I looked at Chapman. She looked at me. I spoke to the first guy who'd come through.

"You think you can handle them?"

He nodded at me with more vigor than I would have given him credit for. The guy's lips smacked and I was able to see his tongue when he spoke. "No problem. Just give me one of those good-looking shotguns will you? I won't use it because that would be too quick for them, and they deserve it slow and bad. The gun would be just in case they start to get uppity."

I turned back to the board members. They had lowered their hands. I made eye contact with them, one after the other. They were looking back at me, alert and expectant. I wondered what they expected. Then I realized it was the same thing they always got for their guilt, some kind of impunity. Some kind of a loophole they could exploit. I was looking at mild concern with an expectation of deliverance.

I handed the Breacher I'd just fired to the guy with no teeth. I was pretty sure he'd like the load. He spoke to me with his eyes on the board members, roving between them. "Thank you, and goodbye mister."

I turned away as the woman executive made a nervous cough and started to say something, but her voice was quickly muffled. By then I was following Chapman's athletic figure out the door. I closed it firmly behind me and joined her on the balcony, looking over the property. The glass was gone and the breeze was crisp. To my right I could see down to a pier. A zodiac boat was bobbing serenely in the calm waters. The sun was not yet up, but it was a new day. There was some commotion behind the closed door. A boisterous board meeting, no doubt the last.

## CHAPTER FIFTY-SIX

CHAPMAN LED me back to the orchard. In the early blue light I could see that the fruit trees were mature. Maybe they had been planted a hundred years ago, maybe more. I tried to cast my mind back to recall when Alaska had been purchased from the Russians. It was sometime in the 1860s or 1870s. We came up to the edge of the orchard, just on the crest with a view on the ocean below.

Chapman pointed and I followed with my eyes, landing upon an area of recently turned soil.

I said, "George Abrams?"

"And others."

"He was a brave man."

"George was one of the good guys."

I looked at her. She was beautiful in the morning light. She smiled, knowing that I was watching her. Strands of blonde hair were blowing gently. The ocean was calm, it was going to be a perfect day.

A siren moaned in the distance. Far off for the time being, but not for very long. I figured we'd get out of there before any commotion. We'd had enough commotion for a good long while. What we needed now was no fuss and no ruckus. I had the phone in my pocket, but I didn't use it. Ellie was a competent operator, and she would do a great job of sorting out the situation up here. It was her jurisdiction, and I hoped that in the end she would get the property for her people. If I was a betting man, I'd put my money on her.

I chin-pointed toward the pier and the zodiac floating there. I said, "What do you think, they leave the keys in that thing?"

Chapman looked over to where I was pointing and understood. She smiled again, this time glancing at me with those steely blue eyes, darting wickedly. She took my arm. "Well, if they didn't leave us the keys, we could always get a screwdriver from the shed, Keeler."

I nodded. I was a couple of steps ahead of her, at least I thought I was. I was already at the part where we caught up with Guilfoyle at Eagle Cove. I pictured that, and then the breakfast rolls and coffee. We weren't going to miss out, which was a good thing. I figured it would only be prudent to stock up on all of the necessary carbs and minerals and fats. There was a whole lot of relaxing to be done on the trip back down to Seattle.

# AN EXTRACT FROM IMPACT

# CHAPTER ONE

The Lincoln handled like a boat, loose and easy and relaxed. The road was wide and I could have floated endlessly among the green lawns and houses, but I'd reached my destination and the long drive up from Alabama was over.

I turned the wheel with two fingers and guided the car to a stop beside a clean curb. The automatic shifter nudged into the park position. I twisted the key back in the ignition and the engine hum fell off. The windows were down and the smell of fresh-cut grass and the faint odor of a two-stroke engine passed pleasantly into the car. Given the quantity of grass in view, I figured the mowing of lawns was a common occurrence in the town of Promise, Indiana.

I leaned forward in the driver's seat and pulled my shirt away from the leather. My lower back had gotten a little hot and sweaty. I stretched. The street was empty. Both sides of it had medium-size houses separated by generous lawns. There was nothing going on that I could see. Nobody walking around either purposefully or aimlessly. Nobody visible at all. It was late afternoon and hot for early summer, maybe eighty degrees in the shade. Humidity was high and the air was close.

I ducked my head and looked to my right through the passenger window at 1250 Springhurst, my destination. Its only distinguishing feature was a sprinkler in the middle of the lawn, doing its rotation. The water hissed and the mechanism ticked as it cycled and spun back to start all over again.

I stepped out of the car and opened the rear door. The guitar case was in the back seat. I reached in and pulled it out by the handle. The sprinkler at 1250 was spitting water in my direction, so I waited for it to finish another circuit before starting up the lawn. White lace curtains were drawn across the two windows, one on either side of the front door. I didn't know who was going to be receiving the instrument, but my job was almost done.

The sprinkler finished its turn and wound back with a rapid clicking sequence. I was about to step off when I heard two gunshots fired in quick succession. After a slight pause, the shooter squeezed a third shot.

The shots were small arms fire, probably a pistol. The triple booms bounced off the facades of the houses facing me, which didn't mean that the weapon had been fired from that direction. Across the street was a good-size yard with bed linens hanging on lines. The white sheets caught whatever meager air currents they could hold, billowing ever so slightly to reveal a woman standing still, looking at something in front of her that I couldn't see. She did not appear to be holding a weapon. There were no other sounds. Nobody was reacting to the shots, and not even an airplane was in the sky.

I opened the Lincoln's rear door and returned the guitar to the back seat. The door clicked quietly shut. I glanced at 1250 again. Whoever this instrument belonged to could wait a couple of minutes, since apparently they'd been waiting for decades.

I turned away and crossed the street to the yard with hanging laundry. A jogger appeared, pounding pavement on the opposite sidewalk, oblivious and sweaty with a bare torso. When he came by, I could see his ears plugged with electronics. I waited for the jogger to pass. The heat was keeping everyone else inside, either in front of a fan or in a sealed, air-conditioned room within easy reach of cool beverages.

I came through the first line of drying sheets and got a good look at the woman before she noticed me. She was in her late forties and wearing a loose summer dress. Her glossy black hair was pulled back into a ponytail. She was slim and tall with dark-brown skin. Her hands hung empty at her sides. Her eyes were fixed on a point on the ground maybe fifteen feet in front of her. I moved forward and saw what she was looking at.

A second woman was face down, her body splayed in an awkward position.

I ignored the standing woman and moved to the casualty on the ground. She had a small pistol loosely held in her right hand, muzzle in the grass. Her fingers moved across the grip, which meant that she was alive. I had a moment's hesitation before I touched the weapon. The police wouldn't like that, but the police weren't there.

I removed the gun from her hand and dropped the magazine. I cleared the chamber and put all the pieces down. Beneath the woman's head, blood pooled among the rich green stalks and seeped into the black soil. Insects had already gotten involved, interested, hungry, insistent. She was breathing raggedly. Her body was moving in a repetitive way, slowly twitching, fingers grasping at nothing.

I turned to the one standing.

"What happened, ma'am?"

Her eyes shifted to me. "She tried to shoot me, then she shot herself."

"Call 9-1-1." The standing woman ignored me. I said it again, "Ma'am, please go inside and call 9-1-1."

The woman on the ground made a sound, something between a moan and a howl, but with meaning and syllables. Two words. "No police."

I examined her dispassionately. Definitely wounded, but conscious and able to express herself. I turned her carefully into the recovery position and took a better look. She'd blown a hole in the left side of her face from the inside out. The wound was engorged with blood, the exposed tissue scorched and inflamed. It probably looked worse than it was, but she might have internal bleeding or hemorrhaging inside her skull from the explosion.

She needed medical attention. I turned to the one standing, tried to figure out if she was in shock. The standing woman gazed into my eyes like she was looking for something.

She said, "Who the hell are you?"

"I was across the street and heard the gunshots."

"That right? Normally people move away from gunshots, not closer to them." She stepped toward the wounded woman. "And don't call me ma'am. Makes me feel like a grandmother and I'm nobody's grandmother."

The wounded woman's eyes were open, staring straight ahead, which for her was into the grass. Her breathing was shallow. She looked to be in her late thirties. Blond hair cut in a bob.

The tall woman knelt down to look. "She doesn't want us to call 9-1-1. Maybe she's got a reason." She motioned to the ground. "She's got a purse." The wounded woman moaned again. This time not as loud. But her words were clear and there was no confusion. "No police. Please."

Which made no sense. If you don't want to attract police, why go out in public firing a weapon at another person, then yourself? But that's exactly what she had done, which meant that her making sense wasn't a reasonable expectation. As a veteran combat medic, I knew that I could provide some form of care right there and then. None of it would be enough if she had brain trauma.

I looked around at the scene, getting my bearings and visualizing what had happened. The younger woman had come up from the street. Maybe first to the front door, then over to the yard when she noticed the tall one hanging laundry. She'd pulled the pistol from her purse, fired twice and missed both times. After that she had inserted the barrel into her mouth and blown her face out.

I was operating under the assumption that the woman had hoped to put a bullet through her brain, not her cheek. It looked like a couple of teeth had been caught up in the blast, which made a tough day even worse.

The wounded woman coughed loudly and rolled into a seated position. She looked ghastly with half of her face shot off. She put out a hand to steady herself and moaned again. I could barely understand the words. "Help me."

The tall woman said, "We can bring her into my house through the side."

I said, "Okay."

She looked surprised that I had agreed.

She said, "But then what?"

"Then you'll see."

## GET A FREE NOVELLA

Building a relationship with my readers is the best thing about writing. I send the occasional newsletter with details on writing, new releases, and other news related to the adventures of Tom Keeler.

And if you register for my Reader Group I'll send you a copy of Switch Back, a Tom Keeler Novella.
   Get your free copy of Switch Back by signing up at my website.

   jacklively.com

See you there.

JL

# ENJOY THIS BOOK?

You can make a big difference.

Reviews are the most powerful tools in my arsenal when it comes getting attention for my books. Much as I'd like to, I don't have the financial muscle of a New York publisher. I can't take out full page ads in the newspaper or put posters on the subway.

(Not yet, anyway).

But I hope to have something much more powerful and effective than that, and it's something that those publishers would kill to get their hands on.

A committed and loyal bunch of readers.

Honest reviews of my books help bring them to the attention of other readers.

If you've enjoyed this book I would be very grateful if you could spend just five minutes leaving a review (it can be as short as you like).

Thank you very much.

JL

## ALSO BY JACK LIVELY

The Tom Keeler Novels

Straight Shot

Impact

The Tom Keeler novels can be read in any order.

# ABOUT THE AUTHOR

Jack Lively was born in Sheffield, in the UK. He grew up in the United States of America. He has worked as a fisherman, an ice cream truck driver, underwater cinematographer, gas station attendant, and outboard engine repairman. The other thing about Jack is that since he grew up without a TV, before the internet, he was always reading. And later on, Jack started writing. All through those long years working odd jobs and traveling around, Jack wrote. He'd write in bars and cafes, on boats and trains and even on long haul bus trips.

Eventually Jack finished a book and figured he might as well see if anyone wanted to read it.

Tom Keeler is a veteran combat medic who served in a special tactics unit of United States Air Force. The series begins when Keeler receives his discharge from the military. Keeler just wants to roam free. But stuff happens, and Keeler's not the kind of guy who just walks away.

Jack Lively lives in London with his family.

**Breacher**

Copyright © 2021 General Projects Ltd.

**Breacher** is a work of fiction. Names, characters, businesses, organizations, places, events, and incidents either are the product of the author's imagination or are used fictitiously. Any resemblance to actual persons, living or dead, events, or locales is entirely coincidental.

All rights reserved. This book or any portion thereof

may not be reproduced or used in any manner whatsoever

without the express written permission of the publisher

except for the use of brief quotations in a book review.

First Print Edition

ISBN 978-1-8380475-7-3

General Projects Ltd.

London, UK.

jacklively.com

Made in the USA
Monee, IL
04 July 2024